MW01533122

LOVE'S RUSHING CURRENT

Toby lifted his gaze and scanned the far bank of the stream where a cluttered grove of pines and aspens grew. His eyes narrowed on an object beneath one of the trees, and squinting more closely, he saw that it was Sarah, nearly camouflaged in her muted-green, calico frock. Only the glint of sunshine off her golden hair had given her away.

She appeared to be dozing, her fishing pole sunk firmly in the bank at her side. No doubt, she was still waiting for her first bite. And smiling at this thought, Toby crossed the stream on the same fallen tree she must have used.

Quietly kneeling down before her, Toby planned to say something. But, seeing the soft rise and fall of her breasts as she slept, the faint dreamy smile on her lips, he felt the almost overpowering urge to take her in his arms and crush her to his chest, to kiss away that soft, slight smile. He bent his head, and his lips caressed hers in a slow, gentle exploration. He heard her quiet, sleepy sigh, and for a moment she yielded to his kiss—but only for a moment. . . .

BESTSELLING ROMANCES BY JANELLE TAYLOR

SAVAGE ECSTASY (824, $3.50)

It was like lightning striking, the first time the Indian brave Gray Eagle looked into the eyes of the beautiful young settler Alisha. And from the moment he saw her, he knew that he must possess her—and make her his slave!

DEFIANT ECSTASY (931, $3.50)

When Gray Eagle returned to Fort Pierre's gates with his hundred warriors behind him, Alisha's heart skipped a beat: would Gray Eagle destroy her—or make his destiny her own?

FORBIDDEN ECSTASY (1014, $3.50)

Gray Eagle had promised Alisha his heart forever—nothing could keep him from her. But when Alisha woke to find her red-skinned lover gone, she felt abandoned and alone. Lost between two worlds, desperate and fearful of betrayal, Alisha hungered for the return of her FORBIDDEN ECSTASY.

BRAZEN ECSTASY (1133, $3.50)

When Alisha is swept down a raging river and out of her savage brave's life, Gray Eagle must rescue his love again. But Alisha has no memory of him at all. And as she fights to recall a past love, another white slave woman in their camp is fighting for Gray Eagle!

TENDER ECSTASY (1212, $3.75)

Bright Arrow is committed to kill every white he sees—until he sets his eyes on ravishing Rebecca. And fate demands that he capture her, torment her . . . and soar with her to the dizzying heights of TENDER ECSTASY!

Available wherever paperbacks are sold, or order direct from the Publisher. Send cover price plus 50¢ per copy for mailing and handling to Zebra Books, 475 Park Avenue South, New York, N.Y. 10016. DO NOT SEND CASH.

California

VOLUME 1
PASSION'S TRAIL

ELIZABETH FRITCH

ZEBRA BOOKS
KENSINGTON PUBLISHING CORP.

ZEBRA BOOKS

are published by

KENSINGTON PUBLISHING CORP.
475 Park Avenue South
New York, N.Y. 10016

Copyright © 1983 by Elizabeth Fritch

All rights reserved. No part of this book may be reproduced in
any form or by any means without the prior written consent of
the Publisher, excepting brief quotes used in reviews.

Printed in the United States of America

Chapter One

The late September afternoon sun sparkled off the river's surface and bathed the green banks of the Humboldt with its warmth. The current moved sluggishly, the water warm and slightly bitter. Still, it was a peaceful, relaxing place; an oasis, of sorts, set amid the barrenness of the northwest Nevada territory.

Samantha Coulter dropped several dark berrylike fruits into the pint pail she carried, then plopped one in her mouth, grimacing at its sour taste but nonetheless welcoming it as the first fresh fruit she had eaten in weeks. She wiped her mouth with the back of her hand, and it came away stained purple; no doubt her mother would make her wash again.

Sighing at this dreary prospect, she hiked up her dusty linsey skirt and trudged to another clump of the prickly bushes with her leggy, adolescent gait. At ten, Samantha was often compared to a young colt; she seemed to be all knees and elbows, gangly yet oddly graceful. But her mother insisted Samantha would grow out of it and someday be a beautiful young woman, with her thick chestnut hair and lively gold-flecked amber eyes. Right now, however, Samantha doubted that time would ever come.

She cast a glance over her shoulder to see how her brother was progressing, and her face pinched into a frown of displeasure. Two years younger than she was, with a cap of unruly flaxen hair and a generous dusting of freckles, he had discarded his pail and was kneeling down, peering through the stunted underbrush. Whatever had caught his attention, he was transfixed in fascination oblivious to everything around him.

Her curiosity aroused, Samantha crept toward him, glancing briefly down the slope at the wagons, drawn into their customary circle, the cattle grazing nearby. She dropped to her knees in the brittle grass beside her brother and gave him a quizzical look. "Lucas, what—?"

He silenced her with a finger raised to his lips, his brown eyes dancing with mischief. He inclined his head toward the river. "Lookee yonder, Sam!"

Frowning once more, Samantha directed her gaze through the tangle of thorny branches and was mildly surprised to discover the enigmatic, always dapper Judd Brannan standing on the bank. His booted feet were planted wide apart, his hands braced on his narrow hips, and he was looking down into the water, laughing. The sunlight glinted off the ivory handle of the newfangled revolver he always wore, as well as the pearl buttons of his waistcoat. He was hatless, and the breeze ruffled his raven hair.

Still puzzled, Samantha glanced once more at her brother. "So it's Mr. Brannan. So what?"

Lucas shook his head impatiently and leaned forward, his eyes bright. "Look!"

Sighing in exasperation, Samantha returned her gaze to

6

the sunlight shimmering on their wet, glistening flesh.

A short, shrill whistle brought Samantha's head up sharply, and she turned quickly to scan the plain below. Her aunt Sarah was standing just at the edge of the rise, a tall, slender outline against the backdrop of faded canvas-covered wagons, the wind blowing her honey-colored hair and snapping the loose skirt of her calico frock against her legs. She raised her fingers to her mouth, and another shrill whistle carried on the breeze.

Samantha poked Lucas in the side and gathered up her pail of berries. "Come on—before she comes looking for us!"

Lucas scrambled to his feet, an impish gleam in his eyes. "Wait till we tell her what we just seen!"

"No!" Samantha wailed, lunging at her brother. She tackled his knees, and he stumbled to the dry grass, his breath escaping his lungs in a rush. Samantha crawled forward a few feet and regarded Lucas narrowly. "We can't tell *anyone.*"

His brown eyes darkened with suppressed rebellion as he got slowly to his knees, carefully examining the contents of his pail. "Why not?"

"Because—". She faltered, suddenly at a loss for words, wondering *why* they shouldn't tell. She liked Maggie O'Brian, in a cautious sort of way. But after four months of traveling in her company all the way from Independence, Missouri, Samantha had come to realize that the Irishwoman cared only for herself. She was selfish and vain and had eyes for every young man in the wagon train. And Samantha didn't like Judd Brannan at all. But unfortunately her aunt Sarah did.

Filled with a sense of vague confusion, Samantha pulled herself to her feet and brushed some of the grass

8

off her skirt. "Just don't tell," she warned her brother, reaching down to offer him a hand.

He glared at the outstretched hand and stood up unaided, his lips pulled into a pout. "But can't we at least tell *Sarah?* She's Maggie's friend."

"No!" Annoyed at her brother's lack of sensitivity in such matters, Samantha moved with awkward haste down the slope, her dark braids bouncing with each hurried step. She doubted that her aunt and Maggie O'Brian were *really* friends at all—especially since Judd Brannan had joined the travelers. There was much about life that Samantha didn't understand yet, but she was perceptive enough to know that Sarah, in her shy manner, was attracted to Judd. And, with all the subtlety of a freight train, so was Maggie.

As Samantha reached the bottom of the hill, she noticed that her aunt's glance held the faintest trace of impatience. Her gray eyes whisked over the pair, taking in the berry stains on their faces and hands and the dried grass clinging to their clothing. For one agonizing moment, Samantha feared that they would be sent back to the river to bathe and interrupt the intimate scene that was taking place there.

"We got berries," Lucas announced, displaying his pail proudly. "Maybe Ma can bake us a pie."

Sarah shifted the rifle she was holding to her other hand, a wry smile tugging at one corner of her mouth. "There's little enough flour and sugar as it is." Her features softened into a warm smile, and she ruffled the boy's hair. "But there *might* be a pinch or two left over."

Lucas's face flushed with sudden pleasure, and he offered a berry to his aunt. She accepted it, tasted it cautiously, and made a face at its bitter tang.

"I'm afraid it'll take more than a *little* sugar to make these sweet," Sarah observed with a twinkle in her eye. "Now let's get back to camp. Your pa and Mr. Pardee are nearly finished fixing Mr. Huntington's axle."

Lucas tilted his head to one side and looked up at his aunt thoughtfully. "There surely have been a lot of breakdowns lately."

"We've come a long way. Wagons wear out."

"And we're almost there!" Lucas let out a sudden whoop of sheer joy. "California's just over them mountains!"

Samantha, lost in thought over the shameless display she had witnessed by Maggie and Judd, let her gaze stray to the distant range of mountains to the southwest, barely discernible. California. She shook her head in wonder. It was a long way from Kentucky—miles and miles of endless prairies and hard walking,—but before this year of 1847 was over, the Coulter family would be through with the dusty wagon tracks and the bland monotony of diet and settled in their new home.

Smiling reflectively as she walked beside her brother, Samantha turned once to cast a glance over her shoulder to the river. Her heart froze in sudden, overwhelming terror. She uttered a frightened little moan and clutched her aunt's arm.

Several yards away—naked, filthy, and emaciated—stood an Indian. His black hair straggled over his shoulders in thick, oily strands, and his dark eyes, sunk deep in his gaunt face, glinted like tiny pinpoints of obsidian. He clutched a bow, though no arrows.

Her eyes wide and fearful, Samantha stole a quick glance at her aunt, whose face was caught in an expression between terror and dismay. Sarah's hands were

10

shaking as she brought the rifle to her shoulder, and the barrel wavered unsteadily. But apparently the sight of the gun was enough, for the Indian turned and bolted away.

Sarah released a trembling gasp and lowered the rifle, leaning on it as if for support. The color gradually returned to her face, but her eyes were filled with ill-concealed anxiety as she exchanged worried glances with Samantha and Lucas. And, as one, they raced back to the protective circle of wagons.

Maggie stretched, then curled back up against the warmth of Judd's body, pleasantly sated from their lovemaking. The bed of dry grass was strangely comfortable, and the unaccustomed caress of the wind of her bare skin was chilly yet invigorating. She traced a finger languidly over his smooth, finely muscled chest, covertly studying his swarthy face and the way his neatly trimmed black sideburns accentuated his lean jaw. He *did* have the look of a scoundrel about him, which was exactly what most members of the party said of him in private speculation.

He had been at Fort Hall—over five hundred miles ago—waiting to join a train to California, explaining that the one with which he had journeyed over the plains had turned off for Oregon. And that—aside from the fact that he hailed from Natchez, Mississippi and was extremely handsome and charming—was all anyone in the Jennings party knew of him. A mystery man, ripe for conjecture from the men and admiring glances from the women.

"Why are you going to California?" she asked.

His faint chuckle was slightly derisive. "Because it's the land of eternal springtime and bountiful harvests."

11

Maggie made a moue. "That sounds like one of the passages from Mr. Hastings' guidebook, I'm thinkin'." She raised up on one elbow, brushing a lock of damp coppery hair away from her face, and regarded him slyly. "Is it runnin' away from somethin', you are? A woman? A debt? A jealous husband?"

His dark brown eyes met hers impassively, and a fleeting look of annoyance passed over his face. But it was replaced quickly by a tolerantly amused smile. "Are all the Irish as inquisitive as you?" Without giving her an opportunity to answer, he rolled her onto her back and traced the ridge of her collarbone with his fingertips. "Why are *you* going to California?"

To find myself a rich husband, Maggie acknowledged to herself, even though she would *never* admit it to anyone else. Besides, the more she heard of California, the less likely it seemed that the men there would turn out to be good prospects for matrimony. "Because my family's going."

"Ah, yes—the entire O'Brian clan," he said with a trace of mockery in his voice. His hand glided over her waist and hip in an absent caress. "How many of you are there—nine?"

"Ten, counting baby Kevin." She watched his hand as it continued its idle exploration, trailing over her flat stomach, his long fingers pausing to outline the hollow of her navel. He had delicate hands for a man, with graceful, tapering fingers—one of the first things she had noticed about him.

"The Irish are a prodigious lot, aren't they?"

Maggie made a murmuring sound of agreement, suddenly acutely aware of the flame of desire slowly beginning to spread through her veins. She knew they should

12

be getting back to the wagons. The sun had dipped low in the sky, and someone might come looking for her. But Judd's touch made her forget everything but the two of them, and she shuddered with longing as his lips brushed one rosy peak of her breast. She closed her eyes, her senses reeling, content with the thought that Judd Brannan would make the rest of this long, arduous journey at least tolerable.

She felt his lips leave her and waited in quivering anticipation for his mouth to claim hers. When at length nothing happened, she opened her eyes, stunned to see Judd leveling his revolver.

The loud crack of the shot ripped through the air, and Maggie, fear leaping into her eyes, struggled to a sitting position. She looked wildly around, confused and frightened, in time to see a scrawny Indian spin around crazily and crumple to the ground.

Maggie recoiled in stark horror, her hand flying involuntarily to her throat. She watched, both fascinated and repelled, as the life's blood pumped out of the gaping hole in the Indian's chest.

Judd was on his feet, tossing her clothes to her and bending to pull on his trousers. "Get dressed! The whole party will have heard that shot, and they'll come looking!"

Maggie's dismay and horror left her in the rush of panic Judd's words had evoked. She snatched up her plaid frock, lurched to her feet, and slipped the dress over her head. She stooped to pick up her heavy leather shoes and lisle stockings, but her gaze was drawn irresistibly to the bloodied corpse of the Indian. A cold shiver of dread crawled across her skin, mixed with a curious sense of exhilaration. A few minutes more, and that mangy brave

13

might have had a swatch of her long flame-colored hair to hang on his belt. The idea sent an intoxicating little thrill through her, and her mouth curved in a furtive, satisfied smile. At nineteen, Maggie O'Brian was a woman who enjoyed excitement, no matter *how* she found it.

Judd buckled on his holster and grabbed Maggie's hand, hauling her away from the river. Unprepared for the sudden movement, she nearly stumbled over the buckled roots of a stubby willow, but managed to keep her balance. The withered reeds and grass hurt her feet, and she berated herself for not putting on her shoes and stockings.

Judd broke through the twisted branches of skimpy cottonwoods and willows and onto the open plain, dragging Maggie along with him. The sight that greeted her made her groan aloud in frustration and curse her lack of good judgment in a trysting place, for six armed men were running up the sage-covered slope from the wagons. How would it look to everyone? There was enough gossip among the travelers as it was already.

Judd slowed his pace slightly and waved encouragingly, and as the two groups drew nearer, Maggie could recognize the men. There was her father, the burly, red-haired Michael O'Brian, and her older brother, Sean; the lean, rangy Roy Coulter; the gregarious Swede, Ole Andersen; the stocky Red Canfield, the party's guide; and quiet, sober Wiley Higgins, the stock tender for Reverend Jennings, the party's nominal captain.

What would all these men think to see her emerging from the river with Judd, shoeless with damp tendrils of hair plastered to her face?

Michael O'Brian swept his daughter into his arms and hugged her to him. Judd was assailed by a storm of ques-

14

tions hurled at him from every man. He held up a hand and shrugged casually. "Just an Indian," he said quietly. "He won't bother anybody again."

"Only one?" Sean asked, letting his gaze rove restlessly along the Humboldt's course. "What was he doing?"

Judd's shoulders lifted in another shrug. "Skulking."

Maggie drew back and looked into her father's square, ruddy face, managing to squeeze a tear out of one corner of her eye. "Oh, Da, it was terrible, it was! I was just about ready to put on me shoes and come back when—" Maggie's lip began to quiver, and she drew a ragged breath, unable to continue. Michael soothed her awkwardly with a big, rough hand, his pale green eyes filled with concern. Maggie's voice quavered, filled with desperation. "If Mr. Brannan hadn't come along when he did—" choking on a sob, she turned her face against her father's shoulder.

Michael O'Brian's gaze moved to the darkly handsome face of Judd Brannan. "It's grateful to you I am, sir."

Judd made a negligent gesture. "Happy to help out."

Roy Coulter scrubbed a hand across his stubbled cheek, his grayish-blue eyes thoughtfully remote. "I think we'd better bring the stock in early this afternoon —in case there's more of them around."

"Heathens!" Sean muttered sourly, his lips drawing back into a snarl. "It's a land cursed with heathens! It's glad I'll be to get to California."

Ole Andersen slung his rifle over his shoulder and nodded his blond head vigorously. "*Ja.* We'll all be glad to get there."

Maggie gave a final loud sniff and drew away from her father. She wiped her eyes and pushed a lock of hair away from her face. ''Can we go back now?''

Michael nodded, a wan smile lighting his somber face. ''Of course we can, girl.'' And he draped a massive arm around her shoulder.

Maggie managed a tremulous smile, secretly pleased with her performance. But as her eyes briefly touched those of Red Canfield's, the smile quickly vanished. His features were almost obscured by an unkempt mane of rusty-gray beard and hair, but his small pale blue eyes glittered with a lewd gleam as he assessed her insolently. His lips drew back in an obscene smile, revealing several gold teeth. Maggie drew herself up indignantly and looked away, an expression of intense disdain on her face.

Of all the members of the Jennings party, Red Canfield was the most offensive, disgusting man Maggie had ever met. And she was sure that now he knew—if no one else did—just what had been going on at the river. Her mouth thinned into an angry line, and a frightened shiver raced over her flesh.

Chapter Two

Sarah Coulter sat on a campstool before the fire in the gathering dusk, absently stirring the pot of beans. The air was cool and sweet and carried with it the promise of autumn, laced with other familiar scents of strong coffee, frying bacon, cattle, and the peculiarly fragrant sagebrush. The wagon—the huge boat-shaped prairie ark that had been her home for the past four months—looked oddly forlorn without its wheels; it now sat propped on two sturdy logs while the wheels soaked in the creek.

At the end of May, when the Coulter family had pulled out of Independence, filled with boundless exuberance for their upcoming trek, the wagon had been new, painted bright colors, and the canvas top a snowy white. Now, however, it bore hardly any resemblance to the gay prairie schooner; the paint had faded and was caked with mud and dust, and the canvas was weathered, stained, and patched in a spot where it had been pierced by a broken rib.

The travelers themselves had fared little better, Sarah reflected morosely. Their faces were browned by sun and

17

wind, their eyes perpetually bloodshot from the ever-present dust. And there had been accidents as well. Several oxen had drowned crossing the Sweetwater, and one of Reverend Jennings's hired men had been caught beneath the wheels and crushed to death; he was buried somewhere back in the Nebraska territory, a place that seemed a lifetime ago.

Lucas's squealing protests at the rear of the wagon broke into Sarah's thoughts, and she glanced over to see her nephew getting his face and hands scrubbed vigorously by his mother, Hetty Coulter. Sarah observed the scene with an amused smile. She was genuinely fond of her sister-in-law, but the woman undeniably had a fierce penchant for cleanliness that bordered on obsession. Where others in the party had packed crates of household goods, family mementos, or outlandish luxuries, Hetty guarded her case of soap as if it were a treasure.

Young Simon scurried over to Sarah and stood cautiously behind her, eyeing his mother warily from a safe distance. At two, he was a miniature version of his father and brother—the same flaxen hair, the same slender bone structure.

Sarah flicked a sidewise glance at the boy, a teasing sparkle in her eyes. "If you don't ever get dirty, you won't have to worry."

Simon considered her dubiously for a moment, then grinned and sat down crosslegged on the ground, picked up a twig and tossed it into the fire.

Sarah's gaze was drawn around the camp, searching restlessly amid the figures at the cooking fires until it came to rest on the lean, sleek form of Judd Brannan, taking his evening meal with the O'Brians. Now that all the earlier excitement had died down and the compliments lavished dutifully on him, he had resumed his normal behavior—mysterious, aloof, soft-spoken. Sarah sighed softly to herself, wishing he would spend some of his time with *her* family.

She envied Maggie for her good looks and high spirits—exactly the type of woman who apparently appealed to Judd Brannan. Sarah knew she was as pretty as Maggie in a subdued sort of way, but she lacked the Irish girl's vivacity, except when her quick temper was aroused. Where Maggie was bold and sassy, Sarah was quiet and reserved. And she feared her shyness had kept this handsome, elusive wayfarer out of her reach.

Sarah could have stayed in Kentucky and married, she supposed. But there was little at home to compel her to stay, and the men she had known were poor and uneducated, with dismal futures ahead of them. When her widowed mother had died five years ago, she had gone to live with her brother and his family. And when Roy decided last winter that he wanted to make the journey to California, Sarah had resolved to go, too.

It was a new land, a land of opportunity. There was no snow to keep a person cooped up inside all winter. Malaria, the dreadful disease that decimated entire families, was unknown in the West. It was said that livestock fared well and the rich soil produced bumper crops. It was a land made for building dreams, but for Sarah—since Judd Brannan had joined the emigrants—that dream had an unfullfilled, bittersweet quality to it.

Hetty set down a plate of hot biscuits, fresh from the camp stove, on a small folding table near the fire. Straightening up, she wiped her hands on her apron and shook her head ruefully. "There's only about thirty pounds of flour left."

19

Sarah looked askance. "But we picked up an extra two hundred at Fort Hall."

"There's no help for it now—except to go on short rations." Hetty shrugged helplessly and walked over to the open chest at the rear of the wagon to fetch the tin plates and cups. Sarah watched her, amazed at how the trip had aged her sister-in-law. At twenty-six, Hetty looked old enough to be Sarah's mother, though she was only eight years her senior. Her hair, once a luxuriant fall of sable tresses, was dull and lusterless. Her arresting brown eyes were now sunken deep, and worry lines radiated out from their corners and creased her forehead. Her skin was dry and sunburned, her hands chapped and red. It had been an arduous journey for Hetty Coulter, and Sarah hoped fervently that the rewards at the end would be worth it.

Roy crawled out from beneath the wagon with a bucket of bear grease which he had been daubing on the axles, hubs, and other moving parts. In contrast to his wife, the trip west seemed to be agreeing with him, and, if anything, he appeared more vigorous and robust than he had in years. Tall and blond, with muscles hardened from years of hard labor, he exuded energy and enthusiasm.

Sarah scooped out the beans onto the plates while Hetty served the bacon from the frying pan. Samantha emerged from the sleeping tent and joined the group around the fire just as her father sat down. The family ate in relative silence, relishing their meal. For even though it was simple, tasteless fare, a body could build up a powerful appetite after a day on the road.

At the beginning, the trek had been a kind of escapade, a novelty, and the sense of accomplishment and seeing new sights had made each day a new adventure. But after a while, monotony soon invaded the days—each one was the same, the routine beginning at dawn and ending at dark. Sarah would be immensely thankful when they finally sighted the Sacramento valley and could set down roots once again.

"I think I'll ask Emmett if he'll share watch with me tonight," Roy said, setting aside his empty plate and pouring a cup of hot coffee from the tin pot. "After that trouble with the Indian this afternoon, I wouldn't want any of his friends to take a notion to get back at us and steal any of the stock."

Hetty wiped young Simon's mouth with a corner of her apron. "Maggie was a lucky girl that Mr. Brannan came along when he did."

Lucas exploded in a fit of giggling. Samantha jabbed him hard in the side with her elbow and shot him a warning scowl. Sarah turned a mystified eye on the pair.

"I'm surprised old Reverend Jennings didn't want to give the fellow a Christian burial," Roy remarked dryly. He lit his pipe and puffed reflectively for a moment. "But I *did* notice him leaving a few of his pamphlets under a rock."

Sarah chuckled softly. "The way he's been handing them out to all the Indians we see, that carton of religious tracts he brought along must be almost empty by now."

Lucas had fetched his pail of berries, but looked up from his selection of the ripest to stare incredulously at his father. "Can Indians read?"

Roy winked at his son and gave him a sly grin. " 'Course not. That's why it's so funny."

Sarah stood up to help Hetty gather up the plates just as several figures crossed the camp and came into the light of the fire. She looked around and had to suppress a grin, for there was the Reverend Preston Jennings himself.

21

In truth, he looked the part of the fire-and-brimstone preacher he professed to be. In his late forties, he was a tall man with an incredibly curly mane of gray hair and fluffy muttonchop side-whiskers. He had a long, severe face with drooping jowls and a fanatical light in his eyes. He always wore the same seedy frock coat, no matter what the weather, and his flat, low-crowned hat was perpetually spotted with bird droppings.

He was perhaps the worst possible man to have been nominated to the captaincy of the emigrants, for his qualifications for the job were dubious. But at the time—miles and miles ago back on the plains—he had been the most likely choice. He was a man of property, with three wagons and a veritable herd of cattle. He was eloquent and educated—and he *wanted* the job. It was purely a ceremonial title, for most of the decisions were made by a majority vote. But the wagon train had taken his name, and the emigrants had become members of the Jennings Party from that day forward.

Sarah inclined her head in polite greeting as she went about her chores and slipped past the men. The reek of stale whiskey and unwashed clothing assailed her nostrils, and her mouth curled in scorn. Only one man in the party smelled like that, and as she bent to fetch Simon's plate, she saw Red Canfield materialize out of the shadows behind the Reverend's towering frame.

He touched the brim of his tattered hat, and his mouth curved into an unpleasant smile. "Evening, Miss Coulter."

Sarah grimaced inwardly at the sound of his raspy voice. Her gaze met his for an instant, then quickly fell away, unnerved by his ogling scrutiny of her. Choking back her revulsion, she managed a tight nod of greeting

22

and hastened over to the wagon. She felt Canfield's eyes on her, and her flesh crawled.

Roy unfolded his lanky form from the campstool and got to his feet. "Well, gentlemen, what brings you by this evening?"

"It's about this nonsense with your wheels," Jennings said, gesturing toward the wagon propped on the logs. His bushy gray brows arched in disapproval. "I told you earlier I wouldn't tolerate another delay, and now both you and Mr. Pardee, here, have disobeyed my orders."

Roy exchanged an amused glance with Emmett Pardee, the husky blacksmith from Arkansas. His gaze returned to Jennings, and he forced patience into his voice, as if addressing a child. "We've been driving in constant drought for over a month now, Mr. Jennings. The wood on those wheels has shrunk so that they barely hold together. We've got a desert coming up, and I intend to get my wagon across it in one piece." He paused to take a puff on his pipe, realized it had gone out, and tucked it into his shirt pocket. "By tomorrow, the water will have swollen those wheels so they'll be as good as new."

Jennings dismissed the explanation with an impatient wave of his hand. "A waste of time!" He turned to Red Canfield. "Don't you think?"

The guide shrugged laconically, hawked loudly, and spat into the fire. "It's just a little stretch of desert—a day of dry driving, at most."

Jennings turned back to Roy, his eyes flashing with smug satisfaction. "You see?" He gestured to the wagon once more. "A waste of precious time, as I said before. And the entire party cannot be held up another day while you two refit your wheels." His gaze took in both Roy and Emmett Pardee. "It's already September twenty-

23

seventh. We're the last train on the road. Our food is running low, and we *still* have mountains to cross."

Roy's glance met Emmett's once more, then swung back to Jennings. "Don't fret about us, Reverend. We'll catch up."

A brief glimmer of indecision flickered in Jennings's eyes; then he nodded curtly. He turned abruptly and marched away, Red Canfield slouching after him.

Roy looked at his friend, a reckless grin spreading across his face. "He's probably conjuring up the wrath of God to strike us down."

Emmett Pardee snorted with laughter and settled his bulk onto one of the stools. He was a barrel-chested man in his late twenties, with powerful arms and thick hands. But his face was gentle and intense, with kind, honest eyes. He was making the journey to California with his wife, three small children, and elderly father-in-law.

Roy indicated the coffeepot with a wave of his hand. "Help yourself." He relighted his pipe and turned to call over his shoulder, "Sarah, fetch that jug of mine, will you?" He returned his gaze to Emmett and gave him a conspiratorial smile. "Picked it up at Fort Hall."

"I don't trust Canfield." Emmett scratched his shaggy brown beard with sausagelike fingers. "He don't seem like much of a guide to me. Kinda vague, if you know what I mean."

Roy nodded solemnly and reached up to take the earthenware jug from Sarah as she approached. "Sarah don't like him neither. Do you, Sarah?"

A mocking light entered her eyes. "I don't believe there's a female on this train that does." She shivered suddenly and chafed her arms, partly from the cold, partly from the image of Red Canfield's leering face. She

24

poured herself another cup of coffee, hoping to ward off the sudden chill she felt, but declined her brother's offer of the whiskey. "I'll be glad when we part company with the likes of him."

Emmett inclined his head in agreement, a faint, amused smile on his lips. "The Reverend had his nerve tellin' us *we're* delaying the party." His eyes narrowed thoughtfully, and his mouth compressed into a hard line. "Who of us refuses to travel on Sundays? Why, if we had all those wasted Sundays back, we'd be in California by now."

Roy nodded absently. "And the three days we held up back on the Platte 'cause his horse had saddle sores, and he wouldn't ride her—and he wouldn't walk her."

"Not to mention it's usually one of *his* wagons that breaks down." Emmett shook his head in exasperation. "Pompous, self-righteous ass!" He glanced over at Sarah and smiled apologetically. " 'Scuse me, ma'am."

Sarah shrugged carelessly and flashed him a dazzling smile. "No need. They're *my* sentiments, too." She took another sip of coffee and grimaced at the bitter grounds that came with it. Her gaze took in the two men with a brief glance. "Well, gentlemen, I think I'll leave you two alone and go see about giving Hetty a hand." And, with a faint, weary smile, she left the fire in a swirl of calico skirts.

Emmett followed her with his eyes, an appreciative smile on his lips as his gaze lingered on her slim, lithe figure and softly rounded hips. "Pretty girl, your sister is," he remarked, reaching for the jug to refill his cup. "Young O'Brian and Peter Andersen seem to think so, too, from what I've observed."

Roy acknowledged the compliment with a nod of his

head. "For a time, I thought she might be interested in Sean O'Brian. But since that fancy man showed up—" A shadow of irritation crossed his rugged features, and he let his words trail off with an expressive shrug.

"I think he's runnin' from the law."

"What makes you think that?"

Emmett shrugged and sipped his drink. "Just a feeling I have. He's too damn smooth for my liking."

Roy swallowed the bitter coffee laced with whiskey, his eyes hooded in thought. *"Whatever* Judd Brannan might be, Michael O'Brian would be wise to keep a closer eye on his daughter." It struck Roy as mighty suspicious that Brannan's hair had been damp and his clothes disarrayed this afternoon after his supposed chance happening upon Maggie about to be scalped. Roy shook his head, annoyed at himself. He was getting to be as bad as the gossipy women on the train. Let the others concern themselves with their own problems. For himself, he had quite enough just getting his family across the country safe and sound.

"I reckon old Jennings is right about not holding up for us tomorrow," Emmett said, bringing Roy out of his reverie, and he looked across the fire at his friend. "We should be able to catch up to them."

"I hope." Roy's thoughtful gaze returned to the fire, its flickering glow turning his skin a burnished bronze. "People talk about the heavy snows in the mountains we still have to cross. I keep thinking about that—the later it gets."

Emmett drained his cup and set it on the table. "Winter's still a long way off, and they say the storms don't commence till close to Thanksgiving. We got plenty of time to make it across." He heaved himself up from the

26

stool and hitched up his belt over his belly. "I'll take the first watch. I'll come wake you at—"

Emmett's words were cut short by an excited shout from the other side of camp. *"Indians!"*

Roy's stomach twisted in knots, and a cold terror spread through his veins. He swallowed dryly and drew in a deep breath, trying to shake off the fear and think rationally.

Emmett was already sprinting across the camp as Roy got to his feet and snatched up his Pennsylvania long rifle from the side of the wagon. His fingers worked clumsily as he fumbled through his pouch for a bullet, and he swore loudly as the metal ball fell to the dusty ground.

Hetty and Sarah raced into the circle of firelight, herding the three children before them. Their eyes were filled with a wild, unreasoning fear, only adding to Roy's own deepening anxiety, but he managed to fight it down.

He grasped Hetty's shoulder and gave her a shove, sending the children with her. "Get under the wagon!" He turned back to Sarah, saw the blind terror in her eyes, but he knew she was the only other member of his family capable of defending the wagon. He pushed the rifle into her hands and indicated the ground beneath the wagon. "Don't waste a shot!"

Simon was whimpering in fear. Lucas was asking excited questions. Beans, the family's setter, loped into the camp, and Samantha pulled him beneath the protection of the wagon bed. Roy waited until his sister had scuttled for cover, then vaulted into the wagon. He threw aside pots and pans, bolts of cloth, and stacks of bedding until he located his flintlock pistol in the trunk, along with powder and shot.

Outside, he could hear the rising clamor of panic and

27

fear coming from the other emigrants. Somewhere a woman had set up a keening wail of terror. Dogs barked, the cattle bawled nervously, and men shouted orders.

Roy crept cautiously to the tailgate, his pistol poised for the slightest movement, wishing he owned one of the new repeating revolvers as Judd Brannan did. He darted a glance to his right and saw the Andersen women huddled under their wagon. Moonlight glinted off the barrel of Ole Andersen's old blunderbuss sticking out of the canvas, and young Peter was silhouetted against the desert sky, armed with a hatchet.

Roy wiped his sweating palms on his trousers and directed his attention back to the farthest side of the camp. He could barely discern several figures creeping out from their hiding places, and as some of the cattle moved restlessly aside, he caught a glimpse of three horses—no, mules—and one lone rider. Sweat beaded on his skin and immediately chilled in the cold autumn night air. Roy suppressed a shiver and continued to watch as a few more emigrants ventured out.

"It's all right, everybody!" he heard Reverend Jennings boom in his deep voice. "It's a white man!"

Roy released his breath from between clenched teeth and felt his muscles go slack with relief. He had come this far; he had no wish to be halted in the wilds of Nevada by a pack of Indians.

Evidently, tonight he wouldn't be.

He jumped down from the wagon, saw others slowly emerging from their protection, and leaned down to peer at his own burrowing family. "It's safe to come out. False alarm."

Sarah shoved the rifle out, and Roy picked it up to set against the axle. Reaching down, he gave each a hand as

28

they emerged, still wary, lastly followed by the dog, who immediately went to investigate the ground near the fire where supper had been consumed.

Hetty gave her husband an impatient, disgusted look and pushed an errant wisp of dark hair away from her face. "What was it *this* time?"

Roy smiled indulgently, knowing full well her disaffection for the pretentious preacher. This would make perhaps the tenth such false alarm since Missouri, and while Roy always found it faintly amusing after any real threat of danger was passed, Hetty begrudged the interruption of her precise routine.

He wiped a smudge of dirt from her cheek with his fingertips. "I don't know." He glanced over his shoulder, noticed the entire party beginning to congregate near Jennings's wagon, and turned back to his wife. "But I think we should go see." He scooped Simon up in his arms and settled the boy on his shoulders.

Lucas's mouth drooped with disappointment. "I wanted to see some Indians!"

Hetty released an exasperated breath and threw up her hands dramatically. Samantha poked her brother in the back. "And get *scalped?*"

Lucas gave her a withering smile. "They don't scalp boys—only girls!"

Samantha compressed her lips and glared, but a tiny renewed glimmer of trepidation shone in her amber eyes.

By the time the Coulters reached Reverend Jennings's wagon, some forty emigrants were assembled in various stages of dress. With some amusement, Sarah noted Ruth Huntington and her daughter-in-law, Alma, clutching blankets around their nightgowns, frilly mobcaps covering their hair. In their state of undress, they somehow no

29

longer resembled the haughty aristocrats of the party, people who seemed too good for the rest of the humble emigrants. And Edgar Huntington, wearing his trousers over a torn pair of long johns and carrying a French dueling pistol, hardly looked like a man who was rumored to have $15,000 sewn inside a quilt.

Adam Trent, the quiet, gentle artist who spent much of his time sketching the countryside, stood clutching a stout club, incongruously wearing a nightshirt and black felt opera hat. Ezra Weeks, Emmett Pardee's father-in-law, complained bitterly and toothlessly of the intrusion to his daughter. Clad in a baggy set of long johns, displaying his bony knees and frail arms, he looked all of his seventy-two years.

The object of all this attention was standing with Reverend Jennings—a tall, lean, bedraggled man, drinking a cup of coffee gratefully. At first glance, the stranger appeared little better than a tired, ragged scarecrow, with masses of touseled, dirty blond hair and beard, wearing a fringed buckskin jacket and high leather boots tucked into heavy corduroy trousers. But Sarah sensed immediately a kind of ruthless power in him. He had the watchful eyes of a hawk, and when he moved, it was with all the grace and sureness of a panther.

Ole Andersen ambled slowly over to Roy. "A hunter," the Swede said. "Wants to join us the rest of the way."

Several of the women and children had gathered around the two pack mules and were exclaiming in wonder at their cargo—two large elks. Sarah's mouth began to water at the thought of fresh game—the first fresh meat in weeks.

Hetty was grumbling pettishly. "I'm going back to

camp with the children. We've had quite enough excitement for one night.''

Sarah nodded absently, her mind still filled with images of roast venison. But as Hetty began to walk away with her three unwilling youngsters, she noticed Roy slip her his pistol, and Sarah shivered once more at the thought of what dangers lurked beyond the boundary of the wagons.

Many of the women were likewise beginning to drift back to their respective wagons, herding excited, now wide-awake children with them, until only Sarah, Mrs. Jennings, and Maggie remained with the men.

Orpha Jennings, a stern-looking woman in her early forties, was busily dishing up a plate of stew for the stranger. Frail and birdlike, with small dark eyes and a perpetual frown, she hovered anxiously around the men like an agitated bee. Sarah repressed a smile at the woman's behavior, for the Jenningses had never been known for their generosity with food before, and she suspected that the two elks had induced this sudden change.

"I heard at Fort Hall that you were the last train on the road this season," the newcomer said, his voice low, with a soft caress in its tone. He lowered his lanky frame onto a campstool and combed his fingers through his disheveled locks, nodding his thanks to Orpha as she handed him a bowl of stew. "I've been riding hard for a week to catch up to you so I wouldn't have to cross the Sierras alone."

"This game," Jennings said, indicating the elk with a wave of his hand. "Where did you find it? We've seen nothing but rabbits and coyotes for miles."

The stranger shrugged lightly. "You have to know where to find it."

Maggie sidled closer to the fire, her long tresses spilling over her shoulders, the color of a fiery sunset in its flickering glow and her green eyes shining like emeralds. She dipped her lashes coyly at the man, and her lips curved in a provocative little smile. "You must be very good at what you do, Mr.—?"

The man looked up, tilting his head to one side and studying her appraisingly, a lazy half-smile playing about his mouth. "Garrett, ma'am. Toby Garrett."

Sarah's eyes flashed with resentment, and angry spots of color flared in her cheeks. Was no man safe from Maggie O'Brian's outrageous flirting? She stole a surreptitious glance at Judd Brannan, leaning against the Jennings's wagon, a wry smile on his lips, regarding the scene with tolerant amusement. At least *he* didn't seem to care.

Frowning in exasperation, Sarah turned her attention back to the stranger.

"We'll be most happy to have you join us, Mr. Garrett," Jennings was saying. "But we're running low on provisions."

Garrett spooned up the last of the stew and lifted his eyes to the older man. "I have some supplies of my own. And you're welcome to any game I shoot."

"Just a minute!" Red Canfield stepped forward and assessed the newcomer with thinly veiled hostility. "As guide, I get two dollars for every unattached person—ten for each wagon." His eyes riveted on the stranger in silent challenge. "Can you pay?"

Toby Garrett met the man's gaze calmly, with a hint of weary indifference. "I can pay." His smile was faint, almost derisive. "Can *you* guide us?"

Canfield's face darkened with suppressed anger. "Of

32

course I can!" He spat a stream of tobacco juice into the fire; it hissed for a brief second on the hot coals. "That's what I'm paid to do!"

Garrett straightened his long legs and stood up, returning the empty bowl to Orpha Jennings with another smile of thanks. His gaze returned to Canfield, his expression inscrutable beneath the tangle of hair and beard. "Then I take it you've had everyone gather in sufficient stores of grass for their cattle? Fill everything they can find to hold water?"

Canfield spluttered in rage. *"What for?* The desert's still two days away!"

"And between here and there is the Humboldt Sink—hardly better than the desert itself. You'll find no water fit for humans there, nor any grass for the cattle." Garrett's eyes swept the men around him, coming finally to rest on Jennings. "You'll need every ounce of water and blade of grass you can find—here."

Jennings looked vaguely bewildered and cast a doubtful look at his guide. "Is that true?"

Canfield snorted in disgust and spat again. *"I'm* running this train!" He turned and thrust a threatening finger at Toby Garrett. "Not him!"

Sean O'Brian caught Sarah's eye across the fire and winked, a sparkle of deviltry brightening his green eyes. She returned his grin, glad that someone else found Red Canfield's belligerent petulance as amusing as she. What little flesh of the guide's face was visible through his beard had turned a deep scarlet, and he resembled a big, overgrown spoiled child, chewing feverishly on his tobacco and glaring at the trapper.

Michael O'Brian ventured forward to stand beside Maggie, still hovering near Toby. The Irishman's brow furrowed in a doubtful frown as he assessed the tall man in buckskin. "Have ye ever been across the desert yourself?"

"No, I haven't. But—"

Canfield cut him off with a triumphant hiss. "You see!"

Michael held up a silencing hand and scowled savagely at the guide. "Just hold your tongue a minute, man. Let Mr. Garrett have his say!"

Canfield's eyes narrowed into fierce slits and fixed malevolently on the Irishman, but he kept silent, choosing instead to direct another stream of tobacco juice toward the fire. It came dangerously close to hitting O'Brian's boot.

"I haven't been across the desert *personally*," Toby said, his gaze sweeping the emigrants speculatively, pausing briefly on Sarah. She thought she detected the faintest trace of a smile touch the corners of his mouth before he looked away, and she flushed. "But I *have* been as far as the Sink," he continued. "The river becomes swampy marsh and then simply disappears." He lifted his hands helplessly, and the chilly breeze snapped the buckskin fringe. "There's no fodder available, and the water is full of alkali. From there on, you've got fifty miles of dry desert."

"It's *not* fifty miles!" Canfield exclaimed furiously, casting him a scathing look. "It's thirty-five at most— one day and one night of dry driving!"

Toby shook his head impatiently, scorn etched in the line of his mouth. "I have friends who have crossed the desert. It's hell on earth—completely desolate—with no water except for some boiling springs halfway across."

Claude Tyrrell, the stock tender hired by Reverend

Jennings, stepped forward. He was a slight, frail man of equally small intelligence, with a sharp, unshaven face and thatch of uncombed black hair. "I think we should listen to this stranger." He flicked a glance at Jennings. "If what he says is true, the oxen won't make it without grass or water."

Red snorted in contempt. "Oxen can go two days without water or grass, and you know it!"

"But they're already weak from the scanty grass picked over by the other trains before us," Tyrrell pointed out.

"He's right," O'Brian agreed. "Some of you have oxen and mules to spare." His gaze rested meaningfully on Jennings and Huntington for a brief moment. "But the rest of us have barely enough. If we lose one or two of the beasts in the desert, we'll have to abandon our wagons."

Ole Andersen nodded agreement. *"Ja.* I think we should take a vote. Stay here tomorrow and prepare—or move on."

A quiet ripple of assent passed through the men. Canfield flung up his hands in disgust and cursed through clenched teeth. Jennings looked around uncertainly and rubbed his forehead in a gesture of weary helplessness.

Maggie ambled over to Sarah and gave her a sly smile. "It seems our Mr. Garrett has stirred up a hornet's nest." Her smile widened to a grin, showing off a row of sparkling white teeth. "I like a man who has opinions and speaks his mind."

Sarah's mouth twitched with grim amusement. You like *any* man, she thought shrewishly. Her gaze moved to Judd Brannan, still leaning negligently against the wagon, his arms folded across his chest, wearing a slight, sardonic smile. So quiet, Sarah mused, and wondered again

35

at the intangibility of the man.

Maggie yawned and stretched her arms langorously above her head. "I think I'll turn in for the night," she said. "Let the men settle this. They never give *us* any say anyway."

Sarah nodded and gazed absently after Maggie as she walked away, her hips swaying provocatively beneath her skirt. Judd moved away from the wagon to speak quietly to her, and Sarah frowned, her eyes glittering in stormy anger. Perhaps if she displayed a little more boldness . . .

She pushed the notion aside and turned to leave. The men's voices were raised in heated argument as they debated the best course of action to take. Sarah glanced back once, and her gaze met that of Toby Garrett. The firelight played across his rugged features, and his eyes narrowed wickedly as they swept the length of her body with deliberate slowness. Sarah dropped her gaze quickly, a rush of color flooding her cheeks, feeling unnerved by the intense stare of the likes of such a filthy, bedraggled man.

She hastened back to her wagon, leaving the men to decide the fate of the party, a fate held in the hands of a group of divergent, incompatible wayfarers thrown together by chance, whose constant petty squabbles would forever seal their dark destiny.

Chapter Three

Judd Brannan's roan gelding topped the rise of a bare, sandy bluff and picked its way carefully down through a field of scattered chunks of sharp black rock. Judd shielded his eyes from the glare of the midafternoon sun, but for miles all he could see was the endless plains caked with alkali, the black basalt hills in the distance, and the bone-white canvas of the wagons. The train was strung out, rambling slowly along the diminishing river in a cloud of dust, nearly invisible for the fine, powdery sand and minute, billowing particles of crushed rock.

Coughing as he approached the last wagon, Judd refastened his handkerchief over his mouth and nose. His eyes watered, he could taste the grit in his mouth, and for the hundredth time he cursed himself for a fool.

If he hadn't been so quick-tempered back at that gambling hall in Natchez, the two Slater brothers would still be alive, and Judd would undoubtedly by now be the husband of Miss Loretta Blaine and the future master of Magnolia Plantation.

He squinted at the wilderness surrounding him, his

mouth twisting in self-mockery. At least the law would never find him out here in this wretched, empty land. If only the Slater boys hadn't accused him of cheating.

A wry smile tugged at the corners of his mouth. Of course, he *had* been cheating; but, still, a man had to defend his good name and honor, no matter how dubious that honor was.

Judd put his heels to the flanks of his mount and caught up with the last wagon, the ramshackle prairie ark of Ole Andersen. The Swede was walking alongside his three yokes of oxen, occasionally cracking his long bullwhip at his side for its pistol noise. Two saddle horses were tied to the back of the wagon, and behind that, seventeen-year-old Peter herded the family's two milk cows.

The young man looked up and waved a greeting, his thick blond curls escaping from beneath his battered straw hat. He was covered with the powdery dust that was everywhere; it clung to his eyebrows, gathered in the creases of his neck, and caked his clothing.

"You look like you took a bath in a barrel of flour," Judd called.

Peter gave him a deprecating shrug. "We should have so much flour to waste, *ja?*"

Judd nodded agreement, but his smile faded and disappeared quickly, replaced by a worried frown. Today was the last day of September, and each day that passed saw the foodstuffs shrink. His own supply, carried in one of Jennings's wagons for a small fee, was almost exhausted, and had it not been for his share of the hunter's two elks, by now he would be subsisting entirely on flour, cornmeal, and beans.

Unbidden, a vision came to him of platters of steamed clams, crisp fried shrimp, and thick, tangy gumbo, the

38

specialty of the Crescent City Hotel in New Orleans. And if he closed his eyes, he could almost smell the heady blend of spices and feel the bubbles from the champagne tickling his tongue.

Angrily, Judd jerked himself back to reality. It would serve no purpose to dream of the unattainable. This was the Nevada territory, a place God apparently had forsaken, and there would be no intimate midnight suppers and fine wines out here.

He nudged his mount forward, pausing to gaze curiously at the sheafs of grass fastened onto the Andersens' wagon. Two days ago, after a discussion that had lasted well into the night, the men had gone out with sickles and scythes, stripping every blade of grass from the countryside. Even Judd had helped, though admittedly he had little experience with such tools. Now that grass was packed away in every conceivable place inside and outside the wagons, and all receptacles—everything that could possibly hold water—had been filled. And because there would be no chance for fuel for cooking, the women had prepared enough food to last the supposed three days it would take the party to reach and cross the desert.

Toby Garrett had spoken the truth in his description of the Humboldt Sink, and Judd shuddered as his gaze swept the terrain. The river spread into swamps and tule marshes, where the water was brackish and fetid. It was warm, sluggish, and unpalatable for either man or beast. There was little grass; only low, green clumps of greasewood, and even that was becoming more scanty with each mile. Judd's face twisted into a grimace, and he shook his head in disgust. What a country!

Movement at the rear of the Andersens' wagon caught his eye, and he turned to see the sunlight shining on pale blond braids and a freckled, sunburned face peeking out from the canvas. Tall, willowy teen-aged Astrid hopped down from the slow-moving van, sank to her shoetops in the loose, sandy soil, and smiled brightly. She was a pretty girl, big-boned and muscular like her parents and brother. A bit too masculine for Judd's liking, but she always had a ready smile and a cheerful word.

Judd slowed his mount and let her catch up to him, shielding her eyes from the sun and smiling up at him. "You like this country?" she asked with a teasing sparkle in her large blue eyes and a wave of her hand that encompassed the barren hills and bleak valleys.

Judd lifted one sleek black brow in amusement. "Do you?"

Her smile widened to a grin, and she shook her head, sending a cloud of fine dust from her long braids. "It must *never* rain here. And the dust"—she gave an exaggerated shudder—"it gets into everything—sifts right into the wagon, and now it's in our food! Mama's inside now trying to protect our things."

Judd feigned a look of sympathy. "We should reach the desert by tonight."

Astrid nodded brisky. "*Ja.* And Papa thinks by tomorrow night we'll be in the mountains."

"Astrid!"

She turned and looked back at her brother, a slight frown wrinkling her high forehead. "*Ja?* What is it?"

"Fetch me a cup of water!" Peter called. "I'm thirsty."

Astrid turned back to Judd and made a small, helpless gesture with her hands. "So my brother is too lazy to get his own drink."

"He's got his hands full." Offering her his most en-

40

gaging smile, Judd touched the brim of his black hat with his fingers. "Good day, Miss Andersen." And, spurring his horse into an easy trot, he rode ahead.

All eleven wagons looked as if they were decorated for some sort of fall harvest festival, with the bundles of dry grass lashed to their sides. In fact, he thought with some amusement, had the grass been green, all they would need were a few sprigs of holly, and the entire train would resemble a Christmas caravan. Though this weather hardly felt like any Christmas Judd had known.

He had removed his jacket and waistcoat, but sweat soaked his back and armpits and dampened the waistband of his trousers. He pulled alongside the Jennings wagon and reached for the dipper hanging next to his water cask. Even though the keg was capped, a fine scum of dust had settled on the surface of the water. Judd drank deeply, ignoring the bitter, chalky taste.

Lester Stone, prodding the oxen, glanced back over his shoulder but made no greeting. A strange one, Judd thought as he resealed the keg. Hired by Jennings as a stock tender, Stone kept to himself almost to the point of total seclusion. A man in his middle thirties, with thinning brown hair and a lean, wiry body, Lester Stone spoke little and smiled even less. His face was flat and blunt, with thin lips and a scar running down one cheek. But it was his eyes Judd noticed most. They were small, close-set, and brown, swimming in slightly jaundiced whites, always restless and shifty. And those eyes were constantly watching—watching everything and everyone. Especially the more prosperous emigrants, the Jenningses and Huntingtons. Their wagons were never safe from Stone's scrutiny, and whatever the man's game was, Judd thought it would do the pilgrims wise to watch him.

41

Judd rode on, past the Huntingtons' three wagons—by far the finest and best equipped. A wealthy furniture shipper from New York, Edgar Huntington was traveling west with his wife, son, and daughter-in-law, grandson, driver, and black servant girl to start a new business in the port of Yerba Buena, only recently coming to be called San Francisco.

Phillip Huntington, the son, dressed in jodhpurs and a fine silk shirt, was plodding through the dust beside the oxen, occasionally halfheartedly poking the beasts' flanks with a stick. He was a sallow young man, with soft brown hair and a neatly trimmed goatee enhancing his thin, ascetic face. But he always seemed drawn and haggard, and lately he wheezed and spluttered incessantly. As Judd passed, Phillip raised his hand in a weak wave, then erupted in a spasm of dry, wracking coughs.

Casting a doubtful, sidelong look at the young man, Judd urged his horse on toward the O'Brians and their brood of children and traveling menagerie of livestock. Two mangy dogs trotted beside Patrick and Daniel, while four-year-old Katie sat in the rear wagon perched beside a coop full of squawking chickens. Molly O'Brian, a small, plain woman with light brown hair and big, friendly brown eyes, tended the cows and extra oxen with her sixteen-year-old son, Kelly. She lifted a hand in greeting to Judd as he passed, then turned to bawl a loud threat to a slow-footed ox. Sean was prodding the team hauling this load.

On the seat of the lead wagon was six-year-old James, cradling his brother Kevin, a child not yet weaned away from his mother's breast, on his lap. Michael O'Brian, his hair and beard covered with the powdery dust, cursed his oxen while Maggie walked at his side. Even with the heat and the difficulty in walking in the loose sand, Judd noticed how easily her body moved beneath her bright calico frock. A wave of brassy-gold hair fell down her back, and even the dusting of sand couldn't obscure its lustrous sheen.

A smug, satisfied smile played around the corners of Judd's mouth. Maggie O'Brian might not be the wealthy heiress to a sugar plantation, but she had other talents that more than compensated for her lack of money and breeding. Still, Judd had to admit he was already beginning to tire of her. She was growing too possessive, and what he had planned to be no more than a pleasant way to pass the time on this journey was becoming far too serious for his liking. Maggie asked too many questions—about his past *and* his future. The past he wanted kept a secret, and the future . . . An annoyed frown creased his brow. His future held no place in it for Maggie O'Brian or any other woman—at least not a woman without substantial means.

Maggie turned around to check on her young brothers and gave a tiny start of surprise to see Judd riding a few yards behind her. A mischievous light came into her green eyes, and her lips formed a pretty pout. "Is it ridin' you're doing, while the rest of us walks?"

He shrugged carelessly. "A man gets tired walking." He nudged his mount forward to walk beside her and slipped the kerchief from his nose and mouth; the dust wasn't so bad near the front of the train. He leaned down in his saddle and gave her a faintly leering smile. "Besides, you give a man enough exercise."

A provocative smile curved her generous mouth, and she eyed him with a bold challenge. "Is it complaining you are?"

A slow, lazy smile spread across his face, and his

43

glance slid suggestively from her face to the rounded curve of her hips. "Never," he said quietly, and, with a sly wink, set his heels to the flanks of his horse.

Perhaps he *still* could continue his relationship with Maggie. After all, they had only another week or two of travel, and then he could be on his way to start a new life for himself in California. He might even slip out of camp a day early and find his *own* way to Sutter's Fort, just in case Maggie had ideas of her own. If she *did* have him in mind for a husband—which he suspected she might—he could be gone before she could cause a scene.

Smiling complacently, he nodded politely to Belle Pardee and her two young sons walking alongside their wagon as he passed.

In the lead was the Coulters' van, and Judd's gaze settled speculatively on Sarah. His eyes traveled her length slowly, comparing her silently to Maggie. She was as straight and supple as a reed and moved with a fluid grace. Her honey-gold hair, gathered with a snip of ribbon, flowed down her back in a rich cascade. Her profile showed her high cheekbones and slightly upturned nose, and despite the wind and sun, her skin was flawless and smooth.

But unlike Maggie, Sarah was shy and undoubtedly as innocent as a newborn babe. Though it might be a tempting idea to try to change all that, Judd thought, and a wicked smile touched his lips.

Sarah felt someone's stare on her back and turned, momentarily unsettled to discover Judd Brannan's inscrutable gaze fixed on her from atop his horse. He smiled, and Sarah felt a hot flush rise in her cheeks, but she managed

44

a faint smile in return.

"You never seem to get tired," he said, a smile of admiration creeping across his lips. "All this walking . . ." He made a sweeping gesture with his hand, his gaze moving deferentially to Hetty. "Both of you."

"You'd be surprised to know how tired we are," Hetty said, and flicked an arch glance at the livestock trailing behind the wagon. "But I suspect *they're* a sight more tuckered than we are."

As if to confirm this statement, one of the cows lifted her head and bawled plaintively.

Sarah stole a wary glance at Judd, wishing she could think of something witty to say. But she *was* tired. The miserable heat, the soft, sandy soil, and the monotony of the scenery all had combined to make this one of the most arduous days of travel so far. She wiped a hand wearily across her face and frowned with disgust at the sweaty, claylike grime that came away on her hand.

"Are Reverend Jennings's wagons still falling behind?" she asked.

Judd nodded. "They're too heavy for this kind of ground." A wry smile flitted across his face. "Must be all those books and Bibles he's taking with him to 'civilize' the Californios."

Sarah matched his smile, an impish gleam in her eyes. "And Mrs. Jennings's organ."

Judd chuckled softly in agreement, removed his hat, and combed his fingers through his black hair, damp with perspiration. And, for the first time since his joining the party, Sarah noted, he looked less than dapper. His shirt was wrinkled and sweat-stained, his trousers powdered with dust. His dark brown eyes, always so clear, were red and swollen from the dust, almost as if he had been cry-

45

ing; his meticulously trimmed mustache drooped over his upper lip like a dead caterpillar.

Everyone was hot and tired. Samantha and Lucas, who ordinarily romped along the roadside, making a kind of game of their trek, had sought the shade of the wagon's canvas with young Simon. The teamsters' voices had dropped to mumbles, and at times it seemed the train scarcely appeared to move. The earth, beaten down by hundreds of wheels and hooves, seemed incapable of sustaining life.

Sarah moistened her dry lips and winced as a salty drop of sweat found its way into a crack. She hazarded another glance at Judd, trying to think of something clever and charming, but her mind was too weary with fatigue.

A flash of bright red calico caught her eye, and as she looked back, she saw Maggie hurrying to catch up with them, her hair streaming behind her, her heavy walking shoes kicking up a cloud of dust. Sarah's mouth tightened, and her eyes flashed with resentment.

"I thought I'd walk along up here." Maggie fell into step beside Sarah and Hetty, her face flushed, her breathing slightly labored. "Me own family's so busy complainin' about the heat, they can't seem to speak a civil word."

Sarah noticed Judd's eyes lingering appreciatively at the rise and fall of Maggie's breasts, and she seethed with an anger she could barely manage to conceal. She gave Maggie a mildly irritated glance. "We're just as hot here."

"But you're *never* as gloomy as the O'Brians when they're in a bad mood." Her smile was warm and ingratiating, and Sarah felt her anger melt away. Despite her ill humor, she couldn't help but smile in return. There

46

was something refreshing about Maggie O'Brian's exuberance that was infectious, regardless of Sarah's brief twinges of jealousy.

A loud stream of profanity erupted a few wagons back, accentuated with a heavy brogue. Maggie looked up sharply and whistled in alarm. "I didn't think his mood was *that* bad."

Judd swung around in his saddle. "One of his oxen's down."

Maggie exchanged an anxious glance with Sarah, then turned to hasten back to her father. Sarah went with her; if nothing else, a prostrate ox was a change in an otherwise dull routine.

When Sarah arrived, nearly the entire O'Brian clan was gathered around the ox. It was down on its forelegs, its head lolling to one side and foam dribbling from its mouth. Michael had forsaken his curses and now was kneeling at its side, talking sweetly to the animal. Daniel dashed up with a pan of water, and, together, he and his father attempted to coax the beast to drink. The ox simply snorted weakly and turned its head away.

Michael scrubbed a hand across his face and muttered a low curse. "It's no use. He's done in."

"We'll make camp here for a short while."

The deep, mellow voice directly behind Sarah startled her, for she had heard no footsteps. She turned abruptly and found herself looking directly at the open neck of a soft calfskin shirt, loosely fastened with thongs, a patch of light, curly hair covering the tanned skin above it. She lifted her eyes slowly, furtively, to study the face of Toby Garrett. His features were shadowed by a wide-brimmed hat, but at least he had trimmed his mangy beard to a semblance of neatness.

"We've reached the end of the Sink anyway," he went on. "A few hours' rest for us and the animals, and we'll start across the desert tonight." He turned and squinted up at Judd. "Why don't you ride down the line and tell the others?" Without waiting for a reply, he stepped forward to help Michael O'Brian unchain the yoke of oxen, and Sarah moved out of the way as Judd cantered off.

The entire train had come to a halt. Reverend Jennings, who had been up front with Toby and Red Canfield, paused on his way back to his own wagons to cluck his tongue sympathetically, then move on.

Michael's heavy brows drew together in a fierce scowl, and he shook his head. "Pious old coot!" He lifted the thick hickory yoke from the necks of his team and handed it to Kelly. "You'd better get the horses out here with some ropes to pull this one out of the way."

Canfield fixed Toby with a cynical stare, a glint of triumphant, sadistic glee in his eyes. "I *told* you it was foolish to waste a day back there cutting grass." He put his hands on his hips, his belly bulging against his greasy shirt. "If we'd have moved out like *I* said, that ox would be across the desert by now."

Toby glanced up, his deep blue eyes like steel. "If we'd done as you suggested, *half* the oxen would be like this one."

Hatred burned undisguised in Canfield's eyes as he gave one last lingering look at Toby, then snorted in disgust and walked away.

Toby's gaze followed the guide for a few moments, a perplexed frown cutting deep furrows in his brow. He shook his head distractedly and turned back to O'Brian. "You might want to dress and cure this meat—if you have the salt to spare."

Maggie gave a repulsive shudder. "Ox meat!" She grimaced as if in pain. "It'd be tough as wood!"

"But it's food, miss." Toby gave her a brief, thoughtful look, then resumed unhitching the second yoke. "There's no game between here and the mountains except snakes and buzzards." He threw another quick glance over his shoulder at her, sardonic amusement in his eyes. "And I assure you—they're even *less* palatable."

Maggie shuddered again and looked helplessly around. But Molly O'Brian was coming toward her with the small bag of the family's remaining salt, and Maggie heaved a resigned sigh. "Ox meat for supper it is then."

Sarah tarried a moment longer, then, with a sigh, turned back to her own wagon. There was much to be done before embarking on the desert crossing, and Roy would need all the help he could get.

Red Canfield walked away from the wagons, his head bent, hands jammed into the pockets of his trousers. He kicked a clump of sagebrush, then glowered at the worn toe of his boot. This was his last pair—the third since leaving Missouri—and he hoped they would last the rest of the journey.

He turned and glared back at the wagons, now alive with activity as the emigrants prepared for the desert. A muscle in his jaw twitched with suppressed anger as he sat down on a large rock and stared morosely at the wasteland of parched grass and sand surrounding him. He picked up a pebble and tossed it into the slimy pool of stagnant water—water so thick with alkali that it didn't even ripple.

Muttering irascibly, he delved into his pocket and withdrew a pint bottle, uncorked it and drank deeply. The raw whiskey soothed his parched throat and helped ease his tension, but he doubted *anything* would lessen his anger at Toby Garrett.

Until the hunter had come along, everyone had listened to Red Canfield. He was their guide, and his word had seemed like the very Gospel itself. The party may not have liked him, but that was a small matter; few people liked Red Canfield. But they *had* respected him—his wisdom, his judgment, his experience at his job.

Red's little eyes crinkled with mocking amusement, and he drank again. Experience! He laughed softly, a harsh, throaty sound. It's true he had been across the country once before—three years ago, with Fremont, then Hastings. But he had gone to Oregon—not California. And for the last five hundred miles, Red had been as unfamiliar with the land as the rest of these simple people.

But the tracks were easy enough to follow, and the occasional sighting of bleached bones or an abandoned wagon told him he was on the right path. Besides, he had a copy of *Hastings' Emigrants' Guide*, just as many of the others did, with information vital to their journey. Leading a wagon train was easy. It gave a man an aura of respectability and pride to be asked an opinion, and Red relished his feeling of authority. The pay was good, the food wholesome, and he had little of the *real* work to do for himself.

But now this Toby Garrett had started to put a seed of doubt in the emigrants' minds, and Red felt he was losing some credibility. Garrett had been right about the water and grass along the Sink, but anything more he said could only be a guess; he had admitted never having crossed the desert himself. Perhaps now he would keep his suggestions to himself. If not . . .

Red swilled the last of the contents of the bottle, carefully recapped it, and returned it to his pocket. Later, when no one was about, he could refill it from Jennings's supply, supposedly for medical emergencies.

His mouth twisted into a humorless smile beneath his whiskers. It had surely been his lucky day when the Reverend had come into the saloon in Independence with a handful of his tracts. Red had convinced him of the need for a trained guide, and Jennings had agreed; his train was the last to depart and he was anxious to have a capable man to lead them and make up for lost time.

That hadn't happened, Red thought maliciously. If anything, they had lost time. What did these farmers and merchants know of travel? They were bumbling, unseasoned wayfarers—a pack of women and children led by a Bible-thumping old fart.

Amused with his thoughts, Red got to his feet and bit off a fresh chew of tobacco. His gaze swept the bare, rugged hills of basalt, devoid of any vegetation except for stumpy clumps of sage, and he shuddered at its arid vastness.

Why were they all so worried about an early snowfall? A little snow would feel mighty good right now—wash away the dust and cool the blood. Though it was hard to keep a man's blood cool with such tempting women as Maggie O'Brian and Sarah Coulter around.

Chuckling lasciviously, he hitched up his belt and ambled back toward the wagons.

* * *

51

The setting sun was gilding the crags to the west as Sarah finished the last bite of her evening meal. It was one of the less savory she had eaten in some time, consisting of dried venison, a hard biscuit dipped in molasses, and one of the last pickles in the gallon jug. Michael O'Brian had generously offered a slice of ox meat, but there was no wood to build a fire on which to cook it. Molly and Maggie, with the help of young Patrick, were still busy cutting strips of the meat and hanging it on the canvas top of the wagon to dry. By tomorrow, it would no doubt make nourishing, if not tasty, jerky.

Sarah picked up her tin cup and washed her supper down with fresh milk. The three cows had been invaluable throughout the journey; but now, with the scanty grass for forage, their milk was drying up. Sarah had only been able to fill two pails from the animals this evening.

With the disappearance of the sun, a chilly wind had sprung up, and Sarah picked up one of the pails and left her place at the makeshift camp to climb into the wagon. Roy had constructed a hinged tailgate for easy access, and Sarah was able to forgo lifting her skirts to climb over the rear as most of the other women were forced to do.

The interior was dim and stank of sweat and stale food, tobacco, and the pungent scent of Hetty's soap. Trunks, bolts of cloth, crates of nails and horsehoes, kerosene lamps, tools, and all manner of supplies were packed along either side, with a narrow passage running down the middle. The canvas was high enough for a person to stand upright in the center of the arch, and as Sarah stood looking around, she shook her head in mute wonder. *How* had they managed to get by all this time with only these meager remnants of their former home life?

Roy had sold his small house in Kentucky, and much

of the money received from the sale had gone into outfitting for the trip. He had purchased the wagon, strengthened it himself by installing strap iron wherever the strain was likely to be the hardest, purchased eight oxen and hundreds of pounds of foodstuffs. Now those provisions were almost gone, and if there were any more delays, Sarah feared that one of the cows might have to be sacrificed to feed the family.

Near the front of the wagon was a churn, and Sarah poured the milk inside, satisfied that at least they would have butter. After a day of the uneven, jouncing motion of the van over the trail, the sweet milk would be transformed into butter. A rather ingenious idea, she had to admit, and one that saved her extra work.

Gathering up her shawl, she made her way back through the maze of goods and paused to look around at her surroundings. The nearby barren mountains were tinged purple by the setting sun. The Humboldt had all but disappeared into dry, cracked sand flats. There was some grass in spots, but it was brittle and dry. Here and there were stagnant, foul-smelling pools of water, white with alkali and unfit to drink.

The air was cool and sharp, and Sarah shivered, pulling her shawl more closely about her shoulders and fastening it with a pin. She hopped down from the van and was surprised to see Toby Garrett standing with her brother near the fire, drinking from a cup.

Sarah wasn't sure if she liked this lean, rawboned stranger or not, though she had barely spoken to him. But there was something about him—perhaps his cool assurance and the almost cynical way in which he seemed to view everything—that was faintly disquieting. And whenever she was around him, she felt strangely unsettled.

As Sarah quietly approached, she saw that he had donned his fringed buckskin jacket once more, and it seemed only to emphasize the width of his shoulders. His fair, tousled hair was streaked by the sun, and his eyebrows were bleached nearly white, making a striking contrast to his deeply tanned skin. His nose was narrow and straight, and despite the blond beard, Sarah detected a suggestion of arrogance in the set of his jaw. But it was his eyes—so intensely deep blue, like sapphires—that Sarah found most remarkable about him.

He turned at her approach, his eyes assessing her in a quick glance. "Miss Coulter," he said, and a faint smile touched his lips for an instant before he returned his attention to Roy. "You might want to put three yokes on your rig for the desert. It'll ease the work and might lessen the chance of eventual exhaustion."

Roy nodded thoughtfully. "They're weak already, and I don't want to end up like O'Brian."

"You'll have to keep a sharp watch on the milk cows, too. If they scent water, they'll stampede."

"Sarah usually sees to the cows."

Toby didn't even glance in her direction as he said to Roy, "You'd best try to help her on the desert."

Sarah bristled in annoyance at being so openly excluded from this conversation. She had worked as hard as any man on this trek west, and she felt herself to be the equal of any of them in most things. Now here was this stranger, obviously dismissing her as just another silly, helpless female.

"I can take care of the cows myself," she said quietly.

Toby turned his head slightly to regard her circumspectly, faint mockery gleaming in his eyes. "This is a little different country. Animals tend to be troublesome."

Sarah faced him with her chin up, a rebellious glint in her gray eyes. "I can *handle* them."

He lifted his cup in mock salute and drained its contents. "I'll remember you said that when you're chasing halfway across the desert after them."

Sarah's lips tightened stubbornly, and she glared at him. "In that case, I *won't* ask for your assistance."

His mouth quirked in sardonic humor. He handed the empty cup to her and executed a smart bow. "Thanks for the milk." He switched his gaze to Roy, and the mockery left his eyes. "I think we should move out in about forty-five minutes. Maybe you'd better tie those cows together." Giving Sarah another slow, taunting smile, he turned and walked away.

Sarah's face was pinched into angry lines as she watched Toby saunter away noiselessly, his knee-high moccasins whispering through the sand. She felt a renewed wave of fury jolt her, and her eyes flashed her angry frustration. "Of all the arrogant, insufferable men!" She grunted irritably and dug her nails into her palms.

Roy let out a sudden rich laugh. "You don't like Mr. Garrett?"

Sarah tossed her head angrily. "Who does he think he is—showing up out of nowhere and giving us orders?"

"So far, everything he's said makes sense."

Sarah sniffed as if to dismiss the matter. Roy put his arm around her shoulder, and she leaned against his side. "Besides," he said. "He doesn't know you like I do. He's probably used to women who can only make pleasant conversation over tea."

Sarah snorted impatiently. "If you ask me, he looks like the only women *he* knows are Indian squaws. And *they* don't drink tea.''

Roy laughed again. "I'm glad to see at least there's another man besides Judd Brannan who's got your full attention."

Sarah drew in a breath in indignation and turned to look into her brother's face. It was a strong face, etched with countless tiny lines from years of hard living, but as she caught the teasing sparkle in his slate-blue eyes, her irascibility dissolved, and an unwilling smile touched her lips. "Let's hitch up the team."

Chapter Four

Maggie sat huddled against a wheel, her heavy woolen cape wrapped close about her, but still she shivered. The morning stars winked feebly in the sky, losing their battle with the invading sun as the first streaks of gray crept across the eastern horizon. Sheltered here against the wagon, protected from the wind, Maggie was at long last beginning to feel a return to her senses. But for the last six hours, the drive across the desert had been a living nightmare.

Unimpeded by trees or mountains, the wind had knifed across her face. The raw, bone-chilling cold of the desert night had penetrated her clothing and stiffened her joints until every step was torture. Her feet sank into the loose sand, and several times she had stumbled like a child learning to walk. The desolation was complete; no crickets chirped, not even a coyote howled. There was only the ominous stillness of the desert—a black, silent infinity lit by brilliant white stars.

The cattle had to be rested often, and Maggie had no way of calculating how many miles they had traversed since sundown. Perhaps they were almost out of this horrible, forbidding wasteland. And when the sun rose, in front of them might be the towering range of the Sierras, filled with cool mountain streams dappled by warm sunshine.

Maggie closed her eyes and shook her head, as if to dislodge the tantalizing images. The wagons had inched along painfully, and she doubted their speed ever made it above one or two miles an hour.

Inside the wagon, she could hear her mother trying to soothe young Katie and James. The blackness of the night, the eerie shapes of the dunes, and the oppressive silence had all combined to frighten the children half out of their wits.

For herself, Maggie thought with longing of being wrapped snugly in a blanket with Judd, feeling his body's warmth next to hers and generating her own kind of heat from his intimate caresses and demanding kisses. Just the mere thought of his touch and the feel of his rippling muscles beneath her fingertips sent the blood surging through her veins, and Maggie found she was already a trifle warmer than before.

She rested her head against the wheel and closed her eyes, her mind a jumble of thoughts, only remotely aware of the other members of her family moving around her. Judd had been with them for nearly two months now, though Maggie still knew very little about him besides the obvious: that he was a witty conversationalist and a superb lover. Maggie preferred to discount the rumors of his unsavory past and liked to imagine instead that he was the dissatisfied son of some wealthy southern planter whose acreage was infinite and bank account even larger. Judd Brannan would make an excellent catch, though

Maggie wasn't entirely satisfied she had snared him yet.

But what other kind of men could she hope to find in California? It was settled sparsely; Indians and Mexicans comprised the bulk of the population. Aside from early settlers like Captain Sutter, she suspected that most of the white men were either old or poor. And Maggie O'Brian had already had her share of poverty back in Ireland.

At least her father had owned his own small parcel of land and not been forced to grovel to one of the haughty English lords. But when the potato crop had failed two years ago, Michael O'Brian had sold his farm and brought his family to America. But the squalid, crowded cities of New York, Boston, and Philadelphia had not been suited to a farmer's nature, and now here they were.

Maggie opened her eyes and sneered in contempt. The sky was beginning to lighten to a pinkish-gray, and she could see nothing in any direction but barren sand dunes and endless miles of desert. America, she thought derisively, and shook her head in irony.

All the same, she would have to work harder on Judd and put all her feminine wiles to work in order to get some kind of commitment out of him. The other men in the train held no particular interest for her. Before Judd's arrival, she had toyed with the affections of Elmore Poole, the driver hired by Edgar Huntington. At twenty-five, Poole was an excitable young man with a high-pitched voice that shot up another octave whenever he was nervous or agitated, a state in which he frequently found himself in Maggie's presence. He was passably nice-looking, with his wavy brown hair and muscular build, but he always stank of sweat and barnyard filth, a distinction which never failed to bring Maggie's desires to a screeching halt.

Adam Trent, the young painter, had been another possibility, but he seemed immune to Maggie's charms, preferring his charcoal and paper to more fleshly matters. Even Peter Andersen, with his Scandinavian good looks and boyish exuberance, had caught Maggie's eye. But for a wordly woman of nineteen, Peter—at seventeen—had seemed a mere boy.

Now this Toby Garrett was interesting, with his loose-jointed stride and watchful eyes. But he was a trapper—a nomad without roots and probably even less money.

Sean came around the side of the wagon and sat down beside his sister, offering her two strips of dried ox meat and a hard wheatcake. Maggie ignored the food and closed her eyes once more.

"Ye should eat, you know," he said. "Da says we'll be moving out soon, and you'll need your strength."

"What I'd really be liking is a cup of hot coffee."

"There's no wood for a fire."

"Or a mug of Da's brew," she continued wistfully. "Michael O'Brian's beer was the best in County Cork."

"All you'll be getting to drink is a few sips of water. We have to save most of it for the animals."

Maggie sighed and took a piece of the jerky grudgingly. She bit into it, tearing off a chunk with her teeth, and chewed thoughtfully for a moment. "I've tasted worse, I suppose. But it's *so* tough and stringy!"

Sean's green eyes sparkled teasingly at her, one unruly curl of reddish-brown hair falling over his forehead. "So would *you*—if you'd been walkin' halfway across this country."

Maggie regarded him wryly from beneath her lashes. "I have."

Sean grinned broadly, and two deep dimples appeared on either sides of his mouth. "Then I'll remember not to dry *your* hide for supper if you should drop along the roadside."

Maggie's stomach knotted with revulsion, and she nearly choked on the stale, tasteless biscuit. She gave her brother an irritated look. "That's a *disgustin'* thought, Sean O'Brian!"

Shrugging, he got to his feet and dusted off the seat of his trousers. The rising sun caught the red highlights in his hair and sillhouetted his large, muscular frame. "Be that as it may—" He left the sentence hanging expectantly and glanced at the other wagons. His eyes returned to Maggie's, and one corner of his mouth twitched in a cajoling, lopsided smile. "Eat up. I see the Coulters and Pardees are already startin'."

Sarah felt the sun's rays cut through the thin material of her dress, scorching her shoulders. Her ankles, calves, thighs—every inch of her legs ached miserably from the toilsome strides she was forced to take through the sand, often sinking up to her shoetops. Sweat trickled into her eyes, ran down between her breasts, and made the calico cling to her skin like insulation, defying the circulation of air—hot though it would be.

The cows, roped together, trailed listlessly behind the wagon, as did the two extra oxen and saddle horses. They were beginning to falter more often now, and in places the sand was so light that the horses sank almost to their knees.

On the other side of the animals, Hetty trudged along, her head bent, a faded poke bonnet ineffectually attempting to keep out the sun. Ahead, Samantha and Lucas toiled through the grainy sand, and Sarah grimaced in silent sympathy when the boy stumbled and fell to his knees. Samantha helped him up, and the two youngsters staggered on through the searing heat of this first day of October.

The children couldn't ride. Only two-year-old Simon was allowed in the wagon, and he sat on the seat whimpering from thirst. Roy prodded the oxen, triple-yoked but still struggling with their burden. His voice, when raised to urge the beasts on, was a hoarse croak, as if his vocal cords had shriveled up in the desert dryness. Even Beans, the setter, shambled pathetically at his master's side, his tail drooping between his legs.

Sarah's throat was parched; her mouth felt stale and cottony, and her tongue stuck to her palate. It was nearly noon, and the last of the water had been consumed an hour ago—all except a pint Hetty was saving for an emergency.

Red Canfield had said a day and a night of dry driving would see them across the desert, Sarah recalled. If that was the case, they should be out of it in another five or six hours. But Toby Garrett had claimed the desert to be nearly twice as many miles across as Canfield. Whom should she believe? Whom *could* she believe? Toby mentioned boiling springs midway across, and they had seen no such springs. If *he* was right, then they hadn't yet even come halfway. Either that, Sarah thought grimly, or they were lost.

She felt a wave of helplessness and depression settle over her. They were moving at a snail's pace. Roy had slowed the oxen to save them, and some of the other emigrants had already passed. The heavier wagons were far behind.

Despite the shade provided by the drooping brim of her straw sunbonnet, Sarah's head throbbed from the heat and the blinding glare. Lifting her head, she squinted at the wide stretch of barren sand. For mile upon mile, there was nothing but the white, desolate plain, stretching away to lonely mountains that held not a hint of green. Dunes alternated with level spaces. The ashlike surface showed only the thinnest scattering of sage. In places, there were chunks of jagged volcanic rock that cut the animals' feet.

The road was a mere scratching of wagon tracks in the sunbaked sand, sometimes strewn with the discards of previous trains. Trunks, cookstoves, anvils, grindstones, harnesses rotted in the heat. A dead ox lay in a formless heap, already bloating under the merciless sun. Idly, Sarah wondered to whom it belonged. The Andersens? The Pardees?

She shook her head miserably and heaved a disheartened sigh. It was hard to remember who was ahead of them, though she vaguely recalled one of Huntington's wagons going by earlier. Shielding her eyes, she peered up into the sky. Cloudless, endless blue with nothing to break its infinity but a flock of buzzards, hovering greedily over the carcass of the ox.

There were no birds to sing, no sound of the wind rustling through grass. Nothing. Nothing except the merciless wastes of sunbaked sand and crusted salt-mud flats. An unearthly land of utterly hopeless unalleviated desolation.

The wagon came to an abrupt halt, but Sarah was so

immersed in her own despairing thoughts that she kept walking until she bumped into Samantha. Sarah blinked, as if suddenly waking, and looked down at the little girl. Her nose was red and blistered from the broiling sun, her lips chapped. She looked imploringly up into her aunt's face, her great amber eyes haunted and sad, and Sarah felt a rush of pity for the child.

Lucas sank down on his knees and buried his face in his hands, his thin shoulders shaking with dry, convulsive sobs. Sarah ground her teeth in sheer frustration, wishing she could somehow produce a bucket of cool water to ease their thirst—and hers.

Roy shuffled wearily back, mopping his face and neck with a kerchief already soaked clear through. "I have to rest the stock—even if I can't water them."

Hetty dragged herself around the rear of the wagon, and Sarah thought her sister-in-law looked worse than the rest of them. There was a profound sadness in the look she gave her children, as if the sight of them caused her pain. Hetty turned silently questioning eyes to her husband, but Roy merely shook his head hopelessly, his shoulders sagging with defeat.

"I don't know," he said tiredly, and made another halfhearted swipe at the perspiration with his kerchief.

Lucas raised his head, his face filled with pain and entreaty. "I'm thirsty, Pa!"

Roy reached down and patted the dusty crown of the boy's battered felt hat. "I know, son. We all are."

Sarah turned a questioning eye on Hetty. "What about the few cups you saved for . . . just in case?"

"I—" Hetty broke off, wrung her hands in anguish, then her voice rose to an angry, tearful shout. "I just don't *know!*"

64

Samantha raised her head and blinked, staring at her mother in bewildered surprise. Hetty turned away from her daughter, choking on an angry sob.

Sarah watched her sister-in-law with mounting confusion and alarm. Her own mind felt dazed and numb with thirst, and for the first time, the uncertainty of their fate filled her with a dull sense of dread. She leaned against the wagon, her eyes closed, fingers pressing against her throbbing temples, then slipped listlessly to the ground.

Were they going to die out here in this horrible wasteland? They had come so far, and now . . . Her uneasiness gave way to a dire sense of foreboding as she stared vacantly around her—the arid, salty sand, the blinding stretches of desolation, the naked mountains of rock looming like luridly sinister sentinels. Would this be the final resting place for them all? This scorched wilderness, where the endless sun blistered sky and earth until they merged into one unbearable plain.

Sarah shook her head in sorrow, unable to fight off the abysmal despair that enveloped her. Hot tears scalded her eyes, blurring her vision, but there were no tears to fall. The landscape seemed to spin in front of her, and a wave of dizziness descended over her. She gave in to her exhaustion and despair, felt herself drifting, floating in a cloudless blue sky.

She thought she had fallen asleep when she felt a strong hand gripping her shoulder. Her eyelids fluttered, and she looked up, her vision foggy. The image slowly swam into focus, and her brother's face took shape. He was pressing something between her lips, and Sarah could vaguely sense a cloying sweetness on her parched tastebuds. She rolled it over her tongue, and the saliva she had thought long-ago dried up flooded into her mouth.

"Sugar," he said. "Suck on it."

Roy moved on, out of her range of vision, and it was too much of an effort to turn her head to follow him. She closed her eyes, let the sugar dissolve, and gradually felt her strength returning.

Judd mopped the sweat from his brow with the back of his hand and squinted down the sluggish string of wagons. Shimmering heat waves blurred the terrain, and Judd had to blink several times to focus. Everyone was ahead of him now—everyone except Reverend Jennings and his overladen prairie ark filled with prayer books and Bibles and Orpha's prized pump organ.

The horse faltered, and Judd felt a tremor ripple through the animal's body where his legs pressed against its sides. Flecks of foam dappled the gelding's muzzle and dribbled from its lips, and it whickered pitiously. Reluctantly, Judd dismounted, detesting the thought of walking, but knowing he had no choice.

But there was one choice he *did* have, he thought mutinously as he glanced back at Jennings's wagon. There was no reason why *he* should perish out here in this arid, barren world of sand and dust. His personal belongings amounted to an extra change of clothing, his razor, and his scant store of food. The horse could transport those items. And his water cask—still relatively full—Judd could carry himself.

Jennings's great, lumbering wagon lurched heavily over the dunes, only to sink inches deep in the loose ashlike sand. It was terrible work for the oxen, and they stumbled beneath their yokes. Jennings himself, looking like some sweating biblical patriarch, had apparently forgotten his piety for the time being and cursed lustily at the animals. His wife toiled beside the wagon, looking pale and drawn, herding her two small children, Ephiram and Hope. Often she had been compelled to carry four-year-old Hope herself, though the woman seemed in little better condition than the exhausted oxen. But it was absolutely out of the question to abandon any of the religious parapheranalia that had been packed clear across the country, so the children were forced to walk.

Judd's mouth hardened in scorn as he tied his mount to the side of the wagon and clambered up inside to retrieve his possessions. An old couple like that had no business having children at their age. Of course, Judd mused cynically, *he* could have offered to carry one of the youngsters. A malicious little smile curved his mouth, and he shook his head in grim amusement.

Tossing his things into a croker sack, he jumped down from the tailgate and returned to his horse, where he tied the bundle to the saddle horn. He removed the cask from the peg on the side of the van, heard the reassuring slosh of water inside, and untied his horse.

Without a word to the Jenningses, he set off across the marshy sand, leaving the captain of the party to labor ahead on his own.

Judd noticed Lester Stone having only a little better luck with the wagon of which he was in charge. Head bent, sullen as always, he prodded the oxen with the butt of his bullwhip, muttering imprecations at the beasts. Cows and mules, stumbling and panting as the merciless sun beat down upon them, straggled behind.

One of Huntington's wagons was ahead of Stone, but as Judd passed, he noticed the left rear wheel wobbling dangerously. Elmore Poole, husbanding the oxen with the help of Adam Trent, looked up as Judd went by, his face a chalky white from the alkaline dust, his eyes red and swollen.

"You've got a loose wheel," Judd called.

The young driver stopped and squinted in a puzzled frown for a moment, as if he didn't understand English. Judd hurried on as quickly as he could before being pressed into service for repairs. What did *he* know of fixing a wheel? Leave that to Pardee the blacksmith or Coulter the carpenter. But *they* were far ahead.

Judd cackled derisively, a hoarse, throaty sound that pierced the eardrums. He shook his head, perplexed, mildly concerned at his behavior. In the last hour, he was beginning to find everything terribly funny, especially other peoples' misfortunes.

Must be the heat, he told himself reasonably, and paused to get a drink for himself and his horse.

Elmore Poole gingerly probed the loose wheel casing with his hands, gripped the spokes, and gave a mighty shake. The wood splintered and cracked, completely rotted from the miles of dry driving. He sat back on his haunches in the sand and scratched his unruly brown hair in dismay.

"Can you fix it?"

Elmore glanced up into the concerned face of Adam Trent. He was a thin young man with a soft face and gentle brown eyes and a full, generous mouth. His hair was long, curling over his collar beneath his hat, and spilled over his forehead in riotous sandy curls. Elmore didn't understand the man's city ways, but he *did* enjoy looking at his pictures and listening to his stories. A bit of a sissy-pants, Elmore had concluded early on, but he was always amiable enough and willing to help.

Elmore switched his gaze back to the shattered wheel, his dark brows knitting reflectively, and ran the back of his hand across his mouth. His breath came out in an exasperated sigh. "Not without help from Mr. Coulter or somebody with the proper tools." He stood up and replaced his tattered hat on his head, peering regretfully down the line of wagons. "I don't know *what* to do. The animals are spent, and there's hardly any water left." His voice had risen stridently, and he gesticulated helplessly. "I can't *leave* Mr. Huntington's things out here!"

Adam shrugged and looked gravely at his friend. "We can't stay here, either. We—" He broke off abruptly and glanced up as Lester Stone strode over to them.

Stone's dark eyes narrowed as he took in the cracked wheel, and he shook his head ruefully. "You'll never get this wagon out of here." He adopted a look of thoughtful consideration, scratching the scar on his left cheek absently. Finally raising his head, he looked at Elmore, his expression respectfully somber. "You'll have to cache most of the things—the valuables." His eyes glittered with an odd light. "I'll help you." Removing his hat and wiping the perspiration from his thinning brown hair, he started back to his own wagon, calling back, "I'll even let you pack some of the stuff out on my mules."

Elmore exchanged a mildly astonished look with Adam Trent. "I don't believe I've ever heard him say so much at one time. And he even offered to *help!*" He gazed after the short-legged, wiry frame of Lester Stone, and a slight satisfied smile touched his lips for an instant. "Maybe after Mr. Huntington gets settled in California, he can send somebody back to dig up what we bury."

* * *

Stone untied the four footsore mules from the tailgate of the wagon and led them back toward Poole. They were mere bags of bones by this time, as were most of the cattle, but what did it really matter? They weren't *his* mules.

A cold smile quirked at the corners of his mouth, his eyes hooded in thought. A shoemaker for most of his thirty-three years and a bachelor for *all* of them, Stone had done his work, kept to himself, and never bothered anyone. But he had never quite managed to save enough funds to open up his own business, and therefore was always on the alert for an advantageous opportunity. Like the time he had almost married the supposedly wealthy widow of the town's undertaker—until he found out it was *she* who was looking for a husband who could bail her out of debt. Just as well, he had concluded wryly, for she was ten years his senior and three inches taller.

Then last winter he had heard of Reverend Preston Jennings's intention to move west and take God's Word to that primitive country. Though Lester knew little more than the average man about livestock, he had offered his services as driver and stock tender. After all, Jennings was known to be one of the more affluent men in Bucks County, and he might be generous. So come last May, Lester had left Pennsylvania for the great, adventurous west.

Lester shook his head in disgust, his upper lip curling in a sneer. For all his prosperity, Jennings was paying Stone only $7 a month plus his meals and, of course, the opportunity of finding eternal salvation. Lester smiled humorlessly. All he had been able to save thus far was $35. And *that* would get him exactly nowhere in California.

Elmore Poole and Adam Trent were unloading Huntington's wagon when Lester returned. He looked around him in dismay at the assortment of heavy side-chairs laid out on the sand, an oak dining table with clawed feet, and a large chest of drawers.

His mouth twisted in disdain. "You can't carry these things, and you can't bury them either." With an air of impatience, he handed over the reins to Adam Trent and hoisted himself into the wagon bed with Poole. *"I'll* decide what to take and what to bury. You help Rembrandt out there pack up." His gaze fell on a pile of tools in the corner, and he handed two shovels to the young man. "You can start digging, too."

Frowning in bewilderment and shaking his head distractedly, Poole threw the spades to the ground and jumped down after them.

Lester stood in the center aisle of the van, trying to let his eyes adjust to its dimness after a morning of glaring sun. The interior was sweltering, for the canvas held in the heat until the place felt like a Dutch oven. Crates and barrels, trunks, and odd pieces of furniture still littered the wagon, and Lester shook his head in wonder at all the things the Huntingtons had chosen to bring with them. But now was not the time to speculate on the eccentricities of the rich, now was the time to make those peculiar quirks pay off for him.

He prowled through the cargo, throwing down items to be buried and those to be packed out on the mules. The food—a half barrel of flour, tins of crackers, some fish packed in brine, and a sack of tea—could be put on the mules, as well as extra bedding, a waterproof groundcloth, and a wooden box full of medicines and herbs. For

71

caching, he decided on clothing, Ruth Huntington's Limoges china, a case of books, a marble clock, and a variety of bronze statuettes.

Lester paused in his pursuits to wipe the sweat from his eyes, his breathing labored, his throat dry. It was intolerably hot and oppressive inside the wagon, and he toyed with the notion of leaving the rest to the buzzards. He had already put aside a chest containing a set of ornate silverware for twelve and two intricately carved sterling candlesticks; these he would hide away with his own goods to be either sold or kept once he arrived in California. Exquisitely crafted and well cared for, Lester imagined they would bring a good price.

Grunting with the effort, he dragged aside a brass-bound trunk and opened the lid. Inside was a sheaf of documents; stock certificates for everything from railroads to sawmills. Lester pressed his lips together in consideration, pondering the value of these papers. He doubted he could sell them without a good many questions asked, so he retied them with their ribbon and tossed them out the back.

He then opened a handsome leather case and discovered, to his delight, a brace of fine French dueling pistols. These he added to his own pile, and after a further inspection of the rest of the trunk, decided he had done enough for the day. Tarrying any longer could prove far more dangerous than the ultimate rewards gained.

He peered over the tailgate and saw Poole and Trent still busily digging in the sand. The mules were already packed and waiting, their heads drooping in the heat. "You go on and take the mules up to Mr. Huntington and tell him what's happened."

Elmore Poole raised his sweat-covered face and

blinked the perspiration out of his eyes. "But we haven't finished with this," he said, gesturing to the half-filled pit.

Lester suppressed a coldly complacent smile. "I'll finish up. You just take the mules and the oxen. I'll be along later."

Again he received that same uncomprehending look from Poole, and Lester ducked back inside the wagon before he erupted in laughter. Either the man was an idiot, or, most likely, he couldn't quite believe that Lester Stone was doing him a kindness.

Chuckling wickedly to himself, Lester gathered up his appropriated items, found a large piece of salt pork wrapped in cloth he had missed earlier, and climbed down from the tailgate. Against the blazing sky and white expanse of sand, he could just make out Poole and Trent herding the cattle ahead in the distance.

Behind him, Jennings's wagon was just overtaking him, and the preacher paused to scrutinize the half-buried goods and demolished wheel. "Where's young Mr. Poole and his friend?"

Lester jerked his head toward the southwest. "Gone ahead with the stock and some of the supplies." He shifted his load in his arms, longing to set down the heavy chest of silver. "I'm just helping out." He flashed the Reverend a simpering smile. "Bein' neighborly, you know."

Jennings nodded with evident satisfaction. "A fine, Christian thing to do, Mr. Stone."

Orpha gave him a rare smile and bobbed her head. "May God bless your charitable heart, Mr. Stone."

Lester remained standing, a sickly, ingratiating smile pasted on his face, until the Jenningses had moved on. He

73

trudged back to his own wagon with his loot. "Don't bless me," he muttered, "bless the Huntingtons for bringing along such nice things."

After depositing his booty inside, he paused to have a drink from the keg of water, his narrowed gaze resting dispassionately on the pile of unburied goods.

"Let the coyotes and snakes have 'em!" he said aloud, recapping the cask and wiping the back of his neck with a bandanna. But even as he uttered the words, he realized there was no one to hear them, for he was now the last one on the trail—and alone.

Suddenly feeling apprehensive and uncomfortable, he slogged through the gritty sand to the front of the wagon and picked up his whip. He cracked the lash loudly in the air—air that had become ominously silent except for his own harsh breathing. Swallowing involuntarily and trying to ignore the goose flesh that had broken out on his arms, Lester snapped the whip again and felt a sweeping sense of relief when the wagon finally lurched forward.

After a short rest and a parsimoniously apportioned tablespoon of water, the Coulters were once again under way. The humans might be slightly revived, but the animals seemed in worse condition than ever. They faltered and stumbled often, and the deep sand forced Roy to stop and rest them every few yards. Hetty had to help him with the oxen, and even Samantha and Lucas were pressed into service, for the beasts simply did not want to move.

Sarah eyed the cows doubtfully, concern clouding her face. They acted listless and lethargic, no longer even bothering to bawl plaintively. Saliva dripped from their

74

mouths, and one heifer had developed a tic, shaking her head violently every minute or so as if an insect had lodged in its ear. Sarah patted them often, speaking to them in soothing tones, telling them fanciful stories of the refreshing mountain springs and shady trees that awaited them just a few miles further. Though, in the back of her mind, she wondered if her tales were more for the animals' benefit, or hers.

Directly overhead, the sun beat down relentlessly on her back and shoulders. Her lips were chapped and puffed; her eyes watered in a never-ending flow from the choking dust. She walked almost mechanically, no longer aware her aching, cramped muscles, her mind dulled by the heat and fatigue. Somewhere deep inside her, she was beginning to feel they would *never* escape this living hell. She tried not to think about it—to force her thoughts to take another direction—but the idea was with her constantly, nibbling away at the edges of her mind.

Her head was bent, eyes focused on the grains of sand that splashed over her scuffed shoetops like . . . like water. She shook off the image quickly, annoyed with herself. But so absorbed in her dismal thoughts was she that she didn't notice Judd Brannan come up beside her until he spoke.

"The next time you're all wrapped up in your quilts, freezing your tail off on a winter's night, you'll remember this place."

Sarah turned her head to regard him, and a tiny shiver went through her at what she saw. Judd no longer resembled the dapper southern gentleman, suave of manner. He had removed his hat, and tendrils of black hair, wet with perspiration, straggled over his forehead. His normally swarthy complexion was a pasty gray, and his eyes were bloodshot, the pupils enormously dilated. He grinned foolishly at her and executed a mock bow.

"I believe we've been formally introduced before, Miss Coulter. Or has my charm struck you dumb?"

Sarah studied him guardedly, suspicion suddenly crowding her mind. His speech was slightly slurred, his eyes glazed and unfocused. "Have you been drinking?"

Judd arched a wondering brow at her, an inane grin on his face. "Only water, my sweet. Only water."

Sarah felt confused and bewildered as she searched his face. "You shouldn't be out in this sun without your hat."

Shrugging negligently, he retrieved the hat from the bundle strapped to his horse and, with a wildly absurd laugh, tossed it into the air. It sailed across the desert and landed on a sloping dune, a black pinpoint amid the stark white sand.

Sarah gaped in mute disbelief, her mind unwilling to reason out Judd's odd behavior as, with deliberate calm, he turned abruptly and began walking slowly toward the hat. Then, as if suddenly pushed from behind, he broke into a ragged run, slipping and tottering over the sand, shrieking at the top of his lungs.

Sarah stood paralyzed with shock for several seconds; then, with a muffled exclamation, gathered her skirts about her ankles and charged after him, calling his name. She stumbled once, nearly losing her balance, but continued to run, passing the discarded hat and lurching over the dunes, gasping for breath, Judd tripped and went down, then tried to crawl a few feet before collapsing on the sand.

Sarah fell to her knees beside him, her chest heaving, her heart roaring in her ears. Her breath came in short, strangled gasps, and her lungs felt raw, as if they were filled with salt.

Judd's head was twisted to one side in the sand. Jaw slack, tongue lolling, he panted like an exhausted animal. Sarah reached out a tentative hand and brushed the hair away from his face. Surprisingly, his skin was cool to the touch, but it had a clammy, unnatural feeling to it. Sarah thought desperately, wondering what to do when Roy dropped to the ground beside her.

"He went crazy or something," Sarah managed to say, and her gaze returned to the unmoving form sprawled on the sand. Judd's breathing was labored, and each breath he exhaled was accompanied by a wheezing moan.

Roy slowly shook his head. "Heatstroke, I guess."

Sarah searched her brother's face with anxious concern. "What can we do?"

Peter Andersen came running up to them, his face flushed, sweat dripping from his tousled blond curls onto his forehead and cheeks. Sarah looked up and exchanged uncomfortable glances with the young Swede.

"Papa says you can put him in our wagon."

"No!" Sarah immediately regretted her outburst and cast a sheepish glance at her brother. *"We* can take him, can't we?"

Roy ran a hand across his face, cutting a path through the sweat and grime, a glimmer of indecision in his narrowed eyes. "He's extra weight for the oxen."

"But—" Sarah bit her lips, breaking off the flow of impassioned pleas she longed to make. With Maggie O'Brian far ahead, here was Sarah's chance to be alone with Judd, no matter that he was half out of his mind from the heat. Perhaps if she could nurse him along for a few miles, show him she had other qualities besides the sultry smiles that Maggie used to bewitch him . . .

But she knew she was being selfish. If it was too much of a strain on the oxen to allow the children to ride, it would be unfair to let this stranger ride. Sarah met her brother's gaze and nodded reluctantly. "I'll go fetch his hat."

Chapter Five

Steaming hot water bubbled and boiled up from fissures in the rocks, spread into small pools, and oozed into the sand. Occasionally there would be a loud rumbling gurgle, and a fountain of scalding water jetted up into the air with a sharp hiss of steam. Then it would stop abruptly, the spout would recede, and the water would settle back into its constant vaporous churning. In some basins, the water was white; in other places clear, while one was deep red. Scattered about the sand around these bizarre pools was evidence of other emigrant trains that had passed before: ox chains, parts of wagons, even a few bleached bones.

Sarah watched in silence as the last jet of steam died away, then hefted the oaken bucket and trudged back toward her wagon. Geyser Spring, someone had called it, and just one more curious vagary of this freakish wasteland. The water was too hot to drink, but if kept in a container until it was lukewarm it could at least relieve the thirst. But so *bitter*, Sarah thought with a slight grimace.

When Judd had run across the desert in his demented

fury, they had only been a mile from the hot springs. Most everyone had arrived by now, and the children delighted in watching the seething water jets.

She paused at the Andersens' wagon where Judd sat in its shade on the ground. He had been given some of the rank, mineral-filled water and several small pieces of dried meat, and now he seemed to be halfway back to normal. He sat with his elbows resting on his drawn-up knees, his head bent, the now all-but-ruined hat perched atop his disheveled black hair.

As Sarah's shadow fell across him, he looked up and managed a faint, strained smile. "I want to thank you for coming after me."

Sarah shrugged lightly, though her pulse quickened its beat a few degrees, and she felt her cheeks burn. Judd Brannan at last begun to notice her. "Are you feeling better now?"

His mouth twisted in self-derision. "After making a fool of myself. I can usually keep a cool head under most circumstances." With a fatalistic shrug, he spread his hands in lame defense. He pushed his hat back on his head and regarded her with enigmatic dark eyes that gave no hint of emotion, but Sarah felt a nervous fluttering in her stomach. "When we get to California—if they have such a thing as a restaurant—I'll take you out for the biggest supper you've ever eaten."

It was all Sarah could do to keep from laughing triumphantly. For two months she had yearned for Judd's attention, and now here he was—inviting her to supper. No matter that he was only just recovering from being half out of his mind from the heat; it was a start, and her senses reeled in giddy delight.

"I'd be very pleased," she managed to say, hoping her

excitement wasn't conveyed in her voice.

He smiled contentedly and nodded his head. "Then it's all settled, then."

Sarah lingered, drawn to his deep, mysterious brown eyes, wondering what he would think if she sat down beside him for a longer chat. Though she was so flustered by his admiring looks and dazzling smile, she doubted she could think of a thing to say. Besides, the stock needed water, and right now the cows were more important than her attempts at flirtation.

Switching the heavy bucket to her other hand, she smiled shyly at Judd. "I'd better go now."

He inclined his head in assent, and, with another brief smile, settled back against the wagon wheel.

Sarah made her way back to the cows, her mind awhirl with turbulent emotions. It was just as well she had work to do, for she would undoubtedly botch things up if she stayed to talk with Judd. Was she *really* shy? Or was she simply unused to carrying on a conversation with a witty, obviously literate man? Back in Kentucky, the few beaus who had courted her were even less educated than she. At least *she* had received several years of schooling, while most of them had none. They were simple farmers or merchants, with no aspirations to anything other than what they were. And the more Sarah thought about it now, the more she came to realize it was only with Judd that she floundered and stumbled over her words.

Perhaps if she tried to see him as she did any other man, her nervous discomfiture would disappear. But it was so *hard* to think of him as a mere mortal, for his darkly handsome looks, glib tongue, and southern sophistication seemed to set him apart from other men.

Sarah's thoughts were rudely shattered when she saw

Toby Garrett talking to her brother. The hunter caught her eye as she passed, and his mouth twisted into a dryly amused smile. Sarah ignored him, continuing on to the rear of the wagon where the livestock was tethered. There was something infuriating about his casual nonchalance, and his arrogant confidence irritated her. Certainly she didn't feel awkward or tongue-tied around *him*. She felt . . .

Oh, what does it matter *what* I feel, she thought testily, and thrust the bucket irascibly under the nose of one of the cows.

The animal drank voraciously, and Sarah had to take the water away before the cow fell ill from too much all at one time. The others had their turn, gulping greedily at the bitter, tepid water. If anything, Sarah thought it might actually be hotter here at the springs, for the steam and the spray brought a trace of humidity to the air that was absent in the rest of the desert. But at least there was water, and, more importantly than that, the springs marked the halfway point in their crossing.

Sarah shuddered, thinking ahead to the miles that lay before them. But at least the sun had passed its zenith, and in a few more hours it would be dark. And as terrible as last night's march had been, it was infinitely preferable to walking beneath the scorching sun.

"I see you were able to keep the cows from running off."

Sarah looked around and met the half-mocking, deep-blue gaze of Toby Garrett. Setting her lips firmly, she gave him a frosty stare. "I *told* you I could manage."

His mouth quirked in caustic humor. "But not Mr. Brannan, from what I've been told. Heard you lit out after him like he'd just stole your last cent."

82

Sarah met his remark with sullen silence and scowled disapprovingly at him. He was wearing a white cotton shirt, darned in several places, and the perspiration molded it to his torso like a second skin. Unwillingly, she found herself inspecting him furtively, noting the broad shoulders that tapered to narrow hips and lean thighs. Salty granules clung to his beard, making it appear lighter than it actually was, and more of the minuscule particles were trapped in the tiny lines radiating out from his eyes. Laugh lines? Highly unlikely, Sarah concluded scornfully. The man seemed to possess no sense of humor, from what she had seen—except perhaps a rather twisted, derisive one.

And that hat he wore! She ran a critical eye over the shabby felt, wondering at its age. It might once have been tan, but dirt and dust obscured its original hue. The crown was darkened by sweat and encircled by a multicolored beaded band with a red feather sticking out of it, drooping in the heat.

Sarah regarded him with a slight frown. "I suppose you're immune to the heat." Without waiting for his answer, she turned and took a handful of grass from the supply lashed to the wagon. She doled it out sparingly to the cows, and, to her surprise, Toby handed her another bunch to feed to the horses.

"Since you're such a first-rate shepherdess," he said in his lazy, drawling voice, and Sarah wondered if there wasn't a hint of sarcasm underlying its tone, "I've decided to let you keep watch on my horse for me."

Sarah turned sharply, her eyes blazing in furious protest. "Why can't you take care of your *own* horse? I have enough to do!"

"I could, I suppose. Except that I've got my mules to

83

see to. And your brother and Mr. Pardee and Mr. Andersen have quietly decided that I should take over the duties as guide—unofficially, mind you.''

Sarah eyed him scornfully. ''I suppose that suits you just fine. Riding in here in the middle of the night out of nowhere, and now you're running the whole show!'' She gave an impatient wave of her hand, then looked coldly into his eyes. ''You *like* that feeling of power, don't you?''

Toby regarded her steadily through lazy-lidded eyes. ''On the contrary, Miss Coulter. I came here wanting only to join your party for the rest of the journey—safety in numbers, you know. Now I find myself with a responsibility I don't particularly want. I can take care of myself, but look around you.'' He gestured expansively, and Sarah's gaze involuntarily followed the sweep of his arm. The emigrants sat apathetically in whatever shade they could find or moved listlessly about their duties. Exhausted, hot, and despairing at their predicament, they were hardly recognizable as the vibrant, aggressive group of travelers that had banded together to cross the plains.

''There must be more than a dozen children here who are too young to care for themselves,'' he went on. ''And probably that many women. I've been able to count only sixteen adult men able to take eleven wagons and scores of cattle across this desert. And some of those—like Mr. Pardee's father-in-law—are practically helpless.'' He took Sarah's chin between his fingers and turned her face back to look at him. ''Would *you* want that responsibility?''

Annoyed at his familiarity, she flinched away from the touch of his rough, callused fingers and faced him with undaunted challenge in her gray eyes. ''I told you—I can take care of myself!''

A smile slowly spread across his face, though this time it seemed genuine, without the sardonic curl to his lips, and Sarah noticed for the first time that his front teeth were rather crooked. "I expect maybe you *can,* at that." His gaze shifted past her shoulder, lowered, then darkened with concern. Still keeping the smile on his lips, he grasped her upper arm in a savage grip, bruising her tender flesh. Her sudden gasp of outrage was quickly silenced by his warning growl, "Don't move until I say!"

Confused and angered, Sarah fought back her impulse to wrench free from his harsh grip only because of the deadly urgency in his voice, a tone that held no room for argument.

His gaze darted to the wagon, then quickly back to the ground behind her. Sarah could feel the tension emanating from him, and a shiver chased itself up her spine for no reason she could imagine. Her arm ached painfully from his viselike hold, but he didn't let go.

Then she heard it. A harsh rattling sound like the toy Simon used to shake to amuse himself. In the next instant, she was pushed roughly away from Toby, propelled by a brutal wrench to her arm. She stumbled and fell to the sand several yards away, her breath escaping in an explosive grunt. Stunned momentarily, she looked around in time to see Toby seize something from the side of the wagon and hurl it to the ground. Sunlight glinted off metal for a brief second; then the object struck the sand with a soft thump.

Sarah blinked and looked around in dazed bewilderment to where the hatchet protruded from the ground. Her eyes widened in disbelieving horror, and, sucking in her breath with a moan, she covered her mouth with both

85

hands. An immense black and tan snake lay in the sand, its long, glossy body severed in two.

White-faced, eyes staring, Sarah lurched to her feet. Her legs felt weak, threatened to buckle. She felt strong hands grasp her shoulders, and she managed to turn her head. Sean O'Brian smiled down at her in gentle reassurance, then wrapped her in his arms and held her tightly to him. Sarah took a deep breath, trying to still the sudden trembling in her limbs and the violent pounding of her heart.

A small cluster of the curious had assembled around the wagon, the children babbling gleefully.

"Can I keep it, Mr. Garrett?" Lucas asked as Toby picked up the reptile gingerly with the flat edge of the hatchet.

"I want it!" Patrick O'Brian whined.

Lucas angrily shoved the older boy aside. "It's mine! It almost bit *my* aunt—not *yours!*"

Toby settled the argument by tossing the lifeless head portion out into the desert. Then he took out his hunting knife, lopped off the tawny rattles, and kicked sand over the rest of the scaly body.

Slipping the rattles into his pocket, he straightened up. Ignoring the curious questions thrown at him from the crowd, he looked at Sarah with faintly casual contempt. "Women and children," he muttered, a heavy undertone of malicious sarcasm in his voice. Shaking his head in perplexity, he wheeled around and stalked away.

Maggie stood off to one side, gazing after him with undisguised curiosity for a moment. Dismissing him with a shrug of her shoulders, she sidled over to her brother and Sarah. "Well," she said with an airy toss of her head, "it's plain to see I don't need to waste my charms

86

on *him!*'' Wicked amusement glittered in her green eyes. ''A fine figure of a man he is, too. 'Tis a pity he's apparently not especially well-disposed to the fair sex.'' She looked at Sarah with a conspiratorial smile. ''But me brother, here, appreciates us.'' Teasing laughter danced in her eyes, and her lips curved into a mischievous smile. ''Now's your chance, Sean. You've got her in your arms—best not let her go.'' Winking meaningfully at her brother, she swept away.

Slightly embarrassed and having once again regained a measure of composure, Sarah drew away from Sean's embrace. She hazarded a glance at the disturbed sand near the wagon and suppressed a shiver.

'' 'Twas lucky you were, Sarah,'' Sean said. ''And lucky one of the cows didn't get bitten, either.''

Sarah stifled a smile at the Irishman's words. Always the farmer, she thought wryly. But at least he put *me* before the cow.

She lifted her gaze up to him, summoning up a wan smile of gratitude. He was a big man, with the same green eyes as his sister and his father's square, ruddy face. Reddish-brown locks straggled out from beneath his cloth cap and curled over the collar of his shirt. ''Thank you, Sean.''

''For what? 'Twasn't me who killed the bloody viper.'' He smiled shyly. ''But you know I'd do anything for you.'' Shifting nervously from foot to foot, he stared at the ground. ''We used to spend a lot of time together, you know. We don't anymore.''

''I know.'' Not since Judd joined the train, she thought dismally. Somehow, since then, Sean's Gaelic good humor and boyish charm had lost its appeal. And now Maggie had her clutches on Judd again, she fumed inwardly as her gaze strayed to the Andersens' wagon. Judd still sat in its shade, while Maggie knelt in the sand, chattering animatedly to him. She had undone several of the top buttons of her frock, and whenever she gestured—which was often—Sarah feared the woman's breasts would spill out of her dress. And no doubt Maggie would like nothing better than to see Sean win Sarah's affections and keep her out of the way as a possible threat to her and Judd.

Sarah's jaw tightened, and her cheeks flushed with resentment as she looked away. Near the boiling wells, she caught a glimpse of Toby, and her eyes flashed with a growing fury. The great frontier hunter with his mocking looks and condescending smiles. He was the most vexing man she had ever met! The few times he had spoken to her, he never failed to provoke her. And how dare he act as if *she* had been the single cause of all the emigrants' misfortunes? Why, the look he had given her had just as much *accused* her of enticing the rattlesnake!

Or were those impressions just an invention of her overtired, heated brain? Sarah ground her teeth in angry frustration and heaved an exasperated sigh. It was too hot to think of anything, and allowing her temper to flare up now would only make matters worse.

Swallowing back her rage, she turned to Sean and managed an artificially bright smile. "I have more things to do before we start out again. I'd better go."

Sean nodded almost grudging acquiescence, but continued to hold her eyes a moment longer. "Just remember, Sarah. I'm here if you need me."

Smiling with feigned cheerfulness, Sarah gathered up her bucket and slogged through the deep sand to the springs.

* * *

Toby squatted near the bubbling pools of scalding mineral water, carefully pouring the now-tepid liquid from a pan into his canteens. He glanced up briefly as Sarah approached the pool farthest away, but she ignored him with studied indifference. Not much wonder, he thought wryly, and for the tenth time since the incident with the snake, he wondered at his hostile treatment of her.

She was hardly to blame; yet the way she had so readily swooned into Sean O'Brian's arms nettled him. Women were all alike—at least *white* women—with their pretended innocence and helplessness. They seemed able to swoon at the slightest provocation, prattled on endlessly about unimportant trivialities, and if you bedded one of them, they expected marriage.

Although Toby had been only fourteen when he last had any real contact with white women, he could remember their ways well enough. After the sudden death of his mother, Toby and his father had left their home in Iowa to roam the uncharted wilderness, and since 1832, Toby had lived among the Indians of the South and Northwest.

Cyrus Garrett had been a lawyer by profession, though he longed secretly for the freedom of the outdoors. He had proved himself to be a competent hunter and trapper, and, although he didn't make a fortune, the sale of pelts to white traders provided well enough for himself and his teen-aged son.

Sometimes Toby thought himself more Indian than white. He knew their customs, spoke several of their languages, and could stalk prey as silently as the most cunning brave. He had lived with the Hopis, the Paiutes, the Bannocks, and most recently the Cayuse in the Oregon territory. It had been there that his father had died of pneumonia, and also there that Toby broke with the Indians after a raid and subsequent massacre of a wagon train last year. Since that time, he had lived by himself, venturing into civilization only when the need for supplies or a woman compelled him—until a few weeks ago, when he had decided to make the mountain crossing to California.

Toby set aside the pan and capped one canteen, his gaze moving speculatively to Sarah as she bent over one of the pools. Her honey-gold hair slipped out from beneath her sunbonnet and tumbled over her shoulders in soft disarray. Her face was fine-boned, with sensuously curved lips and wide-set eyes fringed with dark lashes. And when she grew angry, her nostrils would flare slightly and her cheeks take on a rosy blush.

Toby reached for a second canteen and began to fill it, his eyes narrowed in thoughtfulness. He really shouldn't be so antagonistic and disagreeable with Sarah Coulter. Of all the women in this party, she was probably the *only* one who could hold her own in adversity. The others, well—the others were all too busy playing out their roles as typical females. Why, right this very minute, Maggie O'Brian was trying to seduce that poor fellow Brannan, Toby thought scornfully. No matter that the temperature was well over a hundred degrees and the unfortunate man had collapsed from the heat just minutes before, Maggie was plying her charms. And Astrid Andersen, the Amazonian teen-ager, was standing beside Adam Trent, making calf's eyes at him while he sketched. And the other women—those who had already caught their men—were busy acting the part of harried, overworked wives and mothers.

90

As Sarah stood up, Toby's gaze returned to her. She paused, shielded her eyes from the sun, and peered off in the direction from which they had just come. With her head tilted up and the slim column of her throat exposed, Toby wondered how it would feel to caress that smooth skin and search out her beating pulse with his fingertips. The slight breeze molded her damp calico frock to her body, enhancing her full breasts, gently rounded hips, and long, shapely legs. Her soft, ripe curves beckoned him, and Toby suddenly and unexpectedly became uncomfortable aware of his growing desire.

Annoyed at himself, he returned his attention to the canteen, sloshed water on his thigh accidentally, and cursed beneath his breath. Forcing his wayward thoughts from his mind, he concentrated on the task at hand. Still, his conscience warned him, he *should* try to be a little less belligerent with Sarah. Except that he enjoyed watching those gray eyes of hers sparkle in anger and the way her lips curled into an unconsciously provocative pout when she was aroused. Idly, he wondered whether he dared try to arouse her in some other way than anger, and a slow, lazy smile curved the corners of his mouth at the thought.

Rising from the ground, he strapped the canteens to his mules, then set the pan down for them to drink. A rising commotion near one of Huntington's wagons distracted his attention, and he turned to see the emigrants gathering around some oxen and several mules.

When Toby reached the assemblage, he found Elmore Poole with Huntington's few salvaged belongings lashed to the mules. Trent had come in earlier and explained the situation to Edgar Huntington; but now, for the first time, the wealthy businessman could see the extent of his misfortune as he examined his goods.

Near fifty years of age, Edgar Huntington was a tall, angular man with dark hair graying at the temples. He exuded an air of arrogant superiority, and as he strutted back and forth, bemoaning his losses and slapping a leather quirt angrily against his thigh, he appeared every bit the patrician.

He stopped his agitated pacing abruptly and fixed Poole with an accusing stare. "This is *all* you brought out?"

Elmore Poole nodded glumly. "I had no choice."

Ruth Huntington swept forward imperiously, running her hand over her possessions, her disappointment and dismay clearly evident in the droop of her jaw. At least a decade younger than her husband, she was rather plump, with hennaed hair and a band of shining pearls at her throat. Dressed in a pale blue silk dress—now irreparably sweat-stained—she carried herself with a regal bearing and an aura of aristocracy.

Her cold, haughty gaze moved disdainfully over Poole, and she scowled fiercely at him. *"Where* is my silver?"

"I don't know, ma'am." He spread his hands and shrugged helplessly. "I brung what I could."

She sniffed contemptuously and, pivoting around, flounced over to her son and daughter-in-law. "That silver was to be *yours* someday."

Phillip Huntington made no reply. In fact, he seemed rather intimidated by his mother. Toby had observed the young man in the past, always ready to jump at his parents' commands like a faithful puppy. And his wife, Alma, was exactly the same. A tiny, delicately pretty young woman but with an unhealthy pallor, she spoke little and spent most of her time inside the wagon with her

92

infant son. A perfectly matched couple, Toby thought cynically. And ideal offspring for their dictatorial parents.

Toby shook his head in wonder and drifted away from the crowd. Huntington looked as though he could bluster and complain for the rest of the day, and if the others wanted to listen . . . Toby smiled with amused indulgence. People—"civilized" people—would never change, he thought. No matter how long he had been away from them.

"You'll have to lighten your load!"

Toby's voice sounded unnaturally loud amid the utter silence of the desert. Wheels creaked, axles groaned, oxen wheezed, but no one spoke. Several miles out of the springs, and the wagons were once again spread out along the glimmering, sandy plain. Those with lighter loads had already begun to pull ahead; the heavier wagons brought up the rear.

Red Canfield, leading his horse beside the Andersens' rig in the lead, turned to look back at his interim successor, his eyes cold with hatred. Toby had left his two mules standing loose—too tired to run away—and walked back to the cumbersome prairie ark of Reverend Jennings. It was a monstrous contraption, with storage compartments offset above the wheels and pockets sewn into the canvas top. The oxen—four yokes of them—faltered and struggled with their murderous load, and at times the wheels sank halfway to their hubs in the gritty sand.

Preston Jennings, minus his frock coat but wearing an equally soiled linen shirt, brought his animals to a halt. "There's nothing I can leave behind," he said, mopping his face with a handkerchief.

Toby shrugged impatiently. "Suit yourself. But if you *don't* lighten your wagon, you'll end up killing your oxen and having to leave *everything.*"

Jennings threw up his hands and looked toward Canfield as if for help. Red ducked his head and continued walking, not wishing to be drawn into the problems of the others. Let the miserable old Bible-thumper rot out here, for all I care, Red thought maliciously. Just as long as *I* get out.

It was late afternoon, but still intolerably hot. The desert sun beat ferociously down from above and glared blindingly off the polished white sand. Red had his water keg strapped to his horse, though no food. But he didn't care anymore. He didn't even mind that the trapper had taken his place as guide for the time being. It saved Red from having to concern himself with the well-being of the others—not that he would have—and allowed him the freedom to keep walking. The only thing that mattered anymore was escaping this brutal wasteland before the desert devoured him in all its cruel splendor.

He cast a quick, sidelong glance over his shoulder and saw Jennings and Garrett unloading the pump organ while Orpha stood by with her two youngsters, twisting her hands fretfully. Red uttered a short, derisive laugh, but it changed immediately to a grunt of surprise. He blinked, stared hard across the desert, then blinked again. He gaped in open-mouthed astonishment. Not a hundred yards away was another wagon train rumbling over the glistening sand.

Red stopped abruptly.

So did the other line of wagons.

He shook his head in dismay, his mind whirling in confusion. Narrowing his eyes into slits, he peered warily across the desolate expanse of sand. A dirty, stocky bearded man stared vacantly back at him, the image of himself. Canfield felt a tremor of uncertainty pass through him. A thin shiver of fear ran up his spine.

He squeezed his eyes shut tightly and breathed a fervent prayer. When he looked again, the ghostly caravan was still waiting across the salt plain. Red moaned deep in his throat, and, shaking his head in dumb protest, tugged viciously on his horse's bridle. He reeled forward, stumbling in the sand, and pushed ahead as fast as he could, refusing to look again toward the phantom train.

Sarah trudged beside the livestock at the rear of the wagon. Two of the oxen had already lain down in the sand, never to rise again. The spare pair had been yoked up in their place, but still they moved painfully slowly. The cows stumbled often, and even the horses were beginning to falter. Occasionally Lucas or Samantha would drop back to walk at her side, their glum little faces downcast, short legs struggling through the loose sand.

The water from the hot springs was disappearing fast, and, as before, it had to be doled out sparingly. Sarah's tongue felt swollen, and her lips were puffed and cracked until simply licking them was torture. A hot, dry wind had risen, and it drove the sand like buckshot in her face, tearing and burning her skin. The harsh grit was everywhere—in her hair, her throat, even under her eyelids, despite keeping her lids slitted only enough to see.

The fury of the sun twisted the world into one huge, impossible mirage. Heat waves rippled above the surface of the blinding sand along a track marked by dying, prostrate oxen and discarded goods. Ole Andersen's great iron stove lay half-buried in the sand; Orpha Jennings's beloved organ sat beside crates of primers and hymnals. The stench of decaying, putrid flesh from the bloated carcasses of the oxen invaded Sarah's nostrils, and she fought off a wave of nausea.

She felt weak, and her head throbbed. Sweat stung her eyes, her breath rasped deep in her chest, and she had to fight to concentrate all her efforts on each step she took. Her throat felt agonizingly dry. Roy had given her a flattened bullet to suck on, but it did little to alleviate the raw staleness of her mouth. Thirst burned her tongue and throat, and she swallowed continuously, trying to find some saliva to ease the soreness. She knew she needed to focus her thoughts on something other than her craving for water, but there was nothing but the harsh, alkaline wasteland to look at.

They came to a halt as Roy stopped to assist Emmett Pardee. The blacksmith had pulled his wagon off to the side, his oxen exhausted. Sarah longed to sit down for a brief rest, but she feared she might never rise again. Samantha crept to the rear of the van and sank down in a patch of shade. A heavy sigh broke from her, and her narrow shoulders slumped in weary defeat.

"I thought I saw a lake a little while ago." She twisted a long chestnut braid listlessly between her fingers. "With pretty green trees, and even some ducks."

"I've seen things, too," Sarah said, leaning against the wheel and wiping her forehead with the back of her hand.

"I keep hoping maybe everybody'll see the same thing, and then maybe it'll be real."

Sarah didn't reply. Her throat was too parched to talk

96

above a whisper, and even that hurt. Another Jennings wagon lumbered past, its wheels groaning in protest. Sarah didn't bother to look up. She simply didn't feel she had the strength to even nod a greeting.

Roy shuffled back. Even *he* was beginning to show signs of the strain. His face was burned a livid red from the sun; the whites of his eyes seemed to match his flesh.

"Emmett's got to rest his stock," he said, removing his hat and combing his fingers through his hair. Droplets of perspiration trickled off the sandy locks and ran into the unshaven, dusty stubble on his cheeks. "The old man can't walk anymore. Belle's afraid he'll die out here."

We *all* might, Sarah thought morosely, and a sinking sense of anxiety deepened within her.

Emmett Pardee watched as Roy Coulter's wagon trundled on ahead, and with it seemed to go his last vestiges of optimism. Roy was the only man in the train on whom he felt he could rely for help—his only friend. But Emmett couldn't ask Roy to sacrifice his own family for the sake of another; they would probably *both* die out here if he did.

Emmett released a long-suffering sigh and looked dully around him. The sun was a blood-red ball sinking below the horizon, but it was still excessively hot and would remain so for another few hours. And what difference did it matter whether it was day or night? A man's burning thirst knew no distinction.

Emmett had not been wealthy when he left Arkansas, and he hadn't had the funds to purchase more than six oxen. He still had them, but they were completely played out. But worse than that was his family. Belle was a strong woman, used to hard times, but his three children were failing badly, especially eight-month-old Linus. The child had been cared for most of the journey by Belle's father, Ezra Weeks, but the last two days' hot march had taken its toll on the seventy-two-year-old man. He was as helpless as Linus now, unable to walk, and at times delirious.

He shook his head disconsolately, feeling completely impotent. Their water was gone, and the children whimpered constantly in their misery. A fresh wave of despair and confusion settled over him, and he closed his eyes to say a silent prayer.

Belle came around from the rear of the wagon, wiping beads of perspiration off her face, a worried frown creasing her brow. "Pa's out of his head."

Emmett looked at her closely, concerned. Ten years ago, when they had married, she was a pretty, vivacious girl of seventeen; now she was a mere shell of that happy, carefree woman. She had always been slender, but now she was too thin, with the flesh on her face stretched tight over her prominent cheekbones. Her black hair, already beginning to show threads of gray, was parted in the middle and drawn back severely from her face, giving her a harsh, unfriendly appearance. She had the hands of a man, toughened and callused, and Emmett knew that beneath her loose-fitting faded and patched frock, she had muscles that could compete with a wrestler. Still, Emmett loved her just the same as he had on their wedding day. If she looked like an overworked slattern, he had no one to blame for her hard life but himself.

"How are the children?" he asked.

She looked at him with eyes that were haunted and sad. "Linus ain't hardly moved in his cradle all the time we been stopped here. And Amos—he's cryin' and askin for somethin' to drink. Benjamin ain't so bad, but—'' Her voice broke, and she bit her lip in anguish, lifting dark eyes to him filled with pain and entreaty. "Oh, Emmett, what're we to *do!*"

He drew her into his arms and patted her thin shoulder gently, the sudden flood of emotions that swept over him threatening to choke him. He was filled with a wild sense of desperation, yet powerless to do anything. He felt naked and vulnerable and alone, surrounded by nothing but dry, barren desert for miles in any direction.

He glanced up as Edgar Huntington's huge, lumbering prairie schooner rolled over the marshy sand. It was drawn by eight oxen, and both Huntington himself and Elmore Poole herded them along. Ruth sat atop the seat with her infant grandson, as imperious as if she were a queen riding to her coronation. The child squirmed and giggled, healthy and happy, apparently unaffected by the heat and dust.

Faint, whining sobs came from inside Emmett's own wagon, and he trembled with sheer frustration. Strapped to Huntington's wagon were four large water casks, and as Emmett looked on, Edgar lifted the lid, scooped out a dipperful, and poured water over his head.

Growling with outraged fury, Emmett disengaged himself from Belle's clinging arms and snatched up his rifle. Disregarding his wife's puzzled exclamation of surprise, he stalked across the sand, his eyes smoldering with contempt. His children were dying of thirst, while this arrogant peacock had water to waste!

"Mr. Huntington, I want some of that water."

Huntington turned, moisture dripping down his face and soaking the collar of his finely tailored shirt. His eyes rounded and jaw slackened as his gaze riveted on the barrel of the rifle pointed at his chest. Frowning in disbelief, he raised his eyes to meet Emmett's hostile, accusing stare.

Recovering some of his poise, he fixed the blacksmith with an indignant, faintly condescending gaze. "You have no right to demand anything of me, Mr. Pardee."

Emmett's bearded face had become hard and forbidding with anger. "Maybe not. But my family's dyin'. You—" he jerked his head in the direction of Ruth Huntington, fanning herself in nervous agitation on the seat— "you got plenty."

Huntington bristled defensively. "And I intend to *keep* it."

Emmett's face darkened ominously. "Not if you want to stay alive." His mouth hardened, and his eyes narrowed dangerously. "I'm not a violent man by nature, Mr. Huntington. But believe me when I say I'll shoot you to save my wife and children."

Huntington raised one dark brow impatiently. "Every drop I have is needed for my *own* family."

Emmett gestured contemptuously to the ground where the water was seeping into the sand. "What you're usin' to irrigate the desert might well save my children!" Overcome by a rage he thought he could never feel, he took a step forward and brandished the rifle threateningly. His face became ugly, and his eyes glittered murderously. "You either share your water, or I swear I'll kill you!"

Huntington hesitated a moment, indecision and fear playing alternately across his leonine features. He darted a glance at Elmore Poole, saw that the young driver was evidently not going to help, and his mouth narrowed in grim resignation. "Very well," he said finally, looking at Emmett with utter disdain. "But I intend to speak to Reverend Jennings about this." He shook his head disapprovingly as he took down one of the water casks. "This is most unacceptable behavior."

Emmett lowered his rifle and reached out to take the keg. The sound of the water sloshing inside was like music to his ears, and he could barely suppress a shout of joy.

Instead, he uttered a bitter sound, faintly resembling laughter. "Excuse me if I'm being unneighborly, Mr. Huntington." Faint mockery gleamed in his eyes as they swept the other man. "But I expect if anyone should know about that, it's you."

Chapter Six

Five O'Brian oxen were down, panting and snorting piteously, their shaggy heads lolling in the sand, and for the fourteenth such time since sundown, Michael was forced to halt his family. They were the last of the straggling wagons, and each stop put them even farther behind.

Maggie stood off to one side, holding Kevin in her arms, with Katie, James, and the dogs sitting nearby in the sand, watching the spectral forms of their father and oldest brothers as they tried to rouse the prostrate beasts. The scorching blast furnace of the afternoon had turned to a cold, biting wind with the advent of night, and it nipped at Maggie's face until it felt raw. Overhead, an enormous white moon hung suspended in an endless sky of stars, and Maggie was awed by the absolute desolation of the place.

The men soon gave up trying to rally the dying cattle, and the animals were unyoked. Calculating quickly in her head, Maggie realized, with this latest loss, there would only be four oxen and the milk cows left to haul the two wagons, and she doubted their combined strength would be enough to pull the load.

"We have to leave one of the wagons." Daniel jogged over to her, his blond hair burnished silver in the moonlight. He was a big youth, as were all the O'Brian men, where, in striking contrast, the women were short and small-boned. "Da wants everybody to help. We'll combine the most necessary things into one wagon."

Katie looked hopefully up at her brother. "My doll?"

Daniel smiled fondly and caressed her cheek. "You can be keeping your doll, sweetheart."

Leaving Kevin in the care of the younger children, Maggie began helping unload and repack the goods. Even in its short supply, food seemed to fill up a third of the wagon, and cookware, tools, bedding, and the other necessities of life filled another third.

Maggie paused to wipe a hand across her face, a profound weariness invading her bones. She had tasted only a few sips of water since dusk, and nothing to eat. The tough, dried ox meat was the only food available without benefit of a fire on which to cook, and Maggie couldn't force the stringy beef down her parched throat. But even as tired as she was, she found the strength to protest vehemently when she saw her clothing tossed from a trunk.

Her green eyes flashed with suppressed rebellion and fixed resentfully on her mother. "I *need* those clothes! What will I wear in California?"

Molly O'Brian glowered crossly. Her brown hair fell about her face in tangled wisps, and the eerie gray moonlight gave her the appearance of a half-wild harridan. "We'll not be gettin' to California at *all* if this isn't left behind." She gestured impatiently to the clothing heaped

104

on the sand. "Pick out a couple of things and pack them in the big trunk." One eyebrow arched in a final warning challenge. "And mind ye, girl—no more!"

Maggie's lips curled into a sullen pout as she watched her mother's shadowy form move away. All the lovely dresses she had bought in St. Louis—left out here to rot in the sun! The thought made Maggie grit her teeth in frustrated rage as she bent to sort through her wardrobe, bemoaning each item she cast aside. Perhaps Judd would buy her some new gowns once they reached Sacramento—*if* there were any dress shops, she thought grimly.

Thirty minutes passed while the transfer was being made. Michael and Sean had yoked up the four remaining oxen and two of the cows. All of the chickens had died this afternoon. Still, Molly had kept them, hoping to save them for the next meal. But now she set them on the roadside in their coop, their rapidly putrefying little bodies tainting the air with ripe stench.

Michael handed Maggie a tin cup of water. "Just a drop, girl. There's not much left."

Maggie sipped cautiously, holding the mineral-filled liquid in her mouth for what seemed like an eternity. It flowed slowly beneath her tongue and around her gums before she finally swallowed, letting it soothe her tortured throat.

"I want you to take Jamie and Katie with you in the lead, Maggie, girl. Patrick will have to carry Kevin, and the rest of us have to see to the stock."

Returning the cup to her father, Maggie nodded. At least she wouldn't have to be burdened with a balking animal or carrying a child, she thought testily. She turned to face the southwest and felt her heart constrict in terror.

None of the other wagons were in sight. There was nothing but the blackness of night and the pallid wasteland of unshifting horizons.

Maggie moaned deep in her throat like a wounded animal and, trembling, spun around to her father. "Da! They're all gone! We're lost!"

Michael strode angrily back to her, his eyes narrowed in warning. "Hush your mouth, girl! Do ye want to frighten the children?"

Maggie gave a quick, nervous sob and clutched his arm. "But, Da! How will we find our way?"

"We'll find it," he hissed, and fixed her with an intense scowl. "So just be keepin' your thoughts to yourself." His face softened slightly, and he touched her cheek. "You're a strong girl, Maggie. Stronger than your mother. She's already near the breakin' point with worry. I'm *depending* on you."

Maggie managed a tight nod of acquiescence, but a renewed terror filled her eyes at the sight of the desolation surrounding her. There could be *miles* separating them from the last wagon, and nothing to mark their way. She tried to think, her mind working frantically to recall who had been in front of them. Was it Jennings? She couldn't remember; she felt numbed, her mind a tangle of jumbled ideas. All she knew for certain was the nameless fear that gripped her and the cold feeling of dread that crawled across her skin.

Maggie struggled on through the night, using a heavy blanket as protection against the fierce, biting wind. Overhead, the sky was a canopy of stars, and the moon cast a faint glow on the dunes. The sand was deep and loose, making each step torment. The perspiration on her face attracted the sand like ants to honey and dried in the brisk, arid wind until her cheeks were crusted with the salty granules. Her breathing was labored by fear and exertion until at times she thought her heart and throat would burst.

Occasionally she would come across some abandoned piece of furniture—a feather bed, a rocking chair, a kitchen hutch. Ox chains, yokes, and harnesses littered the sand. But at other times, she stumbled on blindly, with nothing to guide her.

At several points, she was forced to get down on her hands and knees and feel around in the sand for the ox tracks and wheel ruts, sobbing with the effort, sometimes crawling fifty yards until they were located. But she forced herself to go on, knowing that another day of broiling sun would mean the end of the O'Brians and their dream of California.

Sarah sat huddled in a blanket, shivering against the cruel night air. The wind whipped up the grit and dust from the desert floor and pelted her from all sides. Simon, Lucas, and Samantha lay on the ground, sobbing with fear and cold, while Hetty sat next to Sarah, the two women's bodies making an impromptu windbreak for the children. Sarah had put the dog down with the youngsters, hoping his warm, furry body would add to their comfort, but still they cried.

The moon cast black shadows over the silvery sand, the stars fading in the predawn gloom. A mile back, perhaps ten—Sarah had no conception of time and space anymore—Roy had unyoked the oxen near a gully of blackened, blistered rocks. The horses and cattle had seemed beyond the point of exhaustion, frenzied and half-blind with thirst. There was no more water—for either animals or humans—and Roy had been forced to make the decision. They had abandoned their wagon and set out on foot for their very lives.

Sarah had tottered drunkenly across the sand, reeling and stumbling in an effort to keep up with her brother. But she couldn't do it. Nor could Hetty and the children, so they had stayed behind while Roy herded the cattle ahead in search of water, three canteens slung over his shoulder.

Sarah's teeth chattered. Her throat ached and stomach was cramped. She had drunk nothing for eight hours, had not eaten for twenty-four, and she had no idea when she last had slept. She was confused, frightened, and despondent, and all she wanted was to lie down with the children and sleep. Her head sagged forward, and she closed her eyes, a drowsy bliss invading her every cell.

Her head jerked up at the sharp jab of Hetty's elbow. Disorientated and groggy, Sarah looked around. There was nothing but black, endless dunes, shimmering in the moon's pallid glow, and she couldn't suppress the shudder that passed through her.

"We've got to go on," Hetty said.

Sarah groaned in utter despair. To walk another step would be sheer torture, but Hetty was right. They *had* to keep moving. If morning found them still far out on the desert . . .

Sarah's mind shied away from *that* thought. Throwing off her blanket, she pushed painfully to her feet and bent to rouse the children.

* * *

Roy shouted and cursed at his animals, slapping their rumps and urging them on. He still had the three cows, four of his oxen, and one horse; Sarah's mare and Garrett's pinto had run off into the desert, sniffing out some vague scent of water.

Under a black sky splashed with stars, he plodded over the moonswept dunes, passing other emigrants or being overtaken by still others—men driving their cattle, carrying empty water pails, cursing Red Canfield and even Hastings and his guidebook. Women and children trudged along forlornly or huddled, frightened and thirsty, in abandoned wagons. Dead cattle lay about the sand, and deserted wagons loomed up like tombstones in the eerie moonlight.

The ground had grown progressively harder, and a kind of crust covered the earth. Hooves occasionally broke through, and the cattle balked, but Roy urged them on.

Several of the animals stopped suddenly and lifted their noses. They began to bawl loudly, and, before Roy could stop them, they bolted ahead. Roy ran after them, gasping for breath through his parched, raw throat and nearly losing his balance, struggling over the encrusted sand.

The first faint streaks of pinkish gray were staining the sky to the east when Roy fell. The palms of his hands slammed into the gritty earth, tearing away the flesh; his kneecap exploded in pain. His vision doubled briefly, but he shook his head, trying to clear it, then cocked it to one side, listening carefully. Shouting, excited voices and . . . splashing!

Roy blinked, raised his head slowly. Away off to the south were the gray silhouettes of trees—hundreds of them. A shudder went through him, and his voice cracked in a sob of relief. It was the most beautiful sight he'd ever seen.

He lurched to his feet, hobbled forward a few yards on his injured leg, then, regaining his balance, broke into a staggering run. He stumbled almost blindly toward the water, only vaguely aware of three men approaching him, heading back to the desert.

He swayed and went down again, waves of blackness washing over him. Hanging onto his consciousness by only a thread, he struggled to a sitting position, felt strong hands helping him. Cool, fresh water dribbled between his lips and ran down his chin. Through a haze of pain, he was able to make out the features of the two Andersen men and Toby Garrett.

"It's the Truckee River," Toby said, letting Roy drink again. "Only another half mile."

Garrett got to his feet, but Roy caught and held fast to the fringed sleeve of the trapper's jacket. "My family," he managed to croak, and pointed feebly into the bleak, forbidding emptiness of the desert. "Out there."

Toby gave Roy's arm a reassuring squeeze. "I'll find them."

Sarah floated back slowly to consciousness. A hand curved under her neck, lifting her head from its sandy pillow. The sweet scent of water assailed her senses, filled her parched mouth. It was cool, delicious, easing the tortured rawness of her throat. Still slightly dazed, she heard a man's voice cautioning her, and she forced herself to take slow sips.

As the water revitalized her dehydrated body, her mind

110

began to clear. The dipper was removed from her cracked lips, and she found herself looking up into the deeply tanned, blond-bearded face of Toby Garrett. His sapphire eyes were oddly grave and watchful as they studied her, his brow furrowed in a frown.

"Feeling better?" he asked.

Sarah managed a slight nod, but as a flood of memories flashed through her mind, she sat up abruptly and looked around. Hetty and the children were sipping water from a shared tin cup, and even Beans, the setter, was drinking from Samantha's cupped hands. In the gray light of dawn, they were hardly recognizable—dirty, disheveled, sunburned, and blistered. Sarah gaped at them, then cautiously brought a hand to her own stringy, unkempt hair and cracked, swollen lips.

Toby smiled at her with wry amusement. "You look terrible, if that's what you're wondering."

Sarah turned her head sharply to glare at him, her nostrils flaring in indignation. But when she saw the teasing laughter in his eyes, an unwilling smile touched her lips. "I guess I do."

Nodding with exaggerated sagacity, he left the dipper with her and got to his feet. And Sarah couldn't help noticing that, despite the fatigue he must be feeling, he moved with all the supple grace of an animal.

"This is all the water I can leave with you, I'm afraid," he said, refilling the cup and handing it back to Hetty. "But the river's only a little over a mile away, and if you—"

Hetty held up a hand, cutting him off in mid-sentence. "Have you seen Roy?" Her voice was breathless and fearful, as if she had suddenly regained her senses and remembered their plight. "Where's Roy?"

111

"Probably at the river by now. I passed him just a little while ago." Slinging the water bucket over his shoulder, he turned back to Sarah, his hand outstretched, a faintly expectant look in his eyes. Sarah stared stupidly at the hand a moment, as if taking inventory of his fingers, the fine blond hair on its back and wrist, the broken, grimy nails. At length he spoke, his voice almost bantering. "The dipper . . . ?"

With a startled little gasp, Sarah blushed furiously and thrust the copper dipper quickly into his hand. Embarrassed and still slightly befuddled, she hesitantly forced her eyes to meet his. He was regarding her with a tolerantly amused smile, a mocking lift to one brow, and Sarah's cheeks flushed hot in anger.

"There's a little rise just ahead," he said, allowing his gaze to linger a moment longer before turning back to Hetty. "From there you can see the trees at the river. It's not far." And, without another word, he hitched up his pail and strode across the sand.

Sarah gazed after him with an intense scowl, her mouth twisting into a sullen curl. He *still* persisted in badgering her as if she hadn't the sense of a jackass. Even here—in this horrible predicament they found themselves in—he had given her that same look of mocking indulgence that she was beginning to despise.

Sighing irascibly, she brushed the image of his ridiculing smile away. *Now* was not the time to let his hateful attitude provoke her.

She got to her feet shakily, surprised at how weak her legs felt, and helped the children to stand. Samantha seemed the most reluctant to leave, as if she were relaxing and sunning herself on a picnic. Sarah tugged playfully on one of her niece's braids. "You'll have the rest of the day to sit around and do nothing—or maybe even swim, if you like.''

Samantha raised her head and blinked, her amber eyes bright with sudden anticipation. ''Swim?'' Showing more animation than she had in days, she scrambled to her feet and scampered on ahead, pausing to turn and gesture impatiently. ''Come on!''

Judd waded waist-deep into the river to grab the harness of a mule. For over an hour, he had been in and out of the water, hauling out the loose stock. The oxen dashed madly about and blundered down the steep banks into the river; even the horses and cows were completely unmanageable. They wallowed and spluttered, splashed and snorted until they were finally driven back to land. Still, no sooner were they out than they rushed right back in, and it was all the men could do to drag them back. But it was imperative that they be restrained before they killed themselves by drinking too much.

Some of the men behaved little better, shouting and diving and swimming like schoolboys. Judd had paddled around, fully clothed, a good twenty minutes before dragging himself up the bank, though a few hours ago he wouldn't have believed he possessed the energy.

Canfield, Stone, and Pardee had finally improvised a pen for the stock, made from ropes taken from the Andersens' wagon. It, and the Pardees' van, were the only wagons that had come through. The others were still out on the desert, and once the emigrants themselves had safely reached the river, the men planned to take the rested stock out to bring them in.

As more of the exhausted, thirsty pilgrims straggled

into the new camp at the river's edge, Judd settled back under a cottonwood to relax and observe. Most of them drank and then simply collapsed on the ground, too weary even to find a shady spot as Judd had. Canfield sulked, and a few of the emigrants eyed him accusingly, as if the disaster on the desert had been entirely all his fault. Perhaps that opinion wasn't quite fair, Judd mused. But had everyone blindly followed Canfield's advice instead of listening to Garrett, Judd doubted that even a dozen of them would have come through alive.

Now all seemed to be accounted for but the O'Brians. Old Ezra Weeks, Belle Pardee's father, was in a bad way, and little Hope Jennings had had to be carried down to the water by her father and revived. Hip-deep, holding the child in his arms and pouring handfuls of water over her head, his tousled mane of gray hair and beard flowing about his face, Preston Jennings had looked like a modern-day John the Baptist performing some holy rite.

Recalling the scene, Judd smiled in wry amusement at the behavior of their illustrious leader. But the smile faded when he thought of Maggie O'Brian, and his gaze strayed to the trail leading out of the desert. He would miss Maggie and her sharp Irish tongue and voluptuous, willing body, but perhaps it was for the best. He had no intention of honoring the whispered promises made at the height of his passion, and this would save her the hurt and disappointment she was certain to feel.

Judd shook his head in rueful recollection. Yes, he would miss Maggie and her good-natured family. Perhaps he should have been more honest with her, but there was no help for it now. And at least Maggie had had dreams of a bright future to take with her in the end.

He picked up his boots and turned them over in his

114

hands, examining the worn heels and split soles critically. He had worn them into the river while collecting the loose cattle, and they were ruined beyond repair. But he felt no great loss; these had served him well, and he wondered idly, just how many miles they had come.

He glanced up at the sound of footsteps on the gravelly earth and was somewhat surprised to find Sarah Coulter approaching him. She had evidently ducked her head in the river, and her hair hung in wet, dark gold tendrils about her face and shoulders, dripped down her back and chest, dampening the thin calico of her dress and allowing him to see clearly the contours of her breasts.

She smiled shyly at him. "You seem to have found the most comfortable-looking spot around. Do you mind if I join you?"

Judd patted the soft grass at his side. "I'd like the company."

Sarah settled herself beside him, her gaze resting dolefully on his boots. "You'll *never* be able to wear those again."

"I've got another pair." He brushed them aside with an airy wave of his hand, then directed his attention to Sarah's shoes. They were heavy, clumsy-looking brown leather shoes, better suited to a lumberjack. And what he could see of her lisle stockings was snagged and soiled. "Yours look in pretty good shape yet." He exchanged a wry glance with her. "Though hardly the latest fashion."

Sarah's lips formed a distant, self-deprecating smile. "No. I suppose they aren't."

Judd covertly made a leisurely study of her from head to toe—the delicate symmetry of her features, her wide, thickly lashed eyes, slightly upturned nose, her soft, ex-

115

pressive mouth, now cracked and swollen from the punishing dryness of the desert. A button was missing on her dress, and it gaped slightly, revealing a portion of creamy skin.

Judd allowed a thin, leering smile to touch his lips for an instant. Since Maggie was no longer around to provide amusement, perhaps he should replace her with Sarah. She might not be *quite* as willing as Maggie, but Judd had no doubts regarding his persuasiveness. And Sarah *was* interested in him; that much he was shrewd enough to see. Time might prove to be his only enemy, for only the great range of the Sierras was left to cross before they reached the Sacramento valley. Still, it would be a challenge worthy of his talents to corrupt this gentle little creature. As his gaze appraised her openly once more, he decided that the ultimate rewards would be well worth the effort.

He touched her chin with his fingers and turned her head to look at him. Her brows arched in mild surprise, and Judd favored her with a jaunty grin. "Your lips are cracked."

She eyed him somewhat doubtfully. "I know."

He traced the outline of her lower lip lightly with his forefinger, barely touching the flesh. "Such nice lips, too," he said softly.

"There's a jar of salve somewhere in our wagon." Her voice was slightly breathless, and she seemed to stumble over the words.

Judd suppressed a smile at her reaction. His finger trailed over her cheek to the tip of her red, peeling nose. "And your nose is sunburned. And your eyes—" He chuckled softly with teasing mirth. "You look like you've been on a two-day toot with a jug of white lightning.''

Sarah forced an uneasy laugh, watching out of the corner of her eye the path of his finger over to her ear and down the side of her neck. Judd leaned over and brushed his lips against her cheek, grazing it with his tongue, and he heard her sharply indrawn breath.

He sat back and looked at her, his dark eyes glittering. ''Salty, too.''

A mixture of confusion and doubt passed over her face. ''I . . . I suppose I am.''

Judd flashed her a disarming smile, deciding he had taken this far enough for the time being. He was too tired to play this game any longer. Besides, the poor girl seemed so befuddled and flustered . . . He feigned a yawn in order to hide the wicked, self-satisfied smile that threatened. Perhaps this might not be as difficult as he first suspected.

''You're tired,'' she said. ''I should go and let you rest.''

Judd sighed pensively. ''You're probably right. In all likelihood, I'll be needed later on to help bring in the wagons.''

Sarah nodded rather uncertainly and prepared to rise. Judd caught her hand and pressed her fingers urgently. ''Perhaps we can share supper tonight?''

A soft smile played about her mouth, radiant disbelief shining in her eyes. ''Yes,'' she whispered breathlessly, and as Judd released her hand, she turned and hastened away.

Sarah walked back to the river, trying to get hold of her turbulent emotions. She stared thoughtfully at the bright

117

October sun sparkling off the mirrorlike surface, while farther downstream the water foamed white over boulders in a narrow gorge.

Her cheeks held a rosy blush of pleasure, and she felt deliciously dazed. A whisper of a sigh escaped her lips, and at the recollection of the feel of Judd's lips and warm breath on her cheek, she felt her whole body flush with heat. It was a wonderful, sweet feeling. She smiled contentedly and closed her eyes, trying to recapture the moment again.

"What happened to my horse?"

Sarah stiffened at the impatience in the gruff voice that came from her side, shattering her mellow thoughts. She swore silently to herself at this rude intrusion on her privacy and turned sharply to frown darkly up into Toby Garrett's face. Of all the people she *didn't* wish to see at this time, this man was the first on her list.

She raised a challenging brow to him. "I don't know."

"I gave him to you for safekeeping." His mouth became hard beneath his full mustache. "And now I suppose you've *lost* him."

Sarah flung her head back to glare at him. "For your information, the last I saw of your stupid horse—he was with Roy!"

Toby looked momentarily chagrined, as if he couldn't bear to admit that a *man* could lose his horse. And, for a brief, fleeting second, Sarah thought he might actually apologize. Instead, he brushed her explanation away with an impatient gesture. "I guess now I'll have to roam all over this place looking for him."

"I guess you will." Sarah set her lips stubbornly, refusing to allow him to bait her into further argument. As it was, he had already completely spoiled her pleasant memories of moments before.

But in the next instant, another incident suddenly reminded her guiltily of someone she had quite forgotten: Maggie O'Brian.

The low, sleepy voices around the camp rose abruptly in pitch and volume, as excited murmurs raced through the emigrants. "It's the O'Brians!" Jennings shouted.

Sarah whirled away from Toby and peered toward the east. Emerging from the desert trail was the O'Brians' wagon, inching along slowly, animals and humans alike trudging painfully over the crusty earth.

Sarah paled as a wild surge of emotions swept through her. Judd's darkly intense eyes and the touch of his lips had succeeded momentarily in wiping out all thought of Maggie. Until this minute, Sarah hadn't even realized the other woman was absent. Now, as a welter of dizzying thoughts tumbled through her mind, Sarah's face hardened with suspicion. Had Judd been sincere with his ardent looks and flattering words, or had he simply been . . . ?

She hadn't time to complete the thought; as she looked on, Michael O'Brian suddenly broke away from the rest of his family and ran blindly for the river. To Sarah, everything that was happening so swiftly appeared to be in slow motion: The big Irishman reeling dazedly toward her, wild-eyed, his beard and hair disheveled and matted with alkali, waving his arms, alternately shouting Gaelic imprecations and praises to heaven.

He lurched to the river's edge, stumbled down the bank, slipping and sliding on the grass and loose earth, and plunged headlong into the water. He sank from sight for a few moments, then popped to the surface like a cork. Using his battered hat as a dipper, he scooped up the water and drank.

Sarah watched in stunned fascination as Michael O'Brian consumed huge quantities of water. He sat back in the shallows, submerged to his chest, gulping and choking and sobbing until he could hold no more. Then, like some great sea slug, he rolled over and began crawling aimlessly around in circles, shaking his head from side to side and laughing maniacally.

And then Toby was suddenly in the water, trying to pull the half-crazed man to his feet. But in his frenzy, Michael shoved the hunter and sent Toby sprawling on the bank. Wiley Higgins and Emmett Pardee waded into the water, and each grasped O'Brian's arms. But still the Irishman fought them, bucking and flailing like a man possessed, kicking and screaming irrationally as they dragged him up the bank.

He collapsed to the ground and immediately began to retch violently, spewing up what seemed like gallons of water, his whole body shuddering with the effort.

By this time, Sean and Kelly had rushed to their father's aid. A little knot of emigrants had surrounded the Irishman, and they stared with open curiosity, speculation and sympathy sweeping through their ranks.

When the last of O'Brian's paroxysms had passed, Roy cautiously handed a canteen to Sean. "Let him drink— but *slowly* this time."

Sarah watched as Sean held the water gently to his father's lips, and admiration flickered briefly in her eyes. For, despite the young man's own pitiable condition and obvious thirst, he ministered to his father as if he were a helpless child. She was aware that Toby had returned to stand by her side, though she refused to acknowledge his presence. The sour reek of wet buckskin and leather in-

120

vaded her nostrils, reminding her once again of her intense aversion to him.

Maggie stumbled through the crowd and fell to her knees in the grass beside her father and brothers. Her dress was torn and dirty, wild tangles of coppery hair flew in tousled snarls about her face, and her green eyes glittered feverishly. Her skin was ashen, and as she reached out to touch her father's brow, her hand shook uncontrollably.

"Da," she whispered in a quivering, hoarse croak, as if her tongue were swollen to twice its size. She drew in a ragged, convulsive breath, and her head rolled drunkenly to one side on her shoulders.

"Grab her!" Belle Pardee exclaimed in warning. "She's going to faint!"

In one swift, fluid motion, Judd swept forward and caught Maggie's shoulders as she began to sag. He lifted her in his arms as Orpha Jennings rushed forward with a cup of water. She dribbled a few drops between Maggie's cracked lips and over her face.

Maggie began to stir, and her eyes came open slowly. She blinked, peered around dully, then focused on the man in whose arms she was. She put her arms around his neck and pressed her cheek to his shoulder. "Me own darlin' Judd!"

He stroked her hair reassuringly, stealing an uneasy glance at Sarah. The expression on his face was inscrutable, giving not a hint of his thoughts or feelings, but it was all quite obvious to Sarah.

Her back stiffened, and she turned away, striving to compose her features to show as little emotion as possible. For a few joyous moments, she had actually deluded herself into believing that Judd wanted *her*. If it weren't for the others nearby, she could almost have laughed with bitter amusement at her own stupidity. Judd had only turned to her when he thought Maggie was. . . .

Sarah's eyes narrowed suspiciously, an inner confusion and hurt gnawing at her. Perhaps she *was* better off without him—if he was able to turn his affections and charm on and off as easily as that. She didn't know. Every part of her mind rebelled at the thought, but somewhere deep inside her a kernel of doubt lingered.

Hazarding another quick glance across the ring of people, Sarah saw Judd carrying Maggie to the Andersens' wagon, and the last of her spirits plummeted. Sighing with glum, resigned acceptance, she turned away and abruptly collided with the solid wall of Toby Garrett's chest.

Taking her by the shoulders, he held her at arm's length, one brow lifted dubiously, a sardonic twist to his mouth. "It seems you'll have to find someone else to flatter you with pretty words and soulful looks from now on—now that our Mr. Brannan is otherwise occupied."

Sarah gasped in outrage and wrenched free of his grasp. Her face flamed crimson, and a deep, consuming anger swept through her, pushing her past all caution or reason. Trembling with rage, her eyes shooting sparks of hatred, she raised her hands and shoved him with all the strength she could muster.

Unprepared and off-balance, Toby stumbled backward a step, slipped on the slick grass of the riverbank, and toppled into the water with a resounding splash. He landed on his backside in a foot of water and sat staring up at her in dumbfounded surprise. Then, with a flourishing gesture, he swept his hat from his head in mock salute, and his mouth lifted in a caustic smile of grudging admiration.

Sarah fixed him with a venomous glare, turned on her heel, and stormed away, raging inside herself for allowing Toby Garrett to continue to taunt her.

Chapter Seven

Lester Stone leaned negligently against Reverend Jennings's supply wagon, puffing reflectively on the stub of his cigar and gazing thoughtfully around him. The leaves had already turned bright fall colors in many places, while the firs remained a rich verdant green. The air was laden with the pungent odors of lichen and bark, and Lester inhaled deeply, relishing the clean, fresh scents.

Nearby, the river flowed with a soft, lapping sound, broken occasionally by the fretful, muffled cries of one of the O'Brian children or the angry curses of the teamsters. But altogether it was a most pleasant day, Lester reflected contentedly—and very profitable, too.

Once all the emigrants had safely reached the river camp, the party had spent another two days resting on the green banks, searching for lost cattle, salvaging from the desert, and taking stock of their provisions. Food was in dangerously short supply, though the addition of the meat of three wild sheep bagged by Garrett had helped ease the strain on the meager larders. Elmore Poole had shot a number of ducks, and several of the O'Brian boys had snared a basketful of trout.

Three wagons had been left to the mercy of the desert—one each belonging to Jennings, O'Brian, and Huntington. The rest had been brought in, though their loads were considerably lighter than when they had begun.

Lester's lips twisted into a shrewd, cunning smile, and he ran his hand absently over the bulge in his trouser pocket. To add to the rest of his pilfered collection he now had a magnificent ruby and diamond necklace belonging to Ruth Huntington, plus a miscellany of earbobs, bracelets, and pendants. They would no doubt fetch a good price in California, or perhaps—if he should find a woman who especially caught his fancy—make a dazzling gift. All in all, Lester thought smugly, he should be well set to embark on a new life in the virgin land of the west.

The only problem now was getting there.

Much of the stock had been lost or perished on the desert, and, to make the ascent of Truckee Canyon, the emigrants had been forced to double-team oxen borrowed from their neighbors. Even though there had been abundant grazing at the edge of the desert, the animals were in too weakened a condition for the grass to be much help.

This double-teaming was what all the delay today was about, and as Lester flicked his cigar into the bubbling stream, he wondered how much longer it would take. It had been exactly one week since leaving the Humboldt Sink for the desert, and in that time he doubted they had traveled sixty miles. It was that distance yet to the California border; would it take them another week to reach it?

Yesterday they had been forced to ford the river no less

126

than eight times. But it had been a relatively smooth incline at first, running along a high-walled canyon, with plentiful grass on the banks. The wagons and animals had been led up the stream bed, and they had made good progress. But today their route had become steeper, and the narrow gorge was obstructed by rocks, downed timber, and sharp briars.

Hearing Red Canfield's angry, bellowing shouts up ahead, Lester shook his head in contempt. The guide had insisted this was the way, but Lester had misgivings. If this indeed *was* the route to California, why hadn't all the brush and boulders been cleared out of the path by previous trains?

Stifling a yawn, Lester let his gaze wander to the O'Brians' wagon waiting directly behind his. Several of the younger children were playing while Maggie chatted and smiled provocatively at Judd Brannan. Since the desert, the Irish girl had seldom left his side, and Lester envied the younger man. And Michael had recovered sufficiently from his brief spell of madness at the river, though for the rest of that day and all that night, he had lain under a tree like a beached whale.

Voices raised in angry dispute distracted Lester from his thoughts, and he frowned irritably. Jennings had ordered him to stay behind with the slower wagons to lend assistance with his mules, if necessary. Apparently that time had come.

Heaving an annoyed sigh, Stone hitched up his suspenders over his lean ribs and started walking to the front of this last section of the train. Passing Pardee's wagon, he could hear Belle inside talking soothingly to her father; the old man had yet to rally from his ordeal in the desert.

Up ahead, Canfield was arguing vehemently with Ole

Andersen, O'Brian, and Pardee. Red-faced and eyes glittering with rage, the guide gestured angrily with his bullwhip at the sad-faced, lean-flanked oxen yoked to the Swede's wagon.

"You *can* get up over that ridge with these six oxen!" Canfield exclaimed furiously. "It's a waste of time to hitch up more!"

Ole Andersen's normally pleasant features drew into a fierce scowl, but his voice held a note of exaggerated patience. "My animals are tired. *I'm* tired," he added, thumping his massive chest with a large hand. "I need another yoke, or we'll sit here all day. Or maybe slip off this road and fall down the ravine, *ja?*"

Stone cast a wary glance down the steep gorge to his right. Though only about a thirty-foot drop, it was filled with buckled roots, jagged rocks, and clumps of thorny scrub. In places, the trail along the river was slippery, and the oxen had difficulty keeping their footing. The mules, though often sulky and troublesome, had much sounder hooves for this kind of track.

Canfield was obviously holding onto his rage by a thin edge of self-control as he slapped the butt of his whip against his palm. "God damn it, man! It's four o'clock! By the time we wait for you to yoke up another team, it'll be getting dark!"

O'Brian's lips curved into a sardonic smile. "What's the matter, Mr. Canfield? You'd not be a-fearin' the bogeyman, would you now?"

Pardee cackled gleefully, but Canfield scowled darkly.

O'Brian grinned delightedly at the guide's reaction and turned to Lester. "If ye'd be so good as to fetch a couple of your mules, Mister Stone, mayhap we can make it into camp before the ghosties come to frighten the good Mr.

Canfield, here.'' The humor left his eyes as he turned to stare meaningfully at Canfield. ''We've frittered away enough precious time with this arguing.''

Canfield's fists bunched at his sides, and he spat viciously over the ledge. Frowning in disapproval, Stone turned to go back to his mules with O'Brian.

Canfield suddenly let out an enraged bellow, and the loud crack of the whip echoed through the canyon like a rifle shot. An ox screamed. Ole Andersen shouted. The whip snapped again. Axles groaned, wheels creaked, chains rattled. Inga and Astrid whined in fright. The whip sang through the air once again, popped loudly, and another animal bellowed.

Stone spun back in time to see Canfield raise his arm. The lash descended in its arc, cut painfully into dark fur. The ox lurched and reared, slipped on the loose gravel on the ledge.

Ole Andersen barreled into Canfield from the side, and the two men crashed into the flanks of an ox. Canfield threw a handful of dirt in the Swede's eyes, blinding him. The guide struggled to his knees, swung back the whip to strike, and was knocked to the ground from behind by young Peter, pouncing down from the seat.

Canfield slammed against the front wheel with agonizing force. Regaining his senses, he held up an arm to ward off another blow as the elder Andersen charged again. Red's hand struck the brake lever. The wagon lurched, started to slide.

Pardee shouted in warning. Oxen bellowed in panic, hooves slipped on the scree, sending a small avalanche of rocks and pebbles down the canyon wall. Inga screamed in dazed horror, jumped clear of the rolling van, and scrabbled for safety. Ole caught hold of a yoke with both

129

hands and tried to stop the slithering wagon with his own weight, the muscles on his forearms standing out with the effort, sweat running down his face.

Wood splintered, rocks crumbled, terrified oxen bawled—but still the ponderous van continued its unchecked descent, skittering and bumping down the slope. Ole fell to his knees, was dragged several feet, and finally let go, sobbing with sheer, frustrated anger.

The rear wheels went over first, and for a moment the entire wagon seemed suspended in midair before it crashed to the abyss below. There was a terrible cracking as wheels flew from the main body, bows split, canvas tore, oxen bellowed.

"Astrid!" Ole Andersen's voice was a wail of anguish as he scrambled clumsily down the side of the canyon, slipping on the scree, snagging his clothing on the underbrush. Peter climbed down after him, followed by Sean and Michael O'Brian. Inga sobbed hysterically while Molly O'Brian tried to comfort her.

Stone stood on the precipice with the others, watching in silence as the men threw aside goods of all kinds to get inside the ravaged wagon. Two of the oxen had broken free of their yokes and staggered dazedly amid the boulders and scrub.

Lester stole a glance over his shoulder at Canfield. The guide was standing off to one side, a sullen curl on his lips, rubbing his forearm through a tear in his sleeve.

A shout of triumph from below brought Stone's attention back to the matter at hand, and he directed his gaze once more to the canyon floor. Ole was lifting his daughter in his arms and climbing back out of the wreckage. She was dazed but conscious, reduced to a trembling mass of broken sobs.

A cheer broke from the onlookers, and, as Inga waited expectantly on the ledge, Ole made his slow, ponderous way back up the cliff, followed by his son. But, as mother and daughter embraced and babbled in Swedish, Peter's gaze fixed on Canfield, a cold, deadly fury darkening his blue eyes. Withdrawing his hunting knife from its sheath, he moved with slow, measured strides toward the guide, his youthful, handsome face frozen in a mask of pure hatred.

Canfield eyed the young man narrowly, backed up a few paces, and reached for his whip. "Don't mess with me, boy," he said in an ominously low voice. "You're no match for me."

Peter ignored the guide's words, moving ever steadily and purposefully forward. The atmosphere crackled with an almost tangible tension as all eyes turned to stare at the two men. Canfield shook out his whip as the young man continued to advance on him.

The crack of a rifle shot echoed through the canyon. Peter stopped short in surprise and swung his head around to find Toby Garrett at the top of the trail, his rifle pointed at the sky, a knot of men surrounding him.

Peter held up an impatient, cautionary hand. "Keep out of this, Mr. Garrett." His murderous gaze returned to Canfield, and he advanced another step.

Toby lowered the barrel of his gun, aiming it directly at the young man. "There's another shot left in here, Peter. I don't want to use it, but I will."

Peter's eyes flickered with uncertainty. He glanced from Garrett to Canfield, back to Garrett again. Muttering an oath, he flung his knife aside and stalked back to his family.

Reverend Jennings moved with awkward haste down

131

the sloping trail, his stiff, long-legged stride and flapping coattails almost comical. Coulter, Garrett, several of the drivers, and even Huntington followed, taking in the scene with expressions of dismay.

"Your guardian angel was watching over you, my dear," Jennings murmured, patting Astrid's cheek. The girl's lips quivered, and she looked as if she might erupt in a fresh burst of sobs.

In the next hour—after the women and children had been sent ahead—the men worked to salvage some of the Andersens' possession, though the wagon itself was a total loss. Three of the oxen were hauled up the cliff by ropes and yoked to Pardee's wagon, whose own stock was pitiably weak. In return for the use of his animals, Ole Andersen had a place to store what goods he had recovered.

Lester Stone clambered up the hillside from the Swede's wagon, smiling like a contented cat, listening to the sweet music as the pouch of gold *kroner* jingled in his pocket.

It was later than usual that evening by the time the emigrants had finished supper and most of the children had gone off to their beds with little of the usual protest. Several wagons had parked together in a little glade, but the rest of the seven were strung out along the canyon trail, drawn as close to each other as possible for protection.

Maggie sat wrapped in her shawl a few yards from the campfire, shivering in the autumn chill. Thick cloud formations drifted lazily beneath a star-filled sky, and the scent of pine lingered in the evening breeze. Bullfrogs croaked loudly nearby, almost drowning out the crickets, and Maggie sighed wistfully.

Around the fire, some of the men were talking earnestly with Reverend Jennings, regarding Canfield's despicable behavior this afternoon, she supposed. The Andersens had been left with only their oxen and what they could carry, and poor Astrid was scraped and bruised and her wrist was sprained; Inga was completely unstrung. At the thought of the whole episode, Maggie shuddered in disgust. She had truly been sorry to see Toby Garrett break up the fight; Red Canfield *deserved* a knife through his ribs.

Smiling at the image of this in her mind, her gaze wandered to the Huntingtons' monstrous wagon. Phillip's coughing spells had seemed to have become worse since the desert, and, looking at him now, Maggie decided he was indeed a very sick man. Illuminated by the flickering glow of the fire, his face seemed to be all lean planes and hollows, and his eyes were sunken deep and rimmed with dark circles. Alma, looking not much better, sat at his side, cuddling two-year-old Ned on her lap. Both of them gazed as if mesmerized into the flames, their pale, blank faces expressionless—the two most solemn and cheerless people Maggie had ever come across.

She smothered a grin as a thought popped into her head, and she wondered if the two of them ever made love. Certainly they must have at least *once*—Ned was proof of that. But somehow she couldn't quite picture either of them caught up in the furor of ecstasy. They spoke rarely—even to each other—and . . . Maggie restrained an urge to giggle. Maybe they were both too *tired* to talk. And that could also be a cause for Phillip's

133

increasing poor health.

Maggie gave a soft gurgle of laughter at the absurd train her thoughts had taken. She wondered if Phillip had to interrupt things to cough and hawk occasionally, and this new notion brought on another fit of muffled giggling.

Judd turned away from the men around the fire and glanced at her, an eyebrow raised in silent inquiry. Maggie giggled again and covered her mouth with both hands.

Judd broke away from the men and came to sit beside her, regarding her with amused indulgence. "What do you find so funny tonight?"

Maggie shook her head. "I'll tell you later." She managed to sober slightly and turned to study his face. The firelight turned his swarthy skin even darker, and his eyes were like twin glowing coals. His closeness, his lazy smile and enigmatic gaze all made her acutely aware of his masculinity. She longed to reach over and run her hands over the smooth, muscled flesh of his chest beneath his ruffled shirt and feel the silken warmth of his skin next to hers. His dark, liquid gaze met hers, and Maggie felt the heat of desire flooding her veins.

"They want to do something about Canfield," he said.

"Who?"

Judd shrugged. "Andersen. Your father." He took a cheroot from his pocket and struck a match to it. "Some think he ought to be banished—others want him lynched."

Maggie snorted irritably. "They should have let Peter finish the job today."

Judd studied the glowing end of his cigar. "Ah, but that's not a Christian thing to do—so says the good Reverend." He gave her a conspiratorial wink. "Jennings

134

wants him to return the ten dollars Andersen paid him as guide's fee and have done with it.''

Maggie's eyes widened, and her mouth curled in disbelief. ''Ten dollars for what he did!'' Her face twisted into a hateful sneer. ''I'm thinkin' *I'd* vote for the lynching.''

Judd smiled lazily at her, leaned close and let his hand run caressingly over hers. ''Let's not concern ourselves with Canfield *or* his punishment.'' His eyes glittered with open lust as his gaze touched hers. ''Let's go for a little stroll, shall we?''

Maggie nodded almost imperceptibly, a slow, sensuous smile of agreement curving her mouth.

Sarah ambled back into the circle of firelight, Samantha tagging along at her side. She had put Simon and Lucas to bed, but Samantha had refused to join her brothers, stating emphatically that she firmly believed herself to be a grown-up and so should therefore be allowed to sit up with them. Sarah hadn't argued; stubborn little Sam usually got the better of her, anyway. Besides, Lucas had bedded down with the two oldest Pardee boys, and she supposed they would whisper and giggle for at least an hour, excluding Samantha from their secret discussions. Old Ezra Weeks—helpless as he was—was there to keep an eye on the children, as were the two Andersen women.

''What was Mr. Canfield doing back there, sittin' on that big rock?'' Samantha asked.

Sarah shrugged, though she suspected he was getting drunk, from the reek of whiskey in the air and the glint of moonlight on glass bottle. She wondered idly where he got his supply of liquor, but she certainly wasn't about to tarry to ask. Red Canfield unnerved her—had *always* unnerved her for no reason she could define—and after today's episode, he was doubly threatening.

Orpha Jennings offered her a cup of coffee, but Sarah quickly declined, having already tasted the woman's frightful brew and not wanting the opportunity to do so again. But as she steered Samantha in the direction of Roy and Hetty, seated together by the fire, she noticed Judd and Maggie get up and slip into the trees behind the O'Brians' wagon.

A bitter spark of hurt and anger flashed momentarily in her eyes and then was gone. In the last three days, Sarah had resigned herself to the fact that Judd had turned to her only when he thought Maggie was forever lost on the desert. A painful lesson, but one Sarah was thankful to have learned so early. Judd Brannan was obviously a man accustomed to having a woman around him all the time, but the idea that he could disregard Maggie so callously troubled Sarah. But how—and more importantly *should* she—tell Maggie of his heartless attitude?

Samantha sat down beside her father. "I thought you were in bed," he said.

An angry frown flickered across her brow. "Ben Pardee was pullin' my braids."

Roy exchanged an amused glance with his wife as Sarah seated herself on a fallen log. Reverend Jennings was engaged in a heated discussion with his driver Stone and several other men, one of whom was Toby. The firelight threw his face into shadows, making his features appear harsh and cold, turned his beard and hair a tawny shade of orange, his skin a deep bronze. He reminded her of a lion she had once seen at a circus, as confident and agile as any jungle beast.

136

Sarah leaned over to her brother. "What's going on?"

Roy shrugged lamely. "I don't know. I reckon they're still trying to decide what to do about Canfield." He rubbed his knee absently where it was still sore from his fall on the desert. "I think they ought to show *him* the same taste of the whip as he gave Andersen's oxen."

"Now, Roy—" Hetty warned.

"Stop and think about it a minute. What does Ole Andersen have left now?"

"They've still all got each other. And besides, Inga told me they've got a little stash of gold coins they brought over from Sweden with them. Ole was going to build a sawmill with it, but she expects there'll be more than enough for all they'll need to get back on their feet again."

Roy grunted doubtfully as Jennings suddenly threw up his hands and shouted for attention. The hushed chatter died away, and all eyes turned expectantly toward him, standing tall and erect in the glow of the fire, his mane of gray hair almost obscuring his features, his cold, hard little eyes glittering beneath bushy gray-flecked brows.

"We've come to a decision—of sorts," he said in his grandiloquent voice. Sarah had often wondered what his sermons were like, and now she suspected she might be about to find out. "It's obvious we're running low on food—all of us," he went on. "It may take another week—maybe two—to reach Sutter's Fort. That depends entirely on the Lord's guidance."

Sarah suppressed a smile. She didn't think the Lord had been anywhere *near* this wagon train for the last week and couldn't really blame Him.

Jennings looked out over the crowd, his hands clasped before him as if in prayer. "Mr. Garrett has offered to go

137

on ahead and send back supplies.''

"Nooo!" Ruth Huntington wailed, popping to her feet. All eyes turned in surprise to the plump little woman. "He's the only one of us who knows anything about hunting and trapping. If *he* goes, what will we do for fresh meat?''

A ripple of agreement passed through the emigrants. Jennings held up a hand for silence, and, sensing his audience's rapt interest, went on. "Exactly *my* sentiments, Mrs. Huntington. Exactly. *I* suggested sending Mr. Canfield. By doing that, we will rid ourselves effectively of his now-unwanted presence—*and* do ourselves a great service.''

O'Brian shook his head in firm negation. "And *I* say no to that. Ye can't trust the man. Who's to say he won't just keep goin' and never even bother to send back food?''

"That's right!'' Pardee agreed. "He'll light out and leave us high and dry.''

Toby sauntered away from the fire and came to stand a few feet away from Sarah. She eyed him warily, wondering if *he* would desert them, too. The situation *was* desperate. Everyone had been living on short rations for days now, and Sarah had often found herself wondering lately what *would* happen if they ran out of food. They could always kill the cattle, but then what would pull their wagons over the mountains?

"As for Mr. Canfield,'' Jennings continued, "I've decided *not* to send him. For the very same reasons you have given us, besides—as Mr. Stone pointed out—Canfield is the *only* man who knows the way. He *is* our guide, after all. And we must remember that.'' Reverend Jennings strutted back and forth, pausing occasionally to size

138

up his audience. He's *enjoying* this, Sarah concluded with grim amusement. He stopped suddenly and looked around him expectantly. "Mr. Tyrrell has volunteered to go on ahead with my letter to Captain Sutter, which—I'm sure—will give us sufficient credit to advance us the provisions we need. I should imagine we would meet somewhere on the western slope of the mountain. Now"—he paused a moment for dramatic effect—"who else will volunteer?"

Blank, vacant faces stared back at him. Claude Tyrrell stood by, looking small and frail, his black hair an unruly thatch.

"Why must *two* go?" Edgar Huntington spoke, rising up from his seat like a king from his throne. Sarah's lip curled in scorn. She disliked the Huntingtons almost as much as she did Red Canfield.

"Because," Jennings replied, "even though I vouch for Mr. Tyrrell's honesty and integrity, the plain fact is that he has nothing to *compel* him to return. No family, no property—nothing. And civilization, after so many months of loneliness, can tempt even the strongest of hearts."

"Surely you don't expect one of *us* to go?" O'Brian exclaimed. "Men with families?"

"You have grown sons to see to your family's needs."

O'Brian snorted derisively and walked away.

Roy slowly got to his feet. "I'll go."

Hetty's low moan was a howl of dismay. Sarah stared as if he had taken leave of his senses. Samantha put her arms around his waist and looked up at him, her eyes wide and confused. "Pa, you can't *leave* us!"

Roy glanced down at Samantha, smiled, and smoothed her hair. His gaze returned to Jennings. "If I could have a

139

moment to talk with my family, alone?''

Jennings gave a slight inclination of his head. ''By all means.''

Sarah followed her brother in a kind of daze, her mind unable to absorb the words he had uttered.

Hetty's confused shock had turned to anger, and she frowned unhappily. ''How can you even *suggest* such a thing, Roy Coulter? Let one of the others go! It's not your responsibility!''

''It *is* mine. It's my responsibility to see you get safely over the mountains.'' He smiled gently and touched her cheek. ''We're almost out of food. You know that.''

''We can kill a cow!''

''We need those cows to help with the wagon. This way, I can be over the mountains and back with the food in no time. We can't rely on Mr. Garrett to feed us all— the game's already starting to dig in for the winter. This way, I'll *know* help is coming as fast as it possibly can.''

''But we'll never get the wagon over the mountains ourselves,'' Sarah pointed out. ''We need a strong man.''

Roy gazed steadily into her eyes. ''And right now that's not me—with my gimpy knee. I'm better off on a horse than on foot.'' His mouth twitched in a faintly rueful smile. ''Emmett will help you. So will O'Brian, and now that the Andersens have no wagon of their own—'' His voice trailed off, and he sighed. ''Believe me, I wouldn't do this if I didn't think it was best for us.''

Hetty's breath wheezed at the back of her throat, and she rubbed her forehead in a gesture of weary helplessness. Sarah turned away, knowing that what her brother said made sense but unwilling to accept it.

Hugging her arms to her breasts, she paced over to the edge of the clearing, a confused rush of emotions sweeping through her. The idea of being left out here with no man—no *family* man—frightened her. She knew she was capable of doing many things, but there was so *much* she *couldn't* do.

Leaves crackled underfoot, and Sarah spun around. Toby met her eyes briefly, and Sarah scowled. Giving her a tolerant smile, he continued over to Roy. "Mr. Coulter, I'll keep an eye on your family for you—help with the wagon. I told Jennings I'd go, but you heard what he said."

Roy nodded. "It makes better sense that you *do* stay. But if I have your word on looking after my family, I'll feel a lot better about leaving them."

Toby extended his hand. "You have my word, Mr. Coulter. I'll look out for them just like they were my own."

Sarah's mouth narrowed into a grim line, and she swore silently to herself. Of all the men on this train, why *him?*

Chapter Eight

Red Canfield sprawled on a large, flat rock, half-reclining, basking in the warm October sunshine while the others went about their daily tasks. His one chore for the day was completed, he thought wryly, glancing at the shirt he had washed out now hanging from the limb of a spruce, drying in the sun. Naked to the waist, his hairy belly gradually turning a faint pink from the sun's rays, he took a surreptitious pull from his pint bottle. Belching loudly, he slipped the bottle back underneath his hat and let his gaze wander over the camp.

Fertile valleys spread out on either side of the river; the air was rich with the fragrance of pine and wildflowers. Birds sang, leaves rustled in the trees, and occasionally Molly O'Brian would hum an old country tune. Truckee Meadows, they call this place, Red thought, and a twist of his lips passed for what might have been a contented smile. A pretty little spot to stop and rest for a few days.

Garrett had been against tarrying for more than a day to rest the stock, for a few miles to the west stood the great granite domes of the Sierras; fresh snow was clearly visible on the peaks. But everyone was tired after the struggle of ascending the canyon, and Huntington's main wagon hadn't made it all the way; it was three miles back, wedged solidly between the narrow walls of the trail.

Red chuckled maliciously and took another drink. Old man Huntington was fit to be tied. His supply wagon had been crammed full to the bursting point, and still there were more goods back on the trail. He had begged and cajoled and even promised money to anyone who would carry his possessions in their wagons. But no one had accepted his offer. And, for a time, Red feared that Dulcy, the colored maid, might be tossed out to make room for Ruth's wardrobe, but the black girl was still with them.

Red's pale blue eyes narrowed speculatively as they moved to Ruth Huntington, going through trunks of clothing. Fine silks, brocades, and muslins were examined, lamented, and cast aside, and Red chuckled again at the incongruously comical picture the woman presented. Dressed in an elegant silver and gold brocade ball gown, bejeweled and beribboned, she tramped back and forth from the wagon to the trunk, holding her skirts daintily above her ankles, displaying her ugly brown leather walking shoes.

Shaking his head, Red belched softly again and scratched his belly, his gaze straying to Hetty Coulter. She and her daughter were hanging freshly laundered clothes on a rope strung between two trees. Her husband had been gone five days now and ought to be well over the summit of the mountains—unless he got lost or fell off his horse and broke a leg. Red snorted mirthfully at the thought.

The men were busy greasing axles, mending harnesses, and testing wheels. All in all, Red felt he had done a passably good job for a greenhorn. They had left Independence with eleven wagons, and six had made it this far. That was better than half. And if he hadn't lost his temper with the Swede's oxen . . .

Red shrugged mentally and dismissed it from his mind, his gaze settling on Maggie O'Brian, trying to break up a fight between a couple of her brothers, the two Pardee boys, and Lucas Coulter. Her coppery hair swept to her waist in thick, cascading waves, and her breasts threatened to spill out over the top of her bodice as she pulled Patrick away from Amos Pardee.

Red released a long, heavy sigh, and his lips drew back in an obscene smile. She was a voluptuous little thing, with her hair like fire and eyes like emeralds, a waist so small that Red imagined his hands could span it easily. It was a real shame Judd Brannan came along when he did—she had tried every *other* single man before and might eventually have gotten around to Red. Closing his eyes, he shook his head wistfully and gave an appreciative little grunt.

But she was Brannan's woman now, and Red wasn't about to tangle with a man who carried one of those new repeating revolvers. Anyway, once they got to California, Red would be all ready and eager to try out those Spanish señoritas he'd heard so much about. He only hoped they didn't smell as bad as some of the Indian wenches he'd had in the past. But as he got a whiff of himself, he decided it didn't much matter.

Giving a bawdy chuckle, he slipped his bottle from beneath his hat and drank again.

* * *

A worried frown creased Toby's brow as he ran a practiced eye over one of the heifers. A raw, festering patch had developed just above her shoulder where the yoke bit into her hide, and it was growing larger each day. The cows did not fare well beneath the yoke, but after an unsuccessful attempt to team his two mules with the Coulters' oxen, he had reverted to the cattle. Still, this animal's nasty-looking sore didn't seem to be healing.

Dipping his fingers into a jar of salve borrowed from Pardee, he smeared it liberally over the affected area, receiving a mildly irritated glance from a pair of large bovine eyes. "Sorry if it stings, girl. But maybe by the time we hitch you up again, you'll be good as new."

Bending down, he pulled up a handful of grass to wipe the sticky salve from his fingers, his gaze straying inadvertently to the peaks in the west. The sight left him with a vague sense of discomfort and forboding, and he cursed the emigrants silently for delaying here in Truckee Meadows. Yes, they were tired, the animals were tired, *he* was tired. But today was October 12; autumn was here and winter not far behind. They had reached the threshold of California, only perhaps another fifteen miles to go—one day if they made good time; two, at most. And beyond that another twenty miles would see them on the heights of the Sierras and across its towering summit—a summit already capped with snow.

Toby resealed the jar of salve, his gaze dark and brooding, his lips taut. If even a *foot* of snow fell before they got through the mountain pass, it would be difficult going. Almost half the stock had died on the desert, and what remained was weak. The wagons were falling to pieces and needed constant repairs, the emigrants themselves weary and short-tempered.

146

And if *more* than a foot or two was on the ground before they crossed the mountains? A chill crawled up his spine to the base of his neck, and the thin sheen of sweat on his face had suddenly turned clammy.

Annoyed at himself for allowing his imagination to dwell on such grim thoughts, he turned and walked back into camp. Hetty was scolding Lucas, while Samantha looked on and grinned slyly.

"You just had a bath and got clean clothes, and now look at you!" Hetty brushed ineffectually at the mud on the boy's shoulder and scowled at the soiled, torn flap of material at his knee. "You just make extra work for me."

Lucas scuffed his foot in the dust and looked sheepishly up at his mother. "I'm sorry, ma'am."

Giving the boy a final, disapproving look, Hetty lifted her hands in mock surrender. She glanced helplessly at Toby and tucked an uruly lock of her brown hair behind an ear. "I just don't know, Mr. Garrett." She offered him a perplexed half-smile. "Sarah had all three of 'em down to the river earlier and made them take a good bath, and now look!"

"It's hard to keep a boy clean." He flashed Lucas a conspiratorial grin. "I remember how it used to be."

The boy smiled shyly in return and slipped over to sit beside his baby brother in the shade of the wagon.

"I'll be so *glad* once we get settled in a real house somewhere," Hetty said. "A place I can keep swept and dusted and the linens fresh."

"Yes, ma'am." Toby nodded politely, struggling to keep a smile from his face. In the few days he had spent in Hetty Coulter's company, he had discovered her propensity for cleanliness. His own clothes had been washed and mended, and meals were never eaten without first a

147

vigorous scrubbing of hands. Though, in a way, it was nice to feel a part of a family again after so many years. If only Sarah would warm up to him a little.

"Did you shoot any deer or bears today?"

Toby glanced down at Samantha, smiling up at him, her amber-flecked brown eyes wide and filled with curiosity. The child was already beautiful in a kind of reedy, preadolescent way, and he often found himself wondering what she would look like in another five or ten years. Though that was something he doubted he would be around to see. "I set out traps, but they aren't big enough to catch any bears. Maybe a rabbit or a fox. Want to come along while I go check on them?"

Samantha bobbed her head happily, her eyes shining with excitement, but Hetty intervened. "You've got coffee to grind and a dress that needs mending."

Samantha's mouth drooped with disappointment. Lucas looked hopefully at Toby, but Hetty gave him a firm shake of her head. "I need you to gather kindling."

"I'll just get dirtier."

Hetty suppressed a smile. "With your pa gone and Sarah haulin' that rancid bacon and a piece of my twine down to the river to fish, I need you both here to help." Her gaze swept her two oldest children in stern warning. "Understood?"

Samantha nodded reluctantly, but Lucas only scowled.

Toby gave them both a wink, picked up his rifle, and left the camp. Rancid bacon? He shook his head, mystified. Perhaps after he'd seen to the traps, he'd check on Sarah's progress. She was probably *still* waiting for the first nibble on her line.

* * *

148

Toby straightened up from his inspection of the trap, cursing aloud. Nothing. Not even a squirrel or possum had wandered unsuspecting into the steel jaws. He should take his rifle to the glade where earlier he had seen deer droppings, but he had no desire to sit motionless for perhaps hours, waiting. He was restless and edgy, his stomach felt coiled tighter than a watch spring, and the thought of silently stalking a prey today made the feeling intensify.

Disgusted, he eyed the trap narrowly again, hefted his rifle, and picked his way carefully through the tangled underbrush. A flock of wild geese soared overhead in their familiar vee formation, heading to warmer climes for the long winter ahead. A winter, Toby reminded himself grimly, that could descend any day.

As if drawn by some unseen force, his gaze moved to the west. Those mountains were formidable-looking even at this distance—perhaps as great as the Rockies. The sunlight glimmered on their white peaks, made dark shadows in the gorges, reflected off the granite walls.

The hairs on the back of his neck stirred, and he shivered suddenly. If he couldn't persuade the emigrants to move out tomorrow, he *must* convince them to go no later than the next day.

Taking a deep breath and expelling it slowly, he started walking for the river, hoping to divert his mind with Sarah. They would undoubtedly end up squabbling again, with her giving him frosty looks and he laughing at her. But even arguing was preferable to dwelling on the ominous thoughts he couldn't shake of those snow-mantled mountains.

Sarah. He really *should* try to let up on her. She had proved herself capable of most tasks, and she did them without complaint. But he *enjoyed* watching her eyes darken to a smoky gray in anger, the way her nostrils flared, the color that always rose to her cheeks. She had gradually won his admiration, a feeling totally alien to him. Few *men* could earn the respect of Toby Garrett, let alone a woman. And the other emotions Sarah evoked were difficult for him to sort out.

Grunting irascibly at his muddled thoughts, he walked along the bank of the river. The gravelly bed sparkled beneath the swift current, the water splashing and foaming around large boulders. Wild peas grew in disorderly profusion, quail pecked for insects in the grass, but there was no Sarah to be seen anywhere. Perhaps she had given up on her fishing expedition and gone back to camp. Rancid bacon indeed! His mouth twisted with cynical amusement.

He lifted his gaze and scanned the far bank where a cluttered grove of pines and aspens grew thickly. His eyes narrowed on an object beneath one of the trees, and, squinting more closely, he saw that it was Sarah, nearly invisible in her muted green plaid calico frock. Only the shade-dappled sunshine, glinting off her golden hair, had given her away.

She appeared to be dozing, her pole sunk firmly in the bank at her side. No doubt she was still waiting for her first bite, and, smiling at this thought, Toby crossed the stream on the same fallen tree she must have used.

His moccasins made no sound as he walked through the tall grass above the rushing sound of the stream. Sarah slept under a tree, her legs curled beneath her, her dress pulled up to reveal a pale, shapely calf and ankle. Sunlight filtering through the leaves shone on her slim, sunbrowned arms. Her chin drooped onto her chest, her face veiled by a damp tangle of flaxen tresses. Toby caught a vague scent of lemon, and, looking around, discovered a chunk of soap resting on a frayed linen towel beside her clumsy-looking shoes and a small pistol. And, to his amazement, there was a slat-bottomed basket filled with perhaps a half-dozen mountain trout.

Quietly squatting down before her, he planned to say something to startle her. Instead, seeing the soft rise and fall of her breasts as she slept, the faint dreamy smile on her lips, he had an almost overpowering urge to take her in his arms and crush her to his chest, to kiss away that soft, slight smile.

He touched a lock of her hair, letting it slip through his fingers like spun gold and drawing it away from her face. Sarah stirred sleepily, mumbled unintelligibly, and batted at her cheek. Toby suppressed a chuckle and tickled her face with a strand of hair again. Sarah's nose twitched, and her forehead wrinkled in a frown.

No longer able to contain himself, lest he wake her with the laughter that threatened to break free, Toby bent his head, and his lips caressed hers in a slow, gentle exploration. He heard her soft, sleepy sigh, and for a moment she yielded to his kiss.

Then suddenly her hands were pushing against his chest, and she was twisting her face away from his. Toby sat back on his haunches and laughed softly.

Gray eyes flashing with sparks of anger, her cheeks flaming, she swung her arm back in preparation to deliver a stinging slap, but Toby caught her wrist before she could make contact with his face. She tried to wrench free of his grip, but he held firm.

He gave her a crooked smile of amused indulgence. "You don't want to hit me. I might hit you back."

She gazed at him with icy disdain. "I wouldn't be surprised if you *did!*" She attempted to pull free of his grasp again, but he continued to keep her wrist imprisoned between his fingers. She scowled impatiently, her nostrils flaring. "Will you *please* let me have my arm back?"

"Only if you promise to be good."

She grunted doubtfully and gave him a look of cold disapproval. Chuckling again, he released her hand, and she drew it back quickly, as if she had been burned. She rubbed her wrist, her face pinched into a sullen frown, and Toby marveled at the enticing picture she presented with her hair falling in soft disarray over her shoulders and the unconsciously sensuous thrust of her lower lip in its pettish pout. Desire stirred in his loins once more, but he tried to ignore it.

She lifted her eyes to meet his defiantly. "What are you doing over here?"

"I came to see how your fishing was coming along." He indicated the basket with a wave of his hand, then glanced back at her. "I guess I don't need to worry about supper tonight."

Sarah cast a doubtful, sidelong look at him. "Is that a compliment—or another of your condescending remarks?"

Toby shrugged and settled himself more comfortably on the grass, leaning on one elbow and stretching out his long legs. "It's whatever you want it to be." He plucked a blade of grass and rolled it between his fingers, then tossed it aside. When he glanced up, he found her staring at his hat, a tiny frown of displeasure creasing her brow. He regarded her curiously, a hint of amusement lurking in his eyes. "I've seen you looking at my hat before. Don't you like it?"

Her nose wrinkled in distaste. "It's terrible! What happened—did it get run over by a buffalo stampede?"

Toby removed the hat and examined it thoughtfully. "Not quite." He smoothed the feathers, then set it on the grass.

"You need a haircut, too."

He arched a wondering brow at her. "I guess I just don't much meet with your approval today, do I?" She met his comment with a glowering silence, and he shrugged again, suppressing a smile. "At least it's clean, thanks to Hetty's soap."

Her eyes widened in mild surprise. "Hetty? Since when did you two get to be such good friends as to use first names?"

"Not *everybody* feels the same about me as you do."

She gave a short, contemptuous sniff. "I don't feel *anything* for you."

The corners of his mouth twitched in amusement. Then why did you start to kiss me back a minute ago? he mused speculatively. His eyes narrowed in wicked conjecture as they went over her slowly, and he felt he was treading on very dangerous ground. He wanted her. It had been a long time since he had been with a woman, and he wondered whether she knew just how provocative her saucy, quarrelsome attitude and the blazing challenge in her eyes were to him.

He pulled out another blade of grass, trying to concentrate on it, instead of allowing that faint scent of lemon from her skin to tantalize his senses.

"Anyway, it needs cutting," Sarah continued. "Look at it—it's almost down to your shoulders. You look like a girl."

Toby raised his head, his eyes gleaming playfully, and

153

rubbed his whiskers in thought. "The bearded lady, eh? I saw one in a circus when I was a boy."

A reluctant smile tugged at the corners of Sarah's mouth, and Toby was struck by the transformation the smile made. Her soft, expressive mouth curved sensuously, and her eyes glowed with a warm light, innocent yet bold. He sat up beside her and reached out to touch her face, but she flinched away nervously.

She eyed him apprehensively. "I think we'd better get back to camp."

"No." His fingers touched her chin and turned her face until their eyes met. "Not yet." He drew her to him, his hands cupping her face, holding her prisoner, and kissed her with a gentle fierceness. She attempted to shrug out of his hold with a twist of her shoulders, but he didn't relent. He kept her mouth trapped beneath his, savoring the sweetness of her lips. Her hands pressed against his chest in weak protest. Then, with an almost inaudible sigh, he felt her relax, and her lips parted softly under his.

Despite her aggravation with Toby, Sarah felt the first stirrings of response to his kiss, but she managed to cling to a thread of sanity. She squirmed and tried to push him away, but his lips held firm possession of hers, and she felt all her animosity fading gradually. His mouth explored her temples, lingered over her cheek and the lobe of her ear, finally reclaiming her lips, and, with an acquiescent sigh, Sarah gave herself over to his kiss. His lips were soft and warm, caressing hers lightly at first, then deeply and hungrily, making her feel light-headed and no longer in control.

154

Her mind screamed in protest at the betrayal of her body's responses, but she was incapable of resistance. Involuntarily, her hands slid behind his neck, and her fingers brushed against the long, unruly hair curling over his collar and touching his shoulders. His mouth moved to explore the curve of her neck, and the pulse in her throat fluttered wildly beneath his lips. Sarah's heart beat with a frantic rhythm, and she felt a sudden trembling weakness in her limbs as the last vestiges of rational thought fled her mind.

He pressed her back into the sweet-smelling clover, the backs of his fingers caressing her face. His gaze probed hers, an unspoken question in their deep blue depths. Sarah realized he was giving her the opportunity to stop, and she thanked him silently. But she was beyond that now, dazed and breathless and trembling with the sudden, overpowering force of her desires.

She returned his gaze boldly, her lips parting in a soft, beguiling smile, and drew his mouth down to claim hers once more, her pulse leaping in a strange combination of fear and excitement.

His fingers traced down her neck, pausing to unfasten the buttons of her dress with surprising dexterity. His mouth burned a fiery trail to the hollow of her throat, and his tantalizing caresses roused a feverish longing, unfamiliar yet exciting. Sarah was confused at the wild surge of conflicting emotions that swept through her. She didn't even *like* Toby Garrett—*despised* him, in fact—yet she hungered for every touch of his hands and lips.

Her dress slipped away, and Sarah shivered at the sudden, unaccustomed touch of the wind and cool grass against her skin. Toby was removing his shirt, and she stole a furtive glance at his solid, muscular chest, deeply

155

tanned and covered with a downy thatch of light hair.

He turned back to her, his eyes roaming freely over her, and she basked in the ardent admiration of his look, no longer shy. He pulled her into his arms once more, and Sarah pressed herself eagerly to him in wanton invitation. The hard flesh of his body was warm against her bare skin, smelling faintly of leather and sweat, and it was oddly, erotically intoxicating.

His lips touched her shoulder, the silky brush of his mustache and beard making a delightful shiver run through her body. His hands were gentle and practiced as they stroked her, the rough calluses on his palms strangely exciting, awakening her flesh. His hands cupped her breasts to caress their gently rounded fullness, and Sarah felt herself melting beneath his touch. His lips brushed the side of her neck, then moved down to her breasts. Delicately, he ran the tip of his tongue over one jutting peak, and, shivering with pleasure, Sarah thought she would gladly drown in the intensity of these wonderful new sensations.

Her hand ran down over his lean ribs, and she could feel the rippling play of his muscles beneath her fingertips. Aware of his hard, masculine strength, she could almost feel the heat and passion rising from his body.

Reason deserted her as his mouth moved over her ribs, caressing her flesh tantalizingly. He paused for the briefest of moments to let his tongue dip into her navel, then continue its unhurried downward path. A delicious breathlessness attacked her lungs when she felt his hot breath against her quivering flesh, and she shivered in ecstasy at the exquisite torture of his gently insistent touch.

Time and space lost meaning, passing in a daze of excitement as mouths and fingertips explored one another, responded to each other, giving as well as receiving. Sarah felt lost somewhere amid the fiery pleasure that coursed through her veins, as Toby's skillful kisses and caresses evoked fresh waves of desire. Then suddenly there was a sharp, stabbing sensation, an excruciating, tearing pain. A gasping cry escaped her throat.

Toby seemed to freeze, poised above her, and he caressed her face gently, his eyes soft and tender. "It's all right," he said quietly.

All right! Sarah's thoughts screamed the words, her mind seething with anger. She felt as if she were being torn apart, and he says it's *all right!* She had to bite her lip to hold back her scathing words, all her earlier pleasure shattered.

But gradually it began to return with Toby's renewed movements; different this time, but even more enjoyable. Sarah felt a sudden revived stirring of response, sending a glow spreading through her veins, and, unwittingly, she arched her hips to meet him and her body began to move in time with his. She felt deliciously langorous, and she closed her eyes, accepting these curious new sensations without conscious thought and letting them flow over her.

But when Toby's movements stopped abruptly and Sarah felt him leaving her, her eyes flew open, confused and oddly frustrated.

He gave her a sheepish little smile and stretched out on the grass beside her. "I'm sorry," he murmured, drawing her body tightly against his. "It's been a long time."

Sarah frowned in puzzlement but snuggled close to him. Sorry for what? Dismissing the question from her mind, she nestled against the comfort of his encircling arms, feeling drowsily contented now, the vague feeling of dissatisfaction having fled as quickly as it had come. She was aware only of the warmth of his body close to hers, his soft beard against her temple, the almost possessive way his arms tightened around her. The late-afternoon light seeped through the trees, falling in patches across their bodies, and the wind breathed softly through the leaves; a frog leaped off a fallen log and splashed into the river.

Sarah sighed softly to herself and stirred slightly in his arms, feeling strangely detached from reality. If it weren't for her mellow mood and the unfamiliar ache and stickiness between her thighs, she might have believed someone else had been here in her place.

It was bound to have happened sooner or later, she reasoned to herself; though somehow Sarah had never quite pictured it like this—out in the middle of the woods beside the Truckee River, thousands of miles from all that was familiar to her. And with Toby Garrett, of all people! An hour ago, she wouldn't have believed it possible. Nor did she feel particularly guilty with herself or angry with him. She had always been quick enough to lose her temper with him in the past, so why not now?

As if sensing her thoughts, Toby raised up on one elbow and brushed a strand of hair away from her face, his blue eyes sparkling in the half-light. She studied his face, feeling an unfamiliar tenderness for this man she had sometimes hated and even feared.

A faint smile lurked at the corners of his mouth. "Does this mean we have a truce?"

Sarah smiled with feline complacency, a hint of amusement dancing in her eyes. "For the time being."

Chapter Nine

It had been a relatively smooth drive from Truckee Meadows—perhaps the least troublesome in a month. The trail took them across the river, over an easy range of mountains, and into a little valley. They had made good time yesterday, but today—that was another matter altogether.

Sarah cast a pitying glance at the cow. The sore on her shoulder had spread until her hide was a mass of festering, evil-smelling open blisters from neck to forelock. She faltered often, and her lowing cries were almost like a human's mournful wails.

Sarah glanced over the backs of the animals to Hetty, walking on the other side, and gave her a melancholy shake of her head. And, as if sensing something was about to happen, the sick cow fell to her knees, dragging her yoke-mate down with her.

Sarah knelt beside the heifer, faintly nauseous from the suppurating stench, and stroked the animal's nose. "We'll give you a rest, Clarabell." The cow blinked slowly, her eyes glazed and dull, and a dribble of foam

159

slipped out from between her lips. Sighing regretfully, Sarah looked around for the children. "Sam! Bring Myrtle up here. We'll let her pull for a while."

Samantha and Lucas argued for a moment over who would untie the extra cow while Sarah went about unchaining the heavy yoke. She hated the thought of using Myrtle; that particular cow had been tried beneath the yoke before and proved unmanageable. But clearly there was no other choice.

A chilly wind dispelled the warmth of the late afternoon sun. Firs and evergreens grew in dense profusion, and the ground was strewn with their fragrant needles and pine cones. Sarah paused a moment to let her gaze wander, taking in the towering trees and clear blue sky. California—at long last!

They had made camp last night just inside its eastern border near a small creek. Some previous emigrant had posted a sign—crude letters carved into a piece of wagon siding—proclaiming the boundary, and Samantha and Lucas had added their names and the date to a dozen others scratched into the wood.

A splinter stabbed into Sarah's palm, and she withdrew her hand quickly, wincing. She peered at the shard of wood, then carefully tried to pluck it out. She only succeeded in lodging it deeper, and a trickle of blood ran down to her wrist.

"Damn!" She sat back on her heels and tried to grasp the offending fragment between her fingers again.

"You'll only make it worse."

Sarah glanced up and saw Toby standing over her. His ability to sneak up on people so silently unnerved her, and she frowned reprovingly.

"I'll see to the animals first, then you," he said,

squatting down to pull off the yoke. He eyed her circumspectly, one eyebrow raised in teasing mockery. "No arguments today, please."

Her eyes widened in feigned innocence. "Would I do a thing like that?" Rising to her feet, she stood back with Samantha and Lucas while Toby worked.

He had been in a foul mood all day, and it didn't appear that it was improving any. For two days, he had done everything but get down on his knees and beg Reverend Jennings to get the wagons rolling again, reminding him time after time of the lateness of the season and the snow already on the mountains. Canfield had shrugged off Toby's admonitions, saying that there was *always* snow on the Sierras; sometimes, during an especially cool summer, it never melted from one winter to the next. Jennings had acquiesced to his guide's wisdom, and so had most of the others, relishing their brief respite in the peaceful little valley.

And Sarah couldn't deny that it *had* been an enjoyable rest. She and Toby had returned to their secluded grove on the far banks of the Truckee those next two days, but not for fishing. Her cheeks reddened as the memories came rushing back with startling clarity, and she glanced uneasily at Samantha and Lucas. But they were intently watching Toby coax Clarabell to her feet and had failed to notice Sarah's soft, dreamy smile and winsome blush.

She *still* wasn't sure how she felt about Toby. He was every bit as cynical and derisive as before, and at times she felt like scratching his eyes out. But when they were alone together, he made her forget everything but the flaming desire he awakened in her. He seemed to be two different men; tender when alone with her, yet harsh and mocking with others. He was an enigma, and Sarah won-

161

dered whether she would ever puzzle out the two contrasting facets of his personality.

Clarabell wouldn't move, and she was beginning to upset the other animals. Releasing an exasperated breath, Toby walked over to Sarah. "She's completely done in. And that sore on her hide—" His voice trailed off, and he scrubbed a hand through his beard. "We'll have to destroy her."

Sarah caught her breath in astonishment. Samantha let out a wail of dismayed protest.

Lucas tilted his head to look quizzically up at the hunter. "You mean kill her?"

Toby nodded reluctantly. "I'm afraid so. She can't walk, and she hasn't given milk for over a week. She's useless to us—except for meat."

Sarah felt a bitter twinge of sadness close around her heart. Clarabell had been a sweet old thing; good-tempered, and, at times, she seemed almost human. She sighed bleakly. "I suppose—if we have to."

Hetty poked her head out from the canvas. "We don't have any salt left. The meat will spoil."

"Then we *can't* kill her!" Samantha exclaimed, and went to kneel beside the prostrate cow. She stroked the animal's head and spoke quietly. "Get up, Clarabell. *Please!*"

Sarah looked at Toby, and their eyes met. For a fleeting moment, she saw a spark of genuine compassion in their deep blue depths before it was masked by a look of weary indifference.

"I'll have to find someone to help me move her, and then—" He broke off as Huntington's wagon lumbered toward them, filled to overflowing and lurching crazily to one side. Eight oxen drew it, while Huntington cantered

162

alongside on his gray stallion. Ruth rode sidesaddle on a dappled mare, while Alma and the black maid, carrying the child, walked. Phillip and Elmore Poole husbanded five extra oxen and three mules from the abandoned wagons.

Toby stepped into Huntington's path; the stallion snorted and sidestepped nervously. "Mr. Huntington, would you be willing to lend one or two of those oxen to Mrs. Coulter until we reach the Sacramento?"

Huntington flicked a disdainful glance toward the ailing cow and Samantha, his dark eyes expressionless and cold. He pursed his thin lips together thoughtfully, then blew out some air. "I'm afraid not, Mr. Garrett. I may need them later for my own family, and I don't want to risk their lives. I can't sacrifice them."

Toby met the other man's gaze with cool contempt. "And what about Mrs. Coulter? Her husband has gone off to bring back food! What kind of a sacrifice is *that?*"

Huntington watched with satisfaction as his entourage went by, then turned back to Toby, his mouth curling into an unpleasant smile. "There's no guarantee Roy Coulter will return."

Toby's jaw flexed in anger. "His *family* is guarantee enough!"

Huntington waved a black-gloved hand in a negligent gesture. "Men have been known to desert their families before."

Toby's fists clenched at his sides, and he took several menacing steps toward Huntington. Sarah clutched his arm and held him back. "Leave him be, Toby."

He frowned impatiently at her, then turned back to glare at Huntington as the merchant trotted ahead to join his family. "Arrogant bastard."

Sarah continued to hold tight to Toby's arm and expelled a sigh of frustrated acceptance. "Just never mind. We'll get by with the cows."

Hetty climbed down from the wagon with a freshly diapered Simon in her arms. "I appreciate what you're doing for us, Toby. But I've learned in the past—*his* kind never gives for free."

The last wagon rolled up and came to a stop. O'Brian and Andersen eyed the cow sympathetically. "Poor old girl," the Irishman remarked.

Hetty adjusted Simon in her arms and turned to the two men. "If either of you has salt for curing, I'll give you half her meat."

"Salt we have," Ole Andersen said, and gave a self-deprecating shrug. "Not much else."

Toby withdrew his knife and lifted the palm of Sarah's hand. "It'll hurt."

"I know."

She averted her face, steeling herself for the sharp bite of the blade. She sucked in a convulsive breath and clenched her teeth as a needle of pain pierced her flesh, and she grimaced.

"Not so bad." He closed her fist and favored her with a jaunty smile. "Why don't you and Hetty take the children down to that little stream? You can wash out your hand and wait there while Ole and I dress the meat."

"But I—"

Toby silenced her with his fingers pressed to her lips, his eyes softening as they rested on her for a moment. "I'm an old hand at this. Besides, I don't think Samantha should be around—since she's so fond of Clarabell."

Sarah lifted her gaze and searched his face for a hint of sarcasm. She could find none in his craggy features; only compassion and understanding. She felt an unexpected rush of affection, and the emotion surprised her. Summoning up a feeble smile of gratitude, she nodded in acquiescence and went to round up the youngsters.

Maggie stood back with Katie and James while Inga Andersen fetched the salt from the wagon, observing the exchange between Sarah and Toby. A thoughtful frown creased her forehead, her eyes dark and distant. Since when did *they* become so intimate? Whenever she saw them together before, they were usually at each other's throats, engaged in a kind of contest to see which of them could best the other in a war of heated words.

Lost in her thoughts, Sean's booming voice shouting to the oxen startled her, and she almost stumbled when James tugged on her hand. The wagon started forward, leaving three of the Andersens behind to help with the slaughter and dressing of the cow. Astrid, still sore and bruised from her tumble down the canyon, trotted along at Kelly's side. Since the accident, Maggie had noticed that the Swedish girl showed an interest in her sixteen-year-old brother, and Kelly seemed to welcome the attention.

Maggie sighed pensively, her expression remote, preoccupied. They were in California now—almost at the end of their journey—and Judd had not yet mentioned marriage; or *any* kind of a future, for that matter. He was still as aloof as before, seldom even *talking* to her except in the throes of passion, and those were either vague, hollow promises or whispered obscenities. Other times, he spoke of incidental matters: the weather, the other emigrants, the condition of the cattle, or the dwindling sup-

165

ply of food.

Never had he indicated he cared for her in any way other than what mutual pleasure they could derive from one another. And lately, except in the evenings when they would share supper and later slip away into the woods, he spent most of his time at the head of the train with Jennings or Canfield and even sometimes Poole.

Her mouth compressed into a hard line, worry drawing her brows together. Had Elmore told him that he, too, had slept with her? She dismissed the notion with a shake of her head. She doubted it. Elmore didn't strike her as the type who would spread tales, and that had been *months* ago—back in the Kansas territory. Besides, she had never pretended to Judd that she was a virgin.

She rubbed her temples and closed her eyes a moment, trying to collect her thoughts. She had been so *sure* Judd would propose. He was rich—he *must* be. And even if he wasn't, she was certain that with his wits and charm he would be before long. They could have a good life together, but time was running out.

Sighing irascibly, she glanced down at Katie and James, trudging along at her side. At four, Katie had difficulty keeping up, and Maggie slowed her pace a bit. Her only sister in a family of men, Maggie thought, and had they been closer in age, people might have mistaken them for twins. The child had cried long and hard last night at supper, for the meal had been a tasteless, tough one, consisting of the ever-present dried ox meat, some hard crackers, and tea.

"Lucas says his Da's gone to bring us all back food," James said, and eyed his older sister uncertainly.

"That's right," Maggie agreed. "With Reverend Jennings's note of credit." Would they all have to pay Jen-

166

nings back? she wondered. Undoubtedly. That sly old fox would never give anything away for nothing.

"Will he bring back some licorice and horehound candy?"

"I doubt it, Jamie lad."

Molly fell into step beside her children, carrying Kevin in her arms. "Meself," she mused. "I've had me a hankerin' for potatoes. Haven't seen a potato since St. Louis."

Maggie's face pinched into a frown of distaste. She had consumed enough potatoes in her nineteen years to last a lifetime and never cared if she set eyes on one again. But if she didn't persuade Judd to marrying her, she could look forward only to living on a potato farm again, for that was precisely the crop Michael O'Brian intended to harvest in California. Her mouth settled into a determined line, resolved to redouble her efforts to get Judd.

"I took inventory early this morning," Molly said, and Maggie's attention swung back to her mother. The woman's face was drawn and pallid, her brown eyes moist and rimmed with dark circles, and more gray had begun to spread into the short-cropped russet hair. "I figure we've got five days' food left—not countin' the stock."

Maggie shuddered in revulsion at the thought of more ox meat. Even the buffalo steaks back on the plains had been more appetizing than the stringy meat of the draft animals. "I'm thinkin' it's a shame *we* didn't get half of the Coulters' cow."

Molly nodded reflectively. "We've got but a pinch of salt left." A rueful, distant look came into her eyes. "It's prayin' I do every night that Roy Coulter and Mr. Tyrrell

167

will get back soon.''

Maggie murmured a silent agreement, and her gaze lifted to the snow-capped wall of granite directly ahead. A shiver rippled up her spine at the forbidding sight, and goose bumps broke out on her arms.

The afternoon shadows were lengthening, and a biting autumn wind had sprung up as the Coulters came upon Jennings's supply wagon. Its tongue had snapped, and Stone and Higgins had cut a new piece of timber to replace it. The oxen grazed nearby, adding their muffled snorting to the ring of metal against wood as the two men worked with axes and chisels.

Wiley Higgins straightened up and wiped a sleeve across his narrow, unshaven face. He squinted at Toby. ''The Reverend and the others made camp about a mile ahead. I don't reckon we'll get this finished before nightfall.''

Toby directed his gaze to the mountains looming ahead. Low, threatening clouds obscured the snowy summit now, and they rolled gray and ominous in the fading afternoon light. The wind was rising steadily, whistling through the pines and bending the smaller saplings. A vague worry flared up in his mind, and he frowned sourly as his gaze returned to the ferretlike face of Wiley Higgins. ''Just be sure you're ready to move out in the morning.''

Stone leaned against his mallet and regarded Toby intently. A trickle of sweat had caught in the scar on his cheek, glistening in the sun's waning light. ''Maybe you could send back Mr. Pardee. He's good at this sort of thing.''

"I'll see what I can do." Toby cast another uneasy glance at the cloud-mantled peaks, then slapped the ox on the rump. The wagon jerked forward on squeaking axles, and Toby eyed the two teamsters with a warning shake of his head. "Just remember—we move out tomorrow."

Stone waved a hand in understanding and hefted his mallet for another blow.

Ole Andersen rubbed his jaw thoughtfully and eyed Toby with furtive speculation. "Are you thinking what I'm thinking?"

Toby's mouth tightened grimly beneath his beard and full mustache. "About the clouds, you mean?"

The Swede nodded his blond head. *"Ja.* They used to come over the Kjolens just like that before a big storm."

Toby smacked the ox again irritably, urging the beast to more speed, inwardly cursing the emigrants for their incessant delays. He shivered suddenly, despite his buckskin jacket. It wasn't cold enough to snow *here* if a storm did come. But up on the summit . . . A dire sense of trepidation washed over him and settled in the pit of his belly.

Firelight played across the faces of those seated around Toby as he devoured the juicy fried steak ravenously. Sarah and Lucas ate with equal relish, while Hetty cut up small bites for Simon. Only Samantha seemed to have no appetite, and she pushed the food listlessly around on her plate.

Sarah leaned forward, a tacit question in her eyes. "You're thinking about Clarabell, aren't you?"

The youngster raised her head and nodded miserably, a great sadness in her eyes. She glanced briefly at her aunt, then dropped her gaze back to her plate.

"Clarabell was sick," Hetty said, wiping gravy off Simon's chin with a corner of her apron. "She wasn't any good to herself or anyone else anymore."

Samantha frowned sullenly. "She was my friend."

Sarah's smile was faint and slightly wistful. "She was Beans's friend, too." With a nod of her head, she indicated the setter sitting close by Lucas, watching the diners avidly and thumping his tail in the dust. "But *he* knows a good thing when he sees it. We've got a mountain to get over tomorrow, and you'll need your strength."

Samantha's lips set in a firm, uncompromising line. "I can't eat Clarabell!"

Hetty darted an irritated glance across the fire. "Then *go* hungry. But don't expect me to feed you something else because there *isn't* anything else."

Samantha bowed her head, her eyes misting with tears, and stared morosely into the fire.

Sarah glanced helplessly at Toby, but he could offer no suggestions. His mind was elsewhere, his thoughts racing chaotically—the heavy cloudbanks, the increasing bite in the air, the formidable mountain pass ahead, and the broken-down wagons and oxen.

He shrugged laconically, studying Sarah over the rim of his coffee cup. In the glow of the fire, her skin shone like satin, her hair like spun gold. Her gray eyes were luminous, and his gaze fastened eagerly on her soft, expressive mouth. Heat rose to his face as he recalled the taste of those lips and their hungry response to his kisses, and his blood coursed warm in his veins.

Annoyed with these wayward thoughts when there were far more urgent matters to ponder, Toby swallowed the last of his coffee and rose abruptly. "I'd better go check on the stock," he said and wheeled away.

170

He heard Sarah's voice trailing after him as she spoke to Samantha once more. "You remember our chickens back home, don't you? You gave them all names and everything. You ate *them,* didn't you?"

Toby's mouth twisted into an amused smile as he bent to test the ropes and pegs securing the sleeping tent. As he might have predicted, Sarah had erected the shelter with her usual efficiency. There seemed to be little she *couldn't* do, and as he discovered each new ability, he marveled at her capacity to endure out here in this wilderness with so little. Perhaps he had been mistaken about females all his life—or, at least, about *some* of them.

The Coulter women, Inga Andersen, Belle Pardee, and even Molly O'Brian appeared little affected by the hardships, while others, like Orpha Jennings and the Huntington females . . . He shook his head in mocking disbelief.

But still, he wondered whether he had misjudged the human species when he had so abruptly left it back in his early teens. They were petty and small, but they were also good-hearted and strong—not so very much different from the Indians he had adopted. Perhaps life in California among his own race wouldn't be so hard to adjust to as he had first thought it might.

A chilly wind knifed across his face, and he turned up the collar of his jacket, his thoughts returning to the present. Ole Andersen recognized the warning signs of an early storm, but everyone else seemed oblivious to the impending peril.

A fiddle scraped at the far end of camp as Michael O'Brian tuned up his instrument. He heard Maggie's rippling laugh carried on the cold night air; off to his left, Phillip Huntington coughed and wheezed. A baby wailed

171

from Pardee's tent; bawdy laughter came from the direction where Canfield, Trent, and Poole sat.

His head bowed in thought, brow furrowed in a frown, Toby walked through the high grass to the edge of the lake and stared broodingly across its placid surface. In the daylight, it had been lovely and serene, its clear blue waters surrounded by spruce nestled in a grassy valley bordered with groves of tamarack and forests of pine. But tonight the lake seemed black and menacing, the occasional dancing lights of the campfires reflecting on its surface.

Heavy clouds trailed over the moon, and the wind gave a restive howl. Winter was in the air, and the Sierras loomed ominously up ahead.

Before the sun had gone down, Toby had borrowed a horse from Jennings and followed the trail to the pass, through stately forests redolent of sun-sweet earth, through tall pines and firs that towered in the fading afternoon light, beyond which rose a bluff of granite 10,000 feet high. He had halted at the westernmost shore of the lake and stared in awe at the massive, precipitous barrier. To pull wagons up that monstrous mountain was a task to chill a man's heart. Granite ledges, slippery rocks, and sheer rises of ten or more feet marked the trail—a trail not much more than a goat track.

Toby swallowed dryly at the memory. A sinister, all-pervading fear gnawed at his consciousness. He was powerless to shake it off.

Sarah crept silently up beside Toby at the shoreline. She knew he was aware of her presence, but he continued to stare into space, as if lost in another world. She stood

172

at his side without speaking, feeling his warmth, savoring the faint scent of leather and tobacco, listening to O'Brian's gay fiddling. She enjoyed the serenity, but she half-expected Toby to turn his mocking smile upon her at any moment and make some sarcastic remark.

Instead, when he did speak, his voice was tired and the words sounded hollow. "Did you finally talk Samantha into eating?"

She glanced up at him, mildly surprised to find him still gazing into the murky waters of the lake. "A little bit. I think she prefers supper made from a stranger. Maybe you can shoot a deer or something tomorrow."

He shook his head. "Not tomorrow. Tomorrow we've got mountains to get over."

Sarah frowned in faint disappointment. "I'd kind of looked forward to a little rest." Her lips curved into a self-effacing little smile. "I must be getting lazy now that we're almost there."

He turned, regarding her thoughtfully, and Sarah saw the worried, almost haunted look in his eyes. "But we're *not* there yet. And I want you to promise me you'll be ready to leave at the first light. No arguments—even if the others tarry."

The soft urgency in his tone alarmed Sarah, and her sense of well-being turned to nervous concern. "What is it?"

His breath plumed out in a vaporous mist as he sighed heavily. "I don't know. Just a feeling I have." His brooding stare returned to the sky, and Sarah followed the direction of his gaze. A heavy layer of clouds hid the moon. "I feel"—he faltered and shook his head in perplexity—"I feel almost like one of my prey—like *I've* been caught. And this lake and the weather and those

173

mountains and the desert behind us are all the jaws of some huge trap.'' He shrugged lamely and met her eyes, a faint smile playing about his mouth. "I'm probably crazy.''

Sarah felt suddenly cold and uncomfortable as she let her gaze stray toward the black, hulking shadow of the Sierras. Toby's concern was infectious, and she tugged nervously at her lower lip with her teeth. But she attempted to cover it up with a weak, tense laugh. "It's not *supposed* to snow in California. And even if it does—'' Her voice trailed off uncertainly, and she stole another glance at Toby. "It snows at home and melts the next day—at least, *this* early in the season.''

His lips twisted in a half-bitter smile. "I've learned never to trust Mother Nature. She's the most fickle female of all.''

Sarah's gaze shifted back toward the west, and she felt a chill touch the back of her neck. In the light from the campfires, Maggie's skirts twirled in a lively jig with Sean; others clapped in time to the music, and laughter carried on the wind.

A light, misting rain began to fall, and Sarah lifted her face to the overcast heavens. Shivering from apprehension and the cold, she met Toby's gaze briefly; then scurried for the shelter of the tent.

Samantha stirred sleepily in her blankets and sat up, knuckling her eyes. In the gray predawn light, her mother, aunt, and brothers slept quietly, and Samantha was careful not to disturb them as she crawled out of her covers. She hadn't slept well, thinking of poor Clarabell and listening to the patter of raindrops on the canvas, and

174

now she needed desperately to relieve the fullness in her bladder.

Shivering against the cold, she tugged on her coat and pulled aside the tent flap. The rain had stopped, but as she scrambled outside, her eyes widened with surprise and she stared around her wonderingly. A faint pink hue was beginning to stain the pale gray sky, and a light dusting of snow covered the landscape and settled on the tree limbs. A rabbit raced across the ground, leaving tracks in the thin white crust.

Samantha bent down, scooped up a handful of the icy crystals, and let them trickle between her fingers. Laughing delightedly, no longer conscious of her pressing need of earlier, she twirled around, her arms outstretched, reveling in the crisp, clean air and the patterns her feet made in the snow.

Movement by the wagon caught her eye, and she turned. Toby was rising from his blankets beneath the bed, frowning in angry disbelief. He looked sick and mad, Samantha thought, and her brows knitted into a puzzled frown.

She danced lightly across the snow and smiled up at him, her face flushed with pleasure. "Just like Christmas, Mr. Garrett."

Grim lines deepened at the corners of his mouth, and he scowled fiercely. Samantha followed the direction of his gaze until her eyes came to rest on the sheer white wall of the pass. Swirling gray clouds pressed down on its glistening ridges, and a fresh snow pack blanketed the granite domes.

"No, Sam." Toby's voice was weary with melancholy, and his eyes were clouded with despair. "Not Christmas."

Chapter Ten

Light flakes were falling as the wagons followed the north shore of the lake. For the first hour, the children romped in the snow, reveling in its icy purity in contrast to the harsh, blowing grit and intolerable heat of the desert a week ago. A few inches of snow didn't hamper the draft animals and wagons, but as the road wound ever higher, the ground cover grew deeper.

At the head of the lake, the trail suddenly became steep and treacherous. The snow was soft, and the oxen floundered. Progress inched along at a painfully slow pace.

Peter Andersen threw chocks beneath the wheels of the Coulters' wagon to keep it from rolling backward. As soon as the van was secured, Ole would urge the oxen and cows up a few more feet. Then Peter would scramble to reposition the chocks. It was exhausting work, and for each yard of ground made, it seemed to Peter they sank another inch deeper into the snow.

Hetty handed the young man a tepid cup of coffee—the last from the morning's pot—and he drank gratefully. His clothing was wet and muddy, his blond hair a tangled mass of dirty, limp strands straggling over his forehead. Despite the chill in the air, sweat poured down the sides of his face.

"Maybe Sarah or I could spell you for a while," she said.

Peter shook his head. "It's not a job for a woman, Mrs. Coulter." A shadow of a smile crept across his lips as he handed the empty cup back to her. "Besides, your skirts would get in the way."

"We could pin them up."

He gave her a tolerantly indulgent smile, a smile that seemed to age him far beyond his seventeen years. "Just keep my mother company, *ja?* She doesn't like the cold and snow. Her parents and sister died in an avalanche when she was very young, and she always hated the winters at home." His expression grew pensive and distant. "I thought we had left it all behind in Sweden."

Hetty wrung her hands fretfully and turned her gaze to the towering heights looming before her. The heavy cloud mass had risen, and a line of fresh, glistening snow now draped itself across the mountains. Roy was on the other side, somewhere. Perhaps even now he was re-crossing the summit with fresh animals and food. *He* would know what to do.

Hetty stared a moment longer at the snow-swept peaks, then glanced back at Peter. He was a good man, as was his father and Toby Garrett. But how long could she expect strangers to help her and her children?

Summoning up a falsely cheerful smile, she reached out and patted a solid bicep, then turned and trudged away.

* * *

Lester Stone snarled at his mules at the head of the train. Along with Garrett, Higgins, and Canfield, the men were trying to break a trail for the wagons. But the snow was soft and the road had been lost an hour ago in three feet of the powdery stuff.

The mules floundered and fought, more often than not refusing to budge a single step further until a lash was applied to their hindquarters. Then they would rear and bolt ahead, landing in deep snow that sometimes reached their sides.

Stone stumbled and fell to his knees in the soft powder. He swore and pounded the snow with his fist, his sense of rage and frustration increasing with each minute. A man could probably make it over the pass on foot, and the idea had crossed his mind more than once this morning. But a man alone was one thing—a man weighted down with a chest of silver, a few pounds of odd coins, and the rest of the booty he had collected would be just as hampered as with a mule or a wagon.

Still on his knees, unmindful of the wet soaking his trousers and leaking into the soles of his well-worn boots, he lifted his gaze to the trail ahead. Trail? What trail? It was lost, and *he* didn't know the way. Rocks and cliffs merged in the wildest confusion, and a man could wander for days in that labyrinth of granite and ice.

Only Canfield knew the way over the mountains now. Stone's eyes hardened with contempt at the idea of having to put his life in the hands of such a man. Still, he reasoned grimly, Canfield was as unprincipled as he. And if the situation became worse, Stone might be able to persuade the guide to set out with him on foot in return for some of the loot. Two men, each carrying the riches of the other emigrants, *might* make it out.

Stone got wearily to his feet and glared at the mule. He grasped the bridle in preparation of making another few feet, for the time being storing away his thoughts regarding Canfield in the back of his mind.

Patrick O'Brian spread his arms wide and let his body fall forward into a foot of snow. Rising carefully to his feet, he inspected the impression his body had made and grinned broadly. "Look! I made an angel!"

Maggie turned away from her battle with a balky cow and gave an irritated toss of her head. "We'll *all* be seein' angels soon enough if ye don't help me with this cow!"

Sobering quickly, Patrick trotted over to his sister and butted the cow in the rump. The animal leaped forward a few feet, catching Maggie off balance, and knocked her sprawling into the snow.

Cursing lustily, Maggie raised up on her elbow and scowled furiously at her brother. *"Help me up!"* she shouted impatiently and thrust out a hand.

Patrick smiled sheepishly and assisted her to stand. Patches of melted snow soaked her dress, and fresh flakes settled on the scarf covering her hair and the shoulders of her cloak.

She threw her head back angrily and fixed him with a withering stare. "This is *not* playtime, Patrick O'Brian! Now help me with this heathen cow!"

She turned her back on her brother, and her gaze found Judd at the front of the wagon. *He* was as unproductive as Patrick. Instead of helping, he merely walked his horse in the path made by the others, offering no assistance to her father and brothers. Her eyes flashed with a bitter spark of anger and hurt at his lack of support, but she pushed her vexation away quickly. After all, she reasoned to herself, he was probably used to having darkies do all the work for him at home.

"We'll have to double-team!" Michael shouted, holding fast to the harnesses of the oxen while Daniel placed chocks beneath the wheels. When the van was secured, the burly Irishman glanced first in front of him to the Jenningses and Huntingtons, then behind to Coulter and Pardee. The blacksmith was doing fairly well on his own, for he had the addition of Andersen's three oxen pulling his load, and even the old man was able to ride. But he halted his family and offered the use of his animals.

"You go on ahead," Michael told him. "Mrs. Coulter and I can share. No sense in breakin' up your team now that they're workin' together."

"I can't go around you, Michael. I need the trail already cut. I'll just stay here and lend a hand—give the oxen a chance to rest."

While the men worked, the women and children gathered around Pardee's wagon to eat a meager noon meal of dried meat and hot tea brewed over a small fire kindled by two of the O'Brian boys. The snowfall was slightly heavier than it had been earlier, and the powdery flakes clung to hair and beards and clothing while the emigrants ate.

Sarah noticed Maggie's brooding, pettish expression as she watched Judd. He was standing beneath the sheltering branches of a giant pine, casually chewing a piece of meat and sipping tea while his horse dined on pine needles.

Grunting in disapproval, Maggie turned away and scowled fiercely into the sputtering flames of the fire.

Sarah pursed her lips thoughtfully. "Maybe he can't comprehend snow," she ventured. "After all, I doubt it snows much in Mississippi—maybe not at all.''

Maggie's green eyes flashed angrily. ''The Irish have always been hard workers—no matter what the weather. This''—she flung out a hand in contempt, and her voice was a mixture of wonder and disgust.—''this idleness—I don't understand it!''

A hint of a smile flickered across Sarah's face. ''Judd's not Irish.''

Maggie shook her head irritably. *''That's* God's truth!'' She snorted in disdain. ''And I'm beginnin' to think he's not much of a man, either.''

Sarah glanced away from Maggie, trying to keep her face as expressionless as possible. As each day passed, Sarah found herself wondering more and more why she had *ever* found Judd Brannan so appealing. He was still as attractive and probably as charming as ever, but he was soft and weak. First his craziness on the desert, then his dispassionate acceptance of Maggie's possible demise, and now lately his refusal to work. And when she thought back to all the hours she had spent pining for him, her cheeks flushed hot with embarrassment.

Part of her mind wondered whether her new relationship with Toby had changed her attitude toward Judd, but she brushed the notion aside. Toby was still just as disagreeable and cynical as ever. Only their physical relationship had changed; they were still as ready to do battle with words as before. Sarah couldn't deny that Toby excited her or that she enjoyed his lovemaking; but other than the purely sensual reactions he brought out in her, she wasn't sure *what* her feelings toward him were.

No, she told herself. Toby hadn't made her change her opinion of Judd Brannan. Judd was doing that gradually himself.

Draining the last of her tea and, with it, her thoughts, Sarah took Maggie's cup from her and went over to the pot on the fire. The heat felt pleasantly warm, and she wished she could sit for a while and rest. But as she hazarded a glance up along the trail broken in the snow and the rear of Huntington's wagon disappearing around a craggy turn, she sighed in resignation. Judd Brannan could loaf all he wanted; for the rest of them, there was work to be done.

Canfield fell headlong into the snow, twisting his arm beneath him, and a shattering bolt of pain shot all the way up to his shoulder. Cursing loudly, he rose to his knees and flexed his muscles, wincing when he curled his fingers into a fist. He tried a few more times. Deciding that nothing was broken, he turned his head to glare murderously at the temperamental mule that had caused him to fall. The animal gazed blandly back at him, sunk in snow nearly up to its belly.

Disgusted, Red scrambled to his feet and stood a moment, breathing deeply and trying to swallow his rage. Above him, a lacy white mantle was draped across the peaks. Here and there, patches of granite showed through, twisting into weird formations and a maze of impossible passages. The dizzy precipices and yawning chasms defied a logical trail, and whatever path the previous emigrant trains had taken was hidden in the snow.

He removed his hat and ran his hand distractedly through his hair, his brows knitting perplexedly. How could he tell them all he had never been across these mountains before? Even with clear ground, he would have been hopelessly lost without the tracks of other wagons to guide him. But this! He shook his head in angry frustration. At least the confusion of the storm might cover his own inexperience, but he found small comfort in the thought.

He stole a glance over his shoulder and saw Garrett floundering with the mules. A few yards below, Jennings and Higgins struggled with the wagon, but the oxen bogged down in snow to their chests. Orpha stood off to one side with her two youngsters, her head bent as if in prayer.

Canfield snorted derisively. No prayers would get them through this; only a good thaw. And *that* was one thing for which he had no intention of waiting around.

Brushing the wet flakes out of his beard, he slogged back through the soft, powdery snow to Toby, sweating and straining to drag the mules another yard ahead.

"We can't go on like this," Red said.

Toby released his hold on the mule, and the animal ceased its struggle. The hunter wiped the perspiration and melted snow from his face and assessed Canfield coolly. "I'm inclined to agree with you. The wagons will *never* make it over the summit."

Red jerked his head in the direction of Jennings. "Help me convince *him* of that. And the others. They won't want to leave their possessions."

A slight, mocking smile curved Toby's lips. "It's either that or their lives at this point, I'm afraid."

Red bit off a piece of tobacco as the two men made their way back to Jennings, engaged in a fierce battle with two of his oxen. The wagon canted precariously to one side, well up to its axles in snow. "Damn your pagan hearts!" The Reverend thumped one of the oxen behind the ear and spun around in exasperated rage, nearly colliding with Toby.

"We're going to have to abandon the wagons," Toby said. "The snow only gets deeper the higher we climb."

Jennings sucked in his breath incredulously. "Leave the wagons?" His initial surprise turned to anger, and his eyes narrowed defiantly. "Impossible!"

Red spat a stream of brown juice in the snow and eyed the Reverend slyly. "The only thing that's impossible right now is draggin' these goddamn wagons up the mountains."

"The Lord will see us through."

Red spat again. "Hogwash!"

Jennings gaped and shook his head in dismay. He swept his hat from his head and knocked the frozen crystals off its crown. "I think," he said slowly, as if choosing his words carefully, "we should wait until tomorrow and try again. Perhaps the weather will clear and some of this might melt."

"Down by the lake, it might," Toby said. "But not up here."

"Then we'll wait *several* days."

Toby waved a hand impatiently. "And what will we all eat?"

"There's fish in the lake. And *you* can hunt."

"A few chipmunks and squirrels, maybe. The game is already gone, Reverend. We *can't* wait."

Jennings bit his fleshy lower lip in indecision and glanced uneasily at his wife, waiting quietly with her children. Young Ephiram's teeth were chattering, and Hope's lips had turned blue. Jennings's shoulders heaved slightly, and he looked away, confused.

"I'll go on down and tell the others," Toby said.

Jennings nodded reluctantly and, with a dejected sigh,

185

mashed his hat back on his head and turned back to his oxen.

Toby paused on his way back down the trail at the Huntingtons' wagon. Top-heavy, it was buried in snow to its wheel tops, unable to move forward another inch. Huntington, his son, Poole, Trent, and even the black maid were pushing with all their might while Ruth and Alma tugged at the oxen. Little Ned sat atop the seat, gurgling happily.

When Edgar looked up and saw Toby approaching, he halted his efforts and raised a hand for the others to do likewise. Phillip slumped against the tailgate, his breath coming in short, raspy gasps, his head buried in his arms and the snow settling on his trembling shoulders.

Toby flashed a look of concern at the sallow young man, then directed his gaze to the older man. "You're going to have to leave the wagon. Pack what you can onto your mules and oxen. We're going out on foot."

Huntington looked at Toby with imperious contempt. "That's preposterous! I've already left two wagons behind. I'll not leave this one."

Toby was in no mood to argue. He was cold and hungry and exhausted. He studied the merchant with a slightly mocking gaze; his proud, severe face, his graying temples, his elegant clothes. Toby frowned with disdain. "Do as you wish, Mr. Huntington. But I'll not be responsible for you or your family if you don't come with us."

Huntington's mouth opened as if to protest, then closed abruptly, his face flushed with suppressed anger. Gentlemen of breeding never lost their temper publicly, Toby supposed, and his mouth twitched in a wry smile at the thought as he turned away.

Poole and Trent jogged over to him. "We're going with you, Mr. Garrett. When do we leave?"

Huntington blinked, taken completely by surprise, then glared at his driver. "You are in *my* employ, Mr. Poole!"

"I know that, sir." Poole gestured lamely, his melancholy brown eyes confused. "And you've been pretty fair with me, and I appreciate it. But I ain't stayin' here to get snowed in for the winter."

"You *won't* get snowed in! This storm will pass, and the road will be clear again."

Poole looked doubtful. "Maybe. Maybe not. But I ain't riskin' it."

"I'll give you a hundred dollars to stay!" Huntington's voice was low and threaded with desperation.

Poole's eyes clouded thoughtfully for a moment before he shook his head. "I figure my life's worth more than a hundred dollars."

Dulcy had been lingering in the background, listening, and she stepped forward shyly. Barely more than a child herself, she was a tiny little thing in her neat white apron and black skirts, her skin like tarnished copper. She lifted her eyes to Huntington in a timid plea for understanding. "I gwine out wid de menfolks, too, Mista H."

Huntington's face went livid with rage, and, emitting a low snarl, he slammed his fist into his palm. The girl retreated, cringing, behind Adam Trent, then looked beseechingly at Phillip as he joined his father.

The young man's usually carefully groomed goatee was untrimmed, and his face was a pasty, mottled shade. He coughed painfully and spat a glob of bloody phlegm into the snow. Consumption, Toby decided, and he felt a rush of sympathy for the young man. But the elder Huntington seemed unaffected by his son's illness and continued to stare stonily at his two former employees. Probably can't admit the bloodline's been tainted, Toby mused scornfully, and directed his attention to father and son.

"Father, I think we should do as Mr. Garrett suggests."

Huntington stared in angry disbelief. "*You* would leave everything here—for the Indians and wild animals to loot!"

Phillip took a deep, rasping breath. "We can come back for it next spring."

"Come back to *what?*"

Toby suppressed an amused smile. "Mr. Huntington, let me assure you I've seen no signs of Indians hereabouts. As for the animals, the worst they might do is tear or soil your clothing and linens." His eyes shifted from one to the other. "If you're coming, be ready to leave in an hour."

As Toby turned away, Huntington called him back. "It's nearly four o'clock now." He snapped his gold watch shut and replaced it in his vest pocket. His thin lips curled into a sneer. "Do you plan to cross the mountains at night?"

Toby stopped short and muttered a low curse. He hadn't realized it was so late. Traveling at night *might* have its advantages, for the snow pack would harden with the drop in temperature. But in the darkness, they would *never* find their way. Grimly resigned to yet another delay, he nodded reluctantly. "Very well, then. We leave at first light tomorrow."

Adam Trent trotted a few yards after Toby. "Can I take my paints and canvases?"

"If you carry them."

"I have my horse."

Toby nodded absently, suddenly weary of these people and their petty bickering. And he still had the Coulters to see to.

"Is there anything I can do to help?" Trent asked.

Toby regarded the artist thoughtfully, noting the soft, wavy sun-streaked hair, delicate features, and firm, slightly pouting curve to his lips. He may *look* like a girl and sometimes act like one, but at least he was willing to help. He managed a tight smile of gratitude. "Not tonight. But you may be needed to carry someone's child tomorrow—if the snow's still this deep." He glanced up at the darkening sky, filled with thick gray clouds. The snow was already coming down harder, and once again he felt that familiar sinking sensation in his stomach.

Toby sat hunched in a corner of the Coulters' wagon, sipping hot coffee laced with Roy's whiskey, trying to shake off his melancholy mood. Outside, the early dusk of autumn had fallen, and he could hear the gentle patter of the snow as it struck the canvas above him. He cupped the mug in both hands in an attempt to bring some warmth back into his numbed fingers, wishing he were anyplace but here.

Hetty and Sarah had taken the latest news with stolid acceptance, and for the last hour had moved most of their belongings out of the wagon. They would have to sleep inside tonight, for the waterproof blankets normally used as a groundcover for the tent now contained all the Coulters' worldly possessions and what little remaining food they had. Toby had helped them pack, showing them how

189

to make the most economical and secure bundles, and instructed them to add hatchets, a small spade, and other tools they would need for living outdoors for a time.

Simon sat opposite him, playing quietly with a worn rag doll which Toby suspected had belonged to Samantha. The boy would glance at him occasionally with large, curious eyes. Toby would manage a smile, the child would then resume his tranquil play, and Toby could once again return to his thoughts.

The very real possibility that they would indeed be snowed in loomed ever larger with each passing hour. It had snowed steadily, though not particularly hard, all day—but on the heights it could be an entirely different matter. It would be a difficult hike for those in the best of health, and with so many women and children . . . Toby shook his head in dismay.

But there was nothing to go *back* to. The closest settlement was Fort Hall, but it was six hundred miles or more away. It would mean another trek through the desert, and neither the wagons *or* humans were up to that. Better they try to get over the mountains than perish back in that hell on earth.

Toby swallowed the last of the brew, and the fiery fluid soothed his jangled nerves and helped focus his thoughts. He stared into the steady flame of the lamp, turning over the question in his mind that had nagged him all day. If the emigrants *couldn't* scale the pass in the snow, *he* could. There was nothing to keep him here—no ties, no family, no strong emotional attachments. Except that he had pledged his word to Roy Coulter to see to his wife and children until the carpenter returned. And despite his reckless, independent nature, Toby Garrett was a man of his word. He would stay, do his best, and hope that tomorrow saw them over the pass.

A bitter, strangled sound, faintly resembling laughter, came from his throat. The unreality of his predicament was almost comic. For a man who had wanted only companionship for the journey to California, he had certainly got that and more.

Outside, he heard Lucas give a shout of triumph, and the sound of applause. Sarah materialized out of the darkness, an amused smile on her lips.

"Supper's almost ready," she said, kneeling to rummage in the last remaining trunk against the wall.

Toby reached for the jug to refill his cup. "What was all the cheering about?"

"Hetty's going to have to leave her case of soap here. I suppose Lucas thinks he won't have to ever take another bath again."

Toby made a murmuring sound of agreement, not really interested. His gaze roamed leisurely over Sarah, taking in every detail of her supple young body and graceful curves. She was like no other woman he had ever met before. She was efficient and pragmatic, seemingly unaffected by the usual bouts of female weaknesses he had come to think of as part of every woman's nature. She had a quick temper and a lively mind—and she had exacted no promises from him. She had given herself willingly; yet she behaved, for the most part, as if nothing had happened between them. She didn't fawn or cling to him, nor did she seem to expect him to play the courtly suitor. She had made love for the sheer pleasure of it, and Toby respected her all the more for that. At the glade near the river, she had been warm and giving and uninhibited —so unlike the shy, reserved, *sensible* woman she was all the rest of the time.

191

He reached out and let his fingers entwine in her hair, shining like a golden halo in the muted light from the lantern. She turned her head slightly and looked curiously at him.

He continued to toy with a tress of her hair. "Did anyone ever tell you you're quite a remarkable woman?"

A slight sardonic smile twitched at the corners of her mouth, but there was a soft glow in her eyes. "I thought *you* had other opinions of women."

He gave her an abashed grin. "A man can change his mind."

A gentle smile played about her lips, and her eyes shone warmly as they met his. He seemed to be drawn to those eyes, and he couldn't help but wonder if he was staying here because of the promise he had made to Roy, or because of Sarah. It was an absurd thought, of course, but one that wouldn't quite go away even as he cupped her chin in his hand and leaned forward to kiss her softly parted lips.

But when she looked at him again, her eyes were troubled, and a small frown touched her forehead. "We *will* get over the pass tomorrow, won't we?"

He forced a nervous smile to his lips. "Of course." His fingertips caressed her cheek lightly. "And we'll probably run into your brother somewhere on the other side."

Her eyes were tinged with doubt, but she managed a small, tired smile. "Yes." Her voice held a measure of uncertainty as she turned back to the trunk, drawing out a flintlock pistol and a pouch of shot.

"You don't intend to use that on *me,* surely?" he asked.

"Not at the moment." She threw a quick glance over

her shoulder, her eyes twinkling with playfulness. "Not so long as you're behaving."

Hetty climbed up into the van with a platter of steaks, and the aroma of freshly cooked meat assailed Toby's nostrils and permeated the wagon. Samantha and Lucas followed with the coffeepot and a plate of biscuits, kicking clumps of packed snow from their shoes.

Toby ate ravenously, as did they all, and even Samantha seemed to have forgotten that she was consuming the last of Clarabell.

"There's maybe another two pounds of flour left," Hetty said, patting her lips with a napkin. "We transferred it from the big barrel into one of the water kegs. There's a little dried fruit, some beans, molasses, and a tin of crackers." She arched a quizzical eyebrow at Toby. "Think that's enough to see us over to the Sacramento?"

He shrugged. "It'll have to be." *If we ever get there,* he thought morosely, and sopped up the gravy with a biscuit.

"Pa'll be there waitin' with more," Lucas said cheerfully.

Samantha licked her fingers with gusto and nodded firmly. "Pa won't forget us."

Roy stood beneath the shelter of the porch in the fading twilight at Sutter's Fort, watching a half dozen Indians leading horses and mules to a nearby corral. The rain fell in wind-whipped sheets, drenching the workers, cascading off the eaves, and creating deep, muddy puddles on the ground. Ocassionally, silvery flashes of lightning would dance across the sky, illuminating the adobe walls surrounding the fort and the cluster of squat, low buildings inside.

Roy heaved a long-suffering sigh, his gaze moving to the towering mountain range to the east, no longer visible in the gloom. Somehwere out there were Hetty and the children and Sarah. Were they warm and dry? Did they have enough to eat? The unanswerable questions—one after the other—tumbled through his mind, and a wave of despair and helplessness engulfed him.

Captain Sutter had generously offered everything he had at his disposal to help. Sacks of flour and beans were stored in the warehouse. A dozen head of cattle had been slaughtered and the meat dried. There were pack animals and horses for Roy's use, and four Indian guides to help him and Tyrrell recross the mountains. They had planned to leave this morning, but it had been raining since before dawn. The flour would get wet and undoubtedly become moldy, and the meat would dampen and spoil. Roy sighed again disconsolately.

The heavy wooden door behind him swung open, throwing a shaft of yellow light onto the porch. Captain John Sutter emerged into the wind to stand beside Roy and gaze out at the sluicing rain. At forty-four, he was tall and vigorous, with a shock of blond curls and a sleek imperial beard, the picture of a man who was truly the king of California. Before the age of thirty, he had left his family back in Switzerland and traveled to the United States to escape debtor's prison. And by the early part of the decade, he had set up his empire in the Sacramento valley.

Without a second thought, he had accepted Jennings's letter of credit and immediately set about recruiting a party to accompany Roy and Tyrrell. He was kind and sympathetic, and, to Roy, he epitomized Old World charm and hospitality.

194

"Rain down here usually means snow on the mountains," Sutter said, almost as if speaking to himself.

Roy turned and stared at the man. "There was already snow on the summit when we came over."

Sutter returned Roy's gaze, his blue eyes filled with compassion. "A foot or two shouldn't hamper them too much. You say you left them in Truckee canyon almost two weeks ago?" He paused and his brows knitted into a frown, as if mentally calculating time and distance. "They should be over the pass now—maybe near Bear Valley, dug in out of the storm."

Roy grunted doubtfully. "I can't take that chance. I'm leaving tomorrow—rain or no rain."

Sutter placed a beringed hand on Roy's shoulder. "Do as you think you must, my friend."

Roy could only nod, touched by this kindly stranger's genuine concern. A jagged bolt of lightning sizzled and cracked high in the air, and a resounding clap of thunder reverberated off the hillsides. Roy shuddered, unable to push aside the unformed dread that had begun to nibble at the edges of his mind.

Chapter Eleven

The cold gray morning had dawned on the glittering white peaks of the Sierras, and it was still snowing from a leaden sky. Four-foot drifts had piled up during the night, and the wind blew fiercely.

Maggie shuffled awkwardly in the loose powder, numbed with the cold, shielding her eyes against the icy crystals pelting her from all sides. She had pinned up her skirts for easier walking, but, from the knees down, her legs were protected only by her thin cotton stockings.

Unused to the heavy pack strapped to its back, the ox she was herding lay down in the snow and wallowed like a rooting pig. Cursing shrilly, Maggie smacked the animal's back with a stout branch until it finally got to its feet and staggered on.

Daniel, carrying Katie on his shoulders, stumbled in the soft, yielding snow, and the little girl somersaulted into a drift, buried nearly to her shoulders. Half-crying, half-cursing, Daniel dug out his sister and tried to remove as much of the snow as possible from her clothing.

Still battling the unruly ox, Maggie could only stare

helplessly as the mule her mother was leading bucked and reared. Its flanks struck a tree, and the keg of flour strapped to its back cracked and split open. Flour—the last few precious pounds—disappeared in the white snow amid splinters and staves.

Molly balled her fists and raised them in angry surrender. She erupted in a burst of bitter tears, pounding her clenched fists weakly against the wet fur of the mule.

Toby's heartbeat roared in his ears, and sweat slicked his body beneath his heavy clothing. Wading through drifts nearly up to his hips, his legs felt like leaden weights. His chest ached, and his breath rasped in his throat. Sleetlike snow battered at his face, driven by a violent wind; it sifted down his neck and melted quickly from his body heat until he was soaked clear through.

Beside him, Michael O'Brian staggered through the loose powder, and together they were able to break a trail of sorts. But it was impossible to move through the deep snow without the greatest effort, and after only a few minutes, the men fell back to rest while Higgins and Pardee took their places to tackle the deep drifts.

Toby half-collapsed against a tree, sucking in huge lungfuls of frigid air. Far below, the emigrants toiled up the slope, carrying children and driving unmanageable cattle. Despite the trail blazed by him and the others, they were falling ever farther behind. Belle Pardee and her children were barely discernible in the distance, for her old father was unable to keep up.

Having caught up to take his turn at cutting through the snow, Canfield offered Toby a pint bottle of whiskey. He drank gratefully; it burned his throat and warmed the lining of his stomach. Breathing deeply, Toby threw a glance at Canfield. Icy crystals clung to the guide's matted beard and eyebrows, making him resemble some long-extinct creature from the Ice Age.

"How much farther to the summit?" Toby asked, returning the bottle.

Canfield drank, then cast a doubtful glance up the mountain. "Hard to tell."

Toby's face knotted into a frown as O'Brian slogged up to them and snatched the bottle from Canfield's hand. He drank deeply, spilling some on his beard and the collar of his coat. He raised the bottle in mock salute, his lips twisting into a cynical smile. "Ah—'tis a grand place, this California! The land of eternal sunshine!" He handed the bottle back to Canfield and motioned to Toby. "Come along, lad. We've got work to do."

With effort, Toby pushed himself away from the dubious shelter of the tree and forced himself back into the driving snow.

Samantha stumbled, but caught herself before tumbling headfirst into the snow. She had no gloves, and her fingers were growing almost too numb to hold onto the bridle of one of Toby's mules. The fractious animal was too much for her at times, but there was no one to help her. Sarah had charge of an ox, Lucas had the other mule, and her mother had to carry Simon.

The wind had picked up, swirling the snow and obscuring her vision. The storm was getting worse—that much she knew. And when she squinted up ahead, all she could see was the sheer white wall of the pass, looming desolate and menacing. Her legs ached painfully, despite the numbing coldness invading her bones.

The mule suddenly lurched violently, and the rope slipped through Samantha's fingers. The animal bounded out of the makeshift trail and floundered through the soft powder. Samantha scrabbled after him, reeling and tripping through the tumbled drifts, sobbing with exhaustion and angry frustration.

The mule butted into a pine with its shoulder, shaking a small avalanche from the limbs. He bucked and wallowed, rubbing feverishly against the bark until the pack loosened and fell to the ground, spilling its contents onto the blanket of snow.

Samantha fell to her knees and stared dumbly at the clothing and bedding scattered about her. She threw up her hands, and tears of desperation welled in her eyes. A deep, bitter sob cracked in her throat, and her shoulders shook uncontrollably. Hot tears scalded her eyes and trickled down her cheeks, freezing immediately in the icy wind.

She felt a hand gently stroking her shoulder and looked up to find her mother gazing down at her, a great sadness and despair in her brown eyes.

"I'm sorry, Ma."

Hetty patted her comfortingly. "It's not your fault. We'll just repack and be on our way again."

Her mother's words brought on a fresh burst of sobs. "I can't! I'm *so* tired!"

Hetty placed Simon on the ground, bundled in several shirts and his thin cotton jacket. Lucas's knitted cap was atop his head, but it was too large and frequently slipped down over his eyes. The boy sat down immediately and began to pack a snowball in his bare hands.

Samantha shook her head miserably, cold and dispirited. She was trembling, and her teeth chattered, and all she wanted to do was lay down and rest in some safe, warm place.

"Sam, we *have* to go on!"

Dully, Samantha peered at her mother as the woman gathered up their belongings into a bundle. She heard a scream, and her head swung around in time to see Orpha Jennings in much the same predicament Sam had found herself in moments before. One of Jennings's mules was rubbing fiercely against a tree, and a crock of molasses shattered with the force of the impact. A sticky, brown ooze seeped down the bark and dripped into the snow.

Then Samantha smelled smoke, and she directed her attention some fifty yards further up the trail. Edgar Huntington had set fire to a gnarled old dead pine, and his entire family was gathered around the burning tree. Gouts of flame shot up into the sky and licked with hungry abandon at the decayed wood, unimpeded by the blowing snow. Great billows of smoke rose up and filled Samantha's nostrils, and the leaping tongues of fire reminded her once again how cold she was.

Lucas and Sarah, struggling with the cattle, were slowly making their way toward the enticing warmth, as were other emigrants. Samantha got to her feet, dusted the snow from her clothing, and took Simon's hand. As if in a daze, she led the little boy across the snow toward the inviting heat, oblivious to her mother's warning voice trailing after her.

Toby slumped exhausted in the snow and wiped the sweat from his eyes. The labor of trying to blaze a trail through drifts growing increasingly deeper was beginning to take its toll, and it was more difficult at each rest stop to make himself get up and go on again. His ears and nose ached with the cold, and his ragged breath plumed out in front of him like a cloud.

Shivering, he pulled the collar of his sodden jacket more tightly around his neck and gazed restlessly around him. A few jagged pieces of granite showed above the blanket of snow, but the rest of the landscape seemed lost in a world of white ridges and chasms. But the peaks no longer towered so menacingly above him, and he felt certain he was near the summit. Another hour—perhaps less—and *all* the emigrants would be ready to start the descent. And on the other side, the brutal wind and blowing snow might not be so bad. Though, glancing up at the bleak, leaden sky, Toby felt the storm had no intention of abating.

His head jerked up, and he stared in vague bewilderment. Canfield and Pardee were coming back. And a few yards away, O'Brian was getting to his feet and staring off down the trail. Then Toby smelled it: woodsmoke, sweet and pungent, though faint.

Moving away from the boulder against which he had been leaning, he slogged through the powder to gaze in the same direction as the others. Far down the mountain, jets of flame burst high in the air as fire devoured a dead tree. The emigrants streamed toward it, hauling their cattle and children along in their wake, like so many moths drawn to a candle.

Michael O'Brian rubbed his hands together in greedy anticipation. "Ah, 'tis a bit of a rest and a warmin' up we all need." And he set off down the trail at as brisk a pace as the snow would permit. Canfield and Pardee followed, and some thirty feet below, Toby saw Higgins and Poole start back, breaking into a clumsy, shuffling trot.

Toby opened his mouth to call them back, then closed it abruptly instead, choking out a bitter sound. His eyes flew to the crags and gorges and the almost treeless expanse of the heights. The snow fell more heavily, and a gust of wind nearly captured his hat. Shivering again, he looked back at the throng assembled around the burning tree and clenched his fists, crying out loud at this cruel trick nature had played. He had reached the summit—he could be over and on his way down the western slopes of the Sierras in a matter of minutes. But the people whom he had sworn to Roy Coulter he would look after were half a mile back, wasting precious time while the storm increased in its ferocity.

Casting a final, painful glance at the snow-swept summit, Toby muttered a strangled, angry oath and turned to trudge back down the path he had cleared so laboriously, which was already filling with fresh snow.

Sarah sat on a blanket beside Samantha and Lucas, gazing in rapt fascination into the dancing, crackling flames. Snow piled up on her shoulders and the hood of her cape, and from time to time, she shook it off; other than this feeble movement, she seemed incapable of doing anything else.

She was on the verge of collapse, Toby saw, as were most of the other emigrants. And as he knelt beside Sarah and held his hands out to the warmth of the fire, he realized he was equally exhausted. Yet the pass was not far away, and some inner compulsion urged him toward its heights. Once on the other side . . .

He sneered in contempt, angry at himself for feeling so

203

weak, so humbled by the force of nature. The drifts were ten feet high on the summit, and the storm was intensifying. And, despite all his years of surviving in the wilderness, he doubted even *he* could make it alone in this kind of weather.

O'Brian and the others who had been up there with him and displayed such energy to return to the fire now sat listlessly, staring into the burning embers. *They* would be no help now. The drive to go on had all but gone out of them, and, like everyone else, they wanted only to rest and be warm.

Huntington rose up, glancing first at Jennings, then briefly toward Canfield and Toby. His hands were encased in fine, sturdy black leather gloves, and his coat was lined with soft, downy sheepskin. He appeared as unaffected by the storm as a man out for a Sunday stroll.

"My family is staying here," he announced, directing his gaze to Toby once more. "As is Reverend Jennings. It's pointless to tackle the mountain crossing in a storm like this." He gestured expansively around him. "A storm that seems to be getting worse every minute."

Jennings nodded but didn't rise; he sat cuddling Hope on his lap. "Roy Coulter and Claude Tyrrell know we're here. And once they realize our situation, they'll bring plenty of help."

Toby's puzzled and angry frown cut deep furrows in his forehead. "And how *long* do you plan to wait for this help?"

"Until it arrives—or until there's sufficient thaw for us to get over the summit ourselves. It's still very early in the season—this is simply a freak storm. Why, back in Pennsylvania—"

"This isn't Pennsylvania," Toby reminded him sharply.

204

"Nor is it Ireland!" O'Brian snorted in disgust. "It's a cursed land!"

The wind tore at Huntington's elegant beaver hat, and he was forced to hold onto it with his hand. "We have enough cattle to feed us for some time—enough time until help comes." He lifted his grandson in his arms and gave the group one final lingering glance. "I'm staying." And, without another word, he marched awkwardly across the snow in the direction from which they had all come, his family trailing after him.

Poole glanced sheepishly around. "I'm staying, too. At least till this storm blows over." And he scrambled to his feet and trotted after his employer.

"You can't sleep in the wagons!" Toby called furiously after them. Sarah looked at him, mildly startled. He glanced at her, and his lips grew taut with angry frustration. "There's no protection from the weather. You can't build a fire inside a wagon for heat or cooking."

"We can build cabins," Pardee said, shouting to be heard above the rising wind. "We've got the manpower and the tools."

"Do *you* want to stay?" Toby asked him.

Pardee shrugged his broad shoulders helplessly. "I don't have much choice."

Toby glanced at the blacksmith's three small children and aged father-in-law, wrapped in a blanket and shivering toothlessly. He had to agree with the man.

And, one by one, the emigrants slowly left the dying blaze of the fire until only the Coulters and Andersens remained.

Ole frowned unhappily, as if arguing with himself. He finally released a great sigh, and his breath billowed out to be snapped up in the wind. "I've lived in snow all my life. A week or two of this might not be so bad as long as we've got a place to sleep that's warm and plenty to eat.''

"But we *don't* have plenty to eat," Toby reminded. "You've got only three oxen."

"But we'll have four if you'll agree to a trade," the Swede said. "You'll need help building a cabin. Peter and I will give you that help in exchange for one of your oxen. I won't ask for your cows—just one ox. And with us doing the building, you'll have more time to see about finding us fresh game."

Toby groaned inwardly and ground his teeth in frustration. He doubted there would be much game after a storm like this, and if Ole took one of the oxen . . . He calculated quickly; that would leave three oxen, two cows, and the two mules for food. By eating sparingly, that amount of meat should last quite a while. And if not . . . He glanced briefly at the setter, curled up against Lucas. There was always the dog.

Wincing at the thought, he turned to Hetty and raised a questioning brow.

She answered him with a fatalistic shrug. "We haven't any other choice, do we? I can't expect you to try to take us over the mountains all by yourself. But if you want to go on yourself, I'll release you from your pledge to my husband."

The storm was turning into a full-fledged gale, and the wind gusted with a fury, lashing at them with snow crystals that stung like pellets. It would be suicide to attempt the crossing in this weather, and Toby knew it. He glanced at the children, gazing gravely at him, and realized, with some chagrin, that he had become their surrogate father for the time being. And what of Sarah? What was he to her? His eyes searched her face, and she returned his gaze steadily.

"You don't need to stay here, Toby," she said quietly.

He knew she didn't mean a word of it. He could see the fear and apprehension in her eyes, and he suddenly felt a strong surge of protectiveness totally alien to him.

He got to his feet and brushed the snow off his hat and shoulders before bending down to pick up Simon. The wind howled down from the pass, and the air was filled with blowing snow and flying leaves and twigs. Toby glanced one last time toward the pass and saw only the glittering white mountains and icy waste.

He turned away from it, feeling sick and frightened and dismayed. But he composed his features into a mask that gave none of these feelings away, and, managing a jaunty smile, winked at Lucas. "Come on, boy. We've got a cabin to build."

Chapter Twelve

Roy stared in awe up at the snow-packed ridges and forests towering monstrously above him, and a cold sweat broke out over his body in spite of the chilly autumn air. Three miles above Bear Valley, and already he and Claude Tyrrell were feeling the effects of walking through knee-deep, melting snow, carrying packs of close to a hundred pounds.

It had rained steadily for three days, sluicing down in torrents. The road had become a morass, and much of the food had been spoiled. They had been forced to go slowly, crossing swollen creeks and clambering up steep, slippery slopes. Late last night they had camped at the edge of the snow line—much farther down than anyone had expected. This morning, after a few hours' travel it had become evident that the animals could go no farther; they were back at camp with Sutter's Indians. And now, as Roy gazed at the interminable maze of the snow-mantled plains and gorges, he realized, with mounting anxiety and dread, that it would be impossible for Tyrrell and him to continue on by themselves.

They would need more men—each shouldering a lighter pack—and experienced guides. The marks Roy had blazed on trees on his way down would surely be buried beneath the snow now, and he would have no idea where he was going.

He glanced at little Tyrrell, snuffling in his heavy overcoat. Both men had been drenched in the rain, and Jennings's former driver had evidently caught cold. The man was in no fit condition to go on, and Roy knew it would be foolhardy to attempt it alone.

He took a deep breath, then exhaled slowly, trying to calm the churning fear and frustration gnawing at his stomach. There was nothing to do but turn back. Captain Sutter would help. He would recruit more men and more supplies. And in the meantime . . .

Roy cast another uneasy glance at the fearful specter of granite and snow. Sarah and Hetty were not stupid. They knew how to slaughter and dress cattle, had spent every winter of their lives in the snowy Appalachians. And they had Garrett to look out for them, as well as Emmett and perhaps even O'Brian.

It was no longer snowing; that was always a good sign. If this were simply an unusual surprise storm, a week or so of sunny weather might effect enough of a thaw to clear the emigrant road once again. In the meantime, all Roy could do was pray and return to Sutter's fort for more help.

Maggie gazed into the bubbling caldron of ox stew, stirring it listlessly, her brow puckered in a thoughtful frown. The aromatic steam filled the tiny cabin, and if she closed her eyes, she could almost believe she was back home in Ireland. But the minute she opened them and looked around, she realized how absurd the notion was.

Built of pine saplings and roofed with brush, hides, and the canvas taken from the wagon and sleeping tent, it was a miserable little hovel for ten people to live in. One opening served as both door and window, and little light found its way inside. But at least it was dry now that the eight inches of snow on which it had been built had melted and the mud had hardened. There was a fireplace constructed of rocks, and though the ventilation could have been better, it gave off a comfortable warmth.

With so many males available for labor in the family, the O'Brians' cabin had been the first completed, and they had slept indoors for the past two nights while the others still huddled in their tents. The wagons, a mile or so up the trail, were buried too deeply in the snow to move, but Maggie, her mother, and some of the younger children had made the walk several times every day to bring back all they could carry.

Maggie heard a sharp thud on the other side of the south wall, and Kevin stirred fretfully in his sleep. For ease and expediency in building, the O'Brians shared the center wall with the Pardees, though the blacksmith's cabin was only half-completed. He had no one to help him, and no one would offer without the promise of meat in return. Emmett had few enough cattle as it was, so he was forced to take on the task himself.

Now, however, Maggie's father and brothers, the Andersens, and even little Adam Trent were helping. Two days ago—the third since turning back from the pass and the first the sun came out—old Ezra Weeks had succumbed to age and the arduous journey. He had been the

211

first casualty of the trek west, and Jennings had used the opportunity to give one of his most eloquent soliloquies at the impromptu funeral.

Maggie's lip curled in scorn as she stood up and brushed back a lock of hair. Jennings had gotten them all into this mess. Jennings—with his pompous, overblown self-righteousness!

When she thought back to all those Sundays back on the plains when instead of traveling he had held camp meetings, she felt an enormous rage. The arrogant, sometimes fanatical preacher and his interminable delays! If they could have only a handful of those wasted Sundays back, they would probably be in the Sacramento valley by now.

Unable to suppress an involuntary shudder of disgust, Maggie moved to the cradle and looked down at her year-old brother. A few red curls peeped out from under the blanket, and one small fist was clenched tight around a cloth cat. Smiling fondly at the boy, she gathered up her shawl and went outside into the bright October sunshine.

A good deal of bare ground was visible once again around the cabins. Directly across from the O'Brian-Pardee cabin was the one shared by the Coulters and Andersens. A few yards closer to the lake was the Huntington-Jennings hut, and farther down was a ramshackle shanty to house all the single men.

Maggie saw Judd talking earnestly with Higgins and Stone, and she decided to walk over that way. Judd hadn't helped much with the construction, nor had he had much to say to her—to *anyone* for that matter. His face seemed to have changed from the confident, urbane gentleman to that of a haunted man. He looked intimidated and frightened, and he spent much of his time staring off to the imposing wall of mountains to the west.

Huntington's stock—thirteen oxen, two mules, and two horses—was browsing through the grass uncovered by the thaw. Maggie's eyes hardened resentfully. The man and his family could live for *years* on that amount of meat, while others—like her own family—had barely enough for three or four weeks.

She shook off these thoughts quickly. There would be no *need* to stay here that long, so why worry about it? A few more days of sunshine, and the snow on the pass would undoubtedly melt enough for them to get out. It was still deep up there; Toby and some of the others had gone up just this morning. But the sun was pleasantly warm on her shoulders, and even a few birds flitted in the trees. It felt like spring, and the weather helped buoy Maggie's spirits.

She smiled brightly at the three men as she approached, studiously avoiding the many muddy puddles. " 'Tis a bright and beautiful day, is it not, gentlemen?"

Higgins smiled shyly and touched the brim of his battered felt hat. Stone's small brown eyes assessed her quickly, and his lips twisted into what might have been a smile. Judd eyed her guardedly for an instant, then managed one of his most disarming smiles.

Maggie regarded them with open suspicion, but there was a teasing note in her voice. "What are the three of you plotting? Ye all look so mysterious and . . . and guilty."

Judd's smile turned brittle, and he took her elbow. "Let's take a little walk, and I'll tell you all about it." And, giving the other two men a significant glance, he led her toward the lake.

A few of the emigrants were trying their hand at fishing; Hetty Coulter and Inga Andersen were washing clothes. The water sparkled like blue glass in the sunshine, and the wind blew lightly through the tall grass. In the mornings, a thin coating of ice covered the lake, but, for the last two days, it had burned off by noon.

Maggie stopped suddenly and eyed Judd with a provocative challenge, her head thrown back and hands planted boldly on her rounded hips. "Now what is all this about, Judd Brannan?"

"We've decided to go out this afternoon."

"Go out where?" Then, as his meaning suddenly penetrated, she goggled at him. "Over the pass?"

Judd nodded solemnly. "The six of us—me, Stone, Higgins, Canfield, Poole, and Trent."

"That's crazy! Toby Garrett and me father were up there just this mornin'. The snow's still too deep!"

Judd shrugged and sat down on a rock. "I can't stay here."

"And why not? Everyone else is."

A glimmer of fear shone in his eyes, and he looked away, shaking his head. "I just can't."

Maggie reached out a tentative hand and smoothed a lock of his black hair, no longer sure of this man who had shared so much with her. "Is it frightened, you are?"

He laughed, but it was a bitter, sardonic sound, without humor.

Maggie knelt on the grass before him and took his hand—not the smooth hand of a gentleman any longer, but chapped and callused. "Da thinks we can *all* leave in another few days or so. And there's always Mr. Coulter."

Judd turned his head and looked down at her, his dark

214

eyes glittering with an odd light. "We don't even know if Roy Coulter *reached* Sutter's. A hundred things could have happened to him between here and there."

"Exactly why *you* should stay with the rest of us now. It's dangerous on that mountain."

Judd shook his head firmly. "My mind's made up, Maggie. I'm going. If I don't—" His voice trailed off, and a distant look crept into his eyes. "If I don't go now, I know I'll never get out of here alive."

Confused, Maggie's eyes searched his face without understanding This was a side of Judd Brannan that was a stranger to her. Memories flooded back of their lovemaking, the grand dreams she had for a future with him, and she felt a sudden surge of panic. She clutched his hand tighter. "But what about us?"

He tilted his head and looked quizzically at her. "What *about* us?"

"But I thought . . . All those times we—" She shook her head, her mind whirling in confusion. "Judd, darlin', don't you want to *marry* me?"

He looked at her, his eyes dispassionate and remote. "Did I ever *say* that?"

She stared dumbly at him, bewilderment, shock, and anger all mixed in her expression. "But—*Judd!*"

A lazy smile played across his lips, and he patted her hand. "You're a good sport, Maggie. I knew you'd understand."

Completely taken aback, she withdrew her hand from his, as if she could no longer bear his touch. She got shakily to her feet and stared down at him, flushed and trembling with anger. "A good sport, am I? Just another fast tumble in the woods!"

He held up a placating hand. "Now, Maggie—"

Seething with outrage, she swung her arm back and brought the palm of her hand across his face with all the force she could muster. He winced and stared up at her in confused surprise. Maggie glared hatefully at him, her breath coming quickly in short, ragged puffs and treacherous tears stinging her eyes. "I hope you *die* out on the mountain, Judd Brannan! And may God have mercy on your black soul!" Pivoting on her heel and gathering up her skirts, she stalked away.

Judd rubbed his cheek thoughtfully, gazing after Maggie as she marched back to her cabin. Shaking his head in wonder, he shot a surreptitious glance around to see if anyone had witnessed her outburst; apparently no one had.

Sighing pensively, he got wearily to his feet and gazed toward the snow-draped mountains. A few light clouds settled in the highest gorges, but they looked harmless enough. It was the darker, lower ones—far to the north—that worried him most right now. Still, he *had* to go.

Here, he felt trapped—worse than had he stayed in Natchez to await his fate at the hands of the law. He had no food to speak of—only his horse. And if he stayed and they *couldn't* eventually cross the mountains, how long would one footsore, lean-ribbed nag keep him from starving?

No, he resolved firmly. It was insane to stay. He couldn't take his horse out in the snow, but he could leave it with the O'Brians. That way, at least, they would have extra meat if they should need it. It wasn't much, but it made him feel a little less guilty about Maggie.

Casting a final glance at the mountains, he turned and walked slowly back to his shanty to pack up his meager possessions and try to borrow some food.

* * *

Sarah shook out the blanket in front of the cattle tethered to the side of the cabin. Sweet-smelling grass tumbled over the slushy earth, and the animals went for it greedily. She stood back, refolding the blanket, while the oxen and cows ate.

It seemed a lot of extra work, but Toby was leery of letting them graze. It was just one more reason Sarah felt a pang of dread that they might be here longer than everyone was inclined to believe. The emigrants were *all* hoarding food, and no one was willing to share. Their behavior alarmed and frightened her.

Trying to push aside her nagging unease, she walked around to the front of the cabin and saw Toby striding out of the woods with a bundle of grayish fur slung over his shoulder. Sarah paused to wait for him, wondering what his mood might be now.

Earlier, they had had a violent disagreement about putting the cattle out to graze, and, though Toby had won the argument, Sarah felt she had landed some good barbs of her own. Still, despite their frequent disputes, Sarah felt drawn to him. He had the power to stir emotions and responses in her that she had never dreamed existed. Never had she imagined a lover like him—a man who could evoke such a total, overwhelming passion from her in their abandoned moments of ecstasy. She scarcely understood her attraction to him; she only knew that she longed for his touch and often found herself wishing for the freedom they had back on the river. Even when she was angry with him, she was never unaware of that spark of desire smoldering inside her.

"Possums," he announced, displaying the limp bodies. He paused to kick some of the caked mud from his boots before entering the cabin. Sarah smiled furtively; Hetty would be pleased that her admonitions on keeping the place clean had been taken to heart.

She followed him inside. It was dim and cheerless with the three pallets taking up most of the space. Two empty barrels with a piece of wagon siding made up a table of sorts, and smaller kegs served as chairs. There were two lanterns, but once the fuel ran out, Sarah didn't know what they would do for light.

Toby dropped the possums on the table and looked at her with a faintly mocking challenge. "Can you clean them, or should I?"

Sarah bristled slightly under his close scrutiny. "I can do it." She gazed at the lifeless little creatures a moment, then lifted grave, concerned eyes to him. "Tell me the truth, Toby. *Are* we going to be here long?"

"I don't know." He leaned his rifle against the wall and unstrapped his powder horn. He studied her intently for a moment. "If we can avoid another storm for a few more days, we can probably leave. If not—" His shrug was expressive.

"We're here for the rest of the winter, or until Roy brings help." She said the words matter-of-factly, as if detached from the situation, and it surprised her.

"Those clouds to the north don't look good." He sat down and unsheathed his knife, placing it beside the possums. "But even if we *do* have to stay, we've got plenty of cattle to see us through if we go on short rations." His eyes narrowed wickedly as they swept the length of her body with deliberate slowness. "Though if you lose much weight, you won't be nearly as soft to hold."

Sarah managed a smile, although she felt far from in a

good humor. "Mrs. Huntington could live all winter on that roll of fat she's got."

"And she probably won't *have* to. They've got more food than the rest of us combined."

Sarah brushed back a lock of his hair, grateful for his presence. "When I've finished cleaning the game, I'll give you a haircut, if you like."

"Still on that eh?" He turned his face, playfully catching her forefinger in his mouth, holding it gently between his teeth and growling softly. "Don't tempt me, woman. I think—for you—with the right persuasion, I'd even *shave* my head."

Once the possums were cleaned and simmering in the pot, Sarah took a few scraps of fur, her twine, a bent nail, and went down to the lakeside to fish. Only one trout had accepted the bait thus far, but she reasoned that one was better than none.

Samantha had hung out the freshly laundered clothes to dry and joined her. Lucas was gathering pine cones with some of the other boys, for what purpose Sarah couldn't imagine. In the distance, she could hear the familiar ring of axes as several of the men chopped firewood. Pardee had bagged two late-season grouse, and his oldest son was decorating his cap with the feathers.

Altogether, Sarah thought, it was a pleasant afternoon. Shafts of sunlight filtered through the high, broken clouds, and the air smelled sweet and clean. If it weren't for the ominous threat of more snow, Sarah would have been quite content to stay here and wait for Roy's return.

But the threat *was* there: low black masses of clouds moving ever steadily south and east. Another storm was on its way, and Sarah prayed it would pass them by before breaking somewhere over the desert behind them.

She felt a sharp tug on her line and pulled it in as Maggie sauntered over to her. The Irish girl eyed the speckled trout appreciatively and nodded her head.

"I'd never been too fond of fish meself," she said, sinking down on a stump and staring morosely into the lake. "But I suppose it's better than ox meat."

Samantha turned away from her examination of the trout and regarded Maggie curiously. "When's Mr. Brannan leaving?"

Maggie's lips tightened in grim displeasure. "The sooner the better!"

Sarah caught her niece's eye and made a disapproving mouth. Samantha picked up another piece of fur and attached it to the nail, evidently having understood the silent warning. If things had been going right between Maggie and Judd, Sarah doubted the woman would be sitting here. She might well be moping, as she was doing now, but without the look of sheer contempt that sparkled in her eyes.

Sarah tossed the line back into the river, fairly bursting with curiosity over Maggie's strange behavior, but knowing full well she didn't dare ask.

"Since we've already got the possums cooking for tonight, we'll have to save these," she said, indicating the trout and trying to bring up another subject. "But how? We haven't any salt."

"There's a five-gallon crock of pickles," Samantha said. "And only a couple of pickles left. Couldn't you put the fish in that?"

Sarah's brows arched in surprise, and she looked at her niece with new interest. Samantha was no longer just a silly child—she could actually think for herself, and her idea was a good one. Sarah would have to remember to try to treat her as more of an adult in the future. After all, she would be eleven in a few weeks, and a journey like the one they had just completed could age even the most immature.

Maggie's soft grunt of disgust distracted Sarah, and she turned to see Red Canfield slouching over to them. Bundled in a heavy jacket, his belly hanging several inches over his belt, he carried his rifle and had a pack strapped onto his back. He stopped a few feet away and bowed stiffly.

"I just thought I'd come to say good-bye to you ladies," he said.

"Good-bye," Maggie muttered.

Canfield adopted a look of mock disappointment. "Now, is that anyway to treat your old guide?" He grinned crookedly, revealing several gold teeth. His watery pale blue eyes roamed boldly over the two women, glinting with undisguised lust.

Sarah held back a shiver of revulsion at his lecherous gaze and the tobacco juice stains in his rusty beard. She managed a kind of sickly, sneering smile. "Good-bye, Mr. Canfield."

"Not good luck?"

"Good luck." There was a trace of irritation in her voice, and she turned her back on him to resume her fishing. She could still feel his eyes on her, and her flesh crawled.

"Well," he finally said in his raspy, drawling voice, "old Red will never forget the two prettiest ladies I've ever had the pleasure of knowing."

Sarah heard his footsteps receding and cast a sidelong

look at Maggie.

Maggie rolled her eyes and expelled a deep sigh of relief. "Reekin' of whiskey, he was. He'll probably fall flat on his face."

Grim amusement twitched at the corners of Sarah's mouth. "Maybe the snow will wash the filth out of his beard."

Maggie laughed softly in wry satisfaction. Samantha giggled quietly and nudged her aunt's side.

A commotion near the cabins distracted Maggie from her brief mirth, and she turned to see Huntington engaged in a shouting match with his teamster, Poole. The other five men who were going to attempt the mountain crossing milled about to one side, and Maggie scowled when she saw Judd.

"You can't just go off and *leave* us!" Huntington exclaimed. He shook a threatening fist, his saturnine features twisted in rage. "I *need* you! Phillip is sick, and that leaves only me!"

As if to confirm his father's statement, Phillip collapsed in a fit of moist, hacking coughs. Alma put her arm around his shoulder and helped him sit on the ground. Maggie saw blood dribble from one corner of his mouth before he covered it with a handkerchief.

Elmore Poole, holding the bridle of his horse, gazed briefly at the young man, then returned his attention to Edgar Huntington. "I'm sorry for that, sir. But you hired me as a driver—not a nursemaid."

Huntington stared at the man through narrowed eyes. "Mr. Poole," he began, and his tone became deliberately patient, as if dealing with a cranky child. "Your official title may have been driver, but you have performed *many* tasks for me. If you go, *who* will chop firewood?"

Poole gave an impatient shake of his head. "You've got two arms and legs. *You* do it!"

Huntington sucked in his breath, incredulous. The muscles in his face twitched, tightened, and the veins in his neck swelled with anger. "You can't take your horse over the pass. At least leave *him!*"

Poole gaped at the older man, then waved a hand toward the cattle grazing near the cabin. "You got plenty."

Wiley Higgins adjusted his pack more comfortably on his back. "Come on, Elmore. We ain't got all day. You leavin' the horse or not?"

Indecisive, Poole let his gaze roam over the emigrants. The other men had already disposed of their mounts to the neediest; Pardee now had three fine horses to add to his own spivined mare. Poole's glance caught Maggie's for an instant, and he smiled shyly.

He walked the horse across the clearing and handed her the reins. "You might need him in the future, Maggie." And, doffing his hat awkwardly, he strode over to join the other men.

Maggie stared at the bay, her face pinched into a frown. Some token of remembrance, she thought testily. From her two former lovers, she was now the owner of two horses; Judd had left his roan gelding with her father earlier. Her lips thinned into a resentful line, and she swore silently.

All the emigrants had gathered to watch the men depart—all except Huntington, who had returned to his cabin, still unchinked to keep out drafts. Everyone was strangely silent as the little procession moved toward the head of the lake. Judd glanced once in Maggie's direction, but she turned her back on him.

Toby emerged from the woods, carrying an ax, the set-

223

ter trotting at his side. He came up quietly to stand beside Sarah and watched as the six men grew smaller in the distance.

Sarah turned and looked at him. "Why didn't you go with them?"

He shrugged and leaned on the ax handle, continuing to watch the disappearing figures. "I've got the hut all to myself now, anyway."

He felt Sarah's eyes still on him, but he refused to meet them. It was just as well those six were leaving, he thought as his gaze moved to the forbidding black clouds gathering to the west. Another storm was coming. They might scale the summit before it struck. Six healthy men had a chance—women and children wouldn't even get beyond the abandoned wagons.

A chilly wind caressed the back of his neck, and Toby shivered. By tonight or tomorrow, it would be snowing again. The thought drove a cold stab of fear between his shoulder blades. The last chance of escape was going with those men, and, with it, the last vestiges of hope.

He prayed they would make it and alert civilization of the thirty-odd people left in the mountains. And if they didn't make it . . .

Toby realized he had been holding his breath, and let it out through his teeth in a heavy-hearted sigh. At least their departure would be six less mouths to feed during the long winter ahead.

Chapter Thirteen

Maggie rolled over in her blankets and stared up at the darkened ceiling of the cabin. Katie slept quietly beside her, and across the room, Michael snored lustily. Outside, she could hear the soft plop of snow striking the canvas roof and the wind howling fiercely.

It had begun snowing shortly after dark, blowing down from the mountains with increasing fury, lashing the trees and frightening the cattle. Now it was worse, and the cold wind seeped through the cracks in the cabin walls and chilled Maggie to the bone. The fire in the hearth had gone out, but she was hesitant to get up to add more wood. Until she became accustomed to her surroundings, she was fearful she might step on one of her siblings in the dark.

Branches scraped against the walls, thunder rumbled in the distance. Maggie burrowed farther down into her quilts, trying to shut out the maddening noises. But *nothing* could dispel the image she had of Judd, somewhere up in the mountains, unprotected from the fury of the storm.

She was still hurt from his attitude, but worse than the hurt was the fear of being pregnant. It wasn't time to know yet, but now that he was gone and there was no one to turn to if she found herself in such a predicament, she was worried. Before, she had never given the possibility a second thought; but lying here, listening to the storm raging outside, the idea haunted her. She would never live down the shame, and her parents—devout Catholics that they were—would be completely unforgiving.

Shivering, she rolled over and buried her face in the pillow, praying that her worst fears were brought about only by the ferocious storm. But if Judd ever returned, she vowed to make amends with him, regardless of how she *really* felt about him.

Toby lay in the stupor of half-sleep, swathed in blankets near the dying embers of the fire. The wind shrieked outside and whistled through the cracks in the shanty, but something other than the storm had disturbed him. There was a scrape at the door, and Toby tried to sort out the meaning and source of the sound; a sound, he was sure, that was more than a branch snapping in the wind.

The flimsy wooden latch rattled. Toby threw off his covers and came up into a half-crouch in one fluid motion. Snatching up his rifle, he crept to the door. The latch shook again; this time the door pushed inward a little way, but it stuck on the few inches of snow that had blown in under the crack and piled up on the cabin floor.

Toby kicked at the little mound with his stockinged foot, grimacing at the cold. With one hand still holding the rifle, he pulled the door open cautiously.

His heart leaped into his throat, and he stepped back

quickly as a man tumbled inside and fell face down on the dirt floor. A frigid blast of wind and swirling snow swept in, hitting Toby like a splash of ice water. Still wary, but at least having determined the visitor was human and not a stray bear, Toby moved to close the door.

"Nooo!" The prostrate figure cried, scrambling to its feet. "My things are out there!" And the man darted outside.

Recognizing Lester Stone's somewhat nasal voice with its distinctive Pennsylvania twang, Toby expelled a trembling breath of relief and lowered his rifle. Groping in the dark for the lantern and fumbling with a match, Toby managed to get it lighted just as Lester stumbled back inside.

Yellow light flooded the room, and Toby gaped in wordless shock at the sight of the ice-bound wraith before him. Frozen snow clung to the man's clothing, matted his hair, and stuck to his eyebrows. Great clumps of dirty snow clotted his boots, and his face and hands were a bluish-purple. He collapsed onto the floor in front of the hearth, dazed and befuddled.

Toby shut the door and tossed several sticks of kindling onto the fire. Hetty had given him Roy's jug of whiskey, and he splashed a drop in a tin cup. Squatting down, he lifted Stone's head and managed to force some of the strong liquor down the man's throat. Stone blinked, and his eyes seemed to swim back into focus.

"What happened?" Toby asked. "Where are the others?"

Stone drank again and shook his head. "Up there." He made an ineffectual gesture with his hand toward the west wall of the shack. "I couldn't keep up." He slapped his foot against the floor to shake off the loose snow and

227

tugged at his boot. "It's awful up there. I didn't make it to the summit. I suppose *they* have by now. But it's blowing and snowing so bad—" The sentence died as he pulled off the other boot and tried to remove his sodden jacket.

Toby bent to pick up one of the two packs Stone had dragged in. "Are there dry clothes in here?"

"No!" Eyes flashing in panic, Stone spun around. Toby's gaze slid curiously over the bulging canvas pack, but he lowered it back to the floor, puzzled at its substantial weight. Stone managed an uneasy smile. "I didn't take no extra clothes with me." He got to his feet and carefully moved the packs into a corner, then bent to rummage through a small brassbound trunk for dry clothing.

Toby sat down near the fire and studied the other man with open suspicion. The floor was muddy now from the melted snow. "Why did you take such a heavy load with you?"

"Family keepsakes." Stone turned back to him and flashed him an unnaturally pleasant smile. "Things that belonged to my momma and the like. You know?"

Toby nodded, though he didn't believe a word of it. Stone was obviously hiding something, but at the moment, Toby didn't especially care. "Do you think the others will make it?"

Stone tugged a heavy sweater over his head. "Maybe. If they don't get lost." He unbuttoned his trousers and peeled them down over his skinny legs. "I only found my way back from the smell of woodsmoke." He shook out a blanket, wrapped it around his shoulders, and settled down with his back against his packs. "Good night."

Toby considered him dubiously. "Don't you want to sleep in front of the fire?"

Stone opened one eye and peered at him. "Don't want to get overheated. I'm fine right here."

Shaking his head in wonder, Toby blew out the lamp and found his way back to his pallet as the wind screamed outside the cabin.

Sarah opened her eyes to the murky darkness of the cabin and listened. The fierce winds of the night before had abated, and she could hear muffled voices outside. Shivering in her nightgown, she threw off her quilts and dressed quickly, adding as many layers of underwear as she could get on.

The fire had gone out, and she bent to relight it. Her whole body was quaking with the cold, and her teeth chattered.

A shrill scream from outside shattered her concentration, and she dropped the tin of matches. Hetty and the children popped up from their blankets with startled exclamations. Disregarding them and the scattered matches, Sarah stumbled across the floor and flung open the door.

She tripped in the three feet of snow that had piled up around the cabin and fell into a drift. Spluttering, she scrambled to her feet and staggered out into a sterile, snowy world of white. Snow blanketed the ground and nestled in the trees and was still falling.

It was Ruth Huntington who had screamed, and as Sarah slogged through the drifts to where a number of the emigrants were gathering, she saw the reason why. All but two oxen of the Huntingtons' fine herd of cattle had wandered off during the night.

Filled with a sudden, almost mindless terror, Sarah spun around to look for her own stock. She reeled back, covering her face and uttering a moan. Myrtle and Tillie were still tethered to the side of the cabin, but the three oxen and Toby's two mules had evidently chewed through their halters and were gone.

Sarah sank down in the snow on her knees, stifling her sobs with both hands pressed to her mouth as Hetty and the children tumbled out of the cabin. Too stunned to speak, they could only stare wordlessly at the dangling ends of the ropes.

All around, more of the emigrants were discovering the same thing: frightened by the storm, the cattle had panicked and strayed. Only a handful of the animals remained.

Judd had spent the entire night exposed to the fury of the storm, shelterless and exhausted from his climb to the summit. The men had tried to build a fire, but no one had knowledge of how to accomplish this in a raging wind and on top of eight feet of snow. He had sat huddled in his blanket against a tree, unable to sleep, unable to even *think* for the piercing cold penetrating every inch of his body.

Now, at dawn, the other four men were beginning to stir again. eating what little food they had, letting snow melt in their mouths to drink. Judd roused himself sufficiently to tear off a piece of jerked beef he had borrowed from Ole Andersen, but the salt stung the cracks in his lips. Wincing with pain, he ate anyway, letting his gaze roam around his surroundings.

The white cliffs looked the same in all directions— lonely, desolate, forsaken. There was snow everywhere as far as the eye could see, hiding the bases of giant pines and completely enveloping the younger trees. The jagged peaks in the vicinity of the summit were grouped in weird labyrinths, making the entire landscape look eerie and unreal.

Judd shuddered with a quick tremor of fear racing through his body. The emigrant trail was lost beneath tons of snow. They would become hopelessly lost if they went on. The snow was still falling, and Judd's feet were numbed with the cold and wet. Despair settled over him as palpable as the mantle of snow.

Canfield got to his feet and shook the flakes off him like some great, lumbering bear. His head swiveled around on its thick neck, his little eyes squinting against the glare of unbroken white.

"It's this way, I think," he said finally, pointing.

Wiley Higgins cackled irrationally. "You *think!*" And he laughed again.

Canfield glowered at the driver. "I *know!*" He made an abrupt, angry gesture. "Come on! Before it starts in again like it did last night."

Judd stowed away his few remaining ounces of meat and got wearily to his feet. Trent, cradling his roll of sketches wrapped in waterproof canvas, tottered unsteadily around in a circle and fell to the ground. Poole helped the artist to his feet, and as soon as Higgins was ready, they set off.

Canfield took the lead, but with each step he sank two or three feet into the loose, fresh snow. In a matter of minutes, he was panting and wheezing like a man on the verge of a heart attack and had to fall back. Poole took his place, plunging ahead in drifts to his knees. Judd followed the teamster's footprints, but even that was brutally hard work.

Higgins balked at taking the lead when his turn came, so Trent took over. But he was so light that the next man behind him had to break his own trail.

Judd staggered and fell. Snow sifted down his shirt and immediately melted with his body heat. Exhausted, his breath coming in short, strangled gasps, he lay there unable to rouse himself. They would all perish out here. It was impossible to walk in snow this deep, and already the flakes were coming down harder. Fear made his heart pound until he felt it would break through his rib cage, and he choked back a sob caught in his throat.

"Come on, Brannan!" Canfield growled. "Get up!"

Judd shook his head weakly. "I'm going back."

Canfield's mouth twisted into a malicious sneer. "What's the matter? Too much for a fancy-pants like you?"

A brief spark of anger flared in Judd's mind, and his gloved hand moved instinctively for his revolver. But he let his hand fall to the icy ground. His fingers were too numb to pull the trigger; besides, the barrel was probably packed with snow or the firing pin frozen. Fresh tears of frustration welled in his eyes, and the dismay threatened to completely overwhelm him.

"I'm with him." It was Higgins's squeaky voice, muffled by the increasing wind. "I'm going back, too."

Canfield's face turned a deep scarlet. "Why, you little—" Snorting in contempt, he glanced around at the others. "I thought you were all *men!* Seems I got a bunch of old women instead!"

Higgins glared at him sharply, his eyes narrowed. "Who do you think you are anyway, Canfield—God?" He hitched up his pack and looked coldly at the guide. "You're just a fat bully."

The veins in Canfield's neck swelled with anger, and he let out an enraged snarl. His hand snaked out and caught Higgins's collar in a tight grip. His lips curled back to bare his yellowed teeth, and his voice took on a low, threatening quality. "Don't you ever go callin' Red Canfield names again, or you won't live to even have the chance to regret it!"

Canfield gave a mighty shove. Higgins reeled back and went sprawling into the loose snow on the steep slope. He slid down several yards, trying frantically trying to grab onto anything within reach. But as his momentum increased, he tumbled wildly, rolling head over heels down the cliff.

Judd watched Higgins's unchecked descent in morbid fascination, listening to the teamster's tormented screams echoing off the canyon walls. Then there was utter silence, broken only by the fitful moaning of the wind through the trees.

Swallowing dryly, his hands trembling badly, Judd shouldered his pack. Without a glance at any of the others, he waded through the drifts, back toward the lake camp.

Maggie shuffled through the snow amid the thick stands of pine, clutching the collar of her brother's coat tightly to her throat. The raw wind stung her cheeks, and her hands were numb with the cold.

She paused to blow on them in an attempt to bring some feeling back, but her fingers seemed stiff beyond relief. For hours she—and everyone else—had been out combing the forests for the missing cattle. But it was as if the animals had simply disappeared off the face of the earth.

Shivering, Maggie forced herself to go on. It was better to keep moving than to stand still and let the wind and snow pelt her into complete immobility. Far off to her right, she could barely make out Sean's bright yellow scarf, and she felt slightly comforted knowing she was not alone.

Her foot caught on a root buried beneath the snow, and she toppled to the ground, slamming her shoulder into a hard drift. Her breath exploded in a rush of hot, foggy air, and she lay still for a moment, her eyes shining with tears of pain and frustration. Fat, lazy flakes struck her face, clinging to her eyelashes, melting on contact with her warm, rapid breath.

Disgusted, she put a hand out to push herself up. But instead of sinking inches into the fresh snow, she found a solid purchase to brace her weight. Faintly surprised, she settled into a sitting position and brushed some of the loose snow away. Frozen brown fur appeared, and as she shoveled the powder more frantically, the familiar markings of a cow began to emerge.

A cry of joy escaped her throat, and she scrambled to her feet. Cupping her hands to her mouth, she shouted to her brother. "Sean! I've found a cow! Come quick!"

By the time Sean had loped clumsily to her side, Maggie had managed to uncover more of the cow, and it was unmistakably one of their own. Maggie felt a sweeping sense of relief; at least, for the present, she wouldn't have to dine on one of the horses.

Lucas paused in his labor and leaned the shovel against the side of the cabin. The makeshift mittens his mother had fashioned for him from two pairs of socks secured with a leather thong at his wrist were coming loose again. Sighing irascibly, he walked down the slope and disappeared inside the shack.

The fire was burning down, and the boy added another log. Simon was fussing on one of the pallets, and when he spied his older brother, he broke forth with a lusty squall.

Frowning unhappily, Lucas tugged off the socks, laid them carefully on an upturned keg before the fire, and went to investigate his baby brother's complaint. It proved to be wet diapers.

"Why don't you learn to go like everybody else does?"

Simon stopped howling and stared curiously up at Lucas, then grinned, displaying several sprouting teeth. Unable to resist that smile, Lucas returned the grin and went to find clean linens.

His mother, Sarah, and Samantha had been gone most of the day, searching for the missing cattle. It was well past lunchtime, and Lucas was hungry. But his mother had cautioned him not to eat anything she didn't first consent to, so he had gone without.

All of the adults were out looking for the animals, leaving only Phillip Huntington and Orpha Jennings in camp with the children. For a time, Lucas had romped in the snow with Amos and Ben Pardee, Jamie O'Brian, and even Ephiram Jennings, but it was too cold. Besides, Hetty had told him to clear the doorway, and he had shoveled diligently off and on all day. There was now a ramp, of sorts, leading some four feet up out of the cabin to where the snow had piled up in drifts.

After changing Simon's diapers, Lucas poured himself a warm cup of melted snow water from the pan near the fire and one for his brother. He wished Simon could talk more; it was lonely here, hardly better than being by himself.

Hearing voices outside, he tugged the socks on his hands, fastened the thongs by holding one end in his teeth, and trudged outside into the bleak chill. Toby and Ole Andersen were emerging from the woods nearest the lake, leading a limping ox.

Lucas broke into a clumsy run, stumbling through the snow. "Is it one of ours, Mr. Garrett?"

Toby shook his head. "It's Mr. Andersen's."

Lucas's spirits plummeted. He knew how worried and upset his mother had been—as *all* the emigrants were.

"Now at least we have food for a little while," Ole said, glancing down at the boy. "Until your papa comes back with more, *ja?*"

Lucas nodded glumly and looked away. He squeezed his eyes shut tightly, hoping his tears didn't show. Where could his father possibly be? It had been over two weeks since he had left with Tyrrell. Why hadn't he returned? Was he stuck in the snow on the other side? Had he never even arrived at Sutter's? Or, as Lucas had heard a few of the emigrants whisper nastily, had he simply deserted his family?

Toby interrupted the boy's dismal thoughts by clapping a hand on his shoulder. "Have your mother and aunt been back?"

"Not since this morning."

Toby's mouth curved into a secret smile. "I'll bet you're hungry."

"Yes, sir."

From inside his jacket, Toby produced a little bit of brown fur and winked knowingly. "Squirrel stew. How

236

does that sound?''

Lucas grimaced, but at this point he thought he could eat most anything. He eyed the lifeless little creature skeptically, then shrugged.

Toby cleaned the squirrel, threw it in the kettle, and gave Lucas a few bites of dried jerky to chew. He moistened an ounce in water for Simon, and the child seemed to manage the meat perfectly well.

"As soon as I have the time, I'll make a cap for Simon out of this pelt," Toby said. "And one for you out of yesterday's possum," He reached out and flicked Lucas's earlobe. "Your ears are blue."

"They hurt, too.''

"It's the cold. That's why you need a cap." He pushed himself up from the table and donned his jacket. "I'll look for one more hour—then I'll start looking for your mother and aunt and sister. I think we're in for another big blow tonight.''

Lucas stood outside the cabin and watched until Toby had disappeared from sight. Beans loped out of the trees, wagging his tail, and leaped happily up on the boy to greet him. Lucas pushed him away.

"Stop it! You'll knock me down! And you stink like wet fur!''

The setter sat down in the snow and gazed sheepishly at the boy.

Patrick O'Brian came around the side of the cabin across the glade with an armload of kindling. Like Lucas, he had been watching the younger ones while the adults were out looking for the stock. The O'Brians' two mangy curs trotted at his side, and Beans sprinted across the snow, barking.

With a sigh, Lucas turned away. Phillip Huntington

was still working to fill in the cracks between the logs, but as Lucas looked on, the man suddenly keeled over in the snow. Alarmed, the boy slogged through the drifts toward the prostrate man, for he had heard his mother and aunt discussing his illness quietly between themselves in the past.

Lucas's jaw sagged, and he turned away, one hand cupped over his mouth. Phillip lay trembling on the ground near a steaming pool of bloody vomit. The breath rattled out of the man's throat in coarse, hollow gasps, and his face was the same color as the snow around him.

Unable to force himself to look at the vile, reeking mess, Lucas sidled around Phillip and lurched for the door to the Jennings half of the cabin. He pounded loudly, half-sobbing as he called for the Reverend's wife.

Orpha Jennings opened the door and scowled down at the boy. "I'm meditating—and so are my babies. Reflecting upon what sins we have committed that God has visited this catastrophe on us."

Lucas gesticulated helplessly. "It's Mr. Huntington, ma'am! He's sick!"

Orpha stepped outside, gaped at Phillip's form sprawled in the snow, and sucked in her breath, stunned. Hope and Ephiram tumbled out of the shack behind their mother, goggle-eyed and staring.

After a moment of brief confusion, Orpha swept through the snow and bent to touch Phillip's face. He moaned weakly, then seemed to fall back into a kind of stupor.

"Open the door to their side, Eph," she told her son, then turned to Lucas. "And you, boy. Grab his other arm and help me get him inside."

Swallowing his distaste, Lucas took hold of Phillip's

238

arm, keeping his eyes averted from the foul muck in the snow. Together, he and the woman dragged Phillip's unconscious body down the snow ramp and into the cabin. The fire had gone out, and it was cold. Crates, trunks, and furniture took up most of the available space in the cramped interior, and Lucas had to skirt piles of goods to reach the pallet. Grunting with the effort, he finally managed to get the man onto some bedding.

Orpha quickly covered him with blankets, while snapping orders to her two wide-eyed children. Ephiram threw some logs on the fire and searched for a match. Hope had wandered over to the cradle and was peering in at Ned.

"Mama, the baby ain't movin'."

Dropping Phillip's hand, Orpha hastened over to the cradle and picked up the infant. Clad only in a diaper, its flesh had a bluish tinge, and its head lolled listlessly to one side. Orpha cuddled him close to her breast, chafing some warmth back into the half-frozen little body, and muttering imprecations under her breath.

"Mister High-and-Mighty goin' off and leavin' a sick man to care for this poor babe!"

Lucas slipped quietly out the door and loped back to his own cabin, wishing his mother and sister and aunt would return quickly.

After a rather tasteless supper of squirrel stew thickened with a little flour, Sarah sat in the corner of the cabin with needle and thread, taking in a pair of Roy's trousers by the light of a lantern. It was not yet dark out, but the heavy clouds had completely blotted out the sun, and with the door shut, no light entered the hut. The wind

239

gusted savagely, rattling the walls and buffeting the hide roof.

Hetty and Toby sat at the table, discussing the possibilities for the future—a future Sarah shuddered to think about right now. The snow was falling heavily outside, and more snow meant a longer time before a thaw—if one indeed *ever* came.

She pushed these thoughts away and tried to concentrate on her alterations. Even pinned up, her skirts had proven too unwieldy in the snow today, and she had fallen often. Roy had left behind plenty of trousers and heavy shirts which she and Hetty could wear. Samantha had already donned a pair of Lucas's breeches.

A branch slapped against the rear of the cabin, and Simon began to cry. Hetty gathered him in her arms and rocked him while she continued to talk with Toby.

"I'm worried most about him," she said, smoothing Simon's blond hair off his forehead. "A baby needs more than meat."

Toby scrubbed a hand across his face and gazed moodily into the fire. "Meat's all we can get. And not much more of that—unless we uncover the oxen and mules buried out there somewhere in the snow. I've got a crock of wild honey in my things—I'll bring it over for the boy."

Hetty nodded her head absently, and a long, desolate sigh slipped from her. "I'm sorry we got you into this, Toby."

He shrugged off her apology. "It could be worse."

Could it? Sarah wondered dismally, and bit viciously into the thread to sever it. Myrtle had been slaughtered, and parts of her were stacked like cordwood outside the door to freeze and stay fresh in the snow. Toby had demurred at dealing out the same fate to Tillie right away; if there was a thaw, the meat would spoil.

Some of the other emigrants were in worse shape. Ten O'Brians had only a cow to feed them, unless they dispatched Judd's and Elmore's horses into the kettle. Poor Emmett Pardee had only one ox and one horse; the Andersens had one ox. Huntington had his two oxen, and Jennings had an ox and two mules. If you added the few horses Canfield and the others left behind, there was a little more. But *how long* would these few animals have to last?

Anxious and suddenly restless, Sarah rose and carried the trousers to the trunk. "There's quite a few wool shirts in here," she said to Toby. "You're welcome to them—might be a little tight in the shoulders, though."

Toby glanced up at her, and their eyes locked. Sarah saw a great sadness in them and something else she couldn't quite define.

A faint smile flickered on his lips. Then he got slowly to his feet. "I'll put out my traps tomorrow and hope for the best." His gaze lingered on Sarah a moment longer before he picked up his jacket and slipped out the door.

The cold went right through his clothing, chilling him raw, and the air was a frozen fog of darting ice-lances, pelting him in the face. Across the way, through the driving snow, he could barely make out the burly forms of Sean and Michael O'Brian burying their supply of meat.

Stumbling up the ramp, now filling fast with fresh snow, Toby paused to check the four ropes holding Tillie to the side of the cabin. They appeared secure, and, satisfied the cow couldn't chew through them, he bent into the wind and slogged back toward his own shanty.

Hetty and Sarah seemed aware of the need to be frugal

with the food, and he didn't want to caution them to the point of alarming them. They were still hopeful for the return of Roy and supplies; Toby was less confident. His own mind focused only on the burning necessity of conserving what little food they had. It might have to last until spring.

Fear crawled along his skin at the thought, but it was an undeniable fact. There could be no escape from these prison walls of snow—not until the weather calmed and the heavy drifts either melted or hardened enough to walk on them.

Nothing could afford to be wasted. Not bones, not entrails—nothing. The loss of the cattle had worsened the situation drastically, and Toby felt a sudden depression mixed with a black premonition that they would never leave here alive.

A shout, muffled by the wind, brought his head up sharply. Shielding his eyes against the squalling snow, he peered into the gloom and saw movement near the lake. He tried to run, but it was impossible in the soft drifts. But as he drew closer, he was able to discern the bulky shape of Red Canfield; others were struggling behind him, stumbling and reeling drunkenly in the loose powder.

"It's Canfield!" he shouted. "Canfield and the rest are back!"

In a matter of seconds, most of the emigrants had tumbled out of their cabins and gathered around the exhausted, half-frozen adventurers. Their clothing was soaked, ice clung to beards and hair; they seemed dazed and confused.

"Where's Higgins?" Jennings asked.

Canfield staggered and leaned heavily on the Reverend. "Dead. Fell over the cliff."

Poole's face twisted with rage. "You *killed* him!"

Canfield waved a disgusted hand in dismissal and tottered off toward his shanty.

Adam Trent was lying on the snow, blubbering like a baby. Inga Andersen bent over him and touched his face tenderly. Judd was stumbling around in circles, and Maggie caught his arms. He blinked and gazed blankly at her, almost *through* her.

"Judd darlin', it's me—Maggie. Don't ye recognize me?"

He stared at her with dilated, empty eyes and allowed himself to be led to the O'Brians' cabin.

Toby put an arm around Poole's shoulder and steadied him to walk to the shanty. The man trembled convulsively, and strange, gurgling sounds came from his throat.

Wind-whipped snow battered Toby as he shuffled through the drifts. A renewed terror had taken hold of him, and this time it wouldn't yield. Canfield's return had confirmed his worst fears: the Sierras couldn't be breached—even by six strong, healthy men.

They were trapped—hopelessly, irrevocably.

Chapter Fourteen

Sarah was nudged from a dreamless sleep by something unfamiliar worming its way into her consciousness. She lay curled in her blankets, staring at the gloomy interior of the cabin, trying to define what had disturbed her, aware of the bitter cold pervading the room. But there was something else—and as her mind came more fully awake, she realized what it was: Silence. Absolute, utter silence.

For the past two days and three nights, the wind had screamed around the cabin without mercy, and the snow had fallen relentlessly. She and the others had been virtual prisoners in their cabin, unable to venture out into the raging storm. Once—out of sheer desperation—Hetty had attempted to go out to dump the chamber pot, only to be driven back inside immediately by the gale-force winds and pounding snow. That was the last time any of them had attempted even to open the door.

Quietly, Sarah crept out of her blankets and donned two more of Roy's shirts and her shoes; for warmth, last night they had all slept in their clothing. It had been a nightmarish time, huddled together, listening to the banshee winds shrieking around the cabin walls and wondering if they would be buried alive.

They had played checkers by the light of the fire, careful to conserve their precious coal oil for the lamps. They had told stories, reminisced, speculated, and hoped for Roy. The final log had been added to the fire before bed, and the last bite of food consumed yesterday afternoon. The shack reeked of the unemptied pot, the musty, stale air, the setter's droppings in one corner—and of fear.

Sarah bent to lace up her shoes and felt a wave of dizziness wash over her. She sat down hard and waited until the vertigo passed. Gnawing pangs of hunger clawed at her stomach, and she longed for something to ease the emptiness. Even a cup of hot tea would suffice, but there was no fire to heat the water.

The sum and substance of the food she had eaten yesterday consisted of one pickle, tainted with fish reek—the trout had been devoured two days ago—a spoonful of beans, and another of molasses. There remained left perhaps a cupful of the beans and another two of rice—which Hetty was saving exclusively for Simon. If they couldn't dig up Myrtle's meat today . . . Sarah couldn't even complete the thought.

She got to her feet again, and the dog raised his head from his paws and gazed blandly at her for a moment. Creeping quietly to the door, she tugged tentatively on the latch. It squeaked on its hinges—taken from the tailgate of the wagon—and came slowly open. A small avalanche of snow tumbled in at her feet, and the setter growled at this strange intruder.

Picking up the shovel, Sarah stepped cautiously outside. The space Lucas had worked so hard to clear had filled back in, but beyond that, drifts of crisp, clean powder reached nearly to the rooftop. Sarah clambered up the bank, slipping and sliding, dragging the spade with her, until it at last she reached the top.

She lurched to her feet and gazed around in awe. A white carpet of snow covered everything but the tops of the cabins. It weighted down the branches of giant pines, completely obliterated others. Nothing stirred in that sterile silent world except the vapor mist of Sarah's breath.

Hesitantly, she lifted her eyes. The sun grazed the horizon to the east, and there was not a cloud to be seen; the high, blue sky seemed to go on forever.

Sarah gave a whoop of sheer joy and bent to call back into the cabin. "The sun's out, Hetty! Throw me the ax. I'll cut some wood, and you look for Myrtle!"

Three pale, pinched faces appeared at the open door and peered outside disbelievingly. Beans bounded up the bank, barking with glee, and loped over to the nearest tree to hike his leg. Samantha and Lucas squealed with the sudden joy of understanding and capered in the doorway.

At the sound of the first shout outside, Michael O'Brian pulled open the door. Sunlight streamed in, nearly blinding him. Dropping to his knees, he mumbled whispered thanks and crossed himself. Then Sean, Daniel, and Kelly scrambled outside behind their father, hauling hatchets and shovels with them.

Maggie blinked into the sun's brightness and watched the dust motes dance in the air. Beside her, Judd stirred in his blankets and sat up slowly, wiping the sleep from his eyes. Maggie turned her attention to him and was shocked at what she saw—the pallid, untidy ghost of the man who had once so captivated her heart and imagination. His eyes were swollen and red, his face stubbled with the dark growth of four days.

He had been trapped like the others inside the squalid hut since his return from the mountains. But *unlike* the others, he had sat in a kind of dazed stupor, rousing only occasionally—and that was to blubber and wail and bemoan his fate. His outbursts frightened the younger children, angered Michael, and disgusted Maggie.

The dapper, charming gentleman from Natchez had suddenly turned into a sniveling, whining milksop.

Now that the storm had passed, Maggie would be *more* than happy to see him return to his own cabin and take his self-pity with him.

Toby pulled on his heavy boots and glanced with disgust at his roommates. Stone snored peacefully near his mysterious, zealously guarded packs. Trent shivered in his thin blanket, and Poole was curled into a fetal position in one corner. Near the dead fire, Canfield rolled over and farted in his sleep.

Toby's lip curled in a sneer of utter contempt as he reached for his jacket. The cabin reeked of tobacco, stale whiskey, excrement, and urine. Poole had eaten some spoiled meat yesterday and vomited, adding *that* stench to the already overpowering fetor.

The failure to cross the mountains seemed to have snapped the last ounce of hope in both Poole and Trent. During the storm, they had sat listlessly, speaking little, sleeping a great deal, and neither terribly interested in food. It was as if they had lost the will to live, and if they didn't rally soon, Toby feared they never would.

Shouldering ax, rifle, and shovel, he flung open the door and climbed up the snowbank into the bright sunshine.

Sarah's muscles ached as she trudged back to the cabin—shoulders and arms from chopping wood, legs and thighs from wading through the snow. And for all her efforts, she had only enough kindling to get a fire started. But, despite her disappointment with her first attempts at becoming a logger, she felt a sense of well-being that had been conspicuously absent for the last few days. The woods were sparkling and clean, redolent with the scent of pine and clear mountain air. The sky was a beautiful blue canopy, newly washed from the storm, and the sun pleasantly warm.

As she emerged from the forest, she saw Samantha poking around in the drifts at the side of the cabin with a long pole. First she would plunge it deep into the snow, then withdraw it and examine its end critically. Puzzled at this peculiar ritual, Sarah paused with her armload of firewood.

"Take the ax," she said. "I'm afraid it'll fall and cut off my foot."

Samantha leaned her pole against the cabin and removed the hatchet. She eyed the wood skeptically. "That's not much."

"And I'm not Paul Bunyan." She arched a curious brow. "What are you doing?"

"Looking for Tillie. Mr. Garret put a nail on the end— see? And if it comes up with fur stuck to it"—she left the sentence trail with a sly grin—"saves us from digging up

249

the whole place.''

At the mention of Toby's name, Sarah felt a flush of pleasure warm her cheeks. She had missed him during the enforced isolation of the storm—missed his wry remarks, his rugged strength, the comfort of simply having a man around. And the emotion surprised her. She had not been prepared for anyone reaching her innermost feelings, yet slowly—without conscious thought—Toby Garrett was becoming an inescapable part of her life.

''He's smart,'' Samantha said, and thrust the pole into the snow once more.

''Yes,'' Sarah agreed, smiling softly. ''Yes, he is.''

She left her niece to her probing and continued around the side of the cabin. Snow flew through the air in all directions as Toby dug for Myrtle, and Hetty and Lucas cleared the ramp.

''Hey!'' she called. The shovels halted in midair, and three faces blinked up at her. ''If you'll give me a chance to get through, I'll light a fire.''

Hetty and Lucas stepped aside, and Sarah carefully made her way down the snow ramp and into the shack. She dumped the wood into the fireplace and set a match to the bundle of twigs she pulled from her pocket. In a few moments, a cheerful blaze was crackling in the hearth. Simon clapped his hands gleefully, barely visible beneath the layers of clothing and blankets surrounding him.

Taking the big kettle from its hook above the grate, Sarah returned outside to fill it with snow. Across the way, the younger O'Brians were building a snowman, and she noticed Lucas pausing in his labor to gaze longingly over at them. Smiling reflectively, Sarah carried the pot back inside to melt over the fire. At least they could have coffee to fill their empty bellies for the time being.

* * *

Toby ducked his head as he passed through the low doorway. Sarah was standing before the fire, warming her hands, and she turned at his entrance. Honey-gold hair swept below her shoulders in thick, cascading falls, and her cheeks held a rosy blush from the crisp air. Her breasts strained against the plaid wool of the shirt she wore, and the altered corduroy trousers defined her small waist and the softly rounded curves of her hips.

Toby's lips twisted into a wicked smile, and he gave her a humorous leer. "You should wear trousers more often."

She flashed him a faintly provocative look. "You think so?"

Grinning lewdly, he tossed Myrtle's frozen thigh onto the table and swept Sarah into his arms. His lips sought hers, and she responded warmly, sliding her arms about his neck and arching her body against his. He kissed her for a very long time, lazily savoring the taste of her lips, unwilling to let her go. His hands moved over her waist and hips to mold her closer to him, and despite his anxiety and fatigue, he ached with longing for her.

A soft cough from the doorway intruded on his fantasies, and he abruptly released Sarah. Turning, he saw Samantha standing just inside the portal, her head bowed in embarrassment. She peeked up sheepishly, then dropped her eyes again quickly, her cheeks coloring hotly. "I found Tillie."

"Did you leave the pole in the snow where she is?" Toby asked.

Samantha nodded, and her limp, dark pigtails bobbed slightly.

"I'll be out to dig her up in a minute."

The youngster lingered a moment longer, eyeing the pair curiously from under lowered lashes. Then she spun around, and, giggling softly, scampered back up the slope.

Toby's mouth twitched with amusement. "It seems we've provided her with her best source of entertainment in a long while." Turning back to Sarah, he offered her a broad white-toothed grin. "In another few years, you'll have to barge in on *her* and see how she likes it."

Sarah's smile faded, and her eyes clouded with worry. "If there *is* a time like that."

He shook his head in mock reproval and tilted her chin to look into his face. "There *will* be. Don't ever for a minute think there won't."

Sarah looked at him with hurt, frightened eyes. "But how long will two cows *last!*"

"As long as we make them. We'll get out."

Her mouth twisted with bitterness. *"When?"*

"When we can," he said gently, and caressed her cheek with the backs of his gloved fingers. "In the meantime, I think I'll go cut some more wood before I start digging up Tillie." He gave her another smile and turned to leave, calling back over his shoulder, "I'll probably need a saw. Tillie will be frozen solid. If you don't have one, borrow one."

"All of Roy's tools are right here. Anything you need."

This last was said to Toby's retreating back, and, with a sigh, Sarah turned back to the slab of meat on the table. Until it thawed, she could do nothing with it. And, smiling wistfully, she picked it up and dropped it into the pot of now-boiling water. "Good-bye, Myrtle."

252

She stared a moment into the cauldron, feeling the depression creep up on her again. She doubted she could endure another storm like the one just past—the lonely isolation, the howling winds that unsettled her nerves, the close confines of the dingy little cabin, the stench . . .

Thinking of this, she remembered the chamber pot and went to fetch it from the corner. Lucas could clean up after his dog, she decided, carrying the covered enamelware bowl up the ramp. And then there always were Simon's soiled diapers, and she wanted to take a bath, and . . .

A tiny mewling sound escaped from Sarah's throat, and she bit down on her knuckles. With a tremendous effort, she got herself under some kind of control. Toby said they would get out, and she had to *believe* that.

Picking up Lucas's spade, she carried the pot to the edge of the woods and dispatched a most disagreeable task. Perhaps Toby could build them a privy. No, she scolded herself. He had *enough* to do. Besides, who would venture out in the driving snow and freezing wind to use it?

When she returned to the front of the cabin, Ole and Peter Andersen were digging out of their side. And she was shocked to see Dulcy, the Huntingtons' maid, emerge with Inga and Astrid.

"She came to us late last night when the storm let up for a while," Inga explained.

"Why?" Hetty asked, confused.

Dulcy took a deep breath and plunged into her tale with relish. "Mista H.—he say there weren't enough food, an' he weren't gwine to waste it on a nigger." She twisted her apron in her hands in nervous agitation and let out a long sigh. " 'Sides, wid Mista Phillip daid, an'—"

Hetty's eyes widened in stunned disbelief. "Phillip's *dead?*"

The girl bobbed her head quickly. "Yassum. He die de fust night o' de storm. An' they couldn't take him out, an' Miz Ruth—she jes' sat holdin' dat daid man in her arms fer *two days!*" Dulcy's eyes rolled wildly in her dusky face, and she fluttered her hands helplessly. "It scairt me somepin' awful. An' de baby be mighty sick, an' Miz Alma half-crazy wid grief—" The girl broke off suddenly, as if she had run out of breath from this recital. She smacked a hand to her brow and groaned dramatically.

Sarah stared at the young black woman, trying to digest her account.

"We couldn't just leave her out in the cold," Inga said.

"No'm." Dulcy rolled her eyes again and peered at the faces surrounding her. "I went fust to de Reverend's, but he wouldn't let me in. Said dey was prayin' an' couldn't be disturbed."

"A true man of the cloth," Sarah remarked dryly, and she made a face as if she had swallowed something bitter.

Hetty patted Dulcy's shoulder sympathetically, then looked at Inga. "I'm sure we can manage to help you out with a little food for the girl. And Roy will be here soon—"

Sarah swung her gaze to the snow-packed ridges and forests of the mountains—a forbidding glacial barrier that seemed to mock the emigrants in their plight. A shudder ran through her, and she looked away, feeling helpless and insignificant.

The door to Huntington's cabin was pushed outward, and Edgar stumbled clumsily up the bank, carrying something wrapped in a blanket. Phillip, no doubt, Sarah reflected morosely. Poor, sickly frail Phillip, the only member of the family who seemed to have even the *slightest* spark of decency.

Sighing disconsolately, Sarah trudged back down into the cabin and put on the kettle for tea.

". . . and so Phillip Huntington reposes here forever-more."

Maggie pulled her shawl more closely about her shoulders as she half-listened to Reverend Jennings's words. His deep voice carried clearly in the still, crisp air, interrupted only occasionally by a sob or sniffle from the deceased's mother.

The emigrants were all gathered behind the Jennings-Huntington cabin, heads bowed, staring at the mound of snow beneath which Phillip rested. The elder Huntington stood solemnly, an air of lofty assurance in his bearing, no outward sign of grief evident in his haughty features. Alma looked dazed, as if she wasn't quite sure what was taking place.

"And our comrade will dine tonight in Paradise."

Maggie's brow creased into a frown of annoyance. At least the food was bound to be better—and certainly more plentiful—there, she mused testily. No flavorless ox stew at His table, and at the picture of platters of fresh bread and juicy roasts that suddenly danced before her eyes, Maggie's mouth began to water.

A little leftover dried ox meat was all she had consumed today—and for the last few days. It had taken her brothers some time to locate the frozen stack of meat from the cow they had slaughtered, and longer still to find the two horses. These had promptly been hauled back to their own shanties by Judd and Elmore, reclaiming the gifts they had bestowed on their former love.

Maggie's mouth twisted with bitterness, but her expression changed quickly to worry, and that worry set her stomach cramping again. Hopefully—if the weather held—tomorrow her father and brothers could go hunting, though their skills at this were less than proficient. Otherwise . . . She shuddered to think how long one cow would last a family of ten, especially with the hearty appetites of its men.

While Jennings continued to speak, Maggie let her eyes wander over the circle of emigrants. No one seemed to be listening to the last rites; all appeared lost in their own introspective thoughts, no doubt as grim as Maggie's own.

Hetty Coulter, looking drawn and haggard far beyond her years, kept glancing off toward the mountains, as if she expected at any minute to see Roy come galloping down the snowy slopes on a white charger, saddle bags overflowing with tasty morsels of food.

Emmett and Belle Pardee looked absolutely miserable, standing quietly with their three small children. Belle's black hair was uncombed and tangled about her face and shoulders, and she twisted her hands together fretfully. Emmett's bulk had shrunk in the last week, and he no longer seemed the robust, jovial blacksmith Maggie had known back on the plains.

Orpha Jennings stood ramrod straight, gazing proudly at her husband as he spoke. Clad all in black, she reminded Maggie of a crow. Ephiram and Hope glanced furtively at their father, as if they believed he might well be God himself.

Ole Andersen looked bored; once or twice, he stifled a

yawn. Dulcy's eyes—the whites so large in contrast to her complexion—wandered restlessly around her. She grinned vapidly, and Maggie wondered if she was quite all there.

Trent and Poole looked terrible. Unshaven, hollow-eyed, they stared at the mound of snow as if they expected to be the next to join Phillip. Judd looked little better. His clothing was rumpled and soiled, and he fidgeted nervously.

Maggie's lips spread into a tight, disdainful line. He had eaten the O'Brian's food during the storm; the least he could do would be to give them some of his horsemeat in return. No fine weddings for *him*, she thought derisively. He was weak and sniveling—not the kind of man to father the good, stout Irish stock of which the O'Brians were so proud. Thank heavens Maggie's fears of pregnancy had been unfounded.

Stone stood quietly, inspecting his fingernails. He had lost a little weight in his face, and the scar on his cheek was more pronounced, giving him an almost sinister appearance. His eyes darted over the others shyly, assessing them silently.

With a start, Maggie realized that the funeral had come to an end, and the emigrants were drifting away. She turned to follow her brothers when a hand clamped around her arm.

She whirled and found herself looking into the bearded, ruddy face of Red Canfield. His twisted smile more closely resembled a sneer, and Maggie couldn't suppress an involuntary shudder of disgust.

"Pretty boy's lost his appeal, eh?" he asked.

She tossed her head in annoyance. "What do you mean?"

Red inclined his head toward Judd, then resumed his appraisal of her. His pale blue eyes narrowed in a disquieting leer. "The gamblin' man."

Maggie tried to wrench free of his grasp, but his hand only increased its pressure on her arm. "Let me go!"

"In a minute," he said, and she nearly gagged at the fetid, whiskey-scented breath that assaulted her nostrils. "You'll be needing more than one cow to keep you all fed, Maggie." Open lust gleamed in his eyes as they roved over her body impudently, and Maggie felt her flesh shrink away from his gaze. "It'd be a shame to see that fine, smooth skin of yours waste away for lack of something to eat."

Maggie attempted to pull away again, but Red only cackled lasciviously and drew her closer to him.

"I've been wanting you since I first set eyes on you." His gloating gaze made another sweep of her figure, and a repulsive smile twisted his lips. "Remember that, Maggie. And if you're ever hungry, you know who you can come to—and what you have to do to get it."

Horror welled up inside her at the idea, and this time she managed to wrench away, stumbling backward in the snow. Her lips drew back in a grimace, and her green eyes blazed sparks of pure hatred at him. "I'll never be *that* hungry, Mr. Canfield."

Red threw back his head and snorted with malicious laughter. "We'll see, Maggie. We'll see. Remember—it's going to be a long, cold winter." Still chuckling lewdly, he turned and lumbered back to his cabin.

Maggie spun around and staggered after her brothers, waves of revulsion washing over her.

Chapter Fifteen

Roy scowled into the glass of whiskey on the table before him, as if both fascinated and repelled by its contents. A warm fire blazed in the hearth, while outside the rain beat down on the adobe buildings and the wind rattled the shutters. This was the third storm since his arrival at Sutter's fort, and—as he was learning all too well for himself by now—rain in the valley did indeed mean snow in the mountains.

Across the large plank table from him, Captain Sutter sat working on his account books and occasionally sipping from a glass of wine. Tyrrell hunched over a mug of hot rum, more interested in the Mexican serving girl than in the other two men at the table.

Thunder rumbled in the distance, and, wincing, Roy hastily downed the contents of his glass. He, Tyrrell, and a dozen Indians had returned late last night from their second attempt to recross the mountains—as futile a try as the first had been. And with this new storm . . . Roy cringed inwardly and refilled his glass.

"I need *white* men to go with me," he said, looking at

Sutter. "Not these half-witted Indians of yours."

The Swiss set aside his pen and regarded Roy steadily. "They're not half-witted."

Roy brushed the words aside with a wave of his hand. "Superstitious, then."

Sutter nodded. "They *are* that."

"Afraid of the mountains—or the snow. I haven't figured out which it is. Afraid to leave the mules behind when they can go no farther—afraid you'll punish them if one of the animals is lost."

Sutter smiled faintly. "They're very loyal."

"Where *are* all the white men?" Roy asked. "So far, I've seen very few around here. Surely there must be hunters and trappers—men who *know* these mountains."

Sutter poured more wine for himself and leaned back in his chair, steepling his fingers under his bewhiskered chin. "The war with Mexico hasn't been over for very long. Many of the men are down in Monterey trying to set up a government. We hope to become a state in the near future." He paused to take a sip of wine. "The other whites who live around here are mostly all up at Coloma. My partner, Mr. Marshall, and I are building a sawmill there. We'd like to get as much completed before the holidays as possible."

The holidays, Roy thought painfully. It was already November sixth—Samantha's birthday. And Hetty's twenty-seventh had passed unnoticed two weeks ago. Thanksgiving was just around the corner, and then Christmas. He felt helpless, emotionally drained. A month ago—a month that seemed a year—he had left them in Truckee Canyon. Were they still there?

Sutter was speaking again, jarring Roy out of his reverie. "There are men working on the mill who know the

260

mountains." The Swiss permitted himself a faint, reflective smile. "They would probably rather *be* in the mountains than working as laborers—except the pay is steady at the mill."

Sutter broke off as Conchita came into the room in a swirl of colorful skirts. Willowy yet buxom, she bent to stir the fire, her breasts nearly spilling over the top of her loose-fitting peasant blouse. Lifting the kettle, she refilled Tyrrell's mug with hot water and added two lumps of sugar.

She smiled shyly at the driver, then directed her gaze to her employer. "Anything else, *señor?*"

"Not tonight. Sleep well."

Inclining her head deferentially, she replaced the kettle and slipped out the door. Tyrrell followed her with his eyes until the latch clicked softly behind her, then reached for the bottle to add more rum to the steaming water.

"I'll write a letter to Mr. Marshall tonight explaining your situation," Sutter continued. "He can ask for volunteers, and I'm sure you'll have no trouble finding them."

Roy grunted doubtfully.

"They're all hard workers and good men," Sutter added. "A bit rowdy, perhaps." He shrugged. "You can ride up there tomorrow with my letter."

"How far is it?"

"Forty-five, fifty miles."

Another two days at least—in *this* weather, Roy thought dismally. And how many more to recruit the men, then to return here and outfit the expedition all over again?

He put a hand over his eyes and cursed softly, then swallowed the last of his whiskey. It burned his throat but couldn't blot out the pain. *When* would he see his family again?

Toby gazed dispassionately at the three men playing cards on an upturned cracker box in the flickering glow of lighted pine knots. Judd had seemed to rally from his lethargy in the last week, and he spent his time amusing himself with one of the several decks of cards he had in his possession. Now, however, the game was for more than entertainment. The stakes were food—a commodity more precious than gold.

At the mere thought of something to eat, Toby felt the familiar gnawing at his stomach. Since the snow had begun falling again in earnest yesterday morning, he had consumed only a piece of dried meat no larger than his finger; his supply was all over at the Coulters' cabin, and no one here would share. If the storm didn't let up by morning, he would have to make the trek some fifty yards to the other hut. He was already growing weaker, both from the scanty portions and the first stages of malnutrition. It wasn't exactly starvation yet, for there was food available to him with the Coulters. But a diet almost exclusively of lean meat was far from balanced.

Trying to divert his mind, he reached for the fox pelt and his needle and thread. Four days ago, he had been overjoyed to find an adult fox in one of his traps, and the meat had been suprisingly tender. But one fox was hardly an achievement for a man who prided himself on his cunning as a hunter. Pardee had bagged a wild turkey, and Toby suspected that Stone was eating rats to supplement his horsemeat.

Grimacing, he bent his attention to his project. Samantha had no warm clothing besides a light cape. While Lucas's things fit her, the boy had only one coat, and he wore that. Toby was making a vest from the fur so that Samantha could venture outside without half-freezing.

Judd laughed triumphantly and threw down his cards. "A half-pound from each of you," he said, gazing at Poole and Trent.

Toby thought Poole looked as if he might cry at any minute; Trent merely appeared resigned. Both men were going downhill rapidly, as if their failure to get over the mountains had taken away that extra spark of life essential to surviving.

Stone tossed another log on the fire, then settled back in his corner with his whittling. Toby was still curious about the packs he had guarded so secretively, but they were no longer inside the shanty; two days ago, Stone had buried them in the snow and marked the spot carefully.

Judd glanced around expectantly, a week's growth of black stubble on his cheeks, his eyes glittering from dark sockets. "Anyone else for cards?"

Canfield snorted and heaved himself up from his blankets. His beard was matted with filth; his uncut hair straggled into his eyes. "And watch you get fat while the rest of us waste away?" Cackling humorlessly, he lumbered over to the corner, unbuttoned his trousers, and relieved himself.

Shaking his head in disgust, Toby bent back to his fox pelt.

Ole Andersen sat by the fire, weaving lengths of rawhide back and forth between the sides of an oxbow. Since this most recent storm began, he had been working diligently in an attempt to keep his mind from thoughts of their pitifully meager supply of food.

He had carefully sawed the oxbows into strips to preserve their curved shape. Made of hickory, they were sturdy, and their form resembled closely enough the snowshoes he had worn back in Sweden. These makeshift shoes would be clumsy, to be sure, but infinitely more suited to walking on the deep powder than a booted foot. At least the next time he and Peter went out to chop wood, they would have some of their waning strength for the task at hand instead of wasting it tackling the heavy drifts.

Inga stirred the ox meat in the kettle and gazed dully at the rising steam. Astrid slept in her quilts, as she did most of the time. Peter sighed heavily and picked at a torn flap of material on his pants. Dulcy sat rocking on her haunches in a corner, her eyes glazed and staring, occasionally babbling incoherently. The girl's mind had snapped at the onslaught of this last storm. She had turned childish and fretful, often refusing the food offered her.

Frowning pensively, Ole slipped the rawhide through a groove cut into the wood and pulled it taut. His family was still hopeful for the return of Roy Coulter with supplies and help. He himself was no longer so sure.

Emmett Pardee tucked a blanket more snugly around Linus's little body. Eight months old, the child seldom moved, except to cry. Belle's milk had dried up a week ago, and the infant was fed a gruel made from water, sugar, and a little flour. His stomach seemed unable to tolerate the broth of horse meat, and he was growing thinner and paler each day.

Sighing disconsolately, Emmett shuffled back to his pallet and wrapped himself in his blankets, listening to the wind shrieking outside. Ben and Amos were quiet now, but they often cried dismally and asked for something to eat. And their pitiable pleas, in turn, would set Belle to weeping until the cabin fairly resounded with fits of sobbing.

The meat from Higgins's horse would not last forever, and what then? Emmett shuddered and closed his eyes.

Maggie huddled in the stench of the cabin, listening to the storm rage outside. The smells mingled—babies, sickness, and unwashed bodies—until she sometimes thought she would go mad from the confinement of the four walls. Jamie cried constantly, and during the night Kelly had come down with diarrhea. He was terribly weak, and either Daniel or Sean had to help him reach the open pit in the corner that served as a latrine; often he didn't make it in time.

A bough smacked into the side of the cabin, and Maggie winced, hunching down further into the quilt wrapped around her shoulders. Her mother's voice droned on in hushed tones, accompanied by the clicking of her rosary beads. When the storms were at their worst, Maggie had quickly come to realize the heightened religious fervor that seemed to possess the woman; on a clear day, all thoughts of God vanished summarily.

Outside, a wolf howled, and Michael's eyes riveted on the door. Today the wolves had been growing bolder, and Maggie heard them prowling ever closer to the cabin. Her father listened a moment longer, then relaxed and settled back against the wall to wait.

The meat from the cow had lasted exactly ten days, and now all that remained were bones bubbling in the pot—bones that had been boiled over and over again. They still exuded enough juice to flavor the water into a suggestion of soup. If drunk hot, it was slightly comforting but hardly nourishing.

For two days, Maggie had eaten little, and she sometimes felt she was on the verge of losing her sanity from hunger, cold, and despair. She tried to buoy her spirits with the vague hope that it would thaw soon and they could get over the pass. But even these thoughts were becoming increasingly hard to rely on. For now, if a spell of good weather *did* come, might they not be too weak to make the journey?

The O'Brians—once full of good cheer and vitality—now sat glumly in their noisome huddle of filth like condemned prisoners, held captive by a wall of snow and the threat of certain, eventual starvation.

Patrick lay curled up against the two dogs. Last night he had cried bitterly when his father had announced his intention of putting one of the pets into the stewpot. After much histrionics Michael had relented for one day—*if* he could shoot one of the prowling wolves.

He now suddenly came up out of his lethargic half-stupor and reached for his gun. Maggie's eyes went to the big man with the stringy, tangled reddish-brown hair. In even this short span of time, his woolen shirt seemed too large for the once-powerful torso and the seat of his pants drooped almost comically.

He glanced over his shoulder, his green eyes glittering in his pale, bearded face, and motioned them all to silence. "There be one out there," he whispered.

Maggie felt a thin shiver of fear run along her spine,

and a coldness gripped her belly. What if the wolves were as hungry as *she* was? There could be a hundred of them out there waiting—their fangs bared, saliva dripping from their snouts, jaws snapping in ravenous anticipation. Maggie pressed her knuckles to her mouth, her heart pounding furiously, suddenly so terrified from her own morbid imaginings she could hardly breathe.

She stifled a scream as her father flung open the door. He vanished from sight, and Maggie whimpered in utter panic. A shot shattered the silence, followed by a wild high-pitched yelp. And then she heard her father calling for Sean, and the young man scrambled outside.

Maggie stumbled to her feet and pressed herself against the wall, half-expecting at any moment the entire pack of rabid creatures to burst into the cabin and ravage them all. Instead, Sean reappeared, the wind whipping his rusty hair about his face, hauling a mangy gray carcass behind him.

Maggie felt herself go almost limp with relief when her father entered and slammed the door behind him. But in the next instant, a flood of revulsion washed over her as he fell upon the wolf with his knife and slashed the animal's throat. Snatching up a large mug, he held it beneath the pulsing flow of blood, then lifted the cup to his mouth and drank.

Maggie's stomach lurched, and she felt bile rising to her throat as she stared in wonder and disgust at the man she had known as her father—wild-eyed, haggard, blood dripping down his beard and laughing madly.

Chapter Sixteen

Toby let the ax drop to the snow and sat down on the trunk of a tree recently downed by the storm, its branches stripped for fuel. Cutting wood had become increasingly more difficult as he grew weaker; frequently, he was forced to pause to lean against a tree or sit down to regain some of his failing strength.

He looked at Sarah and gave her an apologetic, self-deprecating grin. "I must be getting old."

Sarah's face softened with compassion, and she stepped over the blanket containing the wood he had already cut. Together, they could haul the load back to the cabin and be assured of at least two days of warmth. She seated herself beside him, and the two of them sat in silence, contemplating the vast world of white all around them.

They had been here at the lake for just a little over a month. Today, Sarah reflected somewhat peevishly, was a good day—a day between storms. By now, she had become something of an expert at analyzing the weather. If the wind was from the south or west, soon the great clouds would move in, and there would be snow. These storms generally lasted a few days, followed by a spell of bitter cold. And as the sun gained strength, the snow became wet and consolidated. By then it was usually time for another storm to blow in.

This was one of the cold days, and Sarah shivered, pulling the piece of blanket closer around her head and shoulders. It was a poor excuse for a hood, but it helped keep her ears from aching. Roy's jacket hung on her frame, but it was warm. And every day it seemed she cinched the rope belt tighter around her waist.

She was losing weight at an alarming rate, as were all the emigrants. The meat from the two cows was almost gone—and just about every other scrap of food they had carried in the wagons. The Coulters had subsisted on the scantiest of rations, but they could stretch their supplies only for so long.

Still, they were better off than some, worse off than others. It was Simon she was most concerned about. Despite Hetty's tender ministrations, he was failing. His tiny hands grew thinner, his sad, pleading eyes sank deeper in their sockets, his face had become hollow, his voice faint.

Sarah released her breath in a long, disconsolate sigh, and Toby reached over and took her gloved hand in one of his. "Why such a big sigh?"

Her mouth twisted with bitter amusement. "Why not? Look at us!"

He exchanged a wry glance with her. "I guess we're not a very pretty sight, are we?"

She turned and looked at him. The deep tan he had first had in the desert had faded, and his skin was a pasty, sallow color. His face was drawn and cadaverous-looking, his blue eyes lost in dark hollows. Dejection showed in the slump of his shoulders and his downcast eyes. But at least his beard and hair were trimmed, and he was reasonably clean. Hetty insisted that they all stay as fresh as possible, and Sarah had to admit she felt it helped keep up their flagging spirits.

On sunny days, the bedding was aired, the clothing washed, and the cabin swept. At first it had seemed absurd, but it did indeed keep them busy and their minds occupied.

When Sarah had looked at herself in the mirror this morning—the first glimpse she had of herself in a week—she had been shocked. Her hair hung lank and dull around a face hardly recognizable. Her skin was stretched tight over the bones in her face. Her prominent cheekbones and the hollows beneath gave her a shadowy appearance; her teeth suddenly seemed too large for her mouth. Her wrists were bony, ribs clearly outlined beneath the flesh, and her hipbones jutted. The soft curves and firm muscles of a month ago had completely vanished.

"I suppose I should get back to work." Toby said. But he made no move to get up.

Sarah flicked a furtive, sidewise glance at him out of the corner of her eye. Besides all her other anxieties, she had not had her period. The thought that she might be carrying a baby in her starving condition alarmed her more than the fact itself. She barely got enough sustenance for herself, let alone a child.

She had intended to tell Toby, but, looking at him now, she decided against it. He had enough on his mind; she didn't want to add to his worries. And maybe she *wasn't* pregnant at all. Her body had altered drastically in the recent weeks. Her hair was dry and brittle, her fingernails cracked and soft, her skin was scaly, and her teeth sometimes ached. Elimination of waste varied from bouts of diarrhea to days of constipation. The lack of proper nourishment was gradually changing her in ways she could actually see; perhaps it was doing the same to functions inside her she could only guess at.

"Elmore's about done in," Toby said.

Strange, Sarah thought, how we just accept each other's approaching death like it was a quite ordinary occurrence. Although, in truth, it *was* quite ordinary. The Huntington baby had died, as had little Linus Pardee. Dulcy had been buried just before this last storm, and now Elmore Poole was succumbing.

"I think he just kind of gave up," Toby went on. "He seemed to lose hope and sicken. He just sits in his blankets in the corner, staring at the fire, not speaking. Trent and I've tried to give him some food, but he won't take it."

"And the rest of them over there?"

Toby shrugged. "Canfield's a lazy sonofabitch, but he's still the same. Stone seems fine. Trent and Brannan—" He shrugged again, then shook his head. "But they're all so dirty! The place is worse than a pigsty!"

"Maybe you should move in with us."

His eyes went over her slowly, sparkling with wicked mischief. "And have you tempting me all the time?"

Her lips curled in self-contempt, but her eyes danced playfully. "A bag of bones like me? I doubt I'd even tempt Red Canfield anymore."

"And I doubt I'd have the strength to do anything, anyway." Leaning close, he kissed her lightly. His lips were cold and dry, and Sarah felt that old familiar fear creep up on her once again. It was like kissing a corpse, and her depression came flooding back to engulf her.

Toby got slowly to his feet and picked up the ax. Ole had showed him how to make snowshoes, and they all had a pair now. At first, Sarah had balked at their use. She would sink deep into the loose snow, and it was difficult to lift her feet out. But with a little practice, she could now walk more easily—if not more awkwardly—than before.

A little farther away, Sean and Daniel O'Brian hacked pitifully at a tree. And farther still, Jennings labored to cut wood. The bases of the pines were under ten feet of snow, and sometimes, during a storm, Sarah expected to find the cabin completely buried. Fortunately, the brief thaws and the heat from the fire kept the drifts just below the roof.

"I checked the traps early this morning," Toby said. "As usual—nothing."

Sarah grunted unhappily and rose to gather the branches into the blanket. At the mere thought of food, her stomach cramped. She tried not to think about it, but the hunger was always there, gnawing away in the pit of her belly.

She glanced up and saw Maggie shuffling awkwardly toward her. Clad in a pair of Patrick's trousers and several of Kelly's shirts, she seemed to be lost inside the voluminous folds. Bright, coppery hair flew in loose tangles about her face—a face, Sarah saw, etched with tiny lines and shadowed by deep hollows.

"Da says he'll give ye his gold watch for a tot of your whiskey, Toby," she said, sinking down on the log.

"It's not my whiskey, it's Roy's. But he's welcome to a sip. I don't need a watch."

"It's for Kelly. He's ailin' again. We saved a bit of the

dog stew for him, but he can't keep it down."

Sarah felt a sudden chill of dread. If some unsuspecting animal didn't soon find its way into one of Toby's traps, Beans would have to be sacrificed. And more than the idea of eating dog—Sarah felt she could eat almost anything at this point—was the fear of what the loss of his pet would do to Lucas. He had held up well so far—as had Samantha—but the boy loved that dog.

"Orpha Jennings is sick, too," Maggie observed. "And little Ben Pardee."

"How's Kevin and Katie?" Sarah asked.

Maggie's thin shoulders lifted in a fatalistic shrug. "As well as can be expected. We've been eating bones."

Sarah considered the other woman doubtfully. "Bones?"

Maggie grinned craftily and winked. "If ye boil 'em long enough, they sort of fall apart, and ye can crunch 'em between your teeth."

Sarah frowned with disgust and turned to make a comment to Toby just as he swung the ax. The blade detached from the handle and went flying through the air and skittered into a snowbank. Toby swore angrily and, flinging the handle to the ground, slogged across the snow deeper into the trees after the broken piece.

Sarah sighed and glanced back at Maggie. "I guess this isn't such a good day, after all."

"*Good?*" Maggie threw up her hands and gave a tight, mirthless laugh. "There hasn't been one good day since we came to this horrible place! Me family would have been better off to stay back in Ireland, I'm thinkin'. Eating rotted potatoes would be better than eatin' nothing at all!" Her brief tirade evidently spent for the moment, she cocked her head to one side and studied Sarah, green eyes glittering wildly in almost a suggestion of madness. "I

274

been dreamin' of the little bit of time we spent in St. Louis—and the restaurants we ate at. Why, at the River House, they served the best—"

Sarah held up a hand to interrupt. "Please don't, Maggie. I can't bear to think of food. It only makes it worse."

Maggie lowered her head in mute acquiescence, as if knowing the truth in Sarah's words but unable to restrain her thoughts. A biting gust of wind caught her reddish-gold hair and tossed it riotously about her face. The loss of weight seemed far more pronounced on Maggie, especially on her uncovered hands. They looked almost skeletal, with long, bony fingers and wrists that appeared they might break through the thin parchment skin covering them. And Maggie was a much smaller and more delicate woman than Sarah. In another week or two, would *she* look as bad?

Toby crept up beside Sarah, holding his finger to his lips in warning for silence. "There's a bear in there," he said quietly, gesturing behind him to the woods.

Sarah's heart began to hammer with a mixture of apprehension and excitement. "How do you know?"

"Fresh droppings and tracks." He picked up his rifle and powder and handed her the axe blade. "I'm going in after him."

"Alone?"

A wry smile twisted his lips. "I'll do much better alone than with a whole crowd with me." His gaze shifted to Maggie. "Please don't tell anyone. If they *all* come in after him, they'll frighten him away."

Maggie nodded, though she, too, was clearly excited at this new prospect.

Sarah searched his face with anxious concern. "Be

careful, Toby.''

"I've shot bears before.''

"In the condition you're in *now?*''

He shrugged. "The bear's probably just as hungry as I am.'' He reached out and squeezed her arm gently, then turned and shuffled back into the trees.

Sarah watched him for a moment, a vague worry flaring in her mind. She turned back to Maggie and shrugged helplessly. "If you'll give me a hand taking this wood in, I'll get you the whiskey for Kelly.''

For a moment, Sarah wasn't certain Maggie had heard; she was staring into the woods, her eyes hooded and distant, a dreamy little smile on her pale lips. But then she pulled herself to her feet and gathered up two corners of the blanket. Sarah tucked the parts of the broken ax in her belt and picked up the other corners.

"Bear meat would be quite a treat,'' Maggie observed.

"I've never eaten any.''

"Neither have I. But I'm thinkin' it's *bound* to be better than bones!''

Sarah nodded, her concentration focused on navigating through the snow. The load of wood was lighter than that which she and Toby usually carried, but she could already feel the weight of fatigue dragging at her legs. The cold air hurt her lungs, and her labored breaths turned to vapor clouds before her. Leading the way, she stumbled down the snow ramp and let the bundle of wood fall to the cabin floor.

Breathing heavily, she leaned against the wall, trying to regain some semblance of control over her heartbeat and trembling limbs. Equally exhausted, Maggie slumped onto one of the pallets, her coppery hair falling in tangled disarray about her face, her shoulders heaving.

"Close the door," Hetty said sharply.

Sarah reached behind her and slammed the door. Hetty was drying Simon before the fire, scrubbing his skin until it glowed pink. At the sight of the wasted little body, a wave of sorrow swept through Sarah.

"We should do that for Kevin and Katie, I suppose," Maggie said dully. "Especially Kevin—he's got a rash." Her voice was weary with regret. "Ma and I don't get him changed as often as we should."

Sarah pushed away from the wall and went to fetch the jug of whiskey. Evidently Hetty was in one of her silent moods today, for she didn't bother to comment on Maggie's statement. Hetty's attitudes were often unpredictible, ranging from abandoned gaiety to ugly unpleasantness. Sometimes she would laugh uncontrollably at nothing; other times she would burst into tears; still others she would rant angrily and bemoan their fate.

Sarah took the cup of whiskey and slipped back out the door with Maggie. When Hetty was in one of these moods, Sarah found it best to leave the woman alone. Where Sam and Lucas were, she had no idea. Most likely visiting or gathering pine knots for light.

"Ma's like that, too," Maggie remarked.

Sarah answered with a noncommittal grunt.

"Your place is so *clean* compared to ours," Maggie went on. " 'Course, you've got less people, but still—" In the distance, she noticed Red Canfield emerging from his hut, and her eyes darkened. "I suppose Mr. Canfield still has food. Feedin' only one, that is."

"I suppose. Why?"

Maggie shrugged indifferently, but she pursed her lips in thought. "No reason."

* * *

Hetty finished dressing Simon in clean, warm clothing and placed him on the pallet with Sam's old doll. The soiled clothes she put in a pile to be washed later with her other children's things, once they came in for their sponge baths.

From the small supply of food remaining, she put a pinch of sugar and rice in a cup with some warm broth and gave it to Simon. He drank it happily enough, but obviously the child needed more nourishment than he was receiving. Except for old Ezra Weeks and Phillip Huntington, the youngest children seemed to be affected first. The thought sent a new band of fear to tighten around Hetty's heart, and she sat down at the table, feeling a terrible sense of rage and helplessness.

Sam and Lucas were getting so thin, and now with the last of Tillie just about gone . . . She released her breath in a long, heartsick sigh and gazed glumly about her. Boxes and trunks were piled willy-nilly about the place, as well as wagon parts, a few small pieces of furniture, and Roy's toolbox.

She rubbed nervously at her mouth with the back of a thin, callused hand, her eyes troubled and uneasy. Where *was* Roy?

Had something happened to him crossing the mountains? Perhaps he had been set upon by Indians or attacked by a wild animal. Hetty had heard the malicious whispers of some of the other emigrants: Roy Coulter had abandoned his family for the riches of California. It was said a man could make a fortune there, and there were plenty of pretty, available Mexican girls to warm his bed at night.

Hetty turned her thoughts resolutely away from the sordid rumors, as she did everytime they crept into her mind. That's why she visited the other cabins less than before—to avoid the sly, suspicious looks and raised eyebrows. Roy loved her—had always loved her since they were children growing up in the same little town together. He had married her when she was not quite sixteen and he barely twenty. They had been happy together. Surely he wouldn't throw it all away!

The corners of her mouth quivered slightly, but she fought back the tears. Perhaps Captain Sutter had refused Jennings's note of credit. Roy had not taken much money with him; their small savings were in the trunk. He might have had to work to get the supplies to return over the mountains. So *many* things could have gone wrong, and Hetty was left with nothing but a host of horrible possibilities.

She tried to blink the stinging tears from her eyes, but this time she failed. A choked, wretched sob caught in her throat, and she lay her head in her arms on the table, letting the flood of hot, bitter tears overtake her.

Toby slogged through the forest, following the trail of the bear. The excessive labor of moving the unwieldy snowshoes through the slushy, yielding powder sapped his strength, and often he had to pause to catch his breath. He was weaker than he had imagined; this foray farther afield than he had been in some time was proof of that. The rifle seemed like a fifty-pound iron bar in his hands, his muscles felt like jelly, and waves of dizziness washed over him from time to time.

Still, he *had* to go on. The bear was not very big—he

279

could tell by the tracks. But even that image turned his vague worry into ill-concealed anxiety. However, it also spurred him on. Three hundred or more pounds of bear meat would be a godsend. But there was still the unhappy prospect that the animal might be vicious. He was obviously hungry; otherwise, he would be hibernating with his fellows. And a hungry bear was a dangerous bear.

Pushing his fears aside, Toby drew a deep breath of frigid air and moved on. He staggered clumsily, and the wet snow clung in clumps to his snowshoes. The mantled branches of the trees hung low with the weight of the snow on them, and miniature avalanches cascaded from them whenever he brushed against them.

Then he saw him—thirty yards ahead between a stand of pines. Toby's heart leaped into his throat, and he fell back a step. The bear was larger than he had anticipated—a great black furry beast—reaching to scavenge from the branches of a tree, oblivious to all but his quest for food.

Excitement firing his blood, Toby assessed the situation with practiced care. In his debilitated state, he doubted he could hit the animal from this distance. Spying a group of saplings another ten yards ahead, he crept forward cautiously, cursing the cumbersome snowshoes and his faintness. Sweat beaded and ran into his eyes, and he was certain the bear could hear his ragged breathing.

The animal turned just as Toby dropped to a crouch behind the trees. His vision blurred briefly, and his head throbbed, and for a moment he was afraid he might pass out. But he couldn't, and, with a tremendous effort, he forced his mind and body back into control once more.

Warily, he lifted his head and peered through the branches. The bear had dropped to all fours, its head raised, and was sniffing the air. Toby froze as the great furry head swung in his direction, and he had to fight the urge to turn and run. One shot was all he would have. One shot was the only thing between him and certain death. If he missed or merely wounded the bear, he doubted he would have time to reload. And in his vulnerable condition, encumbered by the snowshoes and slushy powder, he could never hope to outrun the creature.

Evidently satisfied for the time being, the bear lumbered to another tree and rose up on his hind legs to rub his back against the bark. Toby slowly brought the rifle to his shoulder and sighted down the barrel.

The gun wavered crazily in his trembling hands. He closed his eyes and inhaled sharply, commanding his languorous muscles to work. After a moment, he exhaled a cloud of mist and took careful aim once more. The barrel swayed unsteadily again.

Nearly sobbing with angry frustration, Toby moved slightly to one side and slipped the barrel between the crotch of two branches. This time the rifle held steady, and Toby squeezed the trigger gently.

The shot exploded in an earsplitting crack; the smell of gunpowder made Toby choke. The bear reeled backward, struck the tree, and fell heavily to the ground.

Toby got shakily to his feet, his heart hammering in his chest, and stared with disbelieving joy at the prostrate bear. But as he looked on, his triumph turned quickly to fear. In one surprisingly swift motion, the bear rolled over and was on his feet.

Blood glistened on the animal's right shoulder and

dripped into the snow. Toby snatched up the rifle and fumbled for more powder and shot, but his gloved hands worked too slowly, and the bear was advancing on him.

Casting aside the powder horn with a disgusted grunt, Toby unsheathed his knife and held it poised for battle. Always an agile and accomplished fighter with a blade, Toby suddenly let out a bitter, mirthless laugh. Hampered by the snowshoes and as weak as a kitten, how could he possibly expect to fend off a bear twice his size?

Eyes wild, saliva dripping from its muzzle, the animal charged. Toby leaped to one side, stumbling in the snow. The bear crashed into a deep drift at the base of a pine and sat for a moment, stunned.

Encouraged by the flow of blood darkening the snow, Toby scrambled to his feet. And as the bear wallowed and turned, Toby threw the knife. It glinted briefly in the filtered sunlight, then disappeared in the animal's left eye. The bear shrieked, reared up on his hind legs, and batted frantically at the knife.

Toby lunged forward and swung the butt of his rifle like a club. It struck the bear on the side of the head with a sickening thud. The animal fell heavily, and Toby slammed the rifle into him once more. Wood splintered, and the gun shattered.

Toby stumbled backward and fell in the snow, still clutching the broken barrel. He sat still, breathing heavily, his gaze alertly intent upon the bear. His muscles twitched spasmodically, and waves of weakness washed over him. If the bear got up and came after him again, he didn't think he would have the strength to move. He was totally drained both physically and mentally, and he welcomed the lethargy that overtook him suddenly.

The bear stirred once, then lay still. Toby felt a shudder of relief pass through him, and he let the metal barrel fall from his hands. His head slumped forward onto his chest, and he allowed himself the luxury of giving into his fatigue and depletion

He sat there in the snow for some time, completely exhausted, until the melting snow soaking his trousers penetrated his numbed flesh. Rising to his feet unsteadily, he gazed at the bloodstained black fur, suddenly overwhelmed by the enormity of what he had done. More than that was the problem of getting the carcass back to the lake camp.

With laborious effort, Toby slogged over to the stand of saplings to retrieve his powder horn and turned to trudge wearily back to the cabins.

The late afternoon shadows were falling as the men worked over the bear outside the Coulters' cabin. A cold wind had sprung up, and the temperature had dropped considerably. Maggie drew a blanket about her shoulders more closely and directed her gaze toward the west—still cloudless—with a silent word of thanks.

And more than the clear weather, she was thankful for Toby Garrett. For the time being, the O'Brians would have meat again.

Sean, her father, Ole Andersen, and Emmett Pardee had returned to the woods with Toby, armed with stout ropes and a piece of wagon siding. Using the boards as a makeshift sled, they had lashed the carcass onto it and dragged the bear back to camp. For this help, Toby had promised each of the men a generous portion of the

283

meat.

Maggie's gaze moved to Toby now, dressed in dry clothing and sitting by the cabin door. His head was bowed and his shoulders hunched, and he shivered. The two treks into the forest and his bout with the bear had obviously taken a lot out of him. Sarah stood by his side, occasionally speaking quietly to him or refilling his cup with hot, weak tea.

Maggie's mouth curled with resentment. It would be nice to have a strong man to lean on or to give comfort to when he needed it. What did she have—for all her scheming and seductive ways?

Just as these thoughts entered her mind, Judd broke away from the group watching the slaughter and came toward her. His clothes were torn and filthy and hung loosely on his frame. Shaggy black hair straggled over his eyes, and his beard was matted and mangy. His shoulders were stooped, and he shuffled like an old man when he walked.

He smiled in a poor imitation of his once-disarming self. With revulsion, Maggie saw how yellowed his teeth were.

"How are you, Maggie?"

She lifted her shoulders lightly. "How do I *look?*"

Wry amusement glittered in his dark eyes. "Like a red-haired scarecrow."

Maggie pursed her lips in annoyance and ran a critical eye over his greasy shirt, food-spotted vest, and the seam torn out in one armpit of his frock coat. She regarded him with scarcely veiled contempt. "Have ye taken a good look at yourself lately?"

He shrugged negligently and cocked his head to one side to look candidly at her. "I've been thinking a lot about us lately—about what we had together."

Her eyes flickered with suspicion. "And what might that have been?"

He shifted his weight and managed a quick, tight smile. "I was thinking—when we get out of here—we ought to get married."

She stared at him in shock. Only with the greatest effort did she keep her jaw from sagging as her mind attempted to absorb this incredible statement. Three months ago, she would have wept with joy. But now she was filled with all kinds of questions and misgivings, and she eyed him doubtfully. Judd had already shown his true colors. If she *were* to marry him, she could picture quite vividly the life ahead of her. *She* would do all the work, have the babies, clean the house, do the cooking. Mrs. Judd Brannan—resident scullery maid and wet nurse. Her lips stretched into a grimace that wasn't mirth, and she shuddered.

"In fact," he went on, snapping her out of her reverie, "maybe Reverend Jennings could even marry us now."

Amused at this idea, Maggie fluffed her limp hair and struck a pose. "The lovely bride—ninety pounds of marital bliss."

Judd offered her his most engaging smile. "At least the most beautiful bride in camp."

"At least."

His eyes narrowed speculatively, and he cast a sly, furtive glance at her. "And you know—married folks share."

Maggie shot him a coldly suspicious look. "Share what?"

He shrugged nonchalantly, but gestured toward the carcass of the bear. "Food, for instance."

A hot flash of bitter anger swept through her, and she trembled with sudden, overwhelming rage. Her cheeks flushed bright crimson, and she turned slowly and deliberately to face him. Her mouth opened, but no sound came out. Unable to speak, she could only stare hatefully at him before she turned, and, presenting her back to him, marched back to her cabin with all the dignity she could muster.

Tears of rage and humiliation sprang to her eyes, but she fought them back. Judd Brannan wasn't worth the energy of crying over. Let him go back to his squalid little hovel and starve. And she hoped it would be a slow, painful death, so that all that was left to bury would be a shriveled, fleshless skeleton.

She turned back to see what had become of him, and a deep, disturbed frown cut a furrow in her brow when she saw Red Canfield shambling toward her. She sighed impatiently, and her mouth thinned into a tight line. Even *he* was getting thinner and—if it was possible—more slovenly.

Maggie looked at him with weary indifference. "And what can I be doin' for you today, Mr. Canfield? If it's bear meat ye want, ye can be turnin' around and goin' right back where ye came from."

He showed his palms in a gesture of mock innocence and clucked his tongue. "Ah, Maggie. Why do you always think the worst of old Red?"

She scowled intensely at him. "I didn't know there was any *other* way to think of you."

He looked her over with a faintly insolent grin. "I just thought I'd congratulate you on falling heiress to the bear meat. But just remember"—he paused to moisten his lips, and his pale, watery eyes assessed her once again

286

—"I'm *still* the man you come see when that bear meat is gone."

Frowning with distaste, Maggie glared at him a moment longer in silent defiance, then turned and disappeared into the cabin.

Red chuckled with smug contentment and ambled over to the group avidly watching the slaughter. Even in his half-starved state, he wanted Maggie. And would continue to want her until he was too weak to rouse from his blankets. He *would* have her before this was through— even if it was the last thing he ever did in his life.

Edgar Huntington stood at the fringe of the gathering, seemingly no less humbled for the loss of his son and grandson. Though his clothing was still by far the best of all the emigrants, it was now soiled and rumpled. His hair straggled out from beneath his beaver hat in lank, oily strands, and his cheeks were drawn and shadowed. Still, Red thought scornfully, he hadn't changed. His bearing, his every word and gesture seemed calculated to impart a sense of his own consequence.

"I believe we should *all* be entitled to a share of that meat," he said, eyeing the others circumspectly. "After all, we're all here in the same predicament."

Emmett Pardee glanced up, his arms bloodied from the elbows down, and looked coldly at the merchant. "Those weren't your sentiments back on the desert when *I* needed water."

Huntington raised a haughty brow and sniffed disapprovingly. "That was different."

Emmett grinned humorlessly beneath his beard and shook his head. "I figured you'd say somethin' like that." He bent back to his work, making a vicious slash in the bear's belly with his knife.

287

Huntington flushed slightly but remained controlled. "I thought we were all a democratic, fair-minded little society here."

"With *you* as our president," Emmett said, and his eyes crinkled with wry amusement. "I don't know how old Jimmy Polk would like that—you movin' in on his job."

Huntington's mouth tightened, and he looked imploringly toward Toby. "Mr. Garrett, surely you—"

Toby cut him short with an upraised hand and fixed him with a jaundiced eye. "I don't want to hear it, Mr. Huntington."

"But—"

Toby's mouth twisted in an ironic smile. "I remember a time in Truckee Canyon when you refused to lend Mrs. Coulter your extra oxen. Well . . . you kept those oxen, and where are they now?" He gestured expansively with his tin cup. *"Buried* out there somewhere." His blue eyes fixed hard on the older man, and his lips curled in disdain. "If you're hungry—start digging."

Huntington spread his hands in plaintive appeal and shook his head distractedly. "My son has died—and *his* son. My wife and daughter-in-law are broken-hearted. Doesn't anyone *care?"*

Ole Andersen shot him a quick, shrewd glance. "Did you care when you threw your little maid out into the storm?"

Huntington took a handkerchief from his pocket and dabbed agitatedly at his cheeks and forehead, his eyes shifting nervously around him, and for the first time, the man's regal composure crumbled into unconcealed alarm. "But we're running out of food! Think of us—a family who has already lost two of its beloved mem-

288

bers!''

Canfield's lips curled into a sly, sinister smile. ''If you're so hungry—why don't you eat *them?*'' And, chuckling maliciously, he sauntered back to his shanty, leaving Edgar Huntington still spluttering in distressed befuddlement.

Chapter Seventeen

Roy floundered through the deep snow under the weight of his heavy pack, breaking a trail with the eight other men. But the supposedly well-planned relief party was degenerating quickly into a battle of wills: Roy, who wanted so desperately to go on; and Emil Lebec, who was all for turning back.

Yesterday they had reached Bear Valley—Roy's third visit so far—and had gazed up at the precipitous, snow-packed slope to Emigrant Gap. It had been an awesome sight, with uninterrupted expanses of white; enveloping cliffs and forests, filling gorges and ravines. Emil had wanted to turn back then, but Roy's persuasive arguments had prevailed.

Now, however, the situation was changing again. They had reached a lake near the headwaters of the Yuba River, and the men had all but come to a halt. Some sought shelter beneath the pines, others were building a fire on which to cook a meal—a meal, Roy reflected ruefully, unlike any other Thanksgiving past, without family and friends to share.

Emil Lebec was a Canadian trapper who had come to California several years ago and had volunteered at Sutter's sawmill. He was small and slight with hard features and bulging black eyes. And now, as he shuffled through the snow in his heavy jacket and flamboyant red wool stocking cap, Roy was reminded of a weasel.

"It's impossible, *Monsieur* Coulter!" he exclaimed, flinging out an arm expansively. "It is suicide!"

"We *can* make it! You've been in these mountains in winter before."

The Frenchman nodded absently, his eyes half-closed. "That is so. But that was for a purpose for my *own* benefit—fox pelts. And even then, I nearly didn't escape with my life. This time, I might not be so lucky." His shrug was expressive. "I'm risking my life for what?" He lifted his hands in mock defense and turned to make his way back to the fire.

Roy stared incredulously after the little man, numb with shock and disbelief. He had *volunteered,* and now . . .

Sudden rage all but choking him, Roy shuffled clumsily after him. "When you agreed to lead us, you knew the situation!"

The Frenchman turned, smiled unctuously, and offered Roy a cup of coffee. "But I did *not* know how much it had snowed this early in the season."

Roy ignored the proffered cup, barely able to control the anger and pain that trembled through him. "I'll pay you!" His eyes went over the other men, a pleading grimace on his face. "Pay you all!"

Charlie Shaw, a burly, heavily-jowled millwright, gave Roy a significant glance. "We don't know *you*. For all we know, you could be a penniless beggar."

292

Dumbfounded, Roy turned to Tyrrell. "Tell them, Claude! I may not be rich, but I can at least guarantee them *some* money!"

Tyrrell seemed to hunch farther down into his jacket and stared into the fire. "I think Emil's right, Roy." His voice was almost apologetic. "It *is* suicide to go into the mountains any farther. How do we know—" He broke off, glanced briefly at Roy, then looked away again. "How do we know they're even still alive?"

Roy stared at Tyrrell with a bewildered frown and shook his head, fighting to maintain his self-control. He cursed softly in bitter frustration and walked several paces away. When he turned back to the men, his face was filled with an expression of total dismay. "Then that's it. You're quitting. Giving up."

No one met his eyes, and Roy's shoulders slumped in defeated resignation. He slogged over to the river, covered with a thin layer of ice, and stared unseeing at it. His thoughts raced wildly, and he was suddenly assailed by a storm of doubts. Did he *dare* try to go on alone? And if he did and found the emigrants eventually, what good would he be to them? If he had calculated correctly, they all had plenty of food from the cattle to last them. But *he* would only add another mouth to feed, and that could prove to be an added hardship that might well spell disaster.

Overwhelmed by a sense of futility, he felt a presence at his side and turned his head to meet the kindly eyes of Lachlan McTavish. He was a middle-aged man with a paunch, but powerfully built. Thick-necked and ruggedly handsome with a flowing brown beard, he had been one of Sutter's foremen at the Coloma mill and the first to offer his help. A quiet, introspective man, Roy hardly knew him, and knew even less what to expect from him now.

293

"These men," the Scot said quietly, glancing briefly toward the fire. "They're not the ones for this job. They're tavern brawlers and adventurers."

"They're the only ones who volunteered."

McTavish nodded reflectively. "Aye. That's so, lad. But I think—if you were to return to Sutter's now and ask again—you'd find *more* men who'd be willing to come."

"But why—"

"Because it's Thanksgiving, and they wanted to be with their wives and children. They've been working all summer away from their families. Now that construction on the mill has all but stopped for the winter, they've come home. A week or two with their wives and wee ones, and they'll be itching to get away again."

Roy shook his head, unconvinced. "I don't know. We've come this far. To turn back now—"

McTavish put a hand on Roy's shoulder. "It's the only way, lad. These ruffians most likely agreed to come, only figuring to get at the riches your party might be carrying with them. They're no good to you *or* your family."

"Are you sure there will be other men who'll volunteer?"

McTavish's nod was rather noncommittal. "Fairly sure. And if Captain Sutter could sweeten the pot with a bounty, of sorts—" He left the sentence unfinished, withdrew a flask from his jacket and offered it to Roy. "Besides, you'll need snowshoes to get any farther—even that much is plain to me now. And we can cache some of the supplies and food here—save the next party from hauling in so much."

Roy drank gratefully, and tears sprang to his eyes from the potent, burning liquid. He tilted his head and looked speculatively at the older man. "Why are *you* willing to

294

come back and try again?''

McTavish gazed at the river, reflecting a moment, shifting his chew of tobacco from one side of his mouth to the other. "I sent for my own family two years after I'd been here. There was a storm at sea—just off the coast— and the ship went down. I spent almost a year on the beaches, looking, hoping, asking. . . . I know what it's like to wonder—like you.''

The wind howled around the shanty like a wounded beast, whistled through the cracks, and sent pine boughs crashing into its sides. Toby crawled across the litter of filthy bedding to Poole's side, where he was flailing wildly in his blankets and raving for food. Toby gripped the driver's wrists and tried to hold him still, but the man seemed possessed of an inhuman strength born of his delirium. Toby hung on, fighting against his encroaching weakness, until Poole's thrashing ceased and he slipped into a semiconscious stupor.

In the eerie, flickering glow of the lighted pine knots and fire in the hearth, Poole's face was hardly recognizable as the strapping teamster with the thick, wavy hair and sparkling brown eyes. Now those eyes were sunken deep in a gaunt face and had a fierce, demoniacal look to them. And that sturdy body had become a shrunken wreck, with yellowish skin stretched tightly over prominent bones.

Toby relaxed his grip and sat back on his heels, a profound sense of melancholy creeping over him. Poole had surrendered much of his horse meat to Judd in the poker games, and with the loss of that food, he had gradually sunk into a kind of stupefying depression from which he was unable to rouse himself. The attempts of Toby, Trent, and even Stone to get him to eat in the last week had been met with no success, and Poole had gone downhill rapidly. He seldom moved from his bed, and for hours he would stare unblinking at the ceiling; other times he talked to himself incoherently.

Trent staggered across the floor and fell to his knees, nearly spilling the broth of boiled bones. He lifted Poole's head and held the cup to his lips, but the teamster turned his face away.

Trent let out a long, tired sigh and gazed dolefully at Toby. "He's dying."

"He *wants* to die."

Trent smiled bleakly. "Sometimes I don't blame him."

Toby shot a sharp, surprised glance at the artist. The pallor of death was already stealing over his sunken countenance. His eyes were filmed and dull, his sandy hair had begun to fall out and hung in stray wisps around his skull.

"You can't give up like him," Toby said.

Trent looked away, his expression utterly miserable. "Why not? Dying would be preferable to this. When I sleep, all I do is dream about food. Then I wake up and realize I'm here—in this stinking, foul cesspool. It's a torture I'd rather not have to put up with."

Toby could think of nothing to say. His own dreams were confused lunatic visions, and he often woke gasping and salivating uncontrollably. This place, he knew, had much to do with it: Poole's slow death, Trent's lassitude, Judd's recollections of the opulence of various southern cities he had visited, Canfield's grumblings, Stone's silence—and the filth, the stench of unwashed bodies, the ever-present vermin.

Toby shuddered and switched his gaze back to Poole. The teamster's eyes were closed now, and his breathing had settled into a coarse, rhythmic stertor.

"Leastways he's quiet now," Canfield remarked from his sheath of grimy blankets near the fire. "I'm sick of hearin' him yammerin' about food!"

Judd roused from his pallet and peered through a tangle of hair at the guide. "Shut up, Canfield."

"*You* shut up!" Canfield's features twisted into an angry mask. "You're just as bad—babblin' about all the fine ladies and restaurants in New Orleans!" His face took on a closed, forbidding look, and his eyes gleamed with malice. "I ought to take that fancy revolver of yours and make you eat *that!*"

Toby ran a trembling hand across his face and shivered in apprehension. If he stayed here, he knew—with dull certainty—he would become just like the rest of them: either a broken wreck like Poole or an obnoxious hothead like Canfield. Neither was a fate he wanted for himself, but their madness was infectious.

Weary with fatigue and hunger, he rose from the floor and went to gather his few meager belongings into a pile and tie them in his blankets. In spite of the storm raging outside, he *had* to get away from the depression of these men and this dingy hut. If he didn't . . .

Shaking his head to quell his thoughts, he pulled on his jacket and picked up his bundle.

"Goin' for a little walk?" Canfield asked maliciously.

Toby mashed his hat on his head. "I'm going to stay with the Coulters."

Canfield's eyes glinted with wicked amusement. "A little cuddle with your honey, eh?" He uttered a short, cackling laugh. "Watch you don't get blowed away before you get there."

Disgusted, Toby flung open the door and lurched out into the driving snow. He was stunned for a moment by the brutality of the storm. Wind, hail, and snow beat down upon him with an incredible fury. For several seconds, he stood motionless, half-blinded and dismayed by the awesome force of nature. Never in his life had he seen such ferocity—a relentless, punishing show of violence. The fierce, penetrating wind seemed to freeze the very marrow of his bones; it tore his hat from his head and sent it flying away from him to be swallowed up in the turbulent squalls of snow.

Mustering his strength, he leaned into the wind and struck out for the Coulters' cabin, invisible even at midafternoon. He staggered clumsily through the wet drifts, reeling and weaving like a drunk. Darting ice-balls buffeted his face, and he tucked his head down in an effort to ward off their savagery.

Frigid air filled his lungs with each breath and froze the moisture in his nose. The cold numbed his legs, and the wet snow dragged at his feet. He tottered crazily, unable to open his eyes to more than slits. Still, nothing was visible but the swirling, cruel white waste all around him.

To his right, he smelled woodsmoke, and he paused, squinting against the snow. A few sparks blew up and gusted away: Jennings's cabin.

He slogged on, fighting to keep his balance. Clumps of snow stuck to his boots, and he cursed himself for not strapping on the snowshoes, even though he doubted they would be much help.

He stumbled and fell heavily. Sobbing with the effort, he pushed himself to his knees, but his strength was ebbing away rapidly. His foot slipped out from under him, he toppled forward again, and plunged down a slope to come to a painful crashing stop against something solid.

Sarah heard the crack against the cabin door, as did the rest of her family. At first, she dismissed it as a wayward branch, but when the setter roused and went over to sniff the wood, she decided to investigate. Beans pawed the door, whimpering, and set up a feeble barking.

"Get away!" she told the dog, and he moved aside obediently. Sarah flipped up the latch; before she could move, the door swung inward. Toby tumbled in with a fierce squall of snow.

Sarah staggered back and sucked in her breath with an audible gasp, shocked at the sight of this ice-bound apparition before her. And, for a short, confusing space of time, she found herself unable to do anything but stare.

"Close the door!"

Hetty's command seemed to snap Sarah back to reality. She realized that Toby was blocking the door. She bent down to grasp his arm, and he looked up at her, dazed and befuddled. A deep gash was oozing blood from his temple, and she stifled a scream.

With her help, he managed to crawl forward a few feet, where he collapsed once more. Samantha tried to shut the door against the blizzard, but it stuck on the drift that was piling up on the floor. Lucas added his help, and by butting it with their shoulders, the youngsters' combined weight accomplished the task.

Sarah knelt beside Toby, her brow furrowed with concern and alarm. His hair was plastered to his skull in dripping tendrils, the melting snow mixing with his blood and turning it a pale pink as it ran over his cheek and behind his ear. Tenderly, she brushed back the wet locks and winced at the jagged flap of torn skin.

She gave Hetty a stricken look. "Get the whiskey. I think there's still a little left."

Toby's eyelids fluttered, and he moved his head slowly from side to side. "No whiskey." His eyes strained to focus on Sarah's face, then seemed to snap alert, clear and deep blue. He reached for her hand, and a shadow of a smile flickered on his lips, a reminder of the old Toby, the teasing, disagreeable hunter who had so intrigued and repelled her so many weeks ago. "My head hurts bad enough already," he said, pressing her fingers. "I don't need a hangover to add to it."

Sarah laughed softly in relief. For a few agonizing minutes, she had been frightened. If anything should happen to Toby now . . . She gazed warmly into his face with its familiar planes and angles, the firm mouth and slightly crooked teeth. She cared for him—more than she had been willing to admit up to this moment. And the emotion both surprised and pleased her.

The hail hammering on the hide roof unnerved Judd to the point of distraction. Snow wasn't so bad; one seldom heard it strike. But this . . .

Disgruntled, he huddled deeper into his blanket, hunger burning in his belly. Only a little of his horse meat remained. If he had rationed himself judiciously, there would be much more. But Judd was a man who never believed in scrimping on anything.

His gaze strayed to the thin mound beneath the tattered

300

blanket in the corner. Poole had died shortly after Garrett had left, and his body had been lying over there for more than eight hours. Its presence made the hair on the back of Judd's neck prickle, a painful reminder of what they all might expect if relief didn't soon come.

"Can't somebody take him out of here?" His voice sounded more bewildered than annoyed.

Canfield had been engaged in roasting a tiny piece of meat on the fire, and he threw a glance over his shoulder. "What's the matter, fancy man? Dead body make you nervous?"

Judd's mouth hardened in anger, but deep inside he felt fright and pain and confusion. "He'll start to stink pretty soon!"

Canfield turned back to his cooking with a wry chuckle. "One more smell won't much matter in this place."

Stone threw off his blanket and got wearily to his feet. "I'll take him out."

"What're you gonna do with him?" Trent demanded. "Just *leave* him out there?"

Stone flicked an irritated glance toward the artist. "I'm not about to dig a hole and *bury* him—if that's what you mean. The snow'll cover him up."

After donning his coat and gloves, Stone bent to lift Poole's corpse. It was already stiff, and, despite the dead man's loss of weight, Stone was unable to move him.

Judd cringed in his corner as the body dropped back to the floor with a sickening thud.

Stone stared a moment at his arms and hands, as if he couldn't quite believe he had grown so weak. Then he shot an impatient scowl at Canfield. "Get over here and help me!"

The guide bit into his supper and merely shook his

head, grinning humorlessly, grease shining on his lips and in his beard. "I ain't no undertaker."

Snorting in disgust, Judd stood up, felt a brief spell of vertigo, then grabbed a length of rope. He tossed it to Stone. "Tie it around him. We'll have to drag him. *None* of us is strong enough to lift him."

Stone bent to secure the rope beneath Poole's armpits and around his chest. Trent opened the door, and a frigid blast of of wind-whipped snow gusted in. Together, Judd and Stone hauled the corpse across the floor. The body thumped and scraped over the hard-packed dirt. Cold chills of horror washed over Judd, but he tried to close his ears to the slithering, scuffling sound.

Snow and hail pelted him in the face, and the wind tore at his clothes. The cold was intense, and he stumbled in the slushy drifts filling in the pathway. Gritting his teeth against the strain on his flaccid muscles, he staggered up the ramp with Stone, nearly tripping over his own feet.

"Take him around the side!" Stone had to shout above the moaning wind.

Judd wanted only to leave the corpse here and quickly retreat once more to the comforting warm stench of the shanty. But Stone was right: If they left Poole here, one of them would be bound to step on him sooner or later. And if there was much of a thaw . . .

Forcing the image from his mind and summoning up his last reserves of strength, Judd gripped the rope more tightly and bent into the gale.

After a meager Thanksgiving supper of stew—made from perhaps two ounces of meat and flavored with some basil—Sarah sat staring desultorily into the fire. Toby's

302

wound had been cleaned, and a piece of clean cloth tied about his head. He had changed into dry clothing behind a blanket hung for his privacy, but Sarah had caught a glimpse of his naked torso. The chest that had been so broad and powerful six weeks ago was sunken and pale; ribs and spine showed clearly beneath the wasted flesh.

A log broke, sending up a shower of sparks, and Sarah sighed heavily. In the main, she was not a woman prone to self-pity. She could spend hours turning a thing this way and that in her mind until she finally found its brightest side. But now she was totally at a loss to discover any bright side at all to their predicament.

Hetty was agreeable to having Toby move in with them, in spite of its questionable propriety. A man in the cabin might give them all the extra spark to better withstand the hardships. And Sarah was especially grateful to have someone share her pallet. The nights were fiercely cold, and, while Hetty slept with Simon, and Sam and Lucas shared their blankets, Sarah had no other body heat but her own to repel the bitter winter cold.

Unbidden, a hint of a smile touched her lips. The sleeping arrangements had not yet been discussed. What would Hetty say when Sarah announced her intentions?

"Read to us, Sarah," Lucas urged.

"Not tonight." She turned and offered the boy a small, apologetic smile. "It hurts my eyes in this poor light."

Unable to hide his disappointment, Lucas settled back down next to his dog with a weary sigh.

Sarah often read aloud in the evenings, but tonight she had no desire to pick up a book. Hetty could neither read nor write, and the children's skills were woefully deficient. Earlier on in their seclusion, Sarah had worked with them both on their lessons. But their attention wavered, and even Sarah's own ambition ebbed—in that, as in *all* things lately. More often than not anymore, she felt only a black depression, existing merely from one hour to the next in this dismal little hovel.

"Beans is gettin' awful skinny," Lucas remarked. "And he don't do much anymore—just sleeps."

Sarah's eyes met Toby's, and they exchanged rueful glances. They had kept the dog alive this long by feeding him the parts of the slaughtered animals no human would touch—tails, hooves, even the head of one of the cows. Now there was nothing left for the setter to eat, and the day was drawing ever nearer when he would become the sustenance for his masters.

Saddened by the thought, Sarah got tiredly to her feet and crossed the room to her pallet. "I'm going to sleep. Maybe tomorrow the sun will come out."

Hetty stroked Simon's wispy hair, her voice low and defeated. "Maybe."

Toby glanced at Sarah, an eyebrow arched in sharp query. Her smile sparkled mischievously as she patted the blanket beside her.

Hetty's eyes flew open in surprise, and her mouth sagged. "Sarah?" The word was a disbelieving half-whisper.

Toby rose and knelt to bank the fire. Amusement shone in his eyes as they came to rest on Hetty. "Don't worry. A month ago—maybe even last week—I might have had the inclination. But at this point—" He shook his head in self-reproval and straightened up. His eyes glimmered teasingly as they went over Sarah. "My idea of fun anymore would be to snuggle up to a nice plump sow ready for butchering."

Sarah flashed him a look of mock anger, and he gave

her a quick, impudent grin in return.

Lucas and Samantha scrambled for their pallet as Toby lifted the blankets and crawled beneath them beside Sarah. Hetty sat frowning in thought for a moment, her lips pursed into a thin line of disapproval. Then, with a resigned sigh, she snuffed out the lighted pine knot and settled onto her own pallet with Simon.

Sarah wrinkled her nose. "Plump sow indeed!"

Toby chuckled softly and drew her into his arms. She snuggled up to his chest, aware of his heartbeat against her cheek and the roughness of his beard as he brushed a kiss onto her temple. She smiled with dreamy complacency into the darkness. He was warm and strong, and as she closed her eyes and drifted toward a welcome sleep, she felt drowsily contented and secure as the hail continued to drum on the canvas roof.

Chapter Eighteen

The storm lasted almost a week but, on the last day of November, finally ceased its relentless fury. Regardless of the weather, Toby had ventured out alone daily to cut wood for the fire. He had suffered terribly from the cold, and would be completely exhausted by the time he returned to the cabin, dragging a few sticks of kindling with him and panting with fatigue.

Now, on this first day of December, he sat slumped near the fire with Sarah, both regaining their strength from their wood-gathering expedition. The others they had seen while outside were completely disheartened by the calamity that had befallen them all. No longer were there encouraging words passed between the emigrants; only news of the latest casualty. Everyone was sick, and some were so broken by this most recent storm that they had no will to live.

The last of the bear meat had been eaten two days ago, and since then all that remained was a pot of week, flavorless broth. The traps stayed empty, and even the wolves had been conspicuously absent for awhile. Toby knew—even if he had the stamina and borrowed the Coulter's gun—there would be no game to shoot.

He sipped his coffee—there was *still* a little left—and stole a glance at Lucas and Samantha. Their pale, pinched little faces were a stark contrast to the size of their hollow eyes. Arms and legs like sticks, they seldom stirred. No laughing, no play—only despondency and lethargy. Simon was growing weaker by the hour, and Hetty was helpless to do anything for him. All she could do was try to soothe him as best she could with gentle words and tender caresses.

Toby stared glumly down into the black, steaming brew and rubbed a hand across his mouth thoughtfully, his mind filled with indecision and uncertainty. His feeling of angry frustration grew with each passing second of hesitation, but he knew there was no use in delaying the inevitable any longer.

He set aside the coffee cup and got to his feet, his features grim and resolute. Keeping his face as expressionless as possible, he slapped his hand against his thigh. "Come on, Beans." The setter raised its head and gazed dully at him. Toby clapped his leg once more. "Come on, boy."

Lucas stirred as the dog uncurled himself from the boy's side and trotted over to Toby. "Where're you goin' with my dog?"

Toby fought to keep his voice steady, but the words seemed to catch in his throat. "Just out for a little walk."

Horror welled in the boy's face as the implication struck home. *"Nooo!"* Eyes wide and terrified, he scrambled to his feet and lurched across the floor, but Sarah caught him by the shoulders before he could reach the dog. She regarded the boy squarely with icy composure. "It *has* to be."

"No!" Lucas wailed, struggling to break free of her grasp.

Feeling sick and disgusted with himself, Toby opened the door and stepped out into the crisp, bright sunshine. He gave a low whistle, and the setter bounded up the snow ramp after him.

Lucas's strangled, desperate sobs rolled out of the cabin, and Toby felt a stab of remorse for the boy. But there was simply no other way.

He released a dismal sigh and looked down at the dog, sitting in the snow at his feet, thumping his tail happily against the soft powder and gazing eagerly up into his face. A feeling of genuine grief washed over him, and he shook his head regretfully.

Pushing aside his emotions, Toby drew in a determined breath and led the dog toward the woods. And when *this* meat was gone, what then?

Toby shivered as a chill of dread raced up his spine.

Maggie stood leaning against a tree at the edge of the lake, disinterestedly observing Toby and the dog disappear into the woods on the other side. With a sigh, she tightened the collar of Kelly's jacket about her throat and turned back to watch Sean.

For over an hour, he had laboriously chopped a hole through the ice and now sat on a keg with a piece of twine dangling into the cavity. There was nothing to spare for bait, but Maggie hoped that a bright scrap of calico torn from a dress might attract a curious fish—if there were any.

None of the O'Brians knew a thing about the habits of

309

mountain trout. Did they go to warmer waters? Perhaps they even hibernated beneath the frozen surface. Regardless of what the fish of Truckee Lake did in the winter, the family needed food, and the water seemed to be their only hope.

But Sean had been out there for two hours now, and nothing had happened.

Maggie shivered and stamped the snow from her shoes, but she would rather be outside than in. The cabin reeked of vile smells, and half her family was too weak to even get out of bed. Kelly was the worst, and Maggie feared he might be dying. Most of the time he lay in a stupor, his course breathing labored and unnatural. Occasionally he would wake for a few brief moments, only to wail and shriek.

Kevin was failing, a wasted little bundle of flesh. Katie and James often moaned and sobbed for a mouthful of food. And at times, Maggie thought her father showed signs that the privations and horror had disturbed his mental balance. In fact, she wondered grimly, if madness wasn't close upon *all* of them.

For herself, she had slept little during this last storm. The groans of the hungry, the cries of the children, and Kelly's sporadic screams of delirium kept her awake. She found herself simply lying on her pallet without moving, staring at the ceiling, listening to the drumming rattle of sleet-mixed snow against the roof. She spent much of this time thinking of things she hadn't thought of for years, recollecting incidents of her childhood long forgotten. It was easier to remember than to sleep, for when she did, her dreams were filled with frenzied visions of food.

The sun was out, but there was no warmth—only a blinding brilliance of white desolation and bitter cold. A

310

gusty wind had sprung up and whistled through the trees, sending Maggie's breath pluming out in great mists of fog. Her ears ached; her feet and hands felt numb. The sensible thing to do would be to return to the cabin instead of watching Sean's futile efforts. But the cabin was *so* depressing, with its denizens of half-wild, unkempt inhabitants.

Shaking her head miserably, she turned away from the lake and let her eyes wander over the camp. Ole Andersen and his son were coming back with a load of wood, staggering under the weight. Nothing stirred from either the Jennings or Pardee cabin. Maggie briefly toyed with the idea of visiting, but the others' situations might be even more desperate than her own.

Almost furtively, her gaze strayed to the hut at the far end. Smoke billowed up from the lopsided chimney, the only part of the building visible above the deep drifts. Idly, she wondered how Judd was faring. She had not seen him since his untimely proposal of marriage, and at the memory of that conversation, a renewed surge of anger seethed within her.

She was about to turn away when her eye caught movement at the door. Two scrawny, bedraggled figures emerged—Canfield and Stone. They were hauling something up the ramp by ropes, and as Maggie peered more closely, she realized, with a start, it was a body.

A sudden knot of anxiety coiled in her stomach. Was it Judd? She *shouldn't* care—after all, hadn't she wished his death a hundred times? But she *did* care.

She took a few clumsy steps toward the shanty, then stopped short as the body rolled and she caught a glimpse of sandy hair. It was Trent, and she expelled a sigh of relief.

Canfield paused in his labor to rest, and his gaze met hers across the expanse of snow. His lips twisted into a sly, obscene grin beneath his matted beard, a taunting invitation for her to take up his offer.

Maggie's mouth thinned into a scornful line, and she turned away sharply. Not yet. She set her lips stubbornly and drew in a deep breath. She wasn't *that* desperate— yet.

Lucas was quiet, his rage finally spent. He was back in his bed, wrapped in warm blankets, totally exhausted from his outburst. Samantha sat dully in the corner, watching the steam rise from the kettle, grimly resolved to the idea that the liver and kidneys from the family pet were stewing inside it.

Toby sat on a keg while Sarah carefully removed the bandage from his head. The cut was healing nicely, a fact which, in his depleted condition, surprised her. She had received a nasty bruise on her hip over a week ago from a fall in the snow, and it was still as livid as the day after it had happened. Perhaps Toby's resistance was better than hers, she mused, and stepped back to fetch a clean rag.

"Will I live?" he asked, showing her his crooked teeth in a wry grin.

"From that—yes." Sarah bit her lips immediately, annoyed at herself for speaking her doubts aloud. She tried to keep her spirits up—for *her* benefit as well as the children's. But as the days dragged on and their weakness and hunger grew, her sense of hopelessness heightened.

Forcing a cheerful smile to her lips, she turned back to Toby with a strip of linen to wind about his head. *He* felt it, too. He was a different Toby, often quiet and melancholy, with none of the sharp sarcasm that had been so much a part of him. Sometimes he made an effort at his old stinging banter, but it had none of the bite from back on the desert.

Sarah was still concerned that she might be pregnant, but she somehow found the possibility remote. She felt no different than she ever had, except for her increasing fatigue and brief spells of dizziness; these she attributed to her starvation, for everyone had them. Her stomach—when she touched it—was no larger. In fact, it was nothing but a sunken hollow between a jutting pelvis. She was determined not to let it worry her, for she needed no extra anxieties to trouble her now.

"Hetty should come in out of the cold," Toby said. "I don't think it'll get above freezing today."

"That doesn't seem to bother her." Sarah sat down across the improvised table and poured herself a cup of tea made from pine bark. "She's out there every day it isn't snowing. Watching the mountain pass for Roy."

Toby stole a glance over his shoulder at the dozing children, then turned back to Sarah. "I don't think he stands a much better chance of getting to us than we do of getting to him."

Sarah scowled at him, a rebellious spark in her eyes. "Don't talk that way!"

He shrugged helplessly. "I'm sorry. But that's the way I feel."

She knitted her hands together and regarded him solemnly. "But we *have* to believe in something! Roy *will* come with food, and we can build up our strength again, and *then* get over the mountains."

Toby's mouth curved into a sad, distant smile, and there was a hint of tolerant indulgence in his blue eyes.

"If it helps you to think that way—" He let his words trail off softly and reached for his cup just as the door opened.

Sarah looked up and was astonished to see Ruth Huntington entering with Hetty. But not the plump, haughty Ruth Huntington of two months ago. This woman was a mere shell of the once-proud wife of the wealthy furniture dealer. Her hair was tangled and hung in oily strands about her face—a face hardly recognizable, with its sunken, dull eyes and folds of skin sagging from the loss of weight. She wore a bright—but filthy—pink satin gown with torn flounces and ruffles; it hung on her frame like a flour sack.

She lifted tired, apprehensive eyes to Sarah and Toby, eyes that contained not a hint of the condescending arrogance and disdain that were so familiar to Sarah. "Good afternoon," she said softly, and her voice quavered with undefined emotion.

Sarah nodded dumbly in greeting, and Toby managed a brittle smile. *What* could this woman possibly want from them? Sarah doubted this was merely a social call.

"Mrs. Huntington, here, says they're out of food," Hetty said. "And Mister's mighty sick."

Sarah made no comment. This information was hardly news; *everyone* was in the same fix.

"I have money," the woman said, twisting her hands together fretfully. "And I know you have meat. I'll give you a hundred dollars for a pound."

Sarah sucked in her breath in wordless amazement. But her shock quickly changed to bitter resentment. What good would a hundred dollars be out *here?* And when did the Huntingtons ever offer help when the others needed it? Sarah's gray eyes became as hard as granite, and her lips tightened as she directed her gaze to Hetty. She groaned inwardly as, with a sinking feeling, she realized that her sister-in-law was prepared to give the woman the meat. Hetty was too good—too trusting. The Huntingtons *deserved* whatever fate they got.

"Hetty, you're not—?" Sarah's voice was filled with disbelief.

Hetty shrugged, then glanced at Toby, a sly twinkle in her eyes. "What did you do with Beans's head?"

Toby blinked in surprise; then sudden understanding dawned in his eyes. Suppressing a smile, he rose from the table and reached for his jacket. "I'll get it." And, picking up an empty croker sack by the door, he slipped outside.

Hetty turned back to Ruth Huntington, a reckless gleam dancing in her brown eyes and a smug smile on her lips. "I figure that might even weigh *more* than a pound." She thrust out a hand, palm upward, and waggled her fingers suggestively.

In her distress, Ruth produced a strangled laugh and fumbled in her sagging bodice. She drew out a small pouch, and, after counting carefully, placed five gold eagles in Hetty's outstretched hand.

Sarah turned away to hide her smile and busied herself stirring the soup. The money didn't matter at this point —a hundred dollars was less than worthless to them all. But the idea that Ruth and Edgar Huntington were forced to pay such a sum for the severed head of a dog . . .

Sarah stifled a giggle. She had heard of people eating crow before. Perhaps *this* was even more fitting.

The clouds crowded over Sutter's Fort, black and low; now and again, there were a few scattered drops of rain.

Roy carefully wrapped stacks of corn tortillas in a waterproof canvas, then bundled them in the pack he would shoulder tomorrow. At his side, the burly Lachlan McTavish did likewise.

Roy glanced uneasily up at the threatening sky. Another storm was on its way, and despite the haste of the recent days, he doubted they could beat it to the mountains.

He released a sigh of steadfast resolve. "We'll go anyway," he said, more to himself than to the Scot.

McTavish nodded thoughtfully. "Aye, lad, we will." He hefted his pack and started walking across the courtyard to the storehouse "We might have to stop along the way and sit it out, but at least we'll be on our way."

Roy lifted his own bundle and hurried after the big man. It was December 5—two months since he had seen his family. And now—finally—a well-organized relief party was going to get under way. Captain Sutter offered the men $5 a day if they would go, and *this* group of a dozen were more than eager to get started and collect their pay.

The great storehouse doors stood ajar, and the men were busily filling their packs from the provisions laid out on plank tables: jerked beef, coffee, cornmeal, dried fruit, and blankets. These items were for the stranded emigrants; other supplies were gathered for the men. Twelve pairs of snowshoes hung on the wall, completed just yesterday by the Indians. There were hatchets, tins of matches, short shovels. If wild animals hadn't disturbed the caches, there would be even more food waiting in Bear Valley.

In spite of his earlier reluctance, Emil Lebec had agreed to go again, as had Charlie Shaw. Lachlan was

316

coming along, Roy suspected, as a kind of moral support, though he had worked harder than anyone to get the relief party ready. Tyrrell had decided to stay behind.

But it was Hezekiah Perkins, a trapper who had just come into the fort with a load of furs three days ago, who had become their leader. In his middle thirties, he was a tall, gangly man with a small head and wispy tufts of black fuzz above his ears, the only hair on an otherwise bald head. His teeth were large and badly yellowed, his beard stained perpetually with tobacco juice. He spoke little, and when he did, it was with a high-pitched, squeaky voice. Roy was doubtful of the man's abilities, but Sutter—and the other men—all seemed to have the utmost confidence in him. Roy could do nothing but go along with their choice.

"If this storm breaks tonight," Perkins was saying, "we'll leave tomorrow anyway—make camp at Mule Springs till it passes. When the rest of us go into the mountains, two of us will stay at camp with the horses and mules.

Charlie Shaw and another man quickly volunteered for this job. Roy could see the calculating greed flicker in their eyes; $5 a day for sitting with the animals was easy pay.

Perkins shifted his tobacco to his other cheek and spat on the floor. "Captain Sutter says if there's any children needs carried, he'll pay a twenty-five-dollar bounty to every man who totes a young un' out."

The men exchanged avaricious looks. Roy felt the familiar dread and fear lodge in his throat. Would Sam and Lucas be so physically spent as to need to be carried? Were their little shoes still holding up, or had their feet become hopelessly frostbitten? There were so many questions, and Roy could answer none of them. Perkins pushed his coonskin cap back on his head and let his beady black eyes travel over the men. He grunted and spat again. "We've got an early start tomorrow. Soon's you finish up here, turn in." And, grunting again, he left the storehouse, striding awkwardly with his long legs through the mud.

Roy finished filling his pack, then left the shed with McTavish. Lights glowed in most of the rooms of the buildings. Cattle lowed in the distance. A thick, soaking mist had begun to fall steadily from the leaden sky; far to the south, thunder growled like a waking bear.

"Don't worry, lad," McTavish said cheerfully. "You said they had plenty of cattle, so they won't go hungry. The worst they'll be is probably a wee bit cold and scared."

A flash of lightning exploded on the horizon, and the rain increased. Roy shuddered and, picking up his pace, hurried for the cover of the adobe walls of the main building.

Chapter Nineteen

Maggie sat lethargically by the fire, only half-watching the dancing flames. The kettle steamed, but there was nothing in it but boiling snow water. There had been nothing to eat in the cabin for three days—not since Daniel had caught a rat on the first day of the storm.

Outside, the wind screamed down from the mountains, lashing pine boughs against the cabin, tearing at the canvas roof. Inside, vermin swarmed, and the stench of sickness hung thick and cloying.

Kevin was dying. A year old, he lay in his cradle, unwashed, unchanged, unmoving. Jamie was failing, and Kelly was unconscious most of the time. He now lay with his head in Maggie's lap before the fire, his respiration rapid and shallow, his pulse thready. His skeletal hands, resting at his sides, would twitch now and then, the only sign of life.

Sean sat across from her, staring into space, his expression frozen into a mask of fear and disbelief. His rusty hair was tangled, his beard caked with dried spittle, and his eyelids were purplish.

In the center of the floor, Molly repeated every prayer she had ever learned. The rest of her family was gathered around her, raising their voices occasionally to join her. Michael cradled Katie to his chest, a thin, wraithlike child with masses of lusterless coppery hair nearly obscuring her pinched features.

Maggie held nothing but contempt for the religious fervor that had suddenly possessed the other members of her family. There would be no help from God—no help from *anyone*.

Sean raised his head and gazed at her from sunken hollows. "In a couple of weeks, it'll be Christmas." He tossed the wood chip he had been idly fingering into the fire and watched it be devoured by the flames. "I'm thinkin' I'd like a nice stuffed goose with all the trimmings."

Maggie shot him a reproving glance. "Hush your mouth! It's only making things worse with your talk, you are!"

Sean hung his head and sighed heavily. "I know."

Maggie smoothed the filthy hair away from Kelly's brow and gazed sorrowfully down at him. He was so emaciated that it seemed as if only his shriveled skin covered his bones. He looked the worst, though they all were shrunken and drawn, their faces appearing almost ghoulish and sinister.

"If this storm doesn't clear soon, we'll be out of wood for the fire," Maggie said.

Sean waved a languid hand. "What difference does it make if we're warm or freezing? We're *all* dying!"

Maggie choked out a bitter laugh. *She* could get them food—if Red Canfield still had any. And *if* he still wanted her, looking like a slatternly scarecrow. Disgust curled

320

her upper lip, and a hard knot of nausea formed in the pit of her stomach. If it weren't for Kelly and Kevin, she would never go to the man for help—for herself, she would rather sink into the same kind of coma as her brother and die a peaceful death.

Her eyes clouded with indecision, she turned her gaze to the crackling fire once more. When this storm passed . . . She released her breath in a shuddering sigh and was suddenly conscious she was weeping. A frightened part of her mind wished it would *never* stop snowing.

Toby's eyes blinked open in muddled wakefulness. He knew dawn had broken—not from any outward signs, but from some inner sense he had developed over the last eight weeks of living in the windowless cabins. Sarah's faint, even breathing at his side told him she was still asleep.

He closed his eyes again, savoring the warmth of the blankets, unwilling to rise just yet. The wind outside had ceased, and if the storm was finished . . .

What was the sense of thinking about the weather? There was no more food. All that remained now was the wait—the wait for a slow, agonizing death. They would all simply waste away, finally growing too weak to even rouse from the squalor and filth.

"Toby."

Hetty's whispered voice snapped him back from his gruesome thoughts, and he sat up. The woman sat by the hearth, holding Simon in her arms, a look of age far beyond her years in the cruel hollows of her cheeks. Careful not to disturb Sarah, Toby quietly rose and made his way to Hetty's side.

She lifted pleading eyes to him. "He's goin', Toby."

Toby's brow furrowed into a frown of bewildered frustration. The boy was nothing but a small scrap of undernourished flesh and bones, a ghost of the chubby, healthy child Toby had first seen. He had grown so weak, he seldom moved except to cry, and those times were becoming more and more infrequent. Samantha and Lucas were little better, and even Sarah had lately been showing signs that she was giving up.

Toby let out his breath in an exasperated sigh and bent to add a few more sticks of wood to the fire. "I'll take your rifle and go out later." He grimaced in a kind of apology. "I *know* the wolves are out there."

Hetty's shoulders slumped in defeat. "Waiting for us to die." She lifted her eyes, and there was a great sadness in the look she gave him. "I wonder which of us will win—us or them."

Maggie hunched deeper into Kelly's jacket as she made her way across the soft powder toward Red Canfield's hut. She held her head high and shoulders erect, her lips set in a grimly resolute line. She tried to walk with as much poise and pride as she could muster; but, despite her resolve, she tottered unsteadily over the drifts.

Nearly slipping down the snow ramp, she hesitated outside the door, her face clouded with doubt and uncertainty. But she had no other choice anymore—all her options had run out. Two of her brothers were at death's door, and another close behind. Red Canfield was their only hope.

Pushing the forthcoming ordeal to the back of her mind, she brought her fist up and rapped sharply. For several minutes, nothing happened. Perhaps they were all dead inside, and panic began to rise in her.

But just as she was about to turn and retreat back up the incline, the door opened. Lester Stone—unkempt, haggard, and bleary-eyed—stared curiously out at her from a ratty tangle of beard and hair.

Taking a deep, unsteady breath, she spoke with as much authority as she could manage. "I've come to see Mr. Canfield."

Stone blinked his sunken, watery eyes and stepped back. Maggie entered the dingy, dark little hovel, and shock went through her like a cold knife blade. A vile stench assaulted her senses and sent her stomach raging. Amid the litter of blankets and other goods strewn on the dirt floor, she thought she could actually *see* the vermin darting about.

Her gaze fell on Judd, hunched by the fire, a broken, defeated caricature of the man she had known. He glanced up, staring in stunned disbelief. But before he could speak, Canfield materialized from a swath of blankets in the corner.

He stood up—thin, bedraggled, and dirty—and gave her a twisted smile. "So you've finally decided to come see old Red?"

Maggie could not suppress an involuntary shudder of disgust. "I've come for meat."

Canfield threw back his head and cackled lewdly. "And you'll get it, my pretty!"

Maggie's flesh crawled with revulsion. She wanted to turn and flee, but the memory of Kelly and Kevin and Jamie kept her feet rooted to the filthy floor.

Canfield shot a canny leer in the direction of Stone and Judd. "Why don't you two lads go out and chop some wood?'' His pale blue eyes swung back to Maggie and raked her, a faintly leering curl to his lips. ''While the lady and I take care of our business.''

Judd's eyes widened in dismay, and he sucked in a ragged breath. Maggie looked away, her cheeks burning with humiliation. Unable to face the man she had once thought she loved, she fixed her gaze on the kettle simmering over the fire and the aromatic steam rising from it—steam that, in spite of the other odors in the room, smelled of meat.

She was vaguely aware of Judd and Stone donning their coats. Then she heard the door slam shut. Her pulse pounding in her temples and heartbeat roaring in her ears, she lifted her eyes and stared across the room into the twisted, leering face of Red Canfield. Disgust washed over her, and she felt her resolve waver again.

His lips spread into a lecherous grin, and his gold teeth sparkled in the half-light. He beckoned her with a wink and a crooked finger. ''Come on, little lady. I've been waitin' a long time for this.''

Maggie's feet wouldn't move, and a cold terror lodged in her throat. Swallowing hard, she forced a note of false bravado into her voice. ''I want to see the food first.''

Waving a mollifying hand, he bent to pick up a bundle wrapped in an old shirt. Unfolding the cloth, he displayed a large quantity of strips of dried beef.

Maggie's eyes blazed in anticipation, and her mouth began to water uncontrollably.

Canfield gave a snort of amusement and refolded the cache. ''And there's more. *Fresh* meat—kept in the snow just outside the door.''

She turned a quizzical eye on the guide. ''You found one of the heads of cattle that strayed, buried in the snow?''

Canfield winked significantly. "Well . . . you *might* say that. I did do some diggin' in the snow.'' The humor left his eyes, and he held out his hand in invitation once more. "Come over here, girl.''

Maggie forced her legs to cross the floor until she stood a foot away from the man. He stank of sweat and urine and unwashed clothing, and it was all she could do to keep from gagging. He reached out a hand capped by long, grimy nails and touched her cheek. Maggie recoiled as though stung by a wasp.

His face twisted in rage, and he took her shoulder in a painful grip. "I know I ain't much to look at—but neither are you anymore!'' The anger left his face, and his mouth lifted into its familiar lascivious smile. "And old Red ain't got the strength he used to, either.'' One rough fingertip ran over her lips, and his eyes glinted with renewed lust. "But you've got a real fine mouth, Maggie.'' He studied her through narrowed eyes. "On your knees, girl. And take it nice and slow.''

The color drained from her face, and bile rose to her throat. She felt breathless and dizzy and apprehensive. But she managed to fight down her revulsion and knelt meekly on the hard-packed floor. Canfield cackled crudely in triumph, and Maggie steeled herself for what was to come, filled with a hatred that seethed within her.

Judd sat on the rooftop of the shanty, his legs dangling leadenly to graze the drifts with his boots. A smooth blanket of pure white snow covered everything, and it settled fluffy and glistening on the branches. Stone's footprints trailed toward the woods where he had gone with the ax.

For all his quiet, mysterious ways poor Stone was a good soul. He cut most of the firewood, cooked most of the meals, even attempted on a few occasions to clean the hut. Canfield was simply too lazy, and, for himself . . .

Judd wearily wiped one hand across his face and shifted his weight. The cold made it impossible to find a comfortable position, and his head was beginning to throb from the frigid air entering his lungs.

Maggie had been inside with Canfield for over fifteen minutes now. Poor Maggie . . .

Judd let out a short, self-deprecating laugh. He was beginning to think of everyone as poor this and poor that. But that's exactly what they all were: poor, pathetic creatures without hope, reduced to living like animals.

At times, he felt Poole and Trent had had the right idea; just to give up and die. But some inner drive—no matter how faint it was growing—kept Judd from total surrender. If he could somehow manage to stay alive till the spring thaw, *then* he could get out.

The door creaked open below him, and he looked down to see Maggie emerging ahead of Canfield and coming up the snow ramp. She was carrying the guide's shirt rolled into a ball, and her step was proud. As she turned and saw Judd, the expression on her face turned hard and impassive, but there was a sadness in her sunken eyes which even her thick lashes could not hide.

Canfield flashed Judd an arrogant, self-satisfied grin. "Sorry to keep you waitin' out here in the cold so long."

Judd didn't reply, but kept his gaze fixed on Maggie. At Canfield's sarcastic words, a hot flush of shame came into her cheeks, and Judd felt a strange, unfamiliar surge of pity for her.

Canfield squatted in the snow and dug through the

drifts near the ramp. He uncovered a large slab of frozen meat and held it up to Maggie triumphantly. "There you be, my pretty!"

Her eyes came alive suddenly at the sight of the meat, and they glittered with something close to madness. She snatched the steak from Canfield's hands and tucked it into her bundle with the dried jerky. Then, without a word, she turned and slogged back toward her own cabin.

Canfield gave a low chuckle. "Just remember, Maggie!" he called after her. "It's a present from old Red! And from your friend Poole, too!" He laughed again and slapped his thigh at his own twisted humor.

Judd's lip curled in contempt, and he slid off his perch as Maggie bent down, scooped up a handful of snow, put it in her mouth, and spat viciously. Canfield cackled gleefully at her performance just as Stone returned with a few skimpy twigs for the fire.

Canfield unsheathed his long hunting knife and ran it almost caressingly over his thumb to test its sharpness. "I reckon it's time to fill the larder again," he remarked, glancing meaningfully at Stone. "You comin'?"

Stone's features showed his distaste, but he sighed resignedly and handed the wood over to Judd.

There was a malicious slant to Canfield's smile as he turned to regard Judd. "That's right, fancy man. You get the pot boilin' while *we* do all the work."

Unwilling—and unable—to respond to the guide's taunts, Judd scuttled down the slope and into the dismal filth of the shanty.

Toby climbed up into the dreary sunlight with Roy's rifle. It wasn't the fine, accurate weapon that Toby had

327

smashed over the bear's head and shattered in a thousand pieces, but it was serviceable. Now, if he could only find some game.

Heaving a disconsolate sigh, he shouldered the gun and struck out across the snow. He was already exhausted from chopping wood earlier, but Simon's wasted little body and weak cries were so pathetic, he *had* to at least make an effort to find them food.

He stopped in mid-stride, turning an idea over in his mind. His forays for game were always *away* from the lake, and those had proved fruitless thus far. Perhaps he should go *toward* the lake this time. But still . . .

While he was pondering this suddenly weighty problem, Emmett Pardee emerged from the Andersens' half of the cabin with Ole. Both had been solid, robust men, tending toward fat; now they were thin, haggard, and stooped. Ole carried his blunderbuss, and Emmett had his rifle.

"Belle's sick—and so's Amos," Emmett said, looking at Toby with sad, pleading eyes. "I've *got* to find some game today, or they'll both die."

Toby nodded his understanding. The situation was the same with everyone, but Pardee had already lost one son to starvation.

Noticing Ole's intent gaze upon something, Toby followed the direction in which the Swede was looking. The focus of this attention were Canfield and Stone, standing before their hut. And as Toby watched, the two men walked almost briskly around the side of the cabin and disappeared in the back.

Ole scratched his tangled, uncut blond hair and shook his head. "Look at them! *None* of us has that much energy anymore!" He threw a puzzled, dismayed look at

Toby. "They must have food, *ja?*"

Toby shrugged, but his own curiosity was now aroused. Perhaps they had indeed located one of the missing oxen buried in the snow. He himself had tried unsuccessfully many times probing in the drifts with the pole, but had lately given up.

Emmett looked at Toby, bright-eyed and eager, the most animation he had displayed in a long while. "If they've got meat—" Greedy anticipation glittered in his eyes, and he started across the snow at as aggressive a pace as he could manage.

Toby and Ole followed, shuffling clumsily on their snowshoes. It had begun to snow lightly, and fat, lazy flakes flurried about their heads and shoulders. Toby didn't dare hope, but he couldn't help himself. There *was* no game except the wolves, and they usually traveled in packs. Even with Ole and Emmett with him, he seriously doubted they could withstand an attack by creatures just as desperate and hungry as they were. Whatever Stone and Canfield had found, that was the only sensible solution.

Emmett rounded the corner of the hut, and Toby heard his strangled cry of dismay. The blacksmith dropped his gun and reeled back, covering his face with his hands and shaking his head in anguished protest. Toby looked curiously at Emmett, mildly bemused, then stepped behind the shed.

It took him a moment for his mind to register the horror that was suddenly revealed. Gorge rose to his throat; he tasted bile and took a deep breath to keep from vomiting. Ole made a sound that was almost a whimper and spun away. He doubled over and retched until the meager contents of his stomach spilled out into the snow.

Toby drew in his breath with a shudder, and, despite his revulsion, hazarded a glance back at the object of Canfield and Stone's labor. Elmore Poole's naked body lay face up in the snow, its trunk opened from neck to crotch. The heart, kidneys, and liver were gone, as well as a sizable slice of flesh from one thigh.

Grimacing as a fresh spasm of nausea gripped his belly, Toby turned his face away.

"What else were we supposed to *do!*" Canfield's harsh voice rose in defensive challenge. "There *ain't* no other food!"

Toby sucked in a deep breath of frigid air through clenched teeth and shook his head, his senses numbed with shock. He leaned against the wall of the shack for support until his nausea subsided finally, trying to force the picture from his mind.

"But it's not—" Emmett floundered, and a small, choking sound came from his throat—"it's not *right!*"

"Who's to say what's right or not out here!" Canfield shouted, and his voice took on a sharp edge. "It's the only thing left to keep us *alive!*"

Stone spoke almost apologetically. "Why should we deny ourselves what's available for the sake of convention? *I* haven't lost the will to live yet."

Toby glanced uneasily at Ole, still trembling from his bout of nausea. The Swede looked quickly away, unable to meet his eyes. Emmett stared hard at his feet, his heavy brows knitted into a confused, reflective frown.

Were *they* thinking the same things as he was? Toby wondered. Now that the initial shock had passed, he was able to analyze this more logically. Images of Simon lying helplessly in his blankets, crying weakly and incessantly for food flashed through his mind. He was

330

reminded painfully of Hetty's anguished face, Sarah's recent worrisome lethargy, the pitiful pleas for something to eat from Samantha and Lucas, his own gnawing hunger and rapidly diminishing strength.

And as he reviewed the dismal train of events that had led them all to this in his mind, he realized that Stone and Canfield were right. His conscience screamed in outrage at the idea, but—marooned out here in the deep snow, slowly starving to death like trapped rats on a sinking ship—necessity won out. They *must* have food.

Heartbeat pounding, face tight with emotion, he turned back to Stone and Canfield and the mutilated corpse of Elmore Poole. Taking a deep breath and expelling it slowly, Toby unsheathed his knife and knelt in the snow.

He hesitated a moment, fighting back the waves of revulsion that surged through him. At another time, in another place, under different circumstances, he would have been aghast at what he was about to do. Now . . . He closed his eyes a moment in an effort to regain his courage. When he opened them again, Emmett was also kneeling by the corpse.

The blacksmith's eyes were filled with pained sadness. "We *have* to live."

Toby nodded miserably and let the blade touch the pale, frozen flesh of Poole's left leg at the hip. In the back of his mind, he knew he was doing something hideous, but he bore down and began his gruesome task, tearing open a jagged gash of violated muscle and flesh. He bit his lips to smother an anguished moan and forced his mind to go blank.

The knife seemed to have a life of its own as it hacked at cords of resistant flesh, broke through cartilage, gnawed into bone.

* * *

Cold, tired, and filled with self-loathing, Toby pushed open the door to the cabin and entered its warm security. Four thin, wan faces looked up from their listless stupor and fixed their gazes on his buckskin jacket, rolled and carried under his arm.

Sarah's expression turned to something like amazement, and she came up out of her seat with more vitality than she had shown in days. "You found something!"

He nodded, unable to suppress a shudder.

"Let me see!" She reached for the coat, but Toby jerked it away quickly. Her eyes narrowed, and she stared at him in vague bewilderment. There was a hollowness in her cheeks, a faint hardness around her mouth; even the luster of her hair seemed faded. "What is it?" she asked, a note of trepidation creeping into her voice.

"An elk."

Samantha clapped her hands gleefully as Hetty gazed up at him with mute appeal in her eyes, cuddling the emaciated Simon to her shrunken breasts. "Give me a little of the blood now, Toby. It might give the boy strength."

Dead men don't bleed, he thought morosely, and his shoulders heaved slightly. But, with deliberate calm, he forced his eyes to meet hers. "I'll take care of Simon and get the meat cooking. I'd like the rest of you to leave the cabin for just a few minutes." At their confused, skeptical looks, he felt his frustration mount. *"Please!* Just for a little while. Trust me."

He was met by mysterious glances and suspicious frowns, but Sarah reached for her coat. Hetty wrapped Simon in a blanket and lay him on the pallet nearest the fire, then fetched her own warm cloak.

332

Lucas pulled his coonskin cap down over his prominent ears, and his sunken eyes shone with youthful eagerness as he filed past Toby. "Can I have the antlers?"

"I didn't bring them back with me."

Unable to conceal his disappointment, the boy shuffled out the door ahead of his sister and mother. Sarah cast a final, searching look at Toby, but he turned away.

When the door had closed, he let out a long, agonized sigh and unwrapped his grisly goods on the table. He *couldn't* let them know what they were eating—and would *continue* to eat until relief came or they escaped.

Closing his mind to the task at hand, he sliced off several strips of flesh and placed them in the skillet. The meat began to sizzle and pop the minute it was on the fire, and, to his ears, the sound was an irritating as fingernails on a slate.

He stared at the mutilated, dismembered leg for a moment, his mind suddenly filled with a host of misgivings and doubts. But finally, with another disconsolate sigh, he took out his knife and hacked away at the knee. When this odious task was accomplished he slid both halves—calf and thigh—into the big kettle of boiling water and covered it with the lid.

He realized *he* would have to do most of the cooking from now on—another chore to add to his many already. But if it would spare them from learning the terrible truth, it was worth it. Many of the bones could pass plausibly as those of an elk. But what about Elmore's foot?

His mouth curling in scorn, Toby turned back to the skillet and speared a slice, placing it on a plate. He cut it into tiny pieces and put these in a cup of warm water for Simon.

The child was too weak to raise his head, and Toby had

333

to hold him up like a month-old infant. But he drank and even chewed gingerly on the bits of flesh, and Toby felt the first real stirrings of reassurance that what he had done was right.

"There's plenty more where this came from," he told the boy quietly, and his lips twisted with self-derision. Canfield had assured him he knew the location of Adam Trent's body, and when the artist was gone, there was always Phillip Huntington and Dulcy. The children, Canfield had crudely proclaimed, he didn't think were worth the effort of digging up.

A great, hollow sadness pulsed briefly within Toby as he carefully lay Simon back and tucked the blanket around him. Rising wearily to his feet, he turned the meat in the skillet and opened the door.

"Supper's ready," he called, and the words stuck in his throat like sour bile.

Sarah ate with relish and felt a great satisfaction at seeing Samantha and Lucas become more cheerful as they devoured their meal. But when she looked across the table to smile her thanks to Toby, she saw that he had not touched the meat on his plate.

His blue eyes looked distant and haunted in their shadowed sockets, a disturbed frown furrowing his brow. He seemed strangely subdued, preoccupied, staring in dull fascination at a knothole on the surface of the wagon siding, his expression pained, as if pursued by his own private demons.

Sarah reached across the table and touched his wrist lightly, her eyes clouded with concern. He jumped, as if suddenly awakened, and swung his glassy gaze in her direction.

"You should eat," she said quietly.

He seemed to grimace. "I can't."

"You *have* to! I know you're tired, but now that we have food again—" She cut off a bite of her steak and held the fork across to him. "You'll be able to get your strength back now."

Toby stared at the meat speared on her fork, something akin to fear shining in his eyes. As if it was sheer agony to do so, he finally leaned forward and accepted the morsel. He chewed cautiously, his eyes closed, the expression on his face indefinable.

Sarah cast a brief, puzzled look at Hetty and returned her fork to her plate, watching Toby with a mixture of confusion and doubt. Perhaps *his* mind was starting to go with the strain, and she shuddered at the thought.

He swallowed, wiped a hand across his eyes, and, with a grim sigh, picked up his own knife and fork and began to eat.

"Why didn't you bring back the antlers?" Lucas asked him.

"Because it was something extra we didn't need to carry." Toby finished the last of his steak and stood abruptly. He reached for his jacket and moved hurriedly to the door. "I need some air." And, without another word, he disappeared into the chilly December afternoon sunshine.

Sarah gnawed her lower lip, feeling a confusion she couldn't define.

"He's had a terrible responsibility," Hetty said, moving from the table to check on Simon. "It'd be bad enough if we were his kin, but we're strangers."

"Not anymore," Samantha volunteered. "He's like

335

having another pa.''

At the mention of Roy's name, the little group immediately became somber. Sarah gathered the empty plates and stacked them in the trunk; there was no need to wash them anymore, for after every meal, greedy tongues licked them spotless for the last minuscule crumb or drop of juice.

"He seems to be resting easier," Hetty observed, stroking Simon's cheek.

Sarah nodded, standing before the fire and chafing her arms. The silence in the cabin was oppressive and sad, and she was concerned about Toby's peculiar behavior. Guilty—that's how he had looked while he was eating. Guilty and distressed and sick at heart.

Snatching up her coat, she left the cabin and walked up the ramp. Her heavy shoes crunched in the snow, and the air tasted clean and fresh. Smoke billowed up from the other chimneys, and icicles hung in shiny prisms from the eaves.

Toby was sitting on the roof, his bony shoulders hunched forward, staring off toward the massive white domes of the Sierras. Sarah boosted herself up to sit beside him and reached for his hand. He wore no gloves, and his fingers were cold.

"Is anything the matter?" she finally asked.

A faint, sad smile played about the corners of his mouth. "Nothing more than usual."

"You must have gotten off a lucky shot today."

"Lucky?" His voice dropped with bitterness, his eyes hard and cold. "Yes—lucky."

She searched his face for an answer to her unasked questions, studying the deep hollows of his cheeks which even his beard couldn't hide, the jutting bones, the dark circles beneath his melancholy eyes. New lines had appeared on his forehead and at the corners of his eyes, and she saw how much older he looked than when she had first met him.

"Toby—"

He turned, silencing her with a shake of his head. "I've decided something today, and you'll have to promise me you'll help."

She nodded obediently, though she was all to aware of her own limitations.

"We have meat now—plenty of it." His brooding gaze swung back to the mountains, and his eyes took on a faraway look that disturbed her. Heavy black clouds were moving in, filled with the definite promise of more snow. "We can eat better and build up strength. And in another week or two—when I think we're able—we're going to leave this place."

Sarah looked at him wonderingly. "Just us? You and me and Hetty and the children?"

He shrugged. "If the others want to come along, they can. But it'll be every man—or family—for himself. We *can't* stay here any longer. We'll all die if we do!" His voice lowered, and a note of fear crept into it. "And I don't want to die—not *here,* anyway."

Sarah was alarmed at the emotion in his voice. What he said made sense—up to a point. But the emigrant road over the mountains was buried beneath tons of snow, and Toby didn't know the way. Canfield and the others had already tried and failed—and at a time when they still had some stamina left. Now . . . An uneasy feeling clawed at her belly at the thought, and she felt a chill steal over her skin.

"We might die out there, too," she said.

"We might. And we might not. We *might* even make it." He turned her face to him and looked searchingly into her eyes. "But we can't stay *here* to die!"

Her mind was a whirlpool of conflicting emotions and frightening conjectures, but she nodded. She trusted Toby, and he was right—there *was* no hope for them here. Even Hetty seemed to have given up on Roy's returning for them.

"All right," she said quietly. "We'll do all we can to get strong again. But I'm afraid."

His lips curved into a faint, gentle smile. "So am I." He kissed her softly and squeezed her hand in reassurance.

Sarah tried to smile, but could only manage a sort of grimace. Shivering, she turned her gaze toward the west again just as the door to the Jennings's cabin opened. The Reverend—gaunt, pale, his mane of silver hair billowing about his face like a cloud—staggered up the ramp, carrying a body wrapped in a quilt. Ephiram and Hope stumbled after him, mere wraithly shadows of wasted flesh. The children were crying, and Sarah even thought she heard a choked sob come from the Reverend.

A feeling of genuine pity washed over her, but the scene only served to fill her with a renewed determination to leave this camp of death and despair.

"I hope the weather holds when we try to cross the mountains," she said absently, watching as the Reverend carried his wife around the side of the cabin.

Toby nodded gravely, his features set in a grim, haunted mask.

338

Chapter Twenty

Sarah watched dully as Lucas and Toby sat at the table, moving the checkers over the well-worn board. A lighted piece of pitch pine illuminated their game, and its flickering glow alternately threw their lean faces into shadow and light. Samantha and Hetty were outside with a resumption of their vigil of watching the mountain pass for a glimpse of Roy.

A log popped and settled in the hearth, Lucas moved his checker over the board with a scrape; all else in the cabin was silent. A sad, wistful look crept into Sarah's eyes as they shifted to the pallet where Simon had spent his days, swaddled in blankets, fussing occasionally. The pallet was empty now, and Simon was buried in a shallow snow grave behind the cabin. The boy had seemed to rally for a few days after the advent of the meat from the elk; then he deteriorated rapidly. He sank into a kind of coma, his breathing became more strained and irregular, and then finally ceased altogether.

That had been a week ago, during the height of yet another storm. Toby had taken the child out in the midst of the blizzard, but it had been a struggle to get Hetty to part from the lifeless little body. She had wept and cried until she was reduced to a quivering mass of hysterical sobs for almost two days, and Sarah had begun to fear for the woman's own health and sanity. But after her grief was evidently spent, she seemed to come to her senses again, and now was almost back to her usual self.

"You beat me again," Toby said, throwing up his hands in exaggerated defeat. He gave an admiring shake of his head. "You're just too good for me."

Lucas beamed, his eyes totally lost in wide, dark hollows. "Another game?"

Toby nodded. "You set it up." He rose from the table and lifted the lid on the kettle. Steam wafted out and filled Sarah's nostrils with its tantalizing aroma. Toby stirred the contents, examined a spoonful, and replaced the lid. Settling himself back on his keg, he pretended to pore over his first move of the new game.

Toby insisted on doing most of the cooking, which Sarah thought strange but didn't object to. After all, why *should* she protest as long as he kept the kettle full? She suspected his reasons might be to spare them the knowledge of what they were eating—rats, bats, owls, maybe even snakes. It didn't matter, so long as they had food. Every few days he would disappear for a while and return with their supper in a burlap bag. Sometimes it would be steaks, other times meat for stewing, but *always* there was something to eat, and Sarah was grateful to him.

Her strength had begun to return slowly, though by no means was she what could be considered healthy. There was nothing but meat—and lean meat, at that—and often she found herself craving a piece of bread or a ripe apple or a glass of milk so badly she could hardly stand it.

340

Christmas was two days away, and she found it almost impossible to believe they had been here for this long. A shadow of melancholy passed over her face at the memories of former holidays, but these thoughts only made her gloomier. Though she often spent her days in the past, forcing her mind back to warmer and happier times: harvest festivals, church socials, Fourth of July picnics, giant watermelons on warm summer days or hot chocolate on cold afternoons.

She released a soft, doleful sigh and buried her face in her hands. Sometimes the memories helped, but often they only made things worse. Time and space lost meaning, and each minute seemed to drag on for an eternity.

She shook her head in frustrated anger and clenched her teeth against the hatred she felt for this miserable hovel. Toby had promised they would be gone by the new year, and, despite her earlier apprehensions, Sarah was willing to take *any* risk to leave this wretched place.

Lester Stone opened the door of the shanty and stared without recognition at the emaciated shrew before him. She was an unkempt creature, with tangles of greasy brown hair threaded with silver tumbling about a face that seemed composed of thousands of tiny lines and sagging, yellowish skin. Her eyes were dazed and blank, her lips bluish, and it wasn't until she lifted a thin bejeweled wrist in supplication that Lester knew this slattern was Ruth Huntington.

"My husband is very ill," she said, and her voice was a husky, raw whisper. "Our fire has gone out, and neither Alma or I can cut wood. Could you—?" She didn't finish the question, but her eyes were wide and pleading.

341

Stone's dark little eyes narrowed speculatively as they went over the emeralds on her bony wrist and the string of pearls roped around the wattle of flesh at her throat. He cocked his head thoughtfully, and his lips twisted into a cunning smile. He could afford the lady a little help. After all, what were neighbors for?

Assuming a look of patient understanding, he nodded pleasantly to the bedraggled woman before him, then turned to call into the dismal stench of the hut. "Either of you care to help, too?"

Judd mumbled something unintelligible and scrunched up in his blankets by the fire.

Canfield paused in his relentless search for the lice in his beard to grin blearily. "I ain't even got enough energy to fart anymore."

"I'm glad," Judd muttered, and Canfield hooted raucously.

Shaking his head in disdain, Stone gathered up his coat, hat, gloves, and hatchet and left the shanty.

By the time Lester had cut a half dozen lengths of wood, he had to pause to rest. Breathing heavily, he shivered as the biting wind chilled his sweat to ice water. And the logs were ridiculously puny for all his efforts, hardly better than twigs no bigger around than his arm.

Mopping the perspiration from his face before it had a chance to freeze, he leaned heavily against the tree and tried to slow his heartbeat and catch his breath. *Why* was he doing this? It would certainly be easier simply to let nature take its course and wait for the Huntingtons to freeze to death. And, in their weakened state, *that* wouldn't take very long. Then he could move into their cabin and have a place all to himself, away from the two slovens with whom he lived now.

He snorted in contempt. Between Brannan's self-pitying whining and Canfield's temper and sarcastic remarks about their food . . . He shook his head scornfully. Canfield actually thought the ghastly thing they were forced to do was *funny!* He seemed to delight in making bawdy comments about his supper until Stone became so nauseated *he* couldn't eat. He prayed that every time Canfield opened his mouth he would choke on some of that meat he found so amusing and die.

But despite his larcenous leanings, Stone was not ready to murder the Huntingtons, in whatever a roundabout way it might be. And, gathering up his pitiful stack of kindling, he shuffled back to camp.

The Huntingtons' cabin was ice-cold and dim, illuminated only by one guttering candle. Stone threw the wood into the fireplace and managed to get a fire started. A pot of some kind of foul-smelling, gelatinous goo rested near the hearth, and he nearly gagged from its rancid smell.

"Hides," Ruth said, by way of explanation. "We boil 'em and boil 'em, and then let them cool. Sort of like calves-foot jelly."

Stone grimaced and turned away from the kettle. Now that the light was a little better, he let his gaze travel over the room. It was filled with all the baggage from the wagon, discarded, dirty clothing, and soiled linen. Edgar Huntington lay on one of the pallets, unmoving, covered with several quilts. Alma sat hunched in a corner, a peaked, pinched skeleton with snarled wispy blond hair.

Carefully stepping over the litter on the floor, Lester approached the pallet. The erratic rise and fall of Huntington's sunken chest and darting tongue occasionally

343

moistening his cracked lips were the only outward signs of life.

Stone shuddered and turned away, directing his questioning glance at Ruth. "When was the last time you had food? *Real* food."

The woman seemed confused, her hands clutching and twisting the fabric of her dress nervously, as if it was a strain to think. After a few moments of befuddled eyeblinking and lip-chewing, she shrugged helplessly. "Two weeks, maybe three." Her face contorted into a kind of distorted mask, and her eyes took on an irrational gleam. She thrust out a shriveled arm, the band of emeralds glittering in the firelight. "I'll give you *this* for some meat."

Stone appraised the woman shrewdly. "The pearls, too?"

She nodded quickly and fumbled to unfasten the clasp. Lester pocketed the jewels and left the cabin, promising he would be right back.

As he crossed the snowy carpet, an absured, ironic thought popped into his mind, but he pushed it quickly away. They didn't need to know whose liver they were about to receive. It was a fitting sacrifice for a devoted son and husband to make.

Maggie no longer felt any hunger; only a kind of deceitfully pleasant lassitude. Others said she was dying, but she didn't believe them. She felt too peaceful, too comfortable, too serene. She smiled dreamily and let her mind drift, wrapped in a snug cocoon of blankets near the fire on a dirt floor that didn't seem as hard as it used to anymore.

Several days ago, she had felt only a malaise that sapped her spirit and dulled her senses. Now she welcomed the emptiness of her mind, the heaviness of her limbs, the darkness that seemed to envelop her. Sounds drifted in and out of her consciousness—her mother's weeping, her father's occasional outbursts when he would rave for food, Katie's soft whimpering—but nothing really penetrated.

She took several deep, rasping breaths and sank back into her own private world of tranquillity. She felt a warm glow of detachment steal over her, and her lips twitched in a semblance of a smile.

Was this the onset of death? A total surrender to living? A part of her mind wondered at these things, while another part no longer cared. She only knew this unfamiliar delicious lethargy, this dark curtain of peaceful oblivion.

Sarah knelt at Maggie's side, staring in pity and helplessness at the wasted woman before her. Her sallow cheeks were as tight as a death mask against the outline of her skull. She was bloodlessly pale, her pulse weak and thready, her eyes hollow and rimmed with dark circles. She was either comatose or sleeping; no movement was visible except the faint, shallow rise and fall of her chest as she breathed.

The other O'Brians stared dully at Sarah from their pallets; only Sean and Daniel were still able to move about.

Sean fumbled to pour a cup of soup from the pail Sarah had brought when he came to fetch her. His hands shook violently as he handed it to her, and Sarah carefully lifted Maggie's head from the pillow.

345

Maggie felt someone touching her, forcing her head up, and she was vaguely irritated at this intrusion of her pleasant reveries. Something warm pressed against her lips, and they parted involuntarily. Hot, savory broth flooded into her mouth. She swallowed reflexively.

Her eyelids fluttered, and the room swam before her. Hazy shapes materialized out of a mist, and she recognized her brother's voice calling her. But he sounded so far away!

Her skin felt on fire, but great, shaking chills racked her emaciated body. More of the hot, tangy liquid trickled down her throat, and she struggled into a more alert sense of consciousness. The roaring in her ears subsided, and as her glazed eyes were able to focus once more, she was surprised to see Sarah Coulter holding the cup to her lips.

Sean released a whistling sigh of relief and sat back on his heels. Sarah removed the cup, and Maggie dimly heard her tell Sean to give some to the others.

Maggie fought the sudden spinning and nausea and forced herself to sit up. Her lips moved, and when she finally managed to speak, her voice sounded thick and raspy to her own ears. "Have they come?"

"Who?" Sarah asked, bending close.

Maggie took a deep breath and lay heavily back on her pallet, depression washing over her. They *hadn't* come. There was no rescue party; only Sarah Coulter and her damned soup! Why couldn't the woman just have let her die? Why rouse her from that peaceful netherworld only for more misery and despair?

Maggie heard a distant voice sobbing, a sad, heart-wrenching sound. And as the tears stung her eyes and wet her cheeks, she realized they were her own cries.

Sarah's brows drew into a worried frown as she regarded Maggie, then turned her attention to the two brothers, moving languorously among their family members, passing out cups of broth, helping those who were too weak to drink. Her shoulders slumped, and she covered her face with her hands, overwhelmed by fear, frustration, and despondency.

Toby was ready to leave at a moment's notice. He expected another storm any day, but as soon as it had passed, they would be gone. Strips of meat had been dried and stored carefully—enough to last them all for six days; matches, hatchets, even Roy's pistol were packed.

"Mr. Garrett's bringin' us meat," Sean announced.

Michael's head came up from his blankets—gaunt, pallid, eyes glittering wildly, looking like some creature from an age preceding civilized man. "Meat?"

Sean grinned and nodded his head with satisfaction. "Aye—meat."

Sarah got slowly to her feet and tugged on her gloves. She cast one final look around at the unkempt, almost ghoulish faces peering at her, and, suppressing a shudder, left the reeking cabin and trudged up the snow ramp.

The sky was leaden, and a light, misting rain had begun to fall. Clouds of vaporized breath plumed out in great, billowing spirals before her face. The snow was wet and treacherous from the soaking, and it was brutally cold. Still, instead of returning directly to her own cabin, Sarah stood and stared up at the lofty snow-mantled peaks to the west.

She felt a sudden, intense rush of apprehension. It was an awesome, forbidding landscape of snow-packed crags and pathless forests. The idea of attempting to make the crossing in their weakened condition without guide or even compass froze the breath in her throat and sent fear twisting through her intestines. But abruptly a vision of the O'Brians, with their muddled, bleary eyes and sunk into the coma that precedes death, flashed before her, and her mind rebelled.

She didn't want to die like that. She didn't want to die at all! But dying up there on those formidable mountains would be infinitely preferable to wasting away here and having her bones found by the first of next season's emigrant trains. At least they would be *doing* something. And perhaps Toby was right—perhaps they *would* make it. Though, in her heart, she didn't believe it any more than she suspected he did.

Sighing dismally, she turned away, caught a glimpse of Canfield emerging from behind the Jennings-Huntington cabin. He was dragging something, and it left a trail in the snow like a great fat sled runner. She watched as he staggered and tottered through the mushy drifts until he disappeared down the ramp and into the hut.

The temperature was dropping, and Sarah shivered. She blew on her gloved hands, rubbed them together, and started back to her cabin. She saw Toby appear from the same spot Canfield had just been, the ever-present burlap sack clutched in one hand. Evidently their former guide was getting his food supply from the same source as the Coulters.

But what *was* that source—suddenly limitless after weeks and months of scrimping and going hungry? That

348

was a question that had plagued her for weeks—one she didn't know how to answer. And Toby's uncommunicative attitude served only to arouse her suspicions and increase the air of mystery surrounding this unexpected bounty. It also made Sarah vaguely uncomfortable.

Toby slogged through the snow, head bent, intent on his footing. He was *so* thin! And that animallike grace she had admired, that assurance in his step had turned into the stooped, shuffling stride of an old man. The buckskin jacket had been wetted and dried so often that it looked like cardboard, the fringe broken and stiff. His boots, she knew, were worn out, and slush leaked into the soles until he could be out in the cold for only a short time before coming in to warm his feet. What would he do once they were in the mountains?

He seemed surprised to see her. "What are you doing out here?"

She made a gesturing shrug with her hands. "Nothing."

Mocking amusement shone in his eyes, and there was an ironic twist to his mouth. "If you're waiting for the stagecoach, I believe it's running a little behind schedule today."

Sarah's surprised intake of breath changed to a soft chuckle, and a spark of pleasure lit her eyes. She studied his face with its hollow cheeks and eyes gleaming out of dark sockets, then gave him a speculative, mischievous grin. "Is that the old Toby Garrett I hear talking?"

He shrugged negligently, his mouth hinting at a smile. "It's Christmas Eve, isn't it? *Someone's* got to have a little holiday cheer." He slung the sack over his shoulder and kicked a clump of snow off one boot before he took another step. "You go on in and get warm. I'll be back in

349

a few minutes." His blue eyes sparkled impudently at her, and his white teeth flashed in a broad grin. "I've got a bottle of champagne chilling in the snow."

Sarah stared at him wonderingly, saw the teasing grin beneath the tangle of blond beard, and exploded in soft, muted laughter. Pulling her collar up, she hurried back to her cabin, still chuckling. It was good to laugh—something she hadn't done in a long, long time. But as her gaze swung to the massive glacial mountains, she couldn't help but wonder if it would be the *last* time she ever laughed.

Lester Stone tripped descending the snow ramp to the Huntington cabin and slid the last three feet on his skinny behind. Cursing loudly, he picked himself up, dusted the snow off the seat of his pants, and gathered up the spilled firewood. When he entered the gloomy den, both Alma and Ruth were in their beds, wrapped in blankets. Soft, whimpering sobs came from one of them, though he didn't know which. Stepping over the debris, he laid another log on the fire and let the rest drop to the floor.

"He's gone," Ruth said, and her voice was as dead and cold as ice.

Lester glanced up in mild surprise, though he had expected it. He stood amid the clutter of baggage, arms akimbo, wondering what he should do or say.

"Would you take him out?"

Lester grunted irritably. Edgar Huntington had been a big man, and even with the weight loss, Stone doubted he could do it alone. And certainly neither Canfield or Brannan would help—not even for the entire Huntington fortune!

Muttering under his breath, he crossed over to the pallet and lifted the quilt from the dead man's face. Stone's hand stopped in midair as something sewn inside one of the patchwork squares clinked and rolled to one side. Holding his breath, Lester shook the quilt gently. Coins rattled and jingled, and he blinked in nervous anticipation. This must be the infamous quilt everyone had whispered and speculated about for all these months—the one containing the purported fifteen thousand dollars!

Sunken eyes glittering with excitement, Stone turned to the two women peering at him from their blankets. "I might have a little trouble moving him, and it'll probably take some time. Ah—why don't you two ladies go over and wait with Reverend Jennings? He might even have a word or two of comfort for you."

Ruth hesitated, but finally agreed. Alma was less anxious to leave the warmth and security of her bed, but Lester finally managed to persuade her. After the pair were bundled up and had stumbled out of the cabin, Stone returned his attention to the quilt. As he stripped it off the corpse, his hand brushed the lifeless flesh. The touch of the cold, clammy skin chilled him, left him shivering unreasonably for several seconds.

But the musical clink of coins was more enticing than a lover's embrace, and, dragging the quilt with him, Lester sat before the fire and took out his knife. Five patches in each corner contained no less than a dozen gold eagles, but after these were all emptied, he had counted only a little more than five thousand dollars. Hardly the stuff of paupers, but neither was it the fortune he had expected.

He shook the quilt, but no more coins jangled. Annoyed, he balled the ragged coverlet up in preparation to toss it aside when paper crinkled beneath his fingers. Ripping frantically with his knife, he brought forth bank-notes—*negotiable* banknotes—totaling *more* than the anticipated sum.

Lester hooted with joy and tossed the papers into the air, lifting his gaunt, cadaverous face up to let them shower over him. Laughing in sheer delight, he clapped his hands gleefully and began scooping up the notes, pausing once to kiss the stern visage of some obscure bank president engraved on its surface.

"Merry Christmas, Lester!" he shouted and laughed again.

The notes would be lighter to carry, and he could leave the silverware and candlesticks to the wolves. The jewelry, Ole Andersen's gold coins, and now this would be more than enough to make Lester Stone one of the wealthiest men in the Sacramento when he got there.

The smile vanished abruptly, and an angry frown of dismay creased his forehead.

If he ever got there.

Chapter Twenty-One

"It doesn't *feel* like Christmas!"

Toby paused in his woodchopping and leaned on the ax, glancing down at Samantha seated a few feet away on a blanket spread on the snow. Bundled in several shirts beneath her fur vest and wearing a pair of socks for mittens, she looked so frail and tiny. Her dark hair hung in limp strands about her face and shoulders, and her amber-flecked brown eyes seemed lost in deep sockets.

"Oh, I don't know," he said conversationally and swept out an arm. "Look around you. It seems like Christmas to me."

And it was true, he thought, as he let his eyes wander over the landscape surrounding him. The woods were sparkling, newly washed from yesterday's light rain. The snow gleamed in the sunshine and shimmered on the branches of the pines. Icicles glittered in long, icy spikes—a picturesque setting.

There was a tight little frown on Samantha's forehead, and she shook her head. "It's not the same. Last year Pa gave me a pretty new shawl, and we had roast duck for supper and sang carols.''

''*We* could sing carols, I suppose,'' he offered.

She pursed her lips, and her frown deepened. She folded her arms and shook her head firmly. ''It ain't the same!''

Toby shrugged and lifted the ax again. Sam was right —it *didn't* seem like Christmas. It was just one more long, weary day to get through. And another day after this, and another. Scowling, he swung the ax, and it bit deeply into the trunk of the pine.

The storm he had been expecting had not yet come, and—from the look of the sky—wouldn't arrive today. The snow pack had hardened and consolidated—an advantageous condition to begin their trek across the mountains. But if they got two or three days into that maze of canyons and cliffs, and the storm *did* come . . .

Samantha's voice broke into his grim thoughts. ''Do you think they celebrate Christmas in heaven?''

Toby arched a curious brow. ''I don't know. Why?''

She plucked out the needles on a branch one by one, and her face was intent on her task. ''I was thinking about Simon and Kevin and Jamie and Ephiram. Pa always said Christmas was for children. I don't figure maybe Mrs. Pardee or Mrs. Jennings or Mr. Poole or even Kelly O'Brian will miss it much. But the little ones—'' She lapsed into silence and released a heavy, plaintive sigh.

Toby felt a bitter twinge of sadness and pity as he studied the bowed head and thin shoulders. What an unlikely train of thought for a little girl to have, he thought wistfully, and he shook his head with a newfound respect.

Sean and Daniel O'Brian crunched over the thin layer of ice, axes and hatchets in hand.

"Everyone is feelin' much better," Sean said. "Thanks to the meat you brought us. It's grateful, we are."

Toby shrugged aside the thanks, studying the two young men before him. Sean still retained a spark of his vigor, but Daniel, at fifteen, showed all the familiar signs of their ordeal. His face was thin and pallid, his unbearded cheeks hollow and shadowed.

"Sarah said she'd stop in and see how Maggie was doing," he said, hefting his ax once more.

"She gave us a scare," Sean acknowledged, sizing up a nearby pine. "But I think she'll be comin' around just fine by the end of the day."

Toby grunted in reply and swung the ax into the bark with a great thunk. Every muscle ached, and needles of pain jabbed at his toes. Soon, he knew, the discomfort would ebb with the creeping numbness until he felt nothing—not even the sticky warm blood that seeped from the cracks in his feet and caked and froze between his toes.

Roy's throat was dry and his chest ached. His snowshoes dragged over the crusty snow in scuffling steps. The light wind chilled the sweat on his face and chapped his dry, cracked lips. The thirty-pound pack on his back sapped his strength until he thought each step he took would surely be his last.

But he kept moving, shuffling along in a line behind Perkins and Lebec, the others following after him. They had reached the summit yesterday evening, but the barren, windswept heights had offered no fit place to make camp. So they had gone on, down the eastern slope of the pass, and with each yard of ground gained, Roy's despondency and sense of hopelessness increased.

Around every corner, over every rise, he expected to find the emigrants. But they were never there—not even a sign that they had *been* there—only the desolate, unending whiteness.

Lost in his morose thoughts, Roy hadn't realized that the men had stopped, and he walked right into the broad back of Hezekiah Perkins. The grizzled guide turned, scowled fiercely, and then did something quite unexpected. He grinned—a wide, slashing grin bisecting his bushy black beard and displaying a row of horse-sized yellow teeth.

"If I'm not mistaken, Mr. Coulter, that's smoke I see comin' from down there. No chimneys or anything else I can make out—but smoke."

Roy staggered, sucked in his breath audibly, and stumbled forward a few feet to squint down the sloping mountainside. Gray wreaths of smoke billowed up from an unseen source and dissipated in the chilly mist. He swallowed dryly, his stomach churning with a mixture of apprehension and excitement.

"That's Truckee Lake," he heard Perkins say, but he really wasn't listening—*couldn't*, in fact, hear for his heartbeat drumming in his ears. "Froze clean over."

Roy hiked up his pack and started down the trail, wading through drifts, crunching over the harder surfaces of the snow. He could hear the others behind him, grunting and panting to keep up with him, but he was unmindful of the labor of moving through the snow.

Then he was on level ground, and the snow-mantled spruces bordering the icebound lake loomed up on his right. He broke into a clumsy, shuffling run, his snowshoes slapping into the powder with each step and sending up little geysers of slushy ice.

The smoke continued to curl up in wispy spirals, but the baffling origin of these fires still eluded him. He stumbled and nearly fell. Face flushed and chest heaving, he paused to catch his breath and wipe the stinging sweat from his eyes.

He strained to see movement, but there was no sign of life; only the phantom smoke. Cupping his hands to his mouth and drawing in a deep breath of frosty air, he called out loudly, "Hellooo!"

His voice echoed from the steep walls behind him, bounced off the snow-laden trees, and reverberated around the hollow near the Lake.

Toby dropped the ax. His head jerked up, and he blinked in disbelieving shock.

"Hellooo!"

The shout came again, and *this* time he knew it had been real. His gaze flew to Samantha, her head cocked to one side, eyes wider with wonder. She looked at him, and, for an instant, their eyes locked in shared astonishment.

Then she was scrambling to her feet, and they were both lurching out of the woods, Sean and Daniel close behind.

Toby blundered out of the trees, saw dark figures shuffling in an uneven line down from the head of the lake, and fell to his knees. Stunned, he bit his lips to smother a moan of pain as he picked himself up and staggered on.

Despite the cost to his failing strength and the torment to his feet, he felt as if the weight of the world had been lifted from his shoulders. Now there was someone else to take them out of the mountains—men who obviously knew the way. No longer would it be up to him to lead them blindly over the nonexistent emigrant trail, perhaps taking them into a worse fate than what they had escaped from. And more than that—more than *anything*—these men were sure to have food with them. Food—*real* food. Not . . .

Toby stumbled and went down again, but this time he stayed where he was. He blinked glassily, then threw back his head and laughed in sheer relief.

Roy saw the figures running toward him, but it was hard for him to comprehend just who they were. Impossibly thin and ragged, if it hadn't been for the cascade of dark hair blowing free off the child's shoulders and the familiar fringe, ratty and torn, on the man's jacket . . .

Samantha fell headlong in the snow. Roy flung aside his pack and ran the last ten feet, kneeling beside her and gathering her in his arms. She buried her face against his shoulder and began to cry, great, racking spasms convulsing her shoulders.

"Oh, Pa! I *knew* you'd come!"

Roy swallowed back a rush of tears and closed his eyes, rocking her gently in his arms, crooning softly, reassuringly. But confusion and despair wrenched at his heart as his hands touched bony shoulders, closed around a wrist no bigger around than a stick.

"It's all right, Sam. Pa's here, and I won't ever leave you again."

He blinked the tears from his eyes and glanced around. Garrett was still sitting in the snow, half-crying, half-laughing. The two other mangy scarecrows had collapsed beside him, and Roy's face went white with shock as he

358

recognized the rusty hair and cloth cap of Sean O'Brian.

He got unsteadily to his feet and lifted Sam up with him. And as his confused gaze wandered over the camp, he saw other ghostly ragamuffins emerging from their dens under the snow. Filthy, bedraggled, emaciated, they moved sluggishly, as if in a daze. Roy couldn't believe these frightening specters of wasted flesh and tangled hair were the same people whom he had befriended back on the trail so many months ago.

Then Hetty was in his arms, sobbing uncontrollably, her warm tears bathing his shoulder. He saw Lucas and Sarah, lost in the voluminous folds of their heavy clothing, their pinched faces filled with uncertainty and disbelief. The boy's sunken eyes were filmed and distant; he was so thin that there seemed to be no flesh over his bones. He looked frail, fragile, brittle.

Sarah's skin clung tightly to the bones of her face; dark circles obscured her eyes. She seemed confused, her look uncomprehending and blank, as if she couldn't understand what was happening.

Stunned and heartsick, Roy turned his gaze back to his wife, lifting her face to look at him. Her features had hardened; tiny lines were etched in the parchment skin, skin that was a pasty yellow color. Her brown eyes were sunken deep and filled with a nameless grief; threads of gray were interwoven in the matted, uncombed sable locks. His gloved fingers traced the outline of her face, unable to believe his young wife had become this shriveled old hag.

"Simon's"—her voice was weak and distant, raw and raspy as if it was painful to speak—"Simon's dead."

A strangled cry of anguish and sorrow escaped from Roy's throat, and he buried his face against her hair.

Hetty began to weep again, and he stroked her thin shoulder until her sobs turned to sniffles, and he felt a measure of his *own* control returning.

Sarah came to him, looked at him in undisguised affection and gratitude, and gave him a brief hug. Then, squeezing his arm with long, skeletal fingers, she went to see to Toby, still sitting in the snow where he had fallen.

"Food!" he heard someone shout. "They have food!"

Roy looked around at the haggard, starving emigrants. Now that the initial shock of seeing the rescuers had worn off, the mania of the end of deprivation seemed to be working upon them. A ripple of excited voices spread through their ranks, and they pressed forward to surround the nine men from Sutter's, begging, demanding, sobbing. They surged forward, a disorderly, desperate mob of ravenous men, women, and children. Clawlike hands reached out in supplication. Eyes glittered wildly from sunken sockets. Bony shoulders pushed and shoved against each other, all eager to be the first to taste the bounty.

The men of the relief party exchanged nervous glances, alarmed at this demented crowd of emaciated, untidy creatures advancing on them like hideous apparitions from a nightmare.

Standing a head taller than the others, Hezekiah Perkins held up a hand. "There's food for all of you!" He turned to his men, ordering them to distribute dried beef and biscuits to all of them.

Roy saw Emmett Pardee snatch the food from one of the men. At the sight of the meat and sourdough rolls, a light of madness came into his eyes. Horribly thin, a mass of disheveled hair and beard, Emmett dropped into a crouch, glanced furtively around with wild, glassy eyes, and, clutching the food to his chest, ran back to his den and two waiting sons.

Dismayed at his friends's erratic behavior—indeed, the behavior of *all* of them—Roy turned back to Hetty and his children. "I've got food in my pack," he said quietly.

Hetty nodded without speaking, but that same irrational gleam flickered briefly in her eyes. Roy studied her with concern for a moment before fetching his discarded pack. He followed her toward the cabin buried beneath the snow, while the others begged for more food.

The relief party visited each cabin, though they didn't stay long. Roy was forced to tie a handkerchief over his face to filter out the vile stench of the hovels; but even with this protection he often found himself choking back the bile welling up from his stomach.

The emigrants had been forced to live in conditions he didn't believe any human could endure, and they were all in a pitiable state of weakness and exhaustion. They had pleaded for more to eat; food was the only thing on their minds. They were given all the men of the party thought was safe, but it wasn't enough to satisfy them. They begged tearfully for more, but Perkins was firm in his allotment. Eleven were dead, and of those still alive, Roy doubted that Maggie O'Brian, the two Huntington women, and Inga Andersen were strong enough to make the mountain crossing.

Now, much later in the afternoon, after firewood had been cut and doled out, the men were busily engaged in constructing a lean-to in which to pass the night, preferring the freezing cold to the vermin and reek of the cabins.

361

Sarah sat on the floor near the hearth while her brother and Hetty talked quietly and Sam and Lucas sucked contentedly on lemon drops—a tiny treasure Roy had brought especially for his children. He had sat silently with head bowed while the details of their ordeal had been related to him—the cattle wandering off in the storm, the sacrifice of the dog, Simon's death.

Sarah allowed herself to listen to it this one time; she never wanted to hear the story repeated again as long as she lived. She had given up hope of ever seeing the new year dawn. Now she had that hope again, and it burned fiercely within her. There were ten strong, healthy men to lead them out of the mountains, and Roy's descriptions of the fertile Sacramento valley served only to fire her blood all the more.

Toby sat on a keg with his feet soaking in a pan of hot water. He lifted one swollen, inflamed foot, and Sarah raised questioning eyes to him. "More?"

He nodded and closed his eyes, wincing as she poured scalding water into the pan. His feet were masses of puffy, tortured flesh, oozing blood and pus from a multitude of cracks. Sarah feared that he might lose several of his toes, and she knew his pain must be intolerable. Still, he had never even given the slightest indication of his frostbite until today.

"Perkins wants to leave tomorrow," Roy said, and there was a trace of uncertainty in his voice. "I don't think *any* of you are up to it, but a storm might break any day and pin us all down longer. And we didn't bring much food with us."

"A pretty sight, aren't we all?" Toby remarked dryly.

Roy ran a trembling hand over his beard and shook his head. "I didn't know *what* we'd find." His fingers stole across the table and closed around Hetty's. "But I just thank God you're all alive, except—" His voice cracked, and his gaze seemed to turn inward.

An uncomfortable silence descended over the room, tense and oppressive. Sarah chafed her arms and added another log to the fire. Toby removed his feet from the pan of water, dried them carefully, and began applying the same salve he had used on the cow's sore hide.

"Is there snow at Sutter's, Pa?" Samantha asked.

Roy shook his head. "Just green grass and trees. Most of the trees don't even lose their leaves."

The youngsters looked at their father with something close to awe in their eyes. A tree that didn't lose its leaves in winter was beyond their realm of comprehension.

"If we'd known you had nothing to eat—" Roy left the sentence unfinished, and his expression grew thoughtful. "We cached provisions along the way. The first is about two days' march from here." A frown wrinkled his forehead briefly. "Maybe three or four—with the condition everyone's in."

"Toby dried some meat for *our* attempt at crossing," Sarah said, and her mouth curved into a faint, rueful smile. "I'm glad we waited this long to leave. Otherwise, we could have been out there, and—" Her voice trailed off, and she shuddered involuntarily at what might have happened to them. "Anyway," she went on softly, "we can add that meat to what you brought."

"No!" Toby came out of his seat, his face flushed with anger, his hands curling into claws. Sarah gaped at him and watched helplessly as he snatched up the oilcloth pouch filled with jerky. His eyes blazing like spheres of crystal-blue ice and his jaw working tensely, he crushed the package between his fingers until his knuckles turned

363

white. Utter loathing twisted his face into an ugly mask, and, choking out an angry snarl that curled his lips back from his teeth, he flung the pouch into the fire. "Never again!" he exclaimed, and his voice shook with uncontrollable rage as he stood trembling, watching the flames devour the oilcloth covering and char the meat. He turned back, still visibly upset, and slumped into his seat. He buried his face miserably in his hands, and a strangled sound came from somewhere deep in his throat.

Sarah's brows drew into a worried, bewildered frown as she looked at Toby, then exchanged an uneasy glance with Hetty. Roy opened his mouth to speak, but his wife silenced him with a shake of her head and a frowning scowl.

Sarah turned back to Toby, her mind reeling with confusion. What could have possibly brought on his outburst? It simply wasn't like him—unless the relief of finally having the responsibilities lifted from him, the prospect of being out of the snow in a week or so, and the sensation of having a belly full of beans and bacon after being empty for so long had all combined to shatter his long-pent-up emotions.

A rising commotion outside distracted her thoughts, and she turned her attention to Roy as he moved to the door. A cold gust of wind blew in when he opened it, but he went out without bothering to get his coat. Rejuvenated from a decent meal and their lemon drops, Samantha and Lucas snatched up their jackets and followed their father, their insatiable childlike curiosity restored.

Whimpering, agonized sobs came from outside, along with agitated voices. Her own interest aroused, Sarah ventured out into the chilly Christmas afternoon air with Hetty.

Peter Andersen lay in the snow, moaning like a dying animal, rolling from side to side, clutching his belly. His face was as gray as ashes, and a shrill cry of anguish escaped from between his clenched teeth. His father and sister and a number of the men from the rescue party were gathered around him.

Perkins knelt beside him and offered him a tin cup. "Drink this, boy."

Peter moaned again and batted the cup aside. Perkins motioned to one of his men, who squatted down and held the young man's head. Perkins forced the cup to his lips. "Drink it!"

There was genuine fear in Peter's bulging, glazed eyes, and he swallowed obediently, his face twisted into a grimace. Immediately his eyes rolled wildly in his head, and he struggled to sit up. Perkins took hold of his shoulders, and Peter retched violently, his whole body shuddering with hard, racking spasms.

Sarah felt a surge of nausea and turned away as McTavish came over to Roy.

"He stole one of the men's packs and ate all he could hold," the Scot said. "And in his condition—" He glanced back at Peter and shook his head regretfully. "Perkins gave him tobacco juice. I'm hoping that will do the trick."

Sarah winced at the mere idea of drinking tobacco juice and rubbed her arms to ward off the cold. Stealing a glance through the little crowd, she saw that two of the men were carrying Peter down into the cabin, and she retreated quickly into her own.

She could well understand Peter's temptation. She could have eaten until she burst, but Roy had watched them all carefully, cautioning not to overstuff their

365

shrunken bellies. And, remembering Michael O'Brian's episode at the river after the desert, Sarah had steadfastly controlled her urge to gorge herself.

Toby had wrapped strips of cloth around his feet and was pulling on his socks gingerly. "What was it?" he asked, not looking up from his task.

"Peter. He ate too much."

Toby nodded mutely, a grunt his only reply. Sarah paced around the cluttered room, anxiously rubbing her hands together, suddenly uneasy at the prospect of tomorrow's impending journey. She was not strong—a few minutes of exercise had her feeling faint and wheezing like an old racehorse. And the idea of battling mile upon mile of deep drifts on her snowshoes sent a chill of dread streaking up her spine.

Her gaze slid to Toby. He was staring into the fire, his face taut, his eyes narrowed and brooding, and she felt a sudden rush of tenderness tinged with concern. He must be worried, too. After a few miles of walking, she could well imagine what would happen to his feet once the moisture began to seep into his boots.

She went to stand behind him, her hands resting lightly on his shoulders. She stared into the fire a moment, as if mezmerized by its flickering orange tongues. There was a comfortable silence between them, each lost in their own thoughts, until she finally spoke.

"Why did you throw the jerky in there?"

He released a long, weary sigh and reached for her hand, drawing her around until she stood before him. His blue eyes were intense, reflections of the fire's yellow flames dancing in their depths.

"Don't ever ask me about that again," he said softly, and the emotion in his voice surprised her. He took both her hands in his and rubbed them gently. His gaze was steady, searching, faintly melancholy. "I want to forget what's been happening here these last two weeks. So just don't ask me anymore questions." His voice dropped to a husky whisper, a tremor audible in it when he spoke again. "It's better if you never know."

Chapter Twenty-Two

"Maggie!"

Sean's voice was an anguished, frustrated wail as his sister slipped from his guiding hold and crumpled to the snowy ground. He bent to help her to stand once more, but she lay where she had fallen, exhausted, numb with cold, totally spent.

"I can't go on anymore, Sean," she managed to say between harsh, gulping breaths. Her eyes were filled with desperation yet somehow sadly resigned. "You go on with Da and the others. He'll be needin' you for the potato farm."

Sarah turned away, her own fatigue adding to her sense of futility. They had begun their journey three days ago, when the weather was still good. But near noon today, a new storm had thundered down upon them, bringing with it snow and wind and freezing temperatures. The line of weak, broken emigrants—fifteen adults and nine children—were strung out for a half mile, shuffling clumsily on their crude snowshoes or stepping in each other's tracks, with Perkins in the lead and Lester Stone far to the

369

rear.

And to make matters worse, the first cache of food had been ravaged by animals, and the starving emigrants were in as desperate a predicament as they had been before the arrival of Roy and the men.

Sarah shivered and hugged her arms to her body, squinting into the flying flakes to locate the other members of her family. A piercing wind echoed across the mountains and through the desolate stands of pine. The landscape was a jumble of crags, trees, and uninterrupted expanses of white—a bleak, forbidding place.

Choking back a sob of dismay, Sarah sank to the ground and watched as Roy, carrying Lucas, and Hetty and Samantha shuffled toward her. Toby was a few yards behind, head bent into the wind, walking slowly and carefully, as if each step meant pain.

"Why did you throw out the jerky!" Sarah demanded when he slumped in the snow beside her, and she was surprised by the open hostility in her tone. She watched Roy stagger ahead to where McTavish was piling up green logs to make a platform for a fire. But when Toby didn't answer, she turned back to him, suddenly furious that he could waste even one ounce of precious meat. *"Why?* We need it! Look at Maggie!" She flung out a hand in a quick, deprecating gesture. "Look at *us!*"

Toby bowed his head in defeat. "Yes—look at us." He let out a great, long sigh, a vapor mist immediately snatched away in the wind. He shook his head regretfully. "I should have packed you and Hetty and the children out at the first."

Sarah bit back the reply that leaped to mind when Toby shifted his foot; a faint pink spot stained the snow where his shabby boot had been. Sympathy and love flooded

370

her, and she crawled across the icy ground to embrace him. He was shivering, and as she held him, she realized she was, too.

A slaty sky pressed down, and the wind drove the snow in gusts. The men succeeded in building a fire of dry wood on a foundation of green logs, and it crackled noisily. Sarah saw Hetty herding the youngsters closer to it, saw Emmett Pardee with his two sons, saw Ole Andersen with Inga and Astrid; Peter had not left the lake camp with them. After his first binge and subsequent purging, he had sneaked back later that night, uncontrollably ravenous, and gorged himself once more. When he had been found in the morning, he was too far gone to be helped by the tobacco juice and had died an hour before they broke camp.

Now Inga was behaving irrationally. Her fear of the snow and her physical depletion were working together, and she had become childish in the last day. She alternately laughed and wept and babbled in Swedish.

The men were planting large pine boughs in the snow and banking up the drifts to form a windbreak, but Sarah could barely make out their figures in the blowing squalls. A child cried pitiably and begged for food. The wind keened like a ghoul. Sarah's hands and feet were growing numb, but she couldn't find the energy to move. Crystallized flakes settled on her shoulders and uncovered hair, whitened Toby's beard and eyebrows. The sky was leaden, and the fitful gusts of wind caught up thin spirals of snow and twisted them about the huddled, frightened emigrants.

Sarah's heart hammered suddenly as the renewed fear reached deep into her intestines and squeezed. It was madness for them to have left the camp! At least *there*

371

they had been relatively warm and dry, if not well fed. Out here, exposed to the elements, they were not only hungry, but wet and cold as well.

"Toby—?"

He seemed to be dozing, but he roused himself to peer at her. His eyes reflected his deep-seated fear, only increasing her own sense of panic and dread. For the first time, he seemed to notice the fire, and his brows furrowed in a thoughtful frown. "We should go over there and warm ourselves."

She nodded, but neither of them moved. It was too easy to sit, even with the freezing wind and snow lashing them from first one direction, then another.

Movement nearby caught Sarah's eye, and she slowly turned her head to see Canfield slogging up to where Maggie lay, a hairy, gaunt monster with wild eyes and flashing gold teeth. And Sarah was even more surprised to see Judd seated in the snow with Maggie, his shoulders hunched, a thin blanket drawn around his shoulders.

The former guide dropped down beside them and peered closely at Maggie. "What's the matter, girl? You hungry?"

Maggie opened one eye to look at him but didn't respond, and Canfield cackled harshly. "A fine rescue party they are—bringin' us out *here* to starve!" he exclaimed. "At least back there we had meat!" His eyes glittered madly from their sunken sockets and darted furtively around him. His lips twisted into a cruel smile, and, unsheathing his knife, he rose up on his knees. "But we can *still* get it, my pretty!" He pointed with the blade. "How about young master Huntington's widow? She's almost gone." His frenzied eyes came to rest on Sarah, and he smiled a mirthless, wolfish smile, like the grin of a

372

skull without flesh. Sarah felt a shiver of fear ripple up her spine, and she burrowed closer to Toby. Canfield threw back his head and laughed crazily. ''Or one of the *new* men. There's plenty of meat on them!''

Sarah shrank back as Canfield got to his feet and lumbered unsteadily into the circle of emigrants. But the men of the relief party were passing out tiny pieces of jerky and lumps of sugar, and the guide greedily accepted his share, forgetting his deranged ravings for the time being.

But Sarah played his words over and over again in her mind, piecing them together until they all fit. And when she had the only answer possible, a strangled sob cracked deep in her throat. But she pushed the notion aside quickly, refusing to accept its implications. Canfield was crazy; the rest of them were civilized people.

Roy returned to help her and Toby to their feet. A low moan of pain escaped Toby's lips as he moved, but he forced himself to shuffle the few yards to the fire. Sarah ate her portion slowly, trying to make it last, knowing it was all that was left. Perkins had sent two men ahead to the next cache, and, if that had been rifled, on to the next.

The fire roared, sending its warmth around the little cluster of emigrants, and Sarah's chin drooped with profound weariness. She felt a tingling in her limbs, the pins and needles of returning sensation. She had almost drifted off into sleep when Stone came tottering out of the woods, scarcely able to drag his snowshoes over the feathery surface. He collapsed near the fire, weighted down by the bulging pockets of his trousers and jacket.

A thick mantle of clouds obscured the moon. The firelight threw phantom shadows across the forms of the emigrants huddled close to its warmth. Snow whipped about in savage squalls, and the shrill scream of the increasing wind unnerved Judd completely.

He sat wrapped in his ragged blanket, staring into the crackling flames, though each hour that passed saw the logs settle more deeply into a pit hollowed out in the snow by the heat. And in that same amount of time, Judd's vision was growing weaker, more erratic. The leaping orange tongues of flame swam in and out of focus; sometimes there were two or three fires before him, other times his sight dimmed until there was only a dull glow. His eyes watered, and the freezing wind turned the moisture to ice, stinging and burning almost beyond endurance. He rubbed fiercely at them and exhaled sharply in relief when the campfire's image became normal again.

Yesterday—and the day before—the glare of the sun on the endless white wastes had been intolerable. Then today it had been just the opposite: a dark, supernatural world of dim shadows and outlines. A thin film had begun to creep over his eyes shortly before they made camp. It was getting worse.

His senses felt blunted, chilled, dead. The others sat with their blankets as close to the fire as they could get, some dozing. When the flames burned low, one would crawl over and add more fuel. At first, all had been silent, save the storm. Now there were other sounds: the children wailing and shivering beneath their flimsy coverlets, the older ones praying and weeping. And the wolves, never far away, howling through the trees.

The men of the relief party were tiring from the incessant labor of keeping the fire going, from carrying children too young to walk, from their own lack of food. For himself, a great lethargy had settled upon Judd, and he

374

was beginning to wish he could simply let his life slip away out here in this trackless desert of snow and ice. Better that than face the possibility that he might be going blind. A man who knew nothing but how to keep an eye on the cards dealt to him and others—what kind of life could he lead as a cripple?

A shape suddenly materialized out of the darkness and into the light of the fire, and Judd squinted. When he was able to focus he recognized the Amazonian figure of Inga Andersen. And as his vision gradually returned more clearly, he saw that she was doing a most curious thing. She was stripping off her clothing and tossing it aside— layer upon layer of sweaters, blouses, her pinned-up skirt—until she was wearing nothing but a frayed pair of pantalets and one torn stocking.

Judd stared in speechless wonder, too stunned to move, as she danced and capered around the slumbering emigrants, unmindful of the darting snow particles and frigid gale-force winds. Her shriveled skin, stretched like parchment over her large bones, glowed pale and waxy in the firelight, and her eyes glittered wild and insane.

She stopped suddenly, threw back her mane of tangled blond hair, and laughed maniacally. Then, with lightning speed, she raced across the drifts and into the trees.

By the time Judd finally found his voice to alert the others, Ole was already scrambling after her. But the Swede fell headlong into a drift and was too weak and upset to rise. He sat helplessly, floundering, while three of the relief party sprinted clumsily into the woods after the woman.

A fearful whispering spread through the now-awakened emigrants, and Astrid shrieked uncontrollably. Judd ignored them, keeping an eye on the shadowy edge of the

375

trees for any sign of movement, but the darkness soon began to take its toll on his failing vision. Sighing deeply in disgust, he hunched deeper into his thin blanket and closed his eyes to wait.

He didn't have long. The men returned almost immediately with the near-naked woman. She gibbered incoherently and had to be supported between two of them. McTavish added more fuel to the fire in the ever-deepening pit, while another wrapped her in coats and blankets. For an hour they worked over her—chafing her hands and limbs, rubbing her body vigorously—until she began to show some signs of returning awareness.

Judd watched and listened for a time as the night shadows crept through the shimmering, swaying pines and the snow drifted around him. But the whole scene held little interest for him. He had seen and done and been subjected to enough ghastly things in the past two months to last a lifetime. And, allowing his fatigue to claim his mind at last, all he wanted anymore was sleep—a quiet, peaceful sleep, uncluttered with demoniacal dreams.

Toby awoke abruptly as a sharp stab of pain lanced his left foot and went all the way up his leg. Grimacing, he shifted his position beside Sarah and was surprised to see that it was morning. Morning—but hardly lighter than the dead of night. And the blizzard still spread its fury, beating down on the emigrants with relentless ferocity.

He roused himself sufficiently to look more closely at his companions. The fire had sunk below the surface of the snow and gave off little heat. Some sat staring vacantly down into the pit, others slept. Ole cradled his wife to him, Molly O'Brian spoke comfortingly to young

Katie.

The clouds hung heavy; icicles were suspended from every tree. It was still snowing, but, for the moment, the biting wind had abated. The camp was a frigid world of heavy snow and white drifts as far as the eye could see, and Toby shuddered at its awesome isolation and emptiness.

Hunger clawed at his belly; his feet were a steady, throbbing agony. They had been frozen and thawed so many times that he knew they could be nothing but masses of bruised and bleeding flesh. Not yet numb, though, he thought grimly. Not yet dead to pain. His boots were so badly rotted by the constant wetting that they were falling apart. He was drenched to the skin, and his clothing was frozen and hard.

But so was the ground, for during the night the snowpack had consolidated. Walking would be easier— but not in this storm. Evidently, the men of the rescue party thought the same thing, for none were making preparations to move out.

Sneering in scornful frustration, he turned his gaze on the inadequate fire. They would all freeze to death without a fire—if they didn't starve first. Several shovels lay amid the pile of picks and hatchets, and Toby's mind groped back in time for a memory—a memory of a bad winter he had spent years ago with the Indians, and their resourceful method of keeping warm.

He started to rise but sat back hard as the earth began to rock and spin around him. Red-hot coals needled his feet, and he clamped his teeth on his lower lip until the pain subsided, cursing his own debility and weakness.

Sarah roused, shivering, her lips blue. She stared dumbly about her for a moment, then disappointment clouded her face.

"The men haven't come back from the second cache?" she asked, but the tone of her voice clearly indicated she already knew the answer.

Toby shook his head. He could hardly blame them if they kept right on going and *never* came back. It was insanity to attempt to shepherd twenty-four helpless people out of these mountains during the height of a raging snowstorm. If only he hadn't thrown the jerky into the fire . . . Revulsion tightened his lips, and he shuddered even now at the memory.

Roy knelt beside them and furtively gave them each a handful of broken tortillas. Toby cautiously slipped a morsel of the dry, tasteless corn flour into his mouth, savoring it as if it were the finest roast.

"That's all I have," Roy cautioned. "Make it last."

Toby swallowed and tucked the rest into his pocket. But that one tiny bite had seemed to revive him, and this time when he tried to stand, he did so without misadventure. He squinted up at the lowering sky, shook his head, and turned back to Roy.

"The wind's picking up again, and the fire's useless." He hobbled a few steps, willing the pain away, and motioned for Roy to follow him. "That snowbank's frozen solid. We'll dig caves and burrow in."

Sarah lay beside Toby in the hollowed-out snow cave, exhausted from the labor of digging. He had finished most of the work before collapsing, but she had been forced to find a final ounce of strength from some unknown reservoir to complete the task. Now, totally spent, they lay curled together, breathing heavily, trying to draw

378

on each other's warmth. And it *was* growing steadily—and surprisingly—warmer inside the tiny cavern.

Outside, the wind howled, pines swayed, branches lashed about in the flying snow. Some of the others were still digging, and occasionally a voice carried to her above the scream of the wind. Sadly, she reflected, Ole Andersen would need a hollow only large enough for himself and his daughter; Inga had died sometime during the night, from exposure, cold, hunger—and possibly fear.

Sarah's own sense of terror had been increasing with each minute, each darting ice-ball that struck her, each arctic blast of wind that threatened to topple her off her feet. They needed food. It was a difficult and dangerous feat for *anyone* to cross these mountains in the dead of a winter snowstorm, but for starving, weak, ailing people such as themselves . . . In spite of her rising panic, she tried to think clearly. But her exhaustion and hunger made it impossible to think at all.

Toby's rapid, gulping breaths had slowed, though his face was still flushed and his chest heaved. Sarah gently brushed an errant lock of hair away from his forehead and leaned over to place a kiss on the coarse roughness of his beard.

This man—a man she had started out hating—she knew she now loved. For all his brusqueness, he could be tender and giving, strong yet gentle, understanding and at the same time unreasonable.

Sarah sighed wistfully, and her lips quirked in a rueful, faintly ironic smile. No happy family weddings ahead for them, no quiet little cottage with a half-dozen children. Only mile after mile, acre upon acre of snow-swept mountains—bleak, ominous, terrifying.

She scowled deeply, frowning in annoyance at herself. These were exactly the kind of thoughts she should keep from having. And, determined to become as optimistic as she possibly could again, she pushed them resolutely to the back of her mind. She loved him—she refused to accept hopelessness.

Moving her arm carefully, so as to not knock the wall of hard-packed snow and ice in upon them, she dug in her pocket and drew out a few crumbs. She moistened them with snow, rolled them into two balls the size of marbles, and placed one in Toby's mouth.

His eyes came open, and they seemed to smile at her. He didn't chew, but rather let the morsel dissolve. Sarah *couldn't* chew; at least not very well anymore. Since the windfall of the meat a few weeks ago, she had lost five teeth—all in the back, fortunately, so no one knew. But if she ever *did* reach Sutter's Fort and find a bountiful feast laid before her, how would she *ever* manage to eat it?

Amused at this thought and conjuring up images of the plenty that awaited them, she curled up against the warmth of Toby's body and drifted into a dreamless, yet troubled, sleep while the storm raged around them.

Canfield awoke with a sudden start, and he blinked furiously to knock the frozen powder off his lashes and recall his surroundings. Before him, the fire crackled almost serenely, and he followed the plumes of smoke upward. Then he remembered—he was in the snow pit with Stone. They had opted for the heat of the fire rather than the close confines of a hollow with another, possibly equally rank-smelling body. And apparently it had worked: Canfield was no colder than usual, and a few feet away, Stone's chest moved as he slumbered. The pit had kept them protected from the wind, though the ground on which they sat was a slushy, foul stream of ice water.

Red blew on his hands, then folded them across his chest and tucked them beneath his armpits. The wind had died down considerably; in fact, there was hardly a stirring above him. But the snow continued to fall in great, floating flakes.

Hunger cramped his belly. It actually hurt, twisted, seemed to be turning in upon itself for nourishment.

His gaze returned to the fire, his eyes hooded in thought, and he watched the dancing flames for a moment. Inga Andersen's corpse was up there someplace, unburied but undoubtedly shrouded in snow. Inga—with her full, strapping Scandinavian body and well-toned muscles. She had been a fine figure of a woman back on the plains, like a well-fed, purebred heifer . . .

Red's mouth curved into an evil smile, and he nodded complacently to himself. In a few minutes—just as soon as he marshaled his energy . . . Another little smile twisted his lips, obscured by a filthy, rusty beard that reached halfway down his chest. Perhaps he might even share with Maggie. And once she regained her health and they reached the Sacramento, she would be so grateful to him, she . . .

A sound above broke into his thoughts, and his head jerked up. Fear and surprise widened his eyes, and he drew in a quick, rasping breath. For, standing on the ledge of snow not five feet above him was a wolf. The animal slavered uncontrollably, its tongue lolled from its jaws, reddish eyes gazed fiercely down at Canfield. And as he looked on, the beast bared its teeth in an almost

381

mocking grin, and Red saw the bits of flesh and blond hair stuck to its matted wet fur.

His momentary surprise changed to anger, and Canfield's lips drew back into a snarl equal to that of the wolf. "You miserable sonofabitch!" he hissed, springing to his feet with surprising agility. The wolf backed away a few paces, and Canfield fumbled for his knife, his sunken eyes wild with rage. "She's *mine!*"

He scrambled up the sides of the snow pit, slipping and fighting for purchase in the toeholds cut into the ice, gasping with outrage and exertion. With a mighty heave, he hauled himself up and over the lip and lay panting; greasy, uncut hair fell in his eyes, one bearded cheek rested in the snow.

After the briefest of pauses to regain what little strength he possessed, he scrabbled to his knees and looked around. The wolf had retreated almost to the edge of the trees, stood watching him warily, still that near-derisive sneer in its expression. But closer—as Red's eyes made a slow circuit of the silent camp—were perhaps another half dozen of the creatures, busily attacking and devouring their plunder.

A snarl of fury twisted Canfield's face into a hideous mask, and a low sound escaped from his throat, distorted by rage. One of the wolves turned, its muzzle dripping, stared at him. Red lunged forward, flailing his arms. The wolf let the mutilated arm of Inga Andersen fall to the snow and turned to flee into the safety of the woods, the others bounding after him.

Red stared a long moment at the bloodied, mangled pulp and torn scraps of clothing, his temples pounding, the muscles in his jaw working furiously. Then his narrowed gaze returned to the lone wolf and fixed the animal with a murderous stare. As if in challenge, the wolf raised its shaggy gray head, let out a baying howl, then turned and bolted into the trees.

Canfield let out a growling shriek and ran after him, his knife raised high, lurching and floundering in the snow. It clung to his feet in heavy clumps, and he stumbled often, but still he continued through the maze of giant pines and smaller saplings, staggering and weaving like a drunk, his anger pushing him past all caution.

He nearly fell in a heavy drift and caught himself from going down only by embracing a tree trunk. And as he pulled himself erect and, limp with exhaustion, tried to catch his breath, he found himself looking into the glittering, feral stare of the wolf. Not ten feet away, it stood poised, its long yellowed fangs bared, a guttural, purring sound coming from its throat, its eyes like twin red coals.

Canfield's face wrenched with fear, and the breath froze in his throat. All the anger and bravado and indignation drained from his veins like sap from a tree. His legs felt weak, threatened to buckle; a whining moan escaped his lips. His eyes flew to the knife in his hand, and he stared at its gleaming blade with a stricken, horrified expression. A useless weapon for a man in his state of hunger and exhaustion against . . .

He whimpered in stark panic and backed up a step, his eyes darting back to the wolf. The animal matched his step and added one more, advancing two paces on him.

Red's eyes bulged; his jaw trembled; spittle dribbled from his lips. His heartbeat thundered in his ears. He could hear his own breath sobbing in and out of his throat. He stood transfixed, staring at the savage grin of the wolf, trying to summon the strength to flee but unable to force his legs to move.

The animal sprang. Red thrust out his knife hand reflexively, but the weight of the animal struck him with numbing force. He toppled backward, sank several inches into the snow, and floundered. He flung out a hand to retrieve the lost knife, but the wolf pounced again with a ferocious growl, driving the wind from Canfield's lungs.

He clutched the snow-slick fur near the animal's neck, tried to push him away. The wolf strained. Canfield was pinned beneath the writhing furry body. He saw patterns of bursting lights explode in his vision; his muscles grew slack. Slavering jaws snapped viciously, inches from his throat. He could smell the panting, putrid animal breath on his face, smell his own breath, rotten and rank with fear.

Whining in terror, Canfield twisted his head aside and tried to raise his knee to kick the animal's hindquarters. Fetid saliva dripped onto his face, mingling with his sweat. Enormous sharp teeth clicked and snapped. Red pushed, but there was no strength left in his arms.

There was only excruciating pain as knife-edged fangs ripped through flesh, tore out vocal cords, crushed windpipe. Canfield screamed, but only a bubbling sound came from his pulpy, ravaged throat. He felt one moment of brief, devastating torment, then blackness surged over him, and he lay twitching spasmodically as his life's blood pulsed into the snow.

Toby's feet ached with every step, his teeth seemed frozen, clenched in an effort to force the pain away. Still, he continued to shuffle awkwardly on his snowshoes over the soft powder, as he had for most of the morning. He glanced up briefly, saw the bleak expanse of snow-covered jagged slabs, the narrow ledges and precipitous drops, and shuddered inwardly.

The wind had calmed to a gentle breeze, though it was still snowing and the air was bitterly cold. Perkins had decided to push on, in spite of the ever-increasing weakness of the emigrants. The men he had sent ahead should have been back by now, unless they had met the same fate as Canfield.

Revulsion tightened Toby's throat and twisted his lips at the memory. Lebec and another man had found the former guide just before dusk last night; that is, what was left of him. His remains, as well as those of Inga Andersen, had been buried in one of the snow caves. And this morning, frail, delicate Alma Huntington had been awarded the same end.

Now there were fewer of them, and Toby wondered dismally how many more would perish before they reached clear ground and civilization. They were all exhausted and broken, wading through drifts, sinking to their hips. Some of the women had pinned up their skirts to make loose pantalets for easier walking, but they reeled drunkenly across the snow, tripping over their own feet just the same. McTavish had to carry Maggie most of the time, though Toby doubted she weighed any more than a good-sized sack of grain. And Stone, despite his reasonably fair health, kept falling ever farther to the rear.

For himself, Toby simply took one sore, painful dragging step at a time, concentrating all his efforts on the yard of ground directly ahead of him. His feet were frozen, blistered, cracked, bleeding; the cold plunged sharp nails of sheer agony into their marrow with the slightest movement. He staggered often, and sometimes his vision blurred behind a red mist of pain.

An hour ago, they had come across a miraculous sight—a large stream of running water, water so warm it had melted the snow. They had all been forced to cross one by one on a snow bridge, perhaps formed by a blade of grass or a twig. Toby had nearly toppled off, as had Daniel O'Brian and Preston Jennings, but all had made it without mishap.

Toby stumbled, and the ground seemed to waver as he went down, but he held on to consciousness doggedly. Scooping up a handful of snow, he put it in his mouth to let it melt, and the drink seemed to revive him. When the vertigo that rocked and spun the world around him subsided, he struggled to stand. But the pain in his feet was a steady agony, and he cried out in misery.

Still, those warm springs had been an encouraging sign, and he *had* to go on, no matter what the cost. But he was running on stolen energy. And he knew he had no reserves left.

The fine particles of snow cut and stung so that Judd could no longer open his eyes. But what did it matter anymore? He couldn't see anyway. Early this morning, the snow-wrapped forests, the forbidding mountains, the forms of his companions had all gradually faded from view. Now there was nothing but blackness and the icy caress of the wind against his face.

He was frightened by the dark, but more terrified of being left behind. So he had kept on, managing to crawl, stagger, and flounder through the drifts, listening intently for voices, trying to fend off errant branches with outstretched hands.

Waves of dizziness washed over him, and he fell with almost every step. How long since he had eaten? A day— two days? He couldn't remember, but whenever it had been, it seemed a lifetime ago.

Pardee was ahead of him. Judd could hear him panting as he labored through the snow, but he couldn't see him. For some time, he had followed the blacksmith awkwardly, listening, afraid of becoming lost. But as his feet tangled and he tumbled into a deep, glacial drift, he gave a strangled cry of mingled fear and desperation.

They would leave him. Panic assailed him—a wild, unreasoning terror that sent his heart drumming in his ears and compressed the breath in his throat. He sank his teeth into his lower lip to smother his sobs, but the tears came anyway, coursing down his cheeks in salty streaks, freezing in his matted beard. His shoulders trembled violently, and he rocked back and forth in the snow, his keening sounds of grief building in volume and pitch with each shudder and choked sob.

A hand on his shoulder shook him roughly, and he heard Pardee's gruff voice dimly at his side. "Hold onto my belt."

Judd blinked and swung his head in the direction of the voice. There was only intense darkness, but he wiped his face and struggled to his feet, groping blindly for the blacksmith's belt.

Lester Stone faltered, felt dizzy, and his knees buckled. He crumpled into the snow, his breathing harsh and stertorous, and sat still until the pounding of blood in his temples became bearable. The frigid air made his lungs feel raw, his hands were frozen so badly that the skin on his fingers had cracked open. And he was hungry—far hungrier than he could *ever* remember being back at the lake.

His mouth hardened with scorn. Why hadn't Perkins and the others gone after the wolves for food?

At this unwelcome memory, he raised his shaggy head and peered toward the west. Barely discernible was Judd Brannan's tattered black frock coat and Emmett Pardee's filthy plaid wool jacket—the tail end of the line of emigrants. And as he watched dully, those two disappeared over a rise and vanished from sight.

Stone felt his sense of frustration and despair mount. He was weak—growing weaker with each step—and he knew the reason why. Despite all his precautions to distribute it evenly, the gold in his pockets was heavy. For every ounce of gold he carried, he lost that much of his dwindling strength and the others gained a rod of ground on him.

There was nothing left to do but abandon it if he wanted to live. His lips twisted bitterly, and he gave a throaty laugh. All his plotting and scheming had come to this ultimate decision. But what profit was there in being a wealthy corpse?

Releasing an exasperated sigh that plumed into a hazy vapor before his face, he pulled the pouches from his pockets and fumbled to open them for one last look. The gold coins inside gleamed and sparkled, seemed to give off a comforting warmth of their own, and Stone felt an unaccountable sense of loss as he reclosed the bags reluctantly.

At least he still had the negotiable banknotes, and he took some satisfaction from that thought as he scanned the nearby terrain for a likely hiding spot. When spring came, he could return and dig up . . .

No! He shook his head violently and threw up his hands helplessly. If he buried them in the snow, by spring they would be on bare ground, visible to anyone who chanced to come by. Biting his lip in anger and dismay, he realized he would either have to keep the gold with him and run the risk of certain death or leave it to the first comer.

He pushed himself to his feet painfully and tottered across the snow, carefully scrutinizing the pines, searching for niches in the bark. He finally located a well-protected cleft about six feet above the snow level—six feet now, but who could tell how high off the ground when the snow melted?

Shaking his head miserably, he placed the pouches carefully in the crevice. They seemed secure, and tying them with something would only advertise their presence.

Sighing regretfully, he turned to prepare to move on when a faint movement several yards away caught his eye. Fear clutched at his throat and rippled up his spine at the recollection of Canfield's end, and he pressed himself further into the snow-mantled branches. Not daring to breathe, he strained to make out the shape, partially covered by drifting, falling snow. He could see some pink, some pale blue, and as the object moved again, Lester saw that it was Hope Jennings, and he stared at her with stunned disbelief.

He hadn't realized he had been holding his breath until he heard himself expel it sharply. Soft, mewling whimpers were coming from the child now, and as he made his way cautiously over the snow, a barrage of baffling ques-

389

tions raced through his mind. What was the little girl doing out here all by herself? Had they left her for dead? Or had they simply somehow lost track of her?

He knelt down and lifted the child to her feet. Wide brown eyes gazed at him from a pinched pale face framed by stringy dark hair and a ragged blue bonnet. She seemed dazed at first, then flung her arms around his neck and sobbed tearfully. Disconcerted, Stone patted her thin shoulder awkwardly, his mind reeling.

And then—with terrible understanding—he realized what he had just done; exchanged one burden for another. The child couldn't walk, and if he carried her . . .

He pulled her away from him gently and ran a critical eye over her. At four, she was nothing but wasted flesh and jutting bones—perhaps twenty-five pounds at most, probably the same weight as the gold.

Lester's mouth twisted with bitter self-mockery. Still, he couldn't leave her out here to die. Hoisting her up onto his back and summoning up what strength remained, he set out through the drifts after the others.

The snow was beginning to fall harder as the day wore on, but thankfully, the wind was still calm. Sarah's snowshoes were falling to pieces, and she struggled through the blinding drifts, clawing her way painfully forward, sometimes breaking through snow to her waist. She was dizzy, and her knees wobbled, so depleted by the physical ordeal her limbs had begun to tremble erratically and her mind wandered. But she kept on tenaciously, dragging one foot after the other.

The entire Coulter family had begun falling to the rear. Samantha was slow, and, without snowshoes, was forced to step in the footprints of her father. She fell often, and each time Sarah didn't expect her to rise again. Lucas was unable to do much walking for himself, and Roy had to carry him. Hetty floundered in a kind of daze, benumbed, moving half-consciously.

It was difficult to draw a full breath, and what entered Sarah's lungs was raw and cold. Her vision dimmed. Sounds became muted; disjointed images flashed through her mind. A kind of languor was settling over her, dulling her senses, muddling her mind. Walking became mechanical, as if her legs belonged to another.

Toby was a few yards ahead of her, his face flushed, respiration labored, and each breath seemed to come out as a groan; bloodstains in the white snow marked his trail. He staggered crazily, and Sarah watched with detached interest as he sank to his knees. His body seemed to go limp, and he crumpled into a formless heap.

Sarah paused, waiting for him to rise, and taking the opportunity to catch her faltering breath. But unlike all the other times, this time Toby didn't get up. He lay in the snow, his breathing coming in short, choking gasps, eyes closed, his face turning a waxy shade of gray.

Alarmed, Sarah shook off her awful lethargy and stumbled forward the few feet to kneel at his side. His respirations were weak and irregular, and his lips were turning blue.

"Toby." She leaned close, heard the terrible rattle of breath, and a surge of panic rushed through her. "Toby, you *have* to get up!"

His eyelids fluttered, and he peered at her. She saw the fatigue in his eyes, the sadness on his face. A tongue darted out to moisten cracked lips, and a stab of pain clouded his eyes for a brief moment. "My feet. I can't.

You go on." Each word came out slowly, punctuated by a hideous rasping, and Sarah shivered with fear.

She searched her mind frantically, her face a study in helpless despair. If only there were a fire for him to get warm and food to eat! He was strong—he *couldn't* just give up like this! And the thought of all this filled her with such frustrated rage, she felt like screaming.

But her bitter anger helped fire her blood, and she was determined not to let it end like this. Gripping him under both arms and calling up reserves of strength she never knew she possessed, she began to pull him, dragging him through the snow as she stumbled backward.

Ten feet gained—perhaps ten yards—and her head began to swim crazily. The strength ebbed from her arms, and she was forced to let go. Toby's cheek hit the snow, and he lay there, groaning, pain contorting his features.

Overwhelmed by a sense of futility, Sarah fell to her knees beside him, helpless, confused, hanging onto her own consciousness by only a thread. In a kind of stuporous, agonized daze, she watched Roy and Hetty's figures fade into the distance. Then she dropped her head to her hands, tears silently streaming down her face.

For minutes, she sat in the snow next to Toby, wondering at this cruel twist of fate. If she wanted to live, she should go on. But did she really *want* to live without Toby? He had become her whole world, and to think of him lying out here, starving, freezing, in pain . . .

Her mind refused to finish the thought, and she shook her head. She would give it one more try. She had to do *that* much!

She started to rise, felt darkness swirling around her, and sat back down hard, cursing her weakness. The man she loved needed her, and she couldn't even stand up.

When the spinning nausea had faded away and the pulsing at her temples had diminished, she prepared to rise once more. But she stopped again, this time distracted by a confused babble of voices coming from the emigrants up ahead. There were excited, gleeful shouts, and Sarah looked around in frightened bewilderment.

Then she saw Roy and McTavish shuffling hurriedly back to them, Roy waved. "The men have come back! There's food again!"

Sarah stared in numb disbelief. Then her eyes flew to Toby. He had heard, too, and a faint smile had replaced his grimace of pain.

Sarah tore into the dried meat and biscuits, ravenously hungry. She felt another tooth crack, give way, and laughed almost hysterically as she spat it into the snow. McTavish had lifted Toby's head and held a bottle to his lips. Toby drank, coughed, drank again.

Another laugh of relief escaped Sarah's lips, and she handed him a piece of her jerky.

"A wee drop of brandy, lass?" McTavish asked, offering her the bottle.

She nodded, tipped the bottle to her lips and swallowed. Tears sprang to her eyes, and she choked, but the fiery liquid spread a warmth inside her she had not known for months.

"They were pinned down by the storm," Roy explained. "That's why they didn't come back. And the best news is"—he glanced expectantly from Sarah to Toby—"we're only about six miles from the snow line."

Toby grimaced with self-disgust. "A few miles—a hundred miles. I can't walk!"

"You won't have to. Less than a mile away, they say the snow is firm underfoot and the going easy. We'll

393

make a stretcher and carry you.''

Sarah looked at Toby, her eyes bright, feverish and she nodded happily.

A lone figure materialized from the trees, stumbling and weaving. Sarah looked up as Lester Stone collapsed, and Hope Jennings tumbled off his back and into the snow.

Roy and McTavish hurried over to them, and Sarah returned her gaze to Toby, her eyes sparkling, her face glowing with pleasure. ''You see? Everything's going to be all right now.''

Toby picked up the tooth from the blanket of snow and turned it over in his fingers thoughtfully. One eyebrow lifted in teasing mockery. ''I hope they have a good dentist at Sutter's. I don't much know what I'll do with a toothless wife.''

Epilogue

Sarah sat quietly in the office at Sutter's Fort, sipping strong, hot coffee and listening to the conversation going on around her. The only woman present, she said little, preferring the warmth of the fire crackling in the hearth and her own private reflections.

It had been three weeks since coming out of the snow—a long time—but she could still remember vividly her feelings as they had reached a region where the snow lay only in wet patches and oaks were as plentiful as pines. It had been pleasant, rolling country, deer were plentiful, and the sun had shone warmly. The great mountain forests had been left behind forever—but at such a cost! Of the original forty-two members of the Jennings party, twenty were dead. The survivors were scattered at various ranches around the fort, nursing their ills, feeding themselves back to health, and trying to forget.

"I have never known manual labor in my life!"

The vehemence in Preston Jennings's voice startled Sarah, and she looked at him. The white hair and bristly muttonchop sidewhiskers still looked as impressive as before, but his physical appearance had altered drastically. He was a shrunken broken old man; most of the life had gone out of him, leaving only a scaly husk.

"What you need here is a church," he went on. "A *real* church—with a real preacher!"

Captain Sutter nodded his silvery blond head politely. "A church would be most welcome, I'm sure."

"But the rest of us, man!" Michael O'Brian slapped the table with his palm, and his eyes sharply focused on Sutter. "We haven't a cent to our names, and the O'Brians don't take charity. I don't know a blessed thing about working a sawmill!"

Sean sighed heavily, lifted a cluster of grapes from a bowl on the table, and gazed absently at the fruit. "We can learn, Da," he said patiently, then glanced at Roy. "Or maybe you'd teach us how to build?"

O'Brian grunted unhappily before Roy could reply. "He's already *got* a skill—a skill that's *needed!* Besides that, his wife's bringin' in an income of her own—takin' in washin', of all things!"

At this, Sarah had to smile. Hetty had barely recuperated when she began doing the laundry for the single men around the fort, and it was already turning into a thriving business. Most of all, it helped keep her mind off the past.

O'Brian scrubbed anxiously at his beard. "All I know is farmin'."

Sutter refilled his cup from the pewter pot on the table. "The only work *I* can give you is either at the mill or here, building."

The Irishman snorted again. "I'm guessin' even if I *had* land, potatoes don't grow very well here."

Sutter shrugged eloquently. "Not too well. But those"

—he reached across the table and flicked the cluster of grapes still in Sean's hand—"there's land around here I think God created just for growing those."

Sean studied the amber-colored grapes thoughtfully, then turned expectantly to his father. "Da?"

O'Brian grunted and folded his arms across his chest. "What do I know about grapes, either?"

Sarah stifled a yawn as Conchita entered, bearing a platter of freshly baked breads, crocks of creamy butter, and another pot of coffee. The Mexican girl set them on the table, then brought a small tray over to Sarah.

"Take this to him," she said, nodding toward the closed door at the side of the room. "He no eat his breakfast this morning. He just sit and stare."

Sarah sighed irascibly to herself. Toby wasn't rallying as the others were. He was moody, silent, uncommunicative. He rarely ventured out from his little room next to the office, not even with the aid of his crutches.

Managing a smile of thanks for the girl, Sarah took the tray, nodded to Captain Sutter as she passed, and slipped through the door.

The room was a cheerless tiny cubicle, once used as a storeroom. Sunlight streaked through the one barred window, throwing a soft, patterned light on the stark adobe walls, the washstand, a small chest of drawers, rickety table and chair, and the cot.

Toby was seated on this last item of furniture when she entered. He cast a brief glance at her, then returned his gaze to a spot on the far wall. His hair and beard had been trimmed, and his face was beginning to lose its haggard look, though his color had not returned. He wore a faded plaid wool shirt and frayed trousers, donated by one of the local men. A pair of soft moccasins rested on the floor beside his bandaged feet. He had lost three toes on his left foot, and one on the right, and he had been feeling sorry for himself ever since.

Sarah flashed him one of her most cheerful smiles and held the tray out for his inspection. "Fresh bread."

His eyes went sullenly over the food, but all he took was coffee. Suppressing another sigh of frustration, Sarah set the tray on the table and took the other cup for herself. She was seething inwardly with impatience, and her mouth set in a tight, disapproving line. Of all of them, she expected this self-pity from him the least. Even Judd Brannan was adjusting better than Toby.

Frowning, she carried her coffee over to stand by the window, hoping Toby would speak first but knowing he wouldn't. Outside in the courtyard, she could see one of the Indians leading Lucas and Katie O'Brian around on the back of a mare. On the steps, Samantha, Maggie, and Judd sat basking in the crisp January sunshine of this new year of 1848.

Sarah stole a sidelong glance over her shoulder at Toby. He was sipping his coffee, still staring dully at the plank floorboards, and a fleeting look of annoyance passed over her face. She knew his troubles. He was a hunter, the only thing he knew. But now he was crippled, no longer able to stalk his prey quietly and with agility. But he could still *walk*. It wasn't as if he had lost his legs. And in another week or two, he could probably get around without his crutches, if he would only *try!*

They had *all* suffered; some worse than others, but none had come out of the mountains unscathed. She had lost some teeth, but it wasn't a catastrophe. She could and *would* get by. Some of the weight she had lost was returning, and her flesh was beginning to fill out once more. Her hair shone, the sparkle had returned to her eyes; she felt almost her own self again. The lack of food and the poor quality of what she had been forced to eat had caused strange things to happen to her body. Her monthly cycle had not yet returned, and now there was always a nasty whisper in a far corner of her mind, hinting that the deprivation had done far more damage to her than she wanted to think.

Saddened by this thought, she sipped her coffee and returned her gaze to the courtyard. Two men had ridden in. One took their mounts toward the stable; the other—a big man with a bushy beard and wide shoulders—tipped his hat politely to Maggie, kicked mud off his boots, and stepped up on the porch. She heard the outer door to the office open, and Sutter say heartily, "James, what a coincidence! We were just talking about the mill."

Sarah swallowed the last of her coffee and grimaced at the taste of the dregs, Toby's sullenness only increasing her unease. If she could only perk him up. Something more than the loss of his frostbitten toes was tormenting him, eating away at him. She wanted to share his hurt and ease it if she could. But she was helpless until he chose to confide in her.

Against her will, her thoughts returned to something Canfield had said—a sly innuendo, something about their food supply. Sarah shuddered, her mind shying away from the memory, and she pushed it aside firmly.

"Do you still want to marry me?" The question slipped out before she could stop it, and her cheeks flamed at her own brazenness.

An awkward silence stretched between them, and she kept her gaze fixed out the window, unable to turn and face Toby. Roy, the O'Brians, and Jennings emerged onto the porch, and she saw her brother stoop to speak to Samantha.

Toby's voice was brittle with self-contempt. "Do *you* still want to marry *me?* A cripple!"

Exasperated, Sarah spun around, her gray eyes as hard and bright as diamonds as they blazed at him. "You're *not* a cripple! I lost more teeth than you did toes!"

A faint amused smile threatened at the corners of his mouth, but he continued to scowl at her. "It's not the same."

She frowned impatiently, "Four little-bitty toes hardly make a difference one way or the other."

"I'll be gimpy all the rest of my life."

She shrugged indifferently and crossed the room to set her empty cup on the table. At least she had his attention now, and *that* was something. Perhaps if she could make him angry enough . . . No. She didn't want to argue. What she really wanted to do was make love, and at this thought, a flicker of a smile touched her lips.

"Yes." His voice was low and intense. "I still want to marry you. If you'll have me."

Sarah looked up sharply and saw the strange mixture of love and confusion reflected in his eyes. She crossed the room quickly and knelt beside him on the cot. "Of course I'll have you. You're acting crazy! I *love* you."

He took her hand, that wistful, brooding smile returning to his lips once more. "But what kind of a life can I give you? I can't *do* anything!"

It was true, she admitted dismally. He couldn't read, and the only thing he could write was his name. He couldn't clerk in a store, work in a bank, couldn't do *any* of the jobs easiest for a man with two lame feet.

"It doesn't matter," she said. "We'll figure out something.''

He regarded her with a tolerantly amused smile. "As long as we have each other, right?''

Sarah's lips thinned into a grim, disapproving line. She was getting angry again. But, in a way, what he said made a certain amount of sense. The life she pictured before her with Toby—no matter what or where that might be—was nothing like anything she had ever imagined in the past. His strange silences, his odd conveyance of guilt, the self-pity she didn't understand. All she knew was how she felt, and she wanted desperately to be with him for the rest of her life.

She lifted her eyes to his; he was looking at her, and she noted a softening in his eyes. "As long as we have each other.'' She kissed him gently, her lips brushing his with a teasing lightness. He responded with a savage, demanding kiss that left her gasping, and she knew his hunger matched her own.

She drew back and smiled softly at him, then rose from the cot. She went first to the outer door and slipped the latch into place, then to the door leading to Sutter's office to do the same. Low voices came from the other side of the wall, but she ignored them, turning back to Toby with a provocative, almost conspiratorial smile.

She slowly unbuttoned her patched calico frock—a hand-me-down from a neighbor woman—and pulled it over her head. Unembarrassed by her nakedness, she kicked off her sandals, then casually rolled down the tattered lisle stockings.

When she straightened up, Toby was gazing at her. She saw eagerness in his face, a smoldering flame of desire brightening his blue eyes. A slow, sultry smile played about the corners of her mouth as she walked the few feet to stand directly before him, her hands planted on her hips, staring boldly at him with unmistakable meaning. He continued to gaze at her, his eyes, openly appraising, slowly running the length of her.

She took the empty coffee cup from his hand and tossed it aside. It struck the end of the cot, rolled to the edge, and fell to the plank floor but didn't break. He reached for her, his arms encircling her waist, and drew her down beside him. He kissed her tentatively, then hungrily, possessively. His mouth was soft and searching, and she felt her lips part beneath his insistent exploration. She sighed contentedly and closed her eyes, returning his kiss with all the long-suppressed passion of the last three months. He stroked her body with gentle, practiced hands, sending a delicious warmth spreading through her veins.

"Now, that's more like the old Toby Garrett," she whispered against his lips.

A rakish grin lifted one corner of his mouth as he pressed her softly back against the blankets, his eyes glittering, fingers leaving tingling trails of warmth wherever they went. "Surely you didn't think I lost *more* than my toes to frostbite?"

Her lips curved into a slow, beguiling smile as she pressed close to him, wrapping her arms around his neck and arching her body against his. "I certainly hope not."

"Where are we goin' to get the money to buy the land? Will you be tellin' me that?" Maggie asked. She eyed her brother circumspectly, then grunted sourly. "Da was goin' to sell the oxen and wagons for his stake. And where are they now?"

402

"But we don't have to *buy* the land!" Sean exclaimed. "It's ours for the taking."

Maggie's eyes narrowed doubtfully, and she stared across the courtyard toward the stables, the storehouse, the smithy. The sun was pleasantly warm on her shoulders, though it had rained earlier this morning, and new clouds were beginning to move in from the west.

"It's a daft idea, Sean O'Brian!" she said, and her face pinched into a frown. "We know nothin' of makin' wine!"

"Da used to brew up a pretty fair lager."

Maggie snorted disdainfully.

"I've tasted some of the wine from around here," Roy offered "It's not bad."

Judd's face was tilted up to the sky, his eyes wide and staring, letting the sun's rays penetrate his pale skin. "I used to be a bit of a connoisseur of fine wines back in Natchez and New Orleans. 'Course, they were mostly French. Some Italian, too."

Maggie scowled sullenly, watched the two Pardee boys leading a newly shod gelding out of the blacksmith shop and toward the corral. At least Emmett Pardee had found work here. All that the rest of them had was only talk.

Samantha offered her a lemon drop, which Maggie accepted, popping it in her mouth and sucking furiously. They couldn't live off Captain Sutter's charity forever, but this wild notion of starting up a winery . . . She shook her head, exasperated.

"You know," Judd said slowly, "I could be your official taster. I have *some* knowledge of wines. And it's something I could do without needing my eyes."

Maggie glanced sideways at him. He was still gazing

up at the sky, but his hands twisted nervously in his lap. She felt a rush of pity and let her own hand steal over to close over his. He was taking his blindness remarkably well. And she felt a closeness to him she had never experienced before. There was no denying he was an egotistic scoundrel—might have been *once*. Now he was just a pathetic, sad young man, befuddled by a strange new land he couldn't even see. She pressed his fingers gently, and he returned the pressure.

Boots crunched in the dirt, and Maggie glanced up to find Lester Stone. He finished gnawing on a chicken leg, then tossed it negligently aside. A mangy dog rose from the far end of the porch, padded leisurely out to the yard, and retrieved the bone. Maggie winced, remembering a time not so long ago when she would have fought that dog to the death for that bone.

Stone wiped his fingers on a handkerchief and inclined his head toward the office. "Captain Sutter has business?"

Roy nodded. "Mr. Marshall—his partner at the sawmill."

"Very urgent it seemed, too," Sean added.

Stone frowned, pursed his thin lips, and blew out some air. "Oh, well—" He leaned against a post and lit a cigar. "I was hoping the captain could tell me where I could find a bank."

A bank?" Sean glanced wryly at Maggie and winked. "Around *here?*"

Stone shrugged, blew out a plume of smoke.

"No banks around here," Roy said. "Sutter's the only one with any money, far as I can tell."

Samantha gazed up at Stone, her eyes wide with curiosity. "You gonna rob it?"

Maggie suppressed a giggle. Stone smiled at the girl with indulgent humor. "Not exactly."

Sarah stretched like a contented cat, then curled back up against Toby's side, a whisper of a sigh escaping her lips. She could feel the beating of his heart beneath her fingertips, the warmth from the fire in the small stove on her back and shoulders, hear the muted voices from the next room.

Whatever lay ahead for them might not be perfect—certainly not the stuff dreams were made of—but Sarah felt secure in Toby's love. And, with their lovemaking, some of his self-confidence had begun to return. Perhaps now he realized the loss of his toes hadn't made him less a man.

She heard his soft sigh, then an abrupt chuckle. Raising up on one elbow, she peered into his face. "What's so funny?"

His fingertips outlined her lips and traced across her cheek to brush aside the fall of golden hair nearly obscuring her features. His mouth twisted into an amused smile. "I think I'm hungry now. I'm still trying to build up my strength, you know." His eyes twinkled, suddenly alight with boyish glee. "What did you do with that bread?"

She assumed a look of wounded vanity, and her mouth curved into a pretty pout. "I may have started something here I'll be sorry for later. For *weeks* I've been trying to get you to eat more!"

His smile widened to a mischievous grin. "Now I'll probably get as fat as a prize porker." And, drawing her face down, he attempted to kiss her.

But her lips brushed his just tantalizingly, teasing him with a promise of a kiss, before she struggled to sit up and flashed him a saucy smile. Pulling the blanket off the bed and wrapping it around her shoulders, she padded over to the table to get the tray. She returned, bowed low, and handed it to him ceremoniously.

Toby eyed the small loaf of bread and crock of butter greedily "Conchita is a fine cook."

"How do you know? You only *pick* at your food!"

"Still—" He swung his long legs over the bed and reached for his trousers. The corners of his mouth lifted in a wry smile. His eyes gleamed impudently. "My taste buds didn't freeze and fall off either."

Wrinkling her nose at him, Sarah recrossed the room to the door leading to the office. "If Captain Sutter's company's gone, I'll get us some more hot coffee."

Toby was standing, gingerly balancing on his bandaged feet, as he drew the trousers up over his legs. "Like that?" he asked, nodding to the blanket.

She frowned in mock indignation. "I'm just going to listen." And she put her ear to the wooden door.

There was silence for a few moments, and, satisfied the caller had departed, she was about to reach for her dress when a chair scraped next door, followed by some hammering. She turned a mystified gaze on Toby, but he was absorbed in devouring the bread.

"You see?" It was the stranger's voice, deep and gruff, but obviously excited. "You can beat it into different shapes, but you can't break it. And look how much heavier it is than these silver dollars. It's *gold* I tell you!"

Sarah drew in a startled breath and shot a dismayed glance at Toby. He was listening, too, and for a moment they stared at each other with shared wonder and disbelief.

"It's gold, all right." It was Sutter's voice; cultured, slightly accented, but bearing none of the enthusiasm of his friend's. The chair scraped once more. "Tell me again, James."

"I was checking the tailrace on the mill the other morning. It's been clogging up lately. I looked down into the water, and there they were—just as bright and shiny as brass buttons."

"You just reached down and picked them up? Just like that?"

"Just like that. I figured you'd want to know."

"Whom else have you told?"

"Some of the men. I showed 'em to 'em."

Sutter's voice was edged with irritation. "If this gets around, James, I won't have a soul left to help with the building here or over in Yerba Buena. The whole operation will stop abruptly. They'll all be down there at Coloma—every man, woman, and child in the whole of California." There was a pause. Then Sutter spoke again, his tone weary, filled with a mixture of disdain and incredulity. "Gold—on the American River."

Sarah expelled the breath she had been holding and gave a low whistle, her eyes flying to Toby. He had set aside his food and was grinning wickedly, a shrewdly reckless sparkle dancing in his eyes.

Dropping the blanket to the floor, Sarah snatched up her dress and struggled to don her garments as fast as she could.

They gaped, mouths drooped, jaws sagged, eyes wide and staring. Only Samantha seemed unaffected by the news, turning and offering her sack of lemon drops to Sarah and Toby. Sarah waved it away, and, resettling herself on the porch, Samantha grunted irritably and plopped another candy in her mouth, looking curiously from one adult to another.

"Gold?" Sean's voice was a disbelieving half-whisper. "Just layin' around to be picked up?"

Sarah nodded. "That's what the man said. Right below the surface of the river."

Roy pursed his lips in a silent whistle and shook his head in amazement. "I can't believe it." His eyes went to Stone, then over to Ole Andersen who had joined the group, and he shook his head again. "Gold."

Toby shifted so that most of his weight was on his crutches. "You were there. Isn't that where you found McTavish and the others?"

Roy nodded, his brows knitting in confused dismay. "It's such a—desolate place. Who would expect—?" He broke off, shook his head yet another time, completely baffled.

Sean's eyes twinkled with obvious delight as they settled on Maggie. "We'll find ourselves enough money there to buy all the equipment we'll need, build a fine house—" He let out a whoop of sheer joy, dragged his tattered cloth cap from his coppery curls, and threw it in the air.

Sarah felt a nervous fluttering in her stomach, sensed the excitement building among the little group gathered around the porch, a contagious fever to which none of them seemed immune. Even Judd was smiling broadly, his sightless eyes darting from one voice to another.

Roy's gaze sought Toby, his eyes bright, blazing. "I'll leave tomorrow. In a few weeks—whenever you're able to travel—you can bring the women and children and join me. By then—'' He stopped, gave a short bark of laughter, and shrugged happily. ''Who knows?''

Sarah laughed delightedly just as the office door opened. Captain Sutter and the man who had started it all—big, sober-faced Marshall—stepped outside. Sutter took one look at the excited, eager faces that all turned in his direction, and his smile faded. His lips compressed, his high forehead creased into a frown, and he heaved an exasperated sigh.

His blue eyes lingered on Sarah, then moved to Toby. ''You were next door. You heard.'' It was a statement, not a question, and his voice was flat and emotionless.

Sarah nodded. ''We didn't mean to eavesdrop, but—'' She made a lame gesture of apology, though her heart was racing with anticipation, and she could barely contain her excitement.

Sutter rolled his eyes heavenward and sighed again.

Samantha raised an inquisitive gaze to the bearded stranger. ''Could I see the gold, please, mister?''

Marshall's brow lifted in mild surprise. His eyes slid to his employer, and Sutter shrugged resignedly. Marshall glanced warily around him, then dug beneath his heavy coat and drew out a little leather pouch. He shook out several nuggets and placed one in Samantha's outstretched palm. The size of a peach pit, it gleamed and winked in the midmorning sunshine. Anxious, curious faces peered at the brilliant yellow gem.

Ole nodded sagaciously, then grinned. *''Ja.* By golly —it *is* gold!''

Stone's eyes glittered and narrowed into slits as he watched Samantha roll the nugget around in her palm, squeeze it, hold it up to the light. She then handed it carefully back to Marshall. "Thank you, mister,"

Marshall regarded her with open curiosity. "Why such a special interest, little lady?"

Samantha pursed her lips thoughtfully, her face pinched in concentration. "I want to know what I'm supposed to be looking for."

Marshall chuckled softly and replaced the pouch inside his jacket.

Stone was already walking briskly toward the stables, Ole had gone off in search of his daughter, and Sean was still whooping ecstatically as he pounded across the courtyard, dodging the mud puddles and leaping high in the air.

"Well—" Samantha released a heavy sigh, stood up, brushed off her skirt, and tossed her head to shake out her braids. Tucking her candy sack carefully beneath one arm, she stepped off the porch and took Roy's hand. "Come on, Pa. We better go tell Ma and Lucas. We don't want them others to get the jump on us."

Sarah suppressed a smile. Sutter coughed and looked away. Roy arched a wondering brow at his daughter. *"You're* not coming with me."

Samantha regarded him gravely, yet saucy and defiant, her lips set in a stubborn line. "Oh, yes I am. I ain't never lettin' you leave me again. You promised, remember?"

Roy smiled fondly and nodded his head. "So I did. And I won't break that promise now." He glanced at Sutter with an embarrassed, apologetic little grin. "I—"

Sutter waved his words away brusquely. "It's quite all right, Mr. Coulter. I understand." His gaze shifted to Samantha, and, clicking his heels together smartly, he executed a low bow. "And you, young lady. I wish you all the best in seeking your fortune."

410

Samantha dropped a small curtsy in return, her face somber, determined, resolved. "Thank you, sir." And, turning, she tugged impatiently on Roy's hand and started across the courtyard.

Sutter's breath came out in a helpless sigh, and he stroked his mustache absently as he glanced sideways at Marshall. "As I said—every man, woman, and child—"

Sarah noticed Toby delving in his trouser pocket until he finally drew forth the set of polished amber rattles. She stared, gave a little exclamation of surprise. "Are those from the snake in the desert?"

Smiling, he nodded and placed them in her hand. "I saved them—thought they'd bring me luck. Until today, I didn't believe it."

Sarah's fingers closed around the hard, smooth rattles, and she looked at Toby, her face flushed with pleasure, eyes shining softly. "We *will* be lucky, won't we?"

Nodding complacently, he flashed her a smile that exuded confidence, and gave her a knowing wink. "And rich, too."

THE BEST IN HISTORICAL ROMANCE

PASSION'S RAPTURE   (912, $3.50)
by Penelope Neri
Through a series of misfortunes, an English beauty becomes the
captive of the very man who ruined her life. By day she rages
against her imprisonment—but by night, she's in passion's thrall!

JASMINE PARADISE   (1170, $3.75)
by Penelope Neri
When Heath sets his eyes on the lovely Sarah, the beauty of the
tropics pales in comparison. And he's soon intoxicated with the
honeyed nectar of her full lips. Together, they explore the paradise
. . . of love.

SILKEN RAPTURE   (1172, $3.50)
by Cassie Edwards
Young, sultry Glenda was innocent of love when she met handsome Read deBaulieu. For two days they revelled in fiery desire
only to part—and then learn they were hopelessly bound in a web
of SILKEN RAPTURE.

FORBIDDEN EMBRACE   (1105, $3.50)
by Cassie Edwards
Serena was a Yankee nurse and Wesley was a Confederate soldier.
And Serena knew it was wrong—but Wesley was a master of temptation. Tomorrow he would be gone and she would be left with
only memories of their FORBIDDEN EMBRACE.

PORTRAIT OF DESIRE   (1003, $3.50)
by Cassie Edwards
As Nicholas's brush stroked the lines of Jennifer's full, sensuous
mouth and the curves of her soft, feminine shape, he came to feel
that he was touching every part of her that he painted. Soon, lips
sought lips, heart sought heart, and they came together in a wild
storm of passion. . . .

*Available wherever paperbacks are sold, or order direct from the
Publisher. Send cover price plus 50¢ per copy for mailing and
handling to Zebra Books, 475 Park Avenue South, New York,
N.Y. 10016. DO NOT SEND CASH.*

EXCITING BESTSELLERS FROM ZEBRA

PLEASURE DOME   (1134, $3.75)
by Judith Liederman
Though she posed as the perfect society wife, Laina Eastman was harboring a clandestine love. And within an empire of boundless opulence, throughout the decades following World War II, Laina's love would meet the challenges of fate . . .

HERITAGE   (1100, $3.75)
by Lewis Orde
Beautiful innocent Leah and her two brothers were forced by the holocaust to flee their parents' home. A courageous immigrant family, each battled for love, power and their very lifeline—their HERITAGE.

FOUR SISTERS   (1048, $3.75)
by James Fritzhand
From the ghettos of Moscow to the glamor and glitter of the Winter Palace, four elegant beauties are torn between love and sorrow, danger and desire—but will forever be bound together as FOUR SISTERS.

BYGONES   (1030, $3.75)
by Frank Wilkinson
Once the extraordinary Gwyneth set eyes on the handsome aristocrat Benjamin Whisten, she was determined to foster the illicit love affair that would shape three generations—and win a remarkable woman an unforgettable dynasty!

THE LION'S WAY   (900, $3.75)
by Lewis Orde
An all-consuming saga that spans four generations in the life of troubled and talented David, who struggles to rise above his immigrant heritage and rise to a world of glamour, fame and success!

Available wherever paperbacks are sold, or order direct from the Publisher. Send cover price plus 50¢ per copy for mailing and handling to Zebra Books, 475 Park Avenue South, New York, N.Y. 10016. DO NOT SEND CASH.

MORE RAPTUROUS READING!

LOVE'S FIERY JEWEL (1128, $3.75)
by Elaine Barbieri
Lovely Amethyst was on the verge of womanhood, and no one knew it better than the devilishly handsome Captain Damien Staith. She ached with passion for him, but vowed never to give her heart.

CAPTIVE ECSTASY (738, $2.75)
by Elaine Barbieri
From the moment Amanda saw the savage Indian imprisoned in the fort she felt compassion for him. But she never dreamed that someday she'd become his captive—or that a captive is what she'd want to be!

AMBER FIRE (848, $3.50)
by Elaine Barbieri
Ever since she met the dark and sensual Stephen, Melanie's senses throbbed with a longing that seared her veins. Stephen was the one man who could fulfill such desire—and the one man she vowed never to see again!

WILD DESIRES (1103, $3.50)
by Kathleen Drymon
The tempestuous saga of three generations of Blackthorn women, set in the back streets of London, glamorous New Orleans and the sultry tropics of the Caribbean—where each finds passion in a stranger's arms!

ISLAND ECSTASY (964, $3.50)
by Karen Harper
No man could resist her delicate beauty and sweet sensuality. But only one man kindled the flames of desire in the heart of Jade—the one man who resisted her!

Available wherever paperbacks are sold, or order direct from the Publisher. Send cover price plus 50¢ per copy for mailing and handling to Zebra Books, 475 Park Avenue South, New York, N.Y. 10016. DO NOT SEND CASH.

FASCINATING, PAGE-TURNING BLOCKBUSTERS!

BYGONES (1030, $3.75)
by Frank Wilkinson
Once the extraordinary Gwyneth set eyes on the handsome aristocrat Benjamin Whisten, she was determined to foster the illicit love affair that would shape three generations—and win a remarkable woman an unforgettable dynasty!

A TIME FOR ROSES (946, $3.50)
by Agatha Della Anastasi
A family saga of riveting power and passion! Fiery Magdalena places her marriage vows above all else—until her husband wants her to make an impossible choice. She has always loved and honored—but now she can't obey!

THE VAN ALENS (1000, $3.50)
by Samuel A. Schreiner, Jr.
The lovely, determined Van Alen women were as exciting and passionate as the century in which they lived. And through these years of America's most exciting times, they created a dynasty of love and lust!

THE CANNAWAYS (1019, $3.50)
by Graham Shelby
Vowing to rise above the poverty and squalor of her birth, Elizabeth Darle becomes a woman who would pay any price for love—and to make Brydd Cannaway's dynasty her own!

THE LION'S WAY (900, $3.75)
by Lewis Orde
An all-consuming saga that spans four generations in the life of troubled and talented David, who struggles to rise above his immigrant heritage and rise to a world of glamour, fame and success!

A WOMAN OF DESTINY (734, $3.25)
by Grandin Hammill
Rose O'Neal is passionate and determined, a woman whose spark ignites the affairs of state—as well as the affairs of men!

Available wherever paperbacks are sold, or order direct from the Publisher. Send cover price plus 50¢ per copy for mailing and handling to Zebra Books, 475 Park Avenue South, New York, N.Y. 10016. DO NOT SEND CASH.